W9-CMD-261

Malinche's Children

Malinche's Children

Daniel Houston-Davila

University Press of Mississippi / *Jackson*

www.upress.state.ms.us

Designed by Todd Lape

The University Press of Mississippi is a member of the
Association of American University Presses.

Manufactured in the United States of America

11 10 09 08 07 06 05 04 03 4 3 2 1
∞
Library of Congress Cataloging-in-Publication Data

Houston-Davila, Daniel, 1947–
Malinche's children / Daniel Houston-Davila.
p. cm.
ISBN 1-57806-521-6 (cloth : alk. paper)
1. Mexican American agricultural laborers—Fiction. 2. Children of agricultural laborers—Fiction. 3. Mexican American families—Fiction. 4. Mexican Americans—Fiction. 5. California—Fiction. I. Title.
PS3608.O865 M35 2003
813′.6—dc21 2002014444

British Library Cataloging-in-Publication Data available

This book is a salutation to my mother,
Maria de Socorro Matilde Farber Davila Houston,
who always saw the world with a poet's eyes and
whose voice sings in every story, and to my father,
Robert Houston, whose only ship that ever came
in was his family who loved him and kept him
close for all his days and whose presence lingers
between my lines. Dreamers both—they taught
me that hope can be its own reward.

This book is dedicated with cariño especial
to my wife, Sherri, and to my sons, Jason and
Bobby, whose love for me—despite my madness—
fuels all my dreams.

This book is a memorial to
Daniel Onesimo Abrigo, my friend from boyhood,
who took the less-than-perfect hand that he was
dealt and ran with it, defining for all who
crossed his path courage, persistence, faith,
and friendship. He was "a gentleman from sole
to crown . . . ," and I will always miss him.

Contents

Author's Note

Hernán Cortés conquered Mexico, but he and his two hundred conquistadores didn't do it alone. At Cortés's side marched Malinche, who was Aztec by birth, Nahuatl her first tongue. Like a parrot, she picked up the languages of Mexico, having been sold as a slave from her father's house and winding her way, in one form of bondage or another, from Tenochtitlán to the southern reaches of the One World. When gods stepped onto the powdery sands near Cozumel, they demanded women from the Maya there. Malinche found herself again tossed like meat before hungry strangers. Unlike the others in her small band of women, she did not tremble before gods and bemoan her fate, but instead determined which of these smelly strangers held real power in his pale hands. Never content to be merely chosen, she placed herself in shallow sea at sunset as Cortés marched across the sand. Her eyes found his and held them, the parrot saying, "How are you, sir?" in his own tongue, letting him know the value in meat that could speak in tongues enough to bridge worlds. Cortés signed on, and the two marched into Tenochtitlán, followed by an army of tribes made allies only out of hatred the Aztecs had inspired throughout the One World. Malinche's tongue carried Cortés into Moctezuma's palace; Moctezuma and the One World were snuffed out. For this, Malinche is reviled. For this, she is Mexico's "*gran puta*," scorned by the mestizos who forget that from high between her thighs fell forth the first mestizo, planted by a god whose feet Malinche always knew were clay. From this union rose a nation of her children who despise her still for simply making—without any shame at all—the most of circumstances she came upon. Neither this nor that, Malinche walked a tightrope between worlds and made it world enough.

I am Malinche
I am the mother of a nation
I claim all whores
And sons of whores
Who stand between
And carve a place to call their own.
I am Malinche.
These are my children.

Malinche's Children

Chapter 1

Taking Root ~ 1900

Arnulfo had been dreaming. In the dream, he was where his night dreams always took him—wrapped in Gloria's body, the two lying side by side, his face buried between the brown mountains of her breasts, his tongue prizing the moist saltiness gathering there—when he was pulled to wakefulness by an uproar somewhere beyond the dream.

At the shouting outside, he leapt up from his sleeping rug, naked as he always slept in summer heat, his lanza still pointing at the tent top and dreaming on of Gloria. Slipping into his overalls, he stepped from his tent into chaos.

He surveyed the six tattered tents scattered in a wide uneven circle that marked their dusty camp at the edge of Hinton's Norwalk farm. Then, his eyes took in the scene outside, and he saw how a world could change forever in an instant. Before him, rolling in the swirling dust, was proof undeniable that the family they had been was gone.

"Maricón!" The ugly word, a curse, rolled across the flatness of the campsite smacking Arnulfo in the face, flung into the night by Mario Galvan, buried under Negrito's bulk in the pile of spent ashes and overturned stones that had earlier been their campfire. Resounding thuds fanned out over the clearing, the sound of Negrito's black fist, a ham, rising and falling against young Mario's head.

Suddenly, despite his size, Negrito was thrown back, and Arnulfo saw Mario, naked, his yellow skin streaked with charcoal ash, rise up, a phoenix. The much smaller Mario, as if empowered by the sudden turn of events, began to kick at Negrito's body, cursing as he kicked, his voice becoming stronger. "Your hands want to touch a man—" he shouted, his breath lost in a fury of kicks before he found it again and roared on—"then feel these feet of a real man!" And as Mario yelled and rained blows with his feet, Negrito scooted through the rising dust, trying to gain a handhold on the earth to push himself up.

Around the perimeter, all of them watched—compañeros—together ten years or more en los Estados Unidos, picking crops and wandering a wilderness made bearable by memories of home and too-short winter trips back to Mazatlán, a band of almost brothers—but for Mario, young and new, recruited this last trip home. And Arnulfo saw in all their eyes a fire echoed in the tightening coil of their bodies, fists rolled tight and ready. He knew these watching men as he knew no others, for even before they'd been forced to wander in search of work, they'd grown into men together in Mazatlán. But he felt none of the excitement he saw spilling from their eyes, only sadness. The realization that in the scattering blows of Mario's feet—his ugly accusations—they were watching something die.

Then, he saw movement, not the flying feet of Mario, seeming now a man, victorious over Negrito's fallen body, but a slight movement from Paco Valdez, who stood naked save for his shirt bunched over his huevos. And the movement came not from his hands covering his nakedness, but from his bare foot pushing something toward Negrito.

In a flash, Negrito was on his knees, his hand extending through the dust and grabbing at a flash of silver in the moonlight. He flung his free hand back so fast, so hard, that when it collided with young Mario's cojones, the air rushing up Mario's stunned throat spilled into the night as wind, sounding hot and dry like the Santa Anas that blew from the desert bringing madness. Then, Negrito was up, a giant again, a hulking shadow clad only in the billowing cotton undershorts gringos wore. He seemed a bull pawing the earth, but this time it was the bull who had the sword.

Crouching over his own enormous belly, Negrito began the dance around his target every man in the circle had seen before. His arms, enormous, solid from biceps to forearms, were held far out from his body in a menacing circle, one hand fisted, the other clasped as tightly around the handle of Paco's knife, the blade a long, gleaming sharpness in the night.

Mario, sucking the night for air to catch his breath, slowly straightened as he backed away and became again a boy. His yellow skin drained of all color as his eyes followed the tip of Negrito's dancing blade.

"Tell them!" Negrito spat as he advanced. "Tell them that you lied."

"I am no liar," Mario said, no longer roaring.

Arnulfo's eyes moved to Negrito's face. Even with the full moon, he could see only two eyes, pools of equal darkness surrounded by the yellowed whites, but in their depths, he saw a desperation, and he knew the liar.

A flash of movement drew Arnulfo back to Mario as he turned and ran, his yellow nalgas moons retreating into night.

Negrito shouted and chased him, Arnulfo running after them, the others following.

Arnulfo saw Negrito gaining on his prey and heard a growl spill from Negrito's throat as he dove, his free hand taking hold of the boy's ankle, bringing him hard to earth as Negrito scurried up the fallen body, straddling it high, one huge knee on each side of Mario's head, trapping him.

Arnulfo came up on them just as Negrito's knife touched the soft pale skin under Mario's chin. "*Basta!*" Arnulfo ordered.

Negrito shook his head and said, "Enough, my little friend?"—but not to Arnulfo, to Mario.

And Mario nodded.

"Tell them," Negrito insisted.

Arnulfo saw the face flush . . . go slack. "I was mistaken," he said softly.

Negrito cursed, "Cabrón!," rose, and spat. "A man thinks before he speaks." Turning, he walked back to camp.

Before Arnulfo stepped into the circle of tents, he looked up at the moon, brilliant and whole—full, still, when it should have been in pieces. Then, he looked into the silent circle of tents to Negrito's, draped in colorful serapes. He saw him on the stool placed in the loose soil before the tent flap. Negrito was alone, the others wisely seeking sleep. As Arnulfo neared him, he saw the bottle clenched as the knife had been. When he reached Negrito, he squatted in the dust. Negrito looked at him, the eyes naked now. Negrito passed the nearly empty bottle. Arnulfo took it and drank—the tequila fire.

"Where is the little yellow bastard now?" Negrito asked.

"I told him to go to my tent."

"Your tent? Then, get him out, hermano, before he accuses—"

"Stop!" Arnulfo said, their eyes connecting.

After a silence, Negrito said heavily, "I think I'll be moving on . . . mañana." He stood up. "This ain't no life we're living, hombre." He sighed. "I go crazy . . . sometimes . . . wanting to touch someone. Am I the only one?"

Arnulfo thought of his dreams of Gloria. He shook his head no. "But . . . we aren't animals, friend."

Negrito laughed, long and low. "Who told you that? That's all I've ever been. An animal. You know why Rogelio and Gilberto are in Santa Ana?"

Arnulfo lifted his eyebrows.

"There's brown pussy in Santa Ana . . . and those lucky animales have the money this week to buy some." Negrito moved into his tent. Ten minutes later he stepped back out, dressed, his sleeping rug rolled and hanging at his side.

Arnulfo rose from where he'd been squatting, smoking. "Good luck, my brother." They embraced, hard, almost as if each were trying to pull the other into his body.

"Adios," Negrito said and turned. He walked off into the night. Arnulfo watched until his friend was swallowed in the darkness, and he knew then something had to be done before the half-lives they were living destroyed them all.

The patron—Mr. Hinton—did not like being called patron.

"This ain't Mexico. I ain't nobody's patron. You give me a day's labor, I give you a day's wages and a spot to spread your bedroll out at night. How many times I got to tell you that, Arnie?"

For ten years Arnulfo's crew had been coming to this farm at the edge of Norwalk. The first year they'd worked Hinton's land had been chance. They'd been moving up the road to Santa Ana, where Mexicans lived in Colonia Juarez and there were orange trees waiting to be picked, when Hinton on a horse had come barreling down upon them from across a dry harvested field. Arnulfo had thought a gringo on a horse hollering at them could only mean trouble, so he pulled the giant Negrito up next to him to await developments. There'd been eight of them that summer, their first picking season out of Mazatlán, and they'd already covered on foot half of California, moving from farm to farm and heading for the orange trees outside of Santa Ana, each move taking them closer to the border—home.

When the gringo pulled up alongside of them, Arnulfo saw that he was slight, redheaded, and younger than any of them. "Who's the jefe here?" the pale young gringo demanded.

Negrito, who understood English better than the rest of them, pointed at Arnulfo.

"Cómo estás, fella," the gringo said and smiled. "You're just what I'm lookin' for. I got a crop of beans ready to cook in the fields if I don' get 'em picked. You game?"

They never got to Santa Ana that season. They stayed at the Hinton farm right up until the end of November, when he'd trucked them down to Tijuana so they could get back to Mazatlán, that thankful for a band of men who worked like none he'd ever had. So, each year after that they'd come back, forgetting the rest of California as Hinton found more and more for them to do. The dusty flatness had come to feel like home, and their spot near the two giant mulberry trees that rose like miracles from the treeless flats and gave them shade in summer was where they pitched their tents. An irrigation ditch lay between the mulberries and provided water in easy reach.

Over ten years Mr. Hinton had aged with the rest of them. He had gotten a skinny gringa wife with honey-colored hair along the way, followed by three ugly redheaded children, one a boy and Hinton's freckled prize.

But over the years, Arnulfo grew more comfortable with Señor Hinton than he ever had with any gavacho in his memory. Arnulfo's English grew, but it remained so rough and uneven he used it little. Yet, he understood the animated little Hinton, and even trusted him.

One afternoon, Hinton had come upon Arnulfo in the shade of the mulberries where he had just finished lining the irrigation ditch with the metal his patron had heard would slow the evaporation of the precious water.

"Think that'll do the trick, Arnie?" Hinton stood at the edge of the ditch and then turned in a rush without waiting for an answer. He squatted in the loose dark earth under the trees, grabbed a twig nearby and started drawing in the earth. A cigarette dangled from his mouth as he said, "I added this field—beans. Sounds crazy but I'm going to buy up Smith's fields here and here"—he pointed at corners adjacent to his property—"and I'm going to plant flowers. Big demand, they say, for flowers."

Arnulfo was amazed. A flower farm.

"I tried to buy up over here across the road, but somebody named Van Der something is bringing in cows." He laughed. "Flowers and cow shit—some combination, huh, amigo?" He ground out his cigarette. As if from nowhere, his son bounded up and grabbed hold of his father's neck. The child pulled a pack of cigarettes from his father's pocket and put one in his papa's mouth. Hinton grabbed the pack and offered it to Arnulfo. "Smoke?"

Arnulfo took the cigarette.

"What are you," Hinton asked, "one guy short? 'Cause I need every hand I can get."

"We are enough," Arnulfo said.

Hinton slapped his back. "I trust you, Arnie. You get your men out here tomorrow," he said, pointing with the stick over to where the cornfield was adjacent. "Corn's as high as an elephant's ass and the weeds are higher. Clean that out." He stood, shrugging his boy off his back. "How'd you lose that big guy, Arnie? He worked like three men."

"Hay un problem, Señor 'inton," Arnulfo said and then inclined his head toward the flame-haired boy running around them.

"I get you," Hinton said. "Andy, get your freckled ass out of earshot. Arnie wants to talk to me man to man."

Andy ran off. Arnulfo, sucking on the delicious ciragette, squatted and patted the earth. Hinton squatted, too. Arnulfo had been thinking ever since the night Negrito left. "Mujeres," Arnulfo finally said.

"Women? What's women got to do with losing—"

"Womans," Arnulfo nodded. "He misses the *womans*."

Hinton cocked his head, listening.

"Negrito—the others—they are mans," Arnulfo said, and added, "Rogelio Sanchez and the young Mario even have to go Santa Ana every often."

"Why?"

"Putas."

"Putas?" Hinton asked.

Arnulfo stood up and after a moment moved his hips back and forth. Hinton stared and then he went red, red like Arnulfo had never seen red. Then, he burst out laughing, rising and slapping his thighs. "Whores? That's why your boys run off every now and then?"

Arnulfo nodded. "You got putas more near here?"

"They's whores everywhere," Hinton said, "but none round here who'd lay with Mexicans." He lifted his hand to his chin and seemed to be thinking. "This'd cost you, you know, Arnie."

Arnulfo nodded.

"Your boys work better when they've—" Hinton moved his hips.

Arnulfo nodded, suddenly afraid to ask for what they really needed.

"I'll see what I can do."

Sundays everything stopped at the Hinton place. In August the afternoons were so hot and sticky that the men gathered under the mulberries and stayed there until dark. Gilberto Ramirez was propped against one giant trunk and strumming his guitar, the music mournful as Sundays made him feel. Mario was shirtless, lying next to the irrigation ditch, one arm dangling and making circles in the cool water. Every so often, he would lift his hand and fling water at someone. Indio was resting against the far tree, always out of the circle, always quiet. His eyes were closed and his red-brown skin was dry and cool looking. Arnulfo, Diego Reyes, and Gerardo Guggisberg were playing cards. Paco Valdez, Rogelio Sanchez, and Pepe Escalante had gone to Santa Ana the night before.

Guggisberg threw down his cards as Diego laughed and scooped in the wooden chips, saying, "Smile, Guggisberg," but

Guggisberg was staring off into the distance. Then he said, "Arnulfo, look!"

Raising dust, a small black wagon pulled by a single horse was cutting from the road and heading across the flat toward where they sat. All the men save for Indio rose. Mario, youngest and the best-eyed said, "A woman's coming."

"A woman?" Arnulfo asked and squinted, but the wagon was too far off and the dust too thick.

Soon the wagon was close enough. A woman indeed.

"Red-haired," Guggisberg said.

"More red than the hair of Señor 'inton," Diego said.

"She's old," Mario said.

"Maybe she is Señor 'inton's mother," Gilberto suggested.

The wagon drew near and the woman at the reins pulled them back, stilling the single horse. She rose in the wagon. "Who's Arnie?" she asked.

Arnulfo stepped forward. "I—Arnulfo, yo—in what way, señora, I serve you?"

"You speak English."

He nodded. "The little."

The woman, short, redheaded, and round, put her hands on her hips and surveyed the group of them. Arnulfo saw something settle in her face, a resignation that compounded her age. Then, she grimaced, or maybe it was a smile. "Mr. Hinton said you gentlemen was lookin' for a whore."

Arnulfo stayed in the shade of the mulberries as the afternoon wore down. Indio Romero had remained there with him. The others had followed the fat woman to Negrito's seraped tent.

After Arnulfo had helped her down from the wagon, she'd wanted to talk money.

"This is what you want?" Arnulfo had asked his men.

They'd nodded as one—even Mario, who must not have thought her so old after all. Then, running back and forth to tents, they collected pennies, dimes; Diego had two quarters. Three dollars finally was pooled. "Suficiente?" Arnulfo asked, his palm open, the coins heaped.

She took the money, counted it, and then looked up and counted them. "Seven of you?"

Arnulfo stepped back. "No interés I have." Indio, behind him still propped against the tree, laughed. Taking that for a no, Arnulfo said, "Five have intereses."

"Deal." She looked around her. "I don't work outdoors." The men showed her to Negrito's empty tent.

Arnulfo found himself watching the tent into which she'd disappeared. One by one he saw his friends enter. Some in and out in a flash. Others took much longer. "Imagine," he said to Indio as he watched the others milling around the tent waiting their turn. "A gringa who lays with Mexicans."

"A prune," Indio said and spat. "She'd look better if I were younger." Then, he laughed. "But you are not so old, Arnulfo. Your knife must still have a point." Still laughing, Indio walked off into the sun. "Tell them I went hunting rabbits."

Arnulfo closed his eyes. The thoughts of the tent were making him hard. Behind his closed eyes he could think of Gloria—a name that spoke of heaven. Gloria. He eased his head back against the mulberry and wished for sleep and dreams and consummation.

When he opened his eyes, it was dusk. He had been sleeping. His head still against the trunk, he heard a splashing. Lifting his head, he saw the gringa at the irrigation ditch, squatting, naked—her hands in the water. Hunched over, she lifted her wet hands to her face and washed. She had a cloth in her hands, a grey rag that might have once been white. He saw her dip the cloth and bring it to her skin, her face, her neck, her breasts, between her legs. Her skin was white, no pinkness there, but white and flat, crisscrossed with blue veins that marbled her flesh. She was round, but the flesh seemed to hang. He was watching her back, her flaring nalgas.

He heard something above him, moving in the mulberry branches, but he could not take his eyes off the picture of the woman washing at the water. He'd seen Gloria once, naked in their kitchen, squatting before a pail of water as she had washed her body. This woman was not Gloria, a pale reflection, but suddenly she was beautiful, her flesh ample, loose, lovely. "Eres lindisima," he said softly.

At the edge of the irrigation ditch she turned her face and looked at him. "Excuse me?"

"Lindisima . . . eres tú," he said.

She smiled, a tooth missing next to the front teeth taking nothing from the smile. "Sounds lovely, whatever the hell you said."

He saw that her face was lined, but the twilight was kind. The eyes were blue and younger than the face. "Mis boys . . . where are the boys?" Arnulfo asked.

"They went off after rabbits or something. Promised me a feast." She smiled. "I heard lots of promises in my day."

"And still you believe?"

"I never hold my breath," she said and rose. Her breasts were slack and heavy, the nipples so dark they spoke of children, and her belly was loose. Her thighs, as she moved to where she'd set her clothes, danced. At her clothes, she lifted the dress.

"No," Arnulfo said and rose to his knees.

She hesitated.

He dug into his pocket and found the paper dollar. He was to have mailed it to Gloria next week from the post office on Front Street. He pulled it out and extended it to her.

She took it.

"I want—"

She dropped her dress and moved to him. "I usually don't work outdoors, honey." She looked around her into the distance, the sky aflame with sunset. "I guess we are as near to the end of the world as we can get. Who'd see us, sugar?" She squatted in front of him where he waited on his knees. "You look as ready as you'll ever be," she said and reached for the clasp of his overalls. He pushed her hand away.

He stood up and undid his overalls. He stepped out of them, naked—spreading them on the earth like a blanket. Rising, he took off his shirt and set the blue cotton next to the overalls. He extended his hand and she took it. He laid her down on the cloth. "No on the dirt," he said.

She smiled, turning onto her side, her breasts rolling together, inviting him, sparking the fire of memory. He lay down beside her, his brown hands caressing the paleness of her shoulders. He lowered his face to the breasts, large, white, pressed together, and he pushed his face between her breasts and felt them go brown. He sucked in her scent and imagined it Gloria's. He felt her lift a leg and ease it over his hip as he snuggled into the circle made, rising, reaching, slipping up and in. And all the while, he heard it in the trees, the movement, the leaves rustling when there was no wind. He lifted his face at one point but saw her face staring out over his head across the field—placing her far away—and he faltered.

Then, he felt her push him back, and as he rolled, she climbed him, never breaking their connection. Above him she swayed, her breasts like waves rolling onto the beach at Mazatlán as she lowered toward him. As her breasts touched his face, before the world was blotted out he saw a redhead with a freckled face peering through the trees, but his hips had reached that peak of frenzy when even God could call and be ignored. There was a splash—a loud splash and a metallic "thunk"—but Arnulfo's racing hips made the sounds seem insignificant and far away.

When they were done, she climbed off, stood, looked into the irrigation ditch, and screamed.

He jumped up and saw where she pointed in the water. Hinton's boy—his only boy—lay submerged in the irrigation ditch, arms floating, waving up at them, his head at a funny angle where it had thunked against the metal lining they'd placed in the ditch just days before. Arnulfo jumped into the ditch and the water rose to his chest, his feet sinking into mud at the natural bottom, causing the water to cloud.

"You'll lose him," the woman screamed, "don't unsettle the bottom."

Arnulfo went under water, reaching, finding mud, a rock, and then he felt the foot, he grabbed, his hand fisting over the ankle, pulling, lifting, tugging. He rose in the water, his hands sliding up the leg, finding the waistband of the boy's pants and pulling him from the water into his arms. The boy was limp, his freckles faded to almost nothing, the pale whiteness bluish, a deeper blue about the lips. Arnulfo got to the edge and pushed him up onto the dirt embankment. He climbed out and bent over the boy. He saw no movement in the chest. It didn't rise. It didn't fall. The boy, a pale freckled child he'd never liked, went brown before his eyes and became his own son, Manolo. Lowering his face, Arnulfo went down to the turned-up nose and felt for breath. There was none.

And then, he remembered that summer he'd been twelve in Mazatlán and had stopped believing in miracles, when there'd been a boy on the beach, washed up by the waves, thought dead. A stranger, a gringo, white and rich, had been strolling down the beach off Olas Altas, white slacks rolled up over bony knees. The gringo had run to them, who'd given the child up for dead—accepting as always the will of God. But gringos accepted nothing, and that man flipped the child over, turning his head, clearing the mouth with a sweeping finger. Then, the gringo had begun pressing at the child's back, causing water to spit from the child's open mouth. Both hands, pale, long-fingered, had made a fist and struck the child's small back, and the child had started to cough, to breathe—to live again, along with Arnulfo's faith in miracles.

Now, a lifetime later, Arnulfo turned Andy Hinton over onto his belly just as that gringo had so long ago in Mazatlán. Arnulfo scooped his fingers into the child's mouth, clearing it. Then he placed his large brown hands flat on Andy Hinton's back and pressed in imitation of that gringo's pale hands and denied God's claim on his patron's child.

Rising over Andy's body, Arnulfo pressed hard, paused, and pressed again, and as night fell about the mulberry trees, it filled with the soft gurgle of a child's breath, reborn. He saw the boy's back rise and fall.

He felt people around him. Looking up, he saw Mario, dead rabbits flung to the ground at his feet. "Go get Señor 'inton, now!" Mario took off across the dark field, racing.

Arnulfo saw Indio in the shadows. "Take the puta to a tent." Arnulfo stood. He saw the boy breathing, his head turning from side to side, a bruise already forming over the eye that had hit the metal lining in the ditch. He looked up into the web of dark branches. The child had been there, watching. He looked back down at the boy, whose freckles seemed louder, almost as red as before, the face no longer blue, but deathly pale. Arnulfo found his overalls and slipped into them, hooking them at the waist, letting the bib hang. He saw the boy open his eyes.

"My head hurts."

Arnulfo heard a distant shouting. Turning, he saw a horse in the light of the rising moon heading toward them. "Your papa, he coming."

"Don't tell my pa . . . ," the boy said, his words a struggle.

"Be still," Arnulfo ordered.

Hinton rode up, jumped from the horse, took in his boy, the wet clothes, Arnulfo's dripping hair. "What the hell's goin' on?"

"Pa," the boy said, his color high, the bruise a dark relief.

"He fall on the tree," Arnulfo said. "On the water."

The patron knelt by his child, pushed back the red hair to better see the bruise, touching the boy's flesh, Arnulfo saw, as if it were gold. "He was on the water," Arnulfo said. "Still. Floating."

"An' you jumped in, Arnie?"

"He was no breathin'," Arnie said.

"You made him breathe," Hinton said. "How?"

"A way," Arnulfo started, then he stopped and calculated before adding the little lie, "a way we have in Mexico."

Hinton rose and came close, pulling Arnulfo into his arms, and Arnulfo felt a wild trembling pass from the gringo into him. When he stepped back, Arnulfo saw his patron's eyes were wet. "Mil gracias, amigo," Mr. Hinton said and went back to his son, lifting him and carrying him to his horse.

When Mr. Hinton was in the saddle, his wet child cradled before him he said, "How can I thank you, Arnie?"

"I want my Gloria with me," Arnulfo said in a rush, knowing this was the only chance he'd ever have to speak his mind and tell the plan he'd been shaping for days, but just today believed could be, a way to hold his world together by bringing it all here to him.

"You want what?"

"Patrón—"

"Don't call me—"

"Okay, okay," Arnulfo said. "Me and mis mans you need almost all the year. No?"

"Well, yeah."

"Let me bring nuestras womans here to be with us."

"What? You talkin' whores, Arnie?"

"I talking esposas. Mis hombres have womans—babies at the

homes in Mazatlán. Please, we bring our ladies—permitanos por favor, señor."

"Here?" Hinton said.

"Porqué no? I need little space. I build the house."

Hinton hesitated.

"Putas are no good, señor. Wifes is good. Good mans need esposas goods tambien."

Hinton cleared his throat. "I can't take no responsibility for a bunch of women and children."

"Mi responsabilidad—no yours—mi—"

"Your responsibility?" Hinton rubbed his beardless chin, one arm tight around his boy. He appeared deep in thought. "I guess," Hinton finally said, "I could give you this corner—just this little bit—from the edge of the mulberry trees say out to the road."

"Give?"

"Then it would be your responsibility come hell or high water," Hinton said. "Ain't worth a damn anyway—never can get anything much to grow in this corner." The boy in his arm coughed. Hinton looked down at his son, his gaze overflowing gentleness. "I guess I owe you my boy's life, Mr.—" Hinton didn't finish but frowned and looked at Arnulfo.

Arnulfo saw that Hinton had no idea what his name was beyond Arnie. He smiled and said, "Carmelas." Arnulfo bowed with a sweep of his arm and said, "Señor Arnulfo Carmelas," as he realized no gavacho here in the north had ever asked his whole name before.

"Mr. Carmelas," Hinton said, "I am in your debt forever." He reined in his horse, pulled it back, and started to turn away.

"Then, we can bring nuestras womans?" Arnulfo called after him.

"You sure as hell can, amigo," Mr. Hinton said and then rode off, his red-haired boy clinging at his neck.

Arnulfo retreated to the mulberry trunk and sank to the earth, elated. It was dark. The moon was a sliver in the sky—Malinche's moon, his mother had always called this phase of moon, warning him as a boy to fall fast into sleep, for it was on nights like this that Malinche walked—La Llorona, crying over her betrayal of her own children, whom she had left all in pieces never to be whole again. His eyes fixed on the moon, and for a moment he wondered if it were a bad omen, if bringing Gloria and their children here would mean their lives would always be like this sliver of moon, only a piece of the whole their lives might have been had fortune blessed them and allowed them to stay in Mazatlán, washed by the salty whispers of the sea.

He squinted so his aging eyes could better see the moon; he saw—what he hadn't seen as a child—that the lighted sliver was really no piece at all, but just the visible part of the whole that would fatten with the coming days until, in all its glory, it would hang full and rich above him. Peace settled; hope, too. Negrito said they were animals—but more, too, than animals swept by circumstance, helpless before fate. Men could twist circumstance to their advantage if they dared. He thought of Malinche, a shame to all her children, but maybe something of a lesson, too. He remembered even as a child—his mamita bent over a tub of laundry in the middle of the tale of Malinche's betrayal of her Indian brothers—asking why Malinche was with the Spaniards at all. She'd told him she'd been given to them; he'd asked, where was her choice? His mother, at a loss for words, had told him to leave her to her wash. His question though had haunted, as he'd often found himself in circumstances he hadn't chosen but dealt with all the same. His thoughts were broken by the sounds of fire being built in the clearing behind him—Pepe Escalante piling wood and Indio Romero skinning rabbits nearby. The others were gathered at the flap of Negrito's tent, except for Gilberto strumming his sad guitarra.

Arnulfo closed his eyes, his road laid down. He tried to conjure Gloria, but she would not come. She'd be here soon and not in dreams. He imagined the house he'd build her in the garden they would create beneath these huge trees. There would be no ocean. But with Gloria always near, he could live without oceans. He fell into sleep, the scent of Gloria rising all around him, as he felt his soul sinking into this earth embraced by the mulberry's tangled roots.

Chapter 2

La Luna ~ 1910

Sleep far away, she lay in the tall dry grass staring up at the moon. It hung low in the heavens, blotting out the stars. The August air was as hot and heavy as in the daytime and filled as always with the whispers that had followed her all of her life, tugging at her attention, which was now fixed on the face of the moon, as pockmarked as her own.

Lying in the tall weeds, her eyes bored into the moon, and other sounds retreated. Her trained nose could smell the grasses, the scent of yellow grass that never flowered distinct from the greener blades, soft and crowned with tiny blooms. The perfume of dandelion teased her nose and she told herself to find the patch in the morning, for her store was nearly done. She moved her hand through the brittle stabbing grass until she touched her sack, coarse cotton that had once held flour but now held all her bundled weeds, grasses, and flowers—dried and rich, the raw material of magic. She was careful never to use the word aloud. But in her heart, she liked it. What could be more magical than using what grew everywhere, what others scorned as weed or waste but what God and her old teacher had shown her how to harness to ease the pains and fears of people who'd pay for service in corn if not in coin with which she kept herself alive.

Stroking the coarse cotton of the bag, she saw the surface of the moon grow brighter, whiter. The craters, dark rings upon the surface, faded before her eyes as she'd once dreamed the craters scarring her own face might do. That blessing never happened, but others fell—lessening the sting of ugliness. Foremost among them, her name. It finally gave explanation to her oddness, which had from childhood caused neighbors to whisper "madness" and "brujeria" in her direction. That oddness when no longer deniable had forced her mother to take her to a village more barren than their own and leave her in the dark with La Lechuza, famous for her gifts of healing and seeing—all within the Virgin's clean embrace. The old woman had claimed her, seeing no evil, only gifts for her to nurture. That first night with the old woman—after her mother's tearful goodbye—she'd been taken to a graveyard where rows of wooden crosses stabbing a moonless sky had seemed an advancing army to the terrified girl she'd been. As the old woman led her to the farthest corner of the lifeless place, preparing to desert her as her own mama had, she pressed against the woman's bulk, refusing to let go of this stranger who smelled of dry leaves, cornstalks, and tortillas. She'd begged not to be left in the dark, but the woman told her she would wait by the ruin of the graveyard gate and that she had no need to fear the dark, for she carried her own light—she was the moon.

Too terrified to move after the old woman disappeared, she waited for the promised call, knowing it would never come—but then, it came. She set out, wondering how she'd find her way through the thick of crosses. When the dark grew so deep she knew she'd fall, light spilled from her and lit the way to where the old woman—her salvation—waited to scoop her up. La Lechuza had squatted in the dust until their eyes were level. She remembered looking up into old laughing eyes above a gaping mouth, a single tooth that had seemed brilliant in that darkness as La Lechuza had told her she was the moon, naming her. She'd called herself La Luna since—never again fearful of the dark or of the voices that guided her as the moon pulled the earth through its heavens. Luna fell into sleep, alone in a wide empty field and unafraid.

She woke to the sound of cows. Rising to her knees in the grass, she grabbed her sack and saw the line of cows passing not five feet away. She knew they were heading for water, so she followed. She had avoided the roads since leaving Yorba Linda twenty days before, sticking to the fields thick with orange trees that bled into rows of heavy summer corn that in turn became pastureland with cows. She had gained weight, hunger a stranger.

She broke off a piece of salt lick, sucking on it to pass the time until the cows finished at the trough. As the cows drifted away, one lingered. She saw the heavy udder and knew that, with the sun, someone would be coming to gather the cows for milking. Moving slowly to the cow, she approached it face to face, her eyes looking deep into its brown eyes. It made a noise and backed off a foot, its flesh beginning to tremble. So, Luna extended her brown hand and touched the nose, whispering sweetness. She moved around the animal, sliding her palm along its body. Squatting near its rear leg only after all quiver disappeared, she slid her hand under the cow's belly and stroked the swollen udder. She closed her fingers around a teat and pulled, milk arcing through the air. She bent her face close and pulled again, the milk spitting into her mouth. She drank, feeling the heat, the sweetness.

Then, she went to the trough and lowered her face into the water, the coldness pricking. She let her hair down and trailed it in the water, feeling it squeak in her hands as she pulled the thickness through her fingers. As she wound it wet and heavy up on her head, she heard a voice shout gruffly.

"You!"

She turned and saw a man, tall and leathery, his eyes blue and round. He was astride a horse.

"That ain't bathwater, you know."

She didn't understand the noise falling from his mouth. "Inglés," she finally said. "No lo tengo."

"You a Carmelas Mexican?"

"Mexicana?" she asked, grasping the word she understood. "Yo," she said, pointing to her chest, nodding.

"Then you get down the road—out of my fields."

She lifted her shoulders, showing she didn't understand him.

"Carmelas," he said again, more loudly. "Vamoose," he said, pointing to the west. "Carmelas."

She looked in the direction he pointed. "Carmelas?" she asked and pointed.

"You ain't from Carmelas," he said, suspicion fanning in his face. "You a gypsy?"

She knew that word and she knew that gringos bristled at the mention of gypsies. "No!" she insisted. She recalled what the gringos in Temecula had done to the band of gypsies who had wandered into the town that, until then, she'd felt might be her home at last. "Mexicana soy yo . . . no una gipsi—"

"Well," the man said, stepping back. "You get on down the road. Mexicanos belong in Carmelas."

"Mexicanos?" she asked.

"Too damn many for my taste . . . but they're there . . . yeah."

It was still early morning when she climbed through barbed wire out of the field onto a broad dirt road. She looked up it toward the west, seeing nothing in the distance, the road narrowing, bordered on each side by fields. She didn't like to walk on roads, but the chorus behind her eyes insisted otherwise.

She walked in the middle of the empty road, the large flour sack slung over her shoulder, each step causing the coarse cotton to rub against her back, the rustling of the herbs inside causing perfume to rise around her.

When she first saw the houses, they were a cluster that shimmered in the August heat. As she drew closer, she saw that they were small—more huts than houses. She saw, as she approached, three dirt streets, dusty paths cut into the earth. Corn grew in yards, some Mexican style—stalks growing where God wished—others in the gringo fashion—rows neat and straight. She stopped at the second street, feeling the push from within directing her here, a dusty lane crowded with children, the littlest of them naked, that ran like a crooked creek between shacks on each side. In the distance, she saw two giant mulberry trees, circles of shade inviting her beneath them. She turned onto the dusty road and felt a pull stronger than she'd felt in Temecula. She laughed as the noisy children rushed around her, a stranger. "How are you all?" she asked them, noting that some would stare at her face, but never for very long, and not one pointed a finger or said anything at all about the scars there.

She saw women step from houses as news spread of a stranger on their street. She waved and smiled. "How are you?"

"Good," a woman answered. "In what way can we serve you?"

"It is I who will serve you," Luna answered. "Hierbas, hierbas for what ails you."

She got to the mulberry trees and looked up, seeing berries heavy with juice calling. Later, she would climb and feast. She set her sack down, opened it at the neck, and pulled out a serape, colored like a rainbow. She laid it under the trees and began to spread her goods.

The children clustered, asking questions, few she answered. But whenever one came close, she touched the child—her hunger for connection so great—smiling all the while, letting nothing they did bother her, until all of them were crowding close, her scarred face forgotten. She noted their tattered clothes, the pants, the dresses made from bags that had once held beans or flour, but all were clean, these children cared for, loved—essential if she were to stay.

One little girl caught her eye. Round and dark, this child was little different from any of the others and should not have stood out at all. There was nothing special in the face—the body was fit and straight—but Luna's heart felt a heaviness that hung in the air about the child's head, a darkness Luna knew was beyond the power of her healing gifts to ever lift when it would finally fall, claiming the child. Reluctantly, she looked deep into the girl's eyes. "Your name, child?" she could not help but ask.

The little girl's eyes grew round at being singled out. She said, "Claresa Sanchez," laughter at its edges causing Luna's joy to return, for she realized anew it was all God's plan—her healing gifts included, even their limitations. Turning from the child she would never be allowed to help, she looked up and saw the women coming with needs she could find ways to satisfy.

"My Louie coughs whenever the sun goes down."

Luna reached across and lifted a bottle of heavy dust. "The blessed Virgin has stopped your Louie's coughing," Luna said and laughed, passing her a powder wrapped in leaves. "Make him tea with this and give it to him when the sun goes down and once again when the moon is high."

"If there is no moon?"

"The second dose only if there is a moon."

The woman—young, still lovely, a soft brown like Luna once had been—looked hesitant. "I have no money."

"I must eat," Luna said. "Have you tortillas?"

The woman smiled. "I have new masa. I will make you the freshest tortillas you can imagine."

All afternoon the women came to where she sat under the tree. Most lingered, like women everywhere, seeking reason to be out in the air with sisters speaking. As the afternoon grew hotter, most drifted away. Luna began to pack her goods, thankful so much was gone, replaced by a different kind of bounty, for she had corn—ears and ears—and tortillas fresh, still warm, and cheese soft from sun, and tomatoes and chilis, rich, plump, and red that she would dry. It was then that she felt a presence causing her to turn and see a woman in the shadows leaning against the mulberry trunk. Luna recognized her now as a woman who had come close on and off all afternoon, never speaking.

Luna searched the woman's eyes and said, "I have nothing with which to tempt you?" The young woman's eyes filled and Luna felt her breath falter, for she had missed the beauty that now fell from the woman's eyes. This woman's pain, Luna realized, was in her heart.

The woman looked away under Luna's scrutiny and said only, "I thought . . . ," before her voice died.

And Luna knew this one was seeking magic, thinking her a bruja with spells to cast. Gently, so as not to startle, Luna said, "I am what you are seeking, child."

The woman's eyes returned for a moment before dropping to the serape and Luna's array of medicines. "A curandera you are—with medicines," she said and sounded disappointed.

"You wanted magic?" Luna asked.

A desperation filled the younger woman's eyes and Luna said, "All healing's magical, is it not?" Then, she asked, "What is your name?"

"Matilde," the woman said and to Luna the way she spoke her own name was as if she were saying, "and my heart is breaking." Luna knew it was a man. "Your husband," Luna said, naming him.

The woman's eyes went wide. She said, "My husband will not love me."

Luna moved to her and took her hand. The top of the hand was hardly brown, soft as velvet. The palm Luna held was, however, hard from work. Luna backed to the tree and lowered herself to the earth, pulling the woman down beside her. She stroked the soft top of the hand. Luna closed her eyes, concentrating on the whispers rising from the hand, the heat of the fading day heavy at her neck even in the shade. Behind her shuttered eyes, she saw a bed, a small narrow bed, pressed against the wall of a night-dark room. Luna opened her eyes and the heat was almost visible in the shade of the mulberry trees. The woman was staring at Luna, her longing so powerful it threatened. "He loves you."

"When he touches me—there is nothing. He doesn't touch me anymore."

Matilde's hand in Luna's own was flaccid, and the hunger in Matilde's eyes yawned so large it could sow doubt in the heart, the body, of the most certain man. Luna leaned close to Matilde's brown eyes full of question. "Do you believe in the resurrection?"

Matilde nodded.

Luna laughed. "Then do I have something magical for you." She dropped the hand and on her knees went to the sack, and, digging deep, pulled up a can reserved for treasure. She pried it open. Inside, pebbles crystal clear sparkled. These were fresh, made not four days before, when, crossing a stream, she'd found the trees called Woman's Friend by her old teacher when she'd first taught Luna how to draw the sap they'd boil into a see-through block—hard like a stone—that they would shatter into tiny pieces that could be made soft again by fire and hidden in a piece of food a woman might feed a man to make him hard as God surely intended men should be. Shaking some of the contents into her palm, she called Matilde close. "Like gold," she said, for though the tree grew so plentifully along the river bottoms here, in Mexico it was rare indeed. She stared into the woman's eyes and felt such newness that she ached. "A child you are."

"I have eighteen years."

"How long married?"

"Four months. He loved me so that he sent all the way to Mexico for me—to Mazatlán. I have no one here but Gerardo and my Gerardo doesn't love me anymore."

"He loves you. He just fears he lacks the power to make you happy."

"Gerardo? He fears nothing."

Luna smiled. "So they want us to believe. Men are intimate with fear."

"Will this make him able to love me again?"

"Does he like a special sweet?"

"Leche quemada."

"This will do nothing to its taste. When you cook your sweet milk for the candy, light three candles around the stove and think of the blessed Virgin. Stir these in until they go soft and disappear. He will become like stone and think himself reborn. When he sees this proof in flesh, his fear will die."

"You promise?"

"Would a curandera lie?" Luna laughed and then asked, "Do you have a jar at home? Something with a lid to keep out damp?"

Matilde was up and running.

Luna leaned back against the tree, lifted at the sight of the hungry little woman racing home to find a jar to hold magic. From under the tree, she saw in the house next to Matilde's own a dark woman swollen enormously with child being eased through the door to the porch by a woman who was very old. And as she watched the young woman move onto the porch, her hands pressed at the small of her back, Luna saw something in the line of the belly under the cotton dress that set her teeth on edge.

When Matilde returned, Luna could not take her eyes off the pregnant woman on the porch as she poured the resin pebbles into the jar. "The woman there," she asked, leaning her head toward the woman sitting on her porch.

"Chona?" Matilde asked, looking where Luna pointed. "She's

overdue. Her baby doesn't want to budge. You sure this is enough?" She pointed to the five pebbles in the little jar.

"More than enough," Luna said, turning to Matilde as she passed it back. "Sweet dreams." And this one had some money, placing two shiny gringo quarters in Luna's palm.

The day wore down, growing no cooler as the sun sank, turning pink. From where she sat beneath the trees she saw the lane before her tell its tale. The children played, the women wandered about, wash going up and coming down. The woman heavy with child was taken in. Men appeared, the first she'd seen all day, entering the street as evening came, the children being called, the lane finally falling still and empty.

The silence heightened the buzz of voices in her head, directing her to a tiny shack leaning towards where she sat beneath the mulberry trees. It stood forlorn and empty, the walls of wood, rough planks, broken through in places—a tumbledown house calling to her. She closed her eyes, tired from her years wandering, always seeking a place. Her voices told her she would know the place when her hunger finally ceased. Luna could smell the tortillas inside the sack, probably still warm, for the day had been so hot. She could even smell the sharpness of the cheese—but her hunger now was not for food. This hunger had gnawed since she'd lost Lechuza. She closed her eyes and could see the old woman propped before her hut, a single room at the foot of hills in Mexico that took and took and gave so little in return. She saw the pipe glowing in the woman's toothless mouth and yearned for home, feeling no need to move.

Her eyes opened and night had fallen, the darkness thick under the trees. "Señora," a voice called softly. Luna leaned forward and saw Matilde of this afternoon. She was not smiling. "Our magic failed?"

The woman smiled weakly. "No, you are a marvelous curandera. Your medicine worked wonders."

"Then," Luna said, smiling back, "you should not be here with me."

"I wouldn't be—but Chona's Mario pulled me from my husband's bed. The baby just won't come. We've been half this night fighting. The child is winning—I think our Chona's dying. I needed air and on the porch I saw you sitting still beneath our trees and thought with all your magic—medicine—surely you can bring babies into the world."

Luna pushed herself up from the earth. "I can indeed."

They walked in the sweet summer darkness the short distance up the block, the houses that they passed all dark except for a shabby one in the middle of the block, lanterns on the porch. Two men sat upon the steps. A man, young and fair, with hardly any beard at all, lifted his head at their approach. His eyes were bleary, the smell of beer and fear heavy in the air. "I have a curandera," Matilde said and pulled Luna into the light.

The man sitting next to Mario lifted the lantern high and the light spilled across Luna's face as if it were the moon. Luna needed no magic to see in his eyes what he saw when he looked at her; a crone, dirty, bedraggled.

"Who is she?" Mario asked coldly.

"Luna," she answered for herself, giving the only name she ever gave. She stood tall under his gaze. She felt the man's revulsion at the idea of letting her near his woman. Refusing to avert her eyes, she said, "I have come far. The world is dirty. Surely you have water for me to wash, so I can deliver your child into the world."

Mario's color was so light that he turned red. "No," he said. "My mother's there inside. She is enough."

"But Chona's so little, Mario," Matilde argued."This woman knows—"

"No."

"We can only offer, " Luna said, and touched Matilde's cheek, knowing this was a woman who would with years grow too strong for anyone to silence. She turned away, walking up the street, the dust heavy between her toes, heading back to her place beneath the mulberry trees, when she stopped at the empty shack that listed toward the trees and had been calling to her all day. She saw no curtains at the single window. Squinting her eyes, she saw there was no glass in the panes. The house was empty and leaning to the left as if reaching for the trees. She went to the stoop, noting that the wood had broken through in places on the sloping porch. She climbed onto the porch and went up against the rough wood of the house, finding a place stable enough to hold her bulk, and lowered herself to the ground. She would sit and wait. From her place she watched the street, the house into which Matilde had gone, and the men who had denied her entrance.

She slept.

Screams.

She opened her eyes. The night still held, but morning was near. A scream tore through the air. She sat upright and saw the people thick on the porch of the house of the woman who was screaming. Lanterns were lit in other houses, and the street was full of people instead of empty as it should have been. Children hovered on porches staring up at the house from which the screams had come, wakening them.

Luna watched night pass into morning, emptying the streets as mothers pulled their children back to bed and men wandered away to labor. As the sun rose to full morning, the street remained empty, for the children would not be allowed out on this street this day. The screams went on. When the sun was high and hot, the screams were softening, paling, dying.

Luna watched the house and felt the battle going on there. She could imagine Matilde inside demanding that they call the curandera. Finally, she saw him step from his house and look up the street. Their eyes connected. He moved toward her. She looked at her hands as he climbed onto the rickety porch. When his shoes were in her sight, she lifted her head. "My wife . . . ," he said and stopped. Luna heard only his fear that his woman was dying. "The baby won't come out—Matilde says you can work magic."

Luna wanted no such rumors whispered here about her. "I am just a curandera. There is no magic in bringing babies into the world. I feed myself by birthing babies, even those that refuse to come without a struggle."

"Will you . . ."

She was up and moving toward the fading screams. "Water. Do you have water?"

"My mother has hot water behind the house." He led her around the house. She saw an old woman who had no reason to smile today, standing sullen before a pot of steaming water.

At the huge bubbling pot, Luna ladled water into a basin Matilde held. Then, she moved to the side of the house, the only shadow, and pulled her dress down over her arms and washed the world from her flesh. Clean again, she covered herself and moved into the house. Two rooms. She could see the day beyond the wall, the planks so loosely held together.

She stepped into the second room, this roof lower than the other, and the smell that wrapped around her was edged in black. She went to the bed and looked at the woman's face, darker even than Luna's own but ashen—eyes closed. Her wrists were tied to the headboard, her ankles tied with cloth and held by two ladies at the foot of the bed to stop her struggling, the younger stroking the woman's calf gently. Her raised nightgown bared splayed legs, the vagina, torn already.

Luna knelt between the legs at the foot of the bed, watching the vulva, seeing no contractions. "Help her," the young woman to her side whispered. Luna looked at the girl, tears streaming. "Eres tú?"

"Lucita," she said, and Luna had to force her eyes from beauty so naked in its first flower. "She is my sister-friend," Lucita said. "I could not live—"

"Shh," Luna said. "I will help her." She eased her hands into the woman's body, feeling the child inside, pushing the baby back, making more room for her hands. She felt the feet—one kicked—and knew the baby was pointed wrong, the head climbing back up into its mother. She used her hands, spreading the area inside, making room and turning the baby there around. The sweat was dripping from her hair as she finally saw the crown of black damp curls. She pulled out her hands and watched the opening, dilated and ready, but saw no movement, the contractions done. She looked up at Lucita. "The baby is turned right now. I must try to let it come before intervening more."

An hour passed, but the contractions never began again. Time and again, Luna slipped her hands into the woman's body, feeling the child, feeling the beating heart. "It is alive." She glanced up at the mother and saw in the half-open eyes that the woman's heart was failing. "Get her up!" Luna ordered Lucita. The girl did not hesitate. Luna looked at Mario terrified in the doorway. "Help Lucita get your woman out of the bed."

He moved, reaching under his woman's arms and hoisting her. "Where?"

"Stand her up," Luna ordered. He and Lucita held the limp body up, the gown's hem fluttering to the ground as if to cover nakedness. "Lift her gown," Luna told Matilde. "Lucita," she calmly directed, "he can hold her up. You and Matilde use the cloths to spread her legs. Keep her standing." Luna lowered and got between Chona's legs. She looked up and saw the black curls, farther out, more crown exposed, and she felt the baby calling to her, asking for what she alone could give. "I am here, mijo," she whispered to the trapped child. She reached up, her hands sliding expertly into a space already filled, and it felt as if all bones in her hands disappeared. Fluidly, she sank her hands into the woman's body, cupping the child's head and pulling, aided by gravity, working to expel the child. "The head," she screamed and in a rush of life and liquid the child fell into the world and screamed without ever being slapped.

They laid the exhausted mother back in her bed, her mother-in-law bathing her face, already darkening to its normal deep brown. The next hour would tell. When it passed, La Luna's hands touched Chona's sleeping face, fingers telling her the crisis was over. She turned to leave, but Lucita embraced her. "Thank you . . . we came from Mexico together . . . my only friend . . . thank you."

Luna left the room, moving out onto the porch. She stood at the rickety steps and stared up toward the mulberry trees, the shack standing empty in their shade. During the day she'd queried the women about this place—Carmelas, not ten years here, the people hailing from Mazatlán except for one or two families recently arrived from other parts of Mexico, which was already beginning to feel the chaos building now. She wondered how long the shack by the trees would sit empty when Mexico exploded and exiles poured like water from a broken pot. She heard movement behind her.

"Your name?" the father—Mario—asked as he stepped out onto his porch, holding his child, who was already darkening to a brown that would grow deeper than his mother's.

"I told you. Luna." She touched the baby's lips suckling on his papi's yellow finger.

"I have two dollars."

"I want no money."

"I owe you much—much more than money."

Luna stepped closer to him. She knew the man was wondering at the misshapen head, so long and lumpy on one side, which time and a curandera's fingers would mold back into shape. After a long silence, the new father said, "Thank you," and Luna wondered why such simple words were so hard for men to say. "I must show my appreciation. If not money, what can I give?"

"A home would do," she said and felt a retreat of the hunger that had gnawed since she had lost her old teacher. His eyes went wide. She smiled. "I'm tired of walking," she said and stood up, stretching her thick brown arms toward heaven. She started up the street. He followed, his son held in his arms. She stopped before the shack that leaned, empty, toward the mulberry trees. "A house—like this one standing lonely." She climbed the steps, careful of the loose planks. "So near the mulberries, there would be always sweet perfume."

Chapter 3

A Tu Servicio - 1929

Benito Juarez de los Rios y Valles was his name and he let no one forget it from the day he arrived in Carmelas in October of 1929.

"A tu servicio," he said the morning of his arrival, removing his ragged straw hat in an arc that swept the earth as he bowed deeply before the wooden steps leading up to where the old man he'd been seeking sat in a stiff-backed chair appearing asleep though it was too hot for sleep, even on a shady porch, and not yet eleven in the morning. As Benito rose from his greeting, a loud angry banging of cupboard doors came from inside the house, causing the old man's eyes to squeeze shut more tightly. "A tu servicio," Benito said again as he straightened to his full height before the old man, whose eyes slowly opened. He blinked hard, as if the sun reflecting from Benito's large shaved head pained his eyes. Benito placed the straw hat back on his head, and the old man stopped blinking. But then, the eyes grew wide as he stared at Benito, who knew he was a sight in his flowing cotton shirt that had once been white and pantalones that could have held two men his size. He saw fear flicker across the startled eyes and Benito realized he must look like something out of a nightmare, something dark and Indian and not wholly of this world, so he smiled his broadest smile.

"Go away," the old man said, trying to make his voice fierce.

"But I have just arrived—and I intend no harm," Benito said. "Will you not take my hand?" The man struggled up from his chair, hand at his chest, and backed toward the door, when it burst open behind him. A woman—milky brown, not more than a hundred pounds—charged through. Benito felt a tingling of fear, but the woman's target was the old man, who spun to face her.

"Aha! There you are, old man, thinking you can escape from me!" The words flew like bullets. Benito slowly eased backward down a step as she shouted, "This can't go on, Papi!" Her soot-covered arms were waving. "I can't be running over here four and five times a day! I got my house, my kids, my Jose to do for, and then I do it all over here for you. Now you got me putting out *fires*!"

The old man stiffened and looked over her at Benito as if there were less to fear in him. "All this," he said directly to Benito, "over a little smoke from one forgotten pan—"

"Papi, I can't be putting up with this—no more—"

"Who asked you, mija?" the old man shouted back.

"Who asked me!" The woman's roar was so loud that Benito de los Rios y Valles backed off the steps entirely, wanting as always to run from discord.

"I can cook my own food," the old man shouted back.

"But you can't remember you're cooking—you almost burned down the house—"

"If I'd forgotten, the house *would* have burned down!"

"You can't be alone," she said, shaking her head. "No more." Then, she saw Benito.

Clicking his naked heels together noiselessly, he swept his large straw hat from his head and bent so low this time that his forehead touched the first porch step. He said, "Benito Juarez de los Rios y Valles," and as he rose he added, "a tu servicio."

The woman bristled and said, "If you're selling something, this old man hasn't got two tortillas to wrap around cheese." She strode down the steps, raising dust as she crossed the yard. At the edge of the dirt street, she looked back. "Tomorrow, Papi," she said across the barren yard, "I come to get you." Her resolve turned her face to stone. "If I have to carry you, Arnulfo Carmelas, through the streets of this barrio, I will. You are coming to live with me. You've burned your last pot!" said the old man's stringy daughter before she marched up the middle of Pontlavoy.

Behind Benito, Arnulfo sighed heavily, sounding defeated. Then, he looked again at Benito, still holding his sombrero and seeming bewildered. "I'd thought you death, you know—coming upon me as I slept." Arnulfo spat, his spittle landing in the dust just shy of Benito's toes. "I wish you had been death. I would embrace you."

"But I am only Benito Juarez—"

Arnulfo held up his hand. "I know. De los Rios . . ."

"Y Valles," Benito added. "A tu servicio." When the old man said nothing more, Benito put his foot on the first step. "Tío, I have been a long time in coming."

Startled, Arnulfo said, "Tío? Of you?" He looked more closely at Benito, who knew he was fat, dwarf-like, and very brown. "I am *your* uncle? Señor, I know no de los Rios—

"Y Valles," Benito insisted. "I know. But my mother was Carmelas. Margarita."

Looking as if a ghost had swept before his eyes, Arnulfo said, "My sister? Mi palida Margarita? Thirty years gone . . . ," he said, making it sound like a lifetime, "since . . . last I saw her." He shook his head hard and looked at Benito again. "Your mother?"

"Claro, tío. Mi mamá."

The old man closed his eyes and said, "A little girl of nine. That's what I see—tall, long-limbed—a child who never stopped dancing. With skin so light," he emphasized, opening his eyes to look again at Benito's dark face, "she freckled in the sunlight of Mazatlán. What happened?"

Benito listened to his uncle's dismay that one such as he could have come from a mother as lovely as his own, but said nothing.

"Where is your hair?" Arnulfo asked.

Benito smiled, flashing brilliant teeth. "Piojos, tío. "

Arnulfo stepped back.

"Have no fear, tío," Benito assured. "They're gone—with my hair." He slapped his bald, shining head. "My road to you has been long and hard. The people I traveled with not always honest or clean. It has been worth the hardships to finally find you."

"You travel light, nephew," his uncle said, sounding suspicious again.

Benito shrugged, not wanting to think of his misfortunes on the road. "I began with two bags, tío. Lost—both—en route." His smile faded at this distortion of the truth. Suddenly he felt tired, not just from the road north—his foolish trusting of everyone who looked his way—but of it all, his life, the constant moving, arriving always with less than when he started out. His mother—whom he had served all his days, but never really satisfied—had been the only permanence, and she was gone now too.

"You lose your hair to lice, your bags to thieves."

Benito nodded and saw the corners of the old man's eyes turn up as he smiled.

"You're lucky you arrived today. Tomorrow, surely, you'd have lost those pants." Arnulfo turned and opened the screen door—loose at its upper hinge. Before stepping inside, his uncle squinted back at Benito. "My sister's son?"

"Benito Juarez de los—"

"I know," Arnulfo said, cutting him off. "Come in the house. A man can't be too careful these days." He waved up the dusty street. "Carmelas filling with a flood of strangers, all running from Mexico as if it is our obligation to feed them"—he looked suspicious again—"all of them claiming some thread of kinship."

For a moment, Benito was sure the old man was going to chase him off, but he told Benito to come on. He followed his tío up the steps into a small room, no cooler than the porch, but dark, the windows shaded, instantly knowing he and his mother had never lived in lodging so fine as this. Beyond, there was a doorway leading to even more rooms. The floor was wood. Benito's mama had died in a room with a wooden floor in Mexico City. Dust rose through the spaces in the floor as he walked to where his uncle stood staring at a series of photographs along a wall.

"Where is my sister?" Arnulfo asked.

"Dead, tío."

The old man fell silent, one hand touching the edge of a portrait of a woman, soft, smiling, round. "In Mazatlán?" Arnulfo asked.

"No. She left Mazatlán when still a girl—"

Arnulfo turned his head and asked, "Where did my father take her?"

"She was alone, tío—an orphan by then, she told me."

"As God is my witness," Arnulfo said, "after sending for my Gloria, I tried and tried to bring your mother out of Mexico."

Benito felt tears at his eyes, for truth revealed always made him weep. "I believe you, uncle."

"I couldn't write—I did not know how . . . my Gloria neither—"

"But my mother spoke of letters . . . money sent from the north."

Arnulfo nodded. "I sent money until the revolution put an end to that."

"She never spoke much of Mazatlán," Benito said, "except that federales had burned her house, leaving her a girl upon the streets. So, she ran away, tío. She told me she would have run off with a circus—but there were no circuses that year . . . only the revolution and the invitation it offered."

Benito saw his uncle smile. "That is how I remember her, a child pursuing dreams."

"Armies, tío," Benito corrected.

Arnulfo's smile disappeared. "Armies?"

"The revolution," Benito reminded.

"She was a soldier?"

"She followed soldiers." Benito felt alarm at the look filling Arnulfo's face. "Have you not heard, tío, the songs of Las Adelitas?"

Arnulfo put a hand on his heart. "Mi Margarita—following soldiers—"

"And liberty, tío—the reason for it all!"

The old man moved past Benito and in the doorway turned. "Did she find it?" His uncle's eyes brightened wetly and Benito's own filled again—others' tears always calling his own for company.

"She said it is the search, tío, that matters. Things are bad again in Mexico."

"Every day," Arnulfo said, "new ones arrive with horror tales. Soon there will be no place to put them." He wiped his brow. "My sister," he said mournfully.

"The search goes on, tío—"

"Your search," Arnulfo said, blinking his eyes hard, "brings you to me?"

Benito looked at his naked feet. "My mother said you'd take me in."

"Your mother spoke of me?"

"So often, tío, it is as if I know you. She told me—since I was a boy riding behind her on a horse—of how you came north and built a city called Carmelas—"

"A city?" Arnulfo said and laughed. "Four dirt streets, a barrio—"

"That has your name," Benito argued. The old man nodded

after a moment and then walked on through the doorway. Benito followed into a hallway saying, "When we got to the capital, we found a map, but you were never on the map, Carmelas." Ahead of him, Arnulfo snorted. "But then, the very night before she died, she had this burst of brilliance, tío—"

The old man stopped in the narrow hallway. "A brilliance," the old man repeated, "like before an electric light goes out." He said it with familiarity. "It blossoms, mijo—a surge of life."

"Exactly, tío. She sat up in bed and demanded pistachios. I went out into the streets, my heart dancing, for I thought she was getting well. I found pistachios—no easy task for the lateness of the hour and the season."

"She ate them?"

Benito nodded. "And sang, tío—all her favorite songs of the revolution when she was young and needed."

"Your mother?" Arnulfo asked. "The night she died . . ."

"She lasted out the night, singing until dawn. The sun finally came up. The building next door beyond our window, tío, was pink, reflecting sunlight that slid across our room with morning, turning everything to rose. When it touched my mother's toes—" Benito could not finish, and stared wetly into his uncle's eyes.

The old man lifted a hand as thick and heavy as a loaf of bread to Benito's cheek. "Maybe," the old man said, "there is something in the eyes." He dropped his hand, and, turning, walked on into a large kitchen that smelled of smoke and soot. Benito followed, seeing the evidence of fire, a wall charred and black behind a huge, heavy iron stove. The room was large. A table, marred and old, stood in the middle, five chairs circled round. "My family," Arnulfo said. The old man waved a hand behind him toward the pictures on the front room wall. "My wife. My children. Seven. Five born here inside this house. All gone. The flu, 1919. All of them—except for Josefa, the one who smiles."

He turned and went to the heavy stove. "Go out back and bring me wood."

Benito went out the back door, which was hard to open, for the frame was leaning out of plumb. Outside as he gathered wood, he noticed the rows of corn at the back of the yard. He brought firewood into the kitchen, putting it into the stove and seeing, through the wall behind, daylight peeking through in places where the flames had eaten through.

"I feel them around me," the old man said. "Here. How could I leave? Thirty years."

Benito, who had never wanted more than to stay put in one safe place, could not imagine thirty years between familiar walls and in a rush said, "Why, tío, must you go?"

"She is not bad, my Josefa. She talks to me in ways she shouldn't, but she has more than enough plaguing her over on Carmenita where she holds up Jose's roof." He shook his head. "A serious child—smiles were like gold. She had no—"

The screaming woman's face floated before Benito's eyes. "No humor, tío . . . no—"

"Exactly! No sense of humor. And who does she marry?"

"Jose?"

"Exactly. A man for whom life is one big joke. What can she do but smack her kids and kick the dogs and drive me crazy." Arnulfo made his hand into a fist and hit the tabletop hard. "Am I asking her to run over here every two hours? I want peace. Peace and Josefa just don't go together. A little smoke—chisme carries the tale from street to street creating fire."

"The wall is burned, tío. Look, you can see into the yard beyond—"

"Maybe a little fire—who does Josefa think put it out?"

"She loves you and she is afraid," Benito said, his eyes watering again, for who knew better than he how closely love and fear were intertwined.

The old man looked at his tearing eyes, but said only, "Sit. I will feed my sister's son."

"Benito Juarez—"

"De los Rios—I know," Arnulfo said and started rummaging through some cupboards.

"Y Valles," Benito finished for him.

He pulled two plates from a cupboard. He looked at Benito. "Do I appear a man who needs looking after?" he demanded, extending the hand holding the plates and dropping both, which shattered at Benito's feet.

Ignoring the flying pieces of breaking plates, Benito said with a flourish, "I see a man who built a barrio that holds his name!"

"Exactly," Arnulfo said, reaching for two more plates and setting them this time with both hands on the table. Then, he opened the icebox, and Benito saw there was little else of anything to eat save for a block of cheese. "Josefa brought me cheese today. The woman may not smile, but she makes fine cheese." Arnulfo's hand closed on the block of cheese, and he set it on the table before pulling open a drawer and removing a knife. Turning, he waved the knife in the air like a sword and asked, "Your father? Señor de los Rios y Valles? Does he still live?"

"God knows," Benito said, eyeing the cheese hungrily.

"How did you lose contact?" Arnulfo said, setting the knife on the table.

Benito picked it up and cut off a piece of cheese, stuffing it into his mouth. "I didn't. I never knew him."

After a silence, Arnulfo said, "This Señor de los Rios y Valles—"

"He was a soldier," Benito said and laughed. "I know that much. Have you tortillas too, tío?"

Arnulfo took down a towel-covered bowl holding tortillas, saying, "Josefa makes them for me fresh every morning. " He set them in front of Benito, who took one and filled it with more cheese.

"A special soldier?" Arnulfo asked. "This father of yours . . . was he a hero of the revolution?"

"My mother said all soldiers are special, all are heroes—all the revolucionarios who forded the rivers and conquered the valleys of Mexico—I could be proud of any of them!"

Arnulfo asked, "But which, nephew, which soldier was your father?"

Benito was busy eating and answered only after he cut still more cheese and rolled it deftly into another soft corn tortilla. "She told me to consider all of them my father."

Arnulfo went sallow and sat heavily. The only sound at the table was Benito chewing, until Arnulfo asked, "How old are you, muchacho?"

"I was born with the revolution—1910," Benito said and slapped the table hard.

"I hope all your arrivals don't bring such commotion," Arnulfo said. "I am too old for much more fuss."

"I live to serve, tío." Benito thought of all the years providing for his mother, more faithful than any of her soldiers. Between mouthfuls he added, "I am indeed my mother's son."

"God have mercy," Arnulfo whispered and changed the subject. "But what of Mexico, nephew? The only good thing into Carmelas out of Mexico recently is the indio Vicente who grows flowers—as brown as you, mijo, he has a wife pale like a gauchupin—and tells us only nightmare your revolution brings."

"He is mistaken, tío. I carry the revolution next to my heart. My mamá told me—on her death bed, tío, to live as she lived—"

Arnulfo crossed himself.

"To love those who are in need, to make the fallen rise tall again, to use my hands, my body, my soul to give pleasure in this tear-strewn world—"

"Coffee, nephew?" Arnulfo asked, rising from the table, shaking his head. "Josefa brought a pot—"

"Yes, tío. With cream, please," Benito asked, remembering a

soldier who had once long ago given him coffee gold and sweet with heavy cream to keep Benito occupied while he walked Benito's mother into the trees. Surely his tío who lived in a house of many rooms with wooden floors would have such cream.

"In this tear-strewn corner of the world," Arnulfo said, "we're lucky to have sugar." He passed the cup. Benito drank, smacking his lips. Arnulfo sat and faced his sister's son, appraising him again. "Your skin is good, boy," he said, "very dark, but it is bright and clean considering the road you've taken . . . and stretched so tight, nephew, over all your bulk."

Benito went on chewing, for the words sounded almost like praise.

"Clearly," his uncle said, "you have not starved on your journey to me. Vicente Gil arrived here a skeleton."

Benito laughed and pushed his chair back from the table. He lifted his shirt, baring a belly as brilliantly brown as his bald dome and rounder than a barrel, and with both hands grabbed hold of it. "A rock, tío. Feel."

Arnulfo poked and found it hard, solid. "Muscle need not be pretty," the old man agreed.

"So long as it works. That's what my mother always said. Pretty doesn't always bring home fine tortillas," Benito said, laughing and grabbing another from Josefa's bowl, thinking of his labor spent to keep his mother in tortillas, beans, and cheap pulque.

"My sister," Arnulfo said, staring past Benito at his charred wall. "Please tell me she didn't follow soldiers all her days."

Benito set down his half-eaten tortilla and felt his eyes go wet again. Irritated, he batted them, for he knew the tears were proof of the weakness at his core that could surface over anything that touched his heart with pain or beauty, but his mother's life—her end—proved just too much to fight today, so he let the tears spill down his cheeks. "Such happiness, tío, was denied her. We ended up far from the rivers, the valleys that she loved in the capital, closed in by buildings that scratched at heaven. We had a room on Avenida Diez y Seis de Septiembre near el campo militar, but for those soldiers, tío, mi mamita had only disdain. Her revolution was betrayed. It needed her no more, so she had given up on soldiers, keeping room in her heart for only me." He looked up and saw tears spilling also from his uncle's eyes and felt a bond, a shared weakness, that forced them to feel too much, too soon, for anyone and everyone. And in a burst of affection for this man Benito added, "And for you, tío. As she lay dying, a pale flower in my Indian embrace, she whispered—"

"What?" Arnulfo asked, breathless, pulled by Benito's dark intensity.

"'Mijo,' she said, 'give pleasure to my brother's last days, for he is old. Find him, for I feel he needs you.'"

Arnulfo shook his head as if to clear it. "I need you?"

Benito rose in a dramatic swoop. "*You need me!*" He took his uncle's hand and dragged him from the kitchen, through the house and out onto the tired porch, flowers brilliant in the boiling sun in fields across narrow dusty Pontlavoy. "Look at your hands, tío," Benito demanded, holding them palms up.

Arnulfo lifted his hands high before his eyes and scanned them, turning them over in the sunlight.

"They have labored enough. It is time they rested." He pushed his uncle backwards, gently, into his chair. "I am here now, tío. Josefa can't be running over three times a day—"

"She wants me in her house." Arnulfo put his hands over his ears. "She screams, nephew! There is no peace."

"She worries, tío. I will ease her worry. I will bring peace," he said, "to you and Josefa—" and Benito felt a hole fill up somewhere in his middle that had gaped wide his whole life through. He had held his dead mother until her body had gone cold and hard, for she had been all that had ever stood between him and emptiness. She who had been his only connection to blood beyond his own was gone, leaving him alone with nothing save a trail of blood heading north to this uncle. As he'd sat holding her deadness, terror stabbing, he could hear her telling him what she had said more than once—but only when drunk on cheap thin pulque and not really herself at all—that it would take a soldier to follow any trail so faint and that Benito, soft, fat, weak, and foolish, was certainly no soldier. "But I am here, tío," he said almost angrily, contradicting a ghost, "and my walk was hard."

Arnulfo looked up at him and nodded. "I walked it, too."

"But I was afraid, tío—"

"I, too, nephew."

"I was robbed of my bags," Benito confessed, falling to his knees before the old man, "played more than once the fool."

"There *was* a fire, mijo," Arnulfo sighed. "Much more than just a little smoke."

"You put it out."

"And you arrived." He rested his hand on Benito's shoulder.

"I am no soldier, tío," Benito said, lowering his eyes, shame naked in his dark admission, never said before out loud.

His uncle touched his face, lifting it. "Maybe the world has had its fill of soldiers."

"But I can cook," Benito insisted, rising from the floor. "You can't imagine my huevos rancheros, tío. From my mother I learned and she, tío, cooked for armies."

"I am particular about my tortillas." Arnulfo looked up at him, studying. "What do you want of me?"

"To have you honor my connection—to tell me you see your blood when you look—inside—of me."

"An Indian I see—"

"Benito Juarez was an Indian brown as I am."

"But no one to me . . . that Juarez," Arnulfo said, studying Benito's face, and in the old eyes Benito saw a softening. "*You* are more familiar. Something . . . in the eyes." He closed his eyes and leaned back in his chair. His eyes opened. "Josefa said she will take me out of here tomorrow—carry me through the barrio—"

"We will stand up to her. We have walked from Mexico."

Arnulfo laughed. Then, he stopped laughing. "Let me think."

"Claro, tío, and while you think, I will repair that wall behind your stove and mend your sagging doors."

"A carpenter, too, nephew?"

"Jesus should be my middle name."

"I do hate my Josefa worrying—"

"I'm here, tío," Benito shouted, feeling in his rounded shoulders the need for other people's burdens.

"My sister's son," Arnulfo said, sighing sleepily, "Benito—"

"Juarez," Benito added and saw inside his head himself—a boy—clinging to his mother's hips, her black hair flying as they raced with wind on the sleek horse that had been her favorite when she'd been young and had her pick of soldiers, and he heard her remembered voice shout, *"De los Rios y Valles"* as her freckled hand slapped his brown thigh, "y, mijo, don't you ever forget it!"

He saw that his uncle had fallen asleep, so he wandered to the back of the house and whistled when he saw the rows of head-high corn and licked his lips as he thought of the potent brew he could pull from just such corn. Surely, his uncle could use the extra cash. He turned to the house and saw where the fire had eaten up the wall, two planks of wood ruined. He ran his hand over the damage, figuring through his fingers all that the repair would entail. He looked up at the sun and judged the time. Then, he left the yard and moved up Pontlavoy, deciding to make himself known and see if he could find just the wood his tío needed.

His bare feet lifted dust as he walked up the street, flowers in fields to his right; to his left, he passed a shack, no different from his uncle's. The wood was as naked of paint, bleached by sun. But on this porch sat not an old man sleeping, but a young woman—a girl who stole his breath and made him stop still. Her skin was pale, the honeyed gold of his mother's color. She was reading a magazine suspended on her knees, her head bent, her black hair straight, falling in sheets on each side of her face and sweeping the steps. For an instant he did just as he had always done when confronted by a lovely woman. He thought of his squat brownness and felt the old familiar desire to retreat from every battle, leaving life's booty to those who deserved it. But this time, he stopped cold his thinking of a lifetime, ordering it back as a soldier would an enemy, and though he'd never be a soldier, he was a man who had walked across the world and would doubt himself no more.

So, there, in the middle of a dusty road in a barrio called Carmelas, he did what he had seen soldiers do time and again to win his mother. He sucked in air and began to serenade, singing, "Allá en el rancho grande," and, sure enough, the girl's head shot up as he crooned to heaven, "ya donde me vivía . . . ," his voice rising to a note so high, but one he knew would never crack. And in the sharp upward lift of her head, he saw her black hair fall back like water, revealing her face, a vision, eyes that cut his heart, a mouth—a mouth he knew he'd one day kiss and claim. Filling his lungs, he sang, "Hay una chaparita, chiquita y bonita. . . ," and her yellow skin went red.

"Lolita!" A voice called shrilly from inside the house.

She rose, her magazine falling from her lap, her hand rising toward her mouth, but not before he saw her smile. He swept off his straw hat and bowed deeply, elegantly, a bow he'd seen a thousand soldiers cast his mother's way, and shouted as loudly as he had sung, "Benito Juarez de los Rios y Valles. A tu servicio."

Before he lifted his eyes, he heard a woman scream, "Lola Escalante, ven pa ca ahorita!," followed by the slamming of a screen door. When he straightened, she was gone. For today. Whistling, Benito walked up the street that was already his.

Chapter 4

What Lola Wants - 1934

Realizing it was time, Lola Escalante sat up in bed, heart pounding, and looked around the crowded bedroom she shared with her four sisters to make sure everyone was sound asleep. Tiny Chata curled against Lupe, the two snoring softly in the bed they shared across the room, while Linda and Delia, back to back, made no sound in their bed, a foot from Lola's own.

Only then did Lola leave her bed, for if she slipped up, Mama would be up and out of her bed across the hall and Lola's plan would die. As Lola moved across the old wooden floor, she knew God was at her back, for the old planks made no peep, no creak at all.

She stopped before the doorway and ran her eyes over the bedroom walls, the images scattered there almost lost to darkness. But she didn't need light to know the looks that Clark Gable, Joan Crawford, Bette Davis—all the stars of Hollywood—were throwing her way. She'd papered the plain wooden bedroom walls with pictures gathered from Sandy's cast-off *Photoplay*s. Next to the doorway that had never had a door to close, she saw Carole Lombard keeping sentry above the light switch, her smirk even in the darkness enough to make Lola smile. That smirk, Lola had perfected and thrown at Mama more times than she could count.

Before finally leaving her bedroom, Lola touched Lombard's face and then glanced up high above the door to the place of honor that held the photo of Lupe Velez, the actress's dusky skin evident in the black-and-white picture and proof to Lola that even a Mexican could find a place in the heaven that was Hollywood. On tiptoe, she managed to get down the hall, passing Mama's open door without a sound. At the closed front door, she slipped out of her nightgown, her faded cotton everyday dress already on underneath. After slipping her bunched nightgown behind her papa's chair, she put her feet into the sturdy oxfords she'd placed by the door before going to bed, leaving the laces loose. The front door would have been the trickiest maneuver because Papa had never hung it right in the first place and its singing had announced the presence of anyone passing through until Benito from next door had come over not two days ago and rehung it. This night as she opened and then closed the door behind her, there was total silence. Not even the tired screen door protested as she shut it. Surely Benito's arrival out of the blue with a bag of old Arnulfo's tools was a sign God wanted this, too.

After tying her shoes, she slipped her hands into her dress pockets to still their trembling and felt the folded paper note she'd meant to leave on the kitchen sink where Mama wouldn't have found it until after breakfast when she washed dishes. She couldn't go back in, so she pulled out the note and put it in the corner of the tattered screen door, which might even be a better place. Mama wouldn't find it until she came out to sweep the porch, long after Papa was in the fields.

"Estoy yendo con Sandy to the movies in Long Beach. Con cariño, Lola."

That's what the note said. Short. Sweet. She smiled, imagining Mama when she read it and thought of this daughter who dared to take the whole day off to go to the movies—without even asking. Lola knew the fury the note would set to bubbling deep in Mama's chest . . . but she also knew the note would be believed, for Lola had defied her mother in just this way before, leaving Mama with nothing to do but fume.

Turning, she trotted down the steps, no longer afraid of noise. She skipped through the dusty yard, skirting the neat rows of corn Papa had planted, filling their large yard to overflowing. In the street—a dirt trail between the edge of their yard and the flower fields that extended into darkness and bore the grand name of Pontlavoy—she turned and followed the neat row of Papa's corn, full, heavy with ears, tassels waving in the breeze, growing toward heaven as was its destiny.

No different from the corn, Lola was simply allowing God to pull her in the same way toward what certainly had always been her own destiny. She glanced back at Don Arnulfo's house, knowing Benito often rose before the sun, but it was still. She walked briskly, passing the Galvan shack, the last of their street of houses at the very edge of Carmelas, toward the darkness of the mulberry trees and the Hinton field beyond.

She moved off the dirt road into the dark overhang of the two mulberry trees, giant sentries sitting at the top of their four dusty streets. She passed the irrigation ditch at the edge of the trees' shadow, the moon on the water making it look like a swimming pool movie stars had in their own backyards. Then, she stepped into the large field beyond the ditch, which had been full of Hinton corn a week ago and was now naked after the harvesting. Glancing behind, she saw the dark outlines of her barrio and felt its pull. Rejecting it, she turned back, Sandy's house before her. She began to run across the turned earth away from Carmelas toward something she'd always sought and would today discover. She felt the air racing in and out of her body, her breath a locomotive to match the joy in her heart.

Jane Withers. Ed Wynn.

Not her favorites. But stars! Coming to Norwalk. Today. 1934. October 10. The day she'd been waiting for all her life. Front

Street. The train station there. For today it would become Hollywood, just as Sandy had announced weeks ago, and their plan had taken shape. Her head filled with an image of fluttering pages, all the pages of all the movie magazines she and Sandy had ever read. Warner Bros. was shooting a movie, turning Norwalk of all places into Hollywood for a day, making magic and surely making Sandy and her into stars.

This had to be what she'd been waiting for all her life, the reason she'd put everything else on hold. Her mother thought her crazy. She was almost eighteen, with Carmelas boys lined up as if she were a prize for them to pluck, and she would have none of them, driving her mother loco by paying more attention to funny, fat, ugly Benito who had come from Mexico with the ridiculous name that he repeated at every opportunity than the más desirable boys her mama dreamed of. A prize she was, but one they'd never touch before Lola found out what God had held in store for her all these years.

For as long as she could remember, she had been filled with this sense that she was special—chosen—and not just to be some brown man's wife either. She'd had no idea for what she had been chosen—but that had bothered her not at all until recently. Forever, it seemed, she'd been filled with this expectancy. She would stand at the edge of her wooden porch and stare out over the flower fields, the pickers humped here and there, her neighbors, mere dots on the horizon, and she would feel something in the air, something moving towards her, something she could neither see nor hear but almost touch, so heavy it seemed in the air, so full of secret promise. She could remember times she had lifted her hand as if to reach into the sky and grab it, pull it home so she would see, know finally what it held for her, but it remained always out there, over the flower fields, lost in the heat, the dust, the dirt, but there.

And in the past year, with the boys so thick about her door

and Mama telling her life is an hourglass from which the sand was slipping, falling fast, a desperation had begun to take hold, for beauty like hers—the honey drawing boys and promise—was only a quickly passing gift that must be used, her mama said, for once it passed, a woman had so little other currency to attract anything but the likes of the indio next door, Benito.

It was just that desperation that had sent her one dark night one street over to Claresa and La Luna's porch, where, every night at least until the winter cool would drive her inside, the old scarred woman sat long after all the barrio and its gossip had retreated from the streets. And the visit was not easy, for Lola found the dark woman, prized by most in the barrio as their curandera, unsettling.

Lola's unease with the woman who had brought her into the world and nursed her ills off and on throughout the years had nothing to do with the woman's face and its pitted scars everyone said was God's mark and evidence of victory in a childhood bout with smallpox so severe that it would surely have killed anyone not blessed. Lola had seen the woman enough in growing up to look behind the scars. No, it was not the woman's scars; it was her eyes, which seemed to see a person's thoughts, her smell—not unclean, just an odd one that floated about her body like a cloud—and the way the old woman would take a person's hand, her fingers moving over flesh as if eyes were hidden in her fingertips, that unsettled Lola. And then there was the woman's house; a single room, her shack had Christ hanging from every wall with shelves stuck everywhere high and low holding statues of all the saints in heaven, and one corner devoted to the Virgin, with images from wood to clay of the Blessed Mother's thousand faces, all of which set Lola's teeth on edge, too strong a testimony to goodness.

But Lola had gone to her that night—the first time in years—because rumor, chisme only whispered, had it that Luna was magic and could see tomorrow. Approaching the old woman's porch, before she even saw the woman's bulky shadow, she heard La Luna call out, "Lolita, I have been waiting."

Disconcerted, Lola stepped up onto the porch and extended the basket she was carrying, "Señora, I've brought you eggs—a dozen—from my mother's Banti hens, the eggs you prize."

Luna took the basket. "Thank you." Then, she reached up fast and took Lola's right hand, caressing. "Your loveliness shines even here in the dark. Do you know you were beautiful when pulled from the womb—my most beautiful child. Your beauty will never fade, child, even as you die . . ."

Lola gasped.

The old woman laughed in the dark. "Years and years from now." She squeezed Lola's hand, wrapping her leathery fingers tight around it.

Frightened, Lola asked, "My life?"

"A gift is coming—it will be with you always and change your life forever, warming the days of your old age."

From that night, just as Lola's mother trusted in God, Lola trusted in whatever it was that called to her. Indeed, this middle-of-the-night run through an empty field was toward whatever it was that she felt had marked her alone of the Carmelas Mexicans.

Lola's breath, tearing at her throat as she raced across the field, caused her to slow down. She stopped, the field silent, the smell of turned earth rising to her nose. Chosen. Born in Carmelas, but the prettiest child any of them had ever seen—they'd told her, even La Luna, over and over again—prettier even than Sandy Hinton, born the very same day and the first child of the patron who to this day despite the Depression employed almost all of them at some time or another during any given year. "And your skin, mija," her mother told her all the time, "like leche quemada!"

And Sandy Hinton, when she'd grown old enough to wander,

had chosen Lola, of all the girls in Carmelas, as her friend. Standing all these years later in the night in the middle of the naked field, she remembered the first time she'd seen Sandy strutting down the dirt road in front of Lola's house. Lola had been perched on the steps, never allowed then far out of reach of Mama's eyes or voice. The girl in the street had appeared colorless at first, for her hair was as white as her skin. She seemed a white blur as she ran up to the porch—as if it were her own—her pale belly protruding from under the edge of a boy's undershirt. "Let's play." Those had been her first words.

Lola had watched the girl's mouth move, heard the sounds, but understood little, then. "I'm Sandy Hinton, if you please," the ghost-like girl said, hitting her own chest and laughing.

"Sandy," Lola repeated, liking the sounds on her tongue.

"Who're you?" Sandy said, coming close and poking at Lola's chest.

"Lola," she said, drawing back. Sandy grabbed her hand and tried to pull her off the porch. "*Mamá!*" Lola had screamed. Mama was instantly at the door.

"I want to play with her," Sandy demanded and seemed to have no idea how fierce Mama could be; Mama's face tightened, and the words giving permission seemed a lie. Sandy dragged her off, and Lola couldn't believe it. Her mother never let her off the porch. That day she first learned Sandy could do wondrous things, even with Mama—as she often proved throughout the years the girls had grown together.

When Sandy had started school far off in downtown Norwalk, her father—the same Andy Hinton who paid Lola's father's wages—had asked Lola's mother if Lola could start kindergarten too and keep Sandy company. Carmelas girls didn't go to school then. But Lola had gone; such power Sandy had even over Lola's papa.

"What will you wear, mija, with all those rich gavachos?" her mother had asked, trying to frighten her out of going. But Mrs. Hinton had brought a pile of her old dresses to Mama, and Mama had made Lola the finest dresses the Carmelas girls had ever seen, fashioned from Mrs. Hinton's cast-off cloth.

Then later, when Mrs. Hinton had come the first time to see if Lola could stay overnight when she'd been seven, Mama had been horrified at the thought of a girl child sleeping in another's house, but all she'd said was, "Señora 'inton, mi girl es molestación for you. She will stay home."

"She is a godsend, Lupe. Better her than another of these Carmelas Indians. My Sandy has no one to play with."

And Lola had gone, not understanding then the power all the Hintons held over her small wooden house in Carmelas.

So, now, years later, as she ran toward the Hinton house in which she'd spent so much time, it felt in some ways like running home. She got to the Hintons' yard, an expanse of green that went all around the house and was surrounded by fields. She went to Sandy's window and tapped.

The shade was pulled back and the smile of welcome that washed over Sandy's face seemed almost like morning. Sandy pushed up the window. "You're up before the chickens, kid." She popped out the screen, opening it wide enough for Lola to climb in.

"Had to get out before Mama got up."

Sandy went to the light and turned it on. It washed over her cropped hair.

"What have you done?" Lola asked.

"Pixie look. What do you think?" She spun around. "Wait'll you see it after Lorrie fixes it. Spit curls. I'll probably have a movie contract by this afternoon." She ran over to the bed and shook the lump under the covers.

Lorrie sat up, yawning. She smiled when she saw Lola. "Hi, Lo. God, is it still dark?"

"Get up," Sandy ordered. "We got to get to Front Street before anybody else."

Lola went to Sandy's closet and opened it. She kicked off her oxfords. Hanging in the closet was her dress. It shimmered in the light. Navy blue with white polka dots—jersey. The black bra, all lace and dream, hung at the collar along with silk stockings. Her throat closed. Her eyes looked down at the high heels on the closet floor—spectators with heels so high they'd make her mama scream. She closed her eyes.

"What you going to do with your hair, Lola?" Lorrie asked.

"It is long," Sandy said.

Lola turned and saw them eyeing her hair.

"I could do wonders," Lorrie offered.

"She cut mine, I swear to God. She's an artist. If she doesn't get to be an actress, she can become a makeup artist. I'm going to wear a sign. Coiffure by Lorrie Parkhurst." She laughed.

Lola lifted her hand and ran it through the heavy black hair hanging to her waist. "I don't know. I've never cut it—"

"High time," Lorrie tempted.

Sandy jumped across the bed, grabbing her new *Photoplay*. She moved to Lola and fanned the pages before her. "Long hair nowhere, Lola."

Lola closed her eyes, surrendering to destiny.

An eternity later, Lorrie ordered, "Turn around," a whoop barely concealed in her command.

Lola turned, her eyes still closed.

Sandy thumped her back. "Go on, look!"

She opened her eyes and saw someone else in the bathroom mirror.

"Puts us to shame," Lorrie said.

"You're beautiful, Lola," Sandy said in awe.

And she was. Her hair, black, thick, rose from her crown, waving over her ears, following the line of her chin to points that curled up looking like a helmet, sleek and glossy.

"Let me," Lorrie said and wet her fingers, curling the points. "Spit curls like spit curls are supposed to be."

Lola's eyes looked enormous, velvet. Her skin, so much skin, the neck long and naked-looking, was pale, a yellowed gold her mother fought to keep covered from the sun. She had been a girl when she'd awakened. A woman stared out at her from the mirror. She cocked her head and pouted at her image, winking.

The girls behind her squealed.

"A goddamned movie star," Sandy said, envy dripping.

"Get out of here," Lola ordered, pushing them from the small bathroom. "Let me dress."

Alone, she stripped naked and stood brazen before the mirror, marveling at how her color grew paler over her rising breasts, each capped in dusky rose that hardened in the coolness of the room. She lifted her head and stared into the mirror, trying to capture the look Crawford threw at men, a look that seemed to tell them she could eat them if she cared. She slipped the black bra over her breasts. Reaching back, she hooked the bands, which tightened, pulling her breasts together and creating cleavage she'd never had before. Now, she looked back into the mirror and posed. She lifted an eyebrow, widening the size of her enormous brown eyes, and kissed the camera she pretended was behind the mirror. Then, she dressed.

When she stepped into the bedroom, Sandy whistled playfully.

"Where'd you get that great dress?" Lorrie asked.

"I took her to Loman's down in Long Beach," Sandy said.

"How'd you ever afford that?" Lorrie asked.

"Oh, she had bundles saved," Sandy answered for her, "from helping Mama around our house."

Lola stepped into her heels, the feel of the shoe against her silk-covered foot delicious. She turned back to the open bathroom and her breath caught. Heaps of black hair—her own—lay scattered, stark against the white tile. Her hand went to her head. "What will happen when Mama finds out?"

"It'll be too late," Sandy said. "Everything's set. When your mama comes running over here, my mother'll tell her we're in Long Beach riding the roller coaster and going to the movies."

"She'll lie?"

"Course not. She thinks it's the truth," Sandy said. "You know my ma, she wouldn't let me be caught dead with all those harlots and hussies coming to Norwalk today to shoot a movie. So, when I asked her if I could have the car and drive all the way to Long Beach for the day, she jumped at it. That's just what she'll tell your mama. All either of 'em need to know." Sandy laughed and said, "Anyway, you know I can fix anything with your mama!"

So, then and there, Lola pushed all worry away.

They arrived on Front Street early as planned. Hollywood was already there when they arrived, the station platform turned into a sound stage, lights that seemed brighter than the sun as it climbed in the morning sky.

Sandy ran into girlfriends from Excelsior High. She seemed to know everybody. They moved all over the platform amid crowds that grew thicker as the morning passed, and Sandy never let loose of Lola's arm. And from the moment of her arrival on Front Street, Lola felt the presence of her promise closer than it had ever been. Her excitement, constant since waking, rose and fell like the tide on the ocean, as the morning turned to afternoon. The smells, the colors, the noise, the press of people created waves of sensation that rolled in and over her like the sea as she stood on the platform of the Norwalk train station waiting for her dream to unfold around her.

As the day wore on, Lola stood on the platform or strolled arm in arm with Sandy back and forth across the steps of the train station, waiting. The station as if touched by magic had been transformed—lights, hundreds of lights erected in a circle around the tail end of a train car going nowhere, and people, so many people milling, pushing, pulling, shouting, making the air electric. And any of them pushing light could have been stars, though none she'd ever seen in magazines, for they seemed charged, faces flush, agleam as if their closeness to magic and the machines that could remake the world had remade them, too.

Suddenly, she connected the sense of expectancy filling the station with the movie magazines in which she'd immersed herself all these years. Only now did she see how they had always been pointing her to this, and the first inkling had come the day she'd named the dream. She and Sandy had been sitting under the two giant mulberry trees, Sandy leafing through her newest *Photoplay* not long after her fascination with movies had begun. Lola's heart had been untouched by Sandy's passion until she turned the page, revealing Hollywood's newest angel, Lupe Velez—looking nothing like the blonde pale stars on every other page. Suddenly, staring out from *Photoplay,* was a woman with black hair and golden skin, reflections of Lola's own. There under the mulberry trees, August heat rolling about them, Lola felt the same pull that had hovered about her forever, rising this time from the pages of a magazine, in the dusky image of a woman as Mexican as herself.

From then on—even more than Sandy—Lola had been mad about the movies, the cavalcade of stars, the magazines that opened windows on a world never even dreamed of. She devoured the magazines, secondhand.

One magazine a week, bought over Sandy's mother's protests of tight money and the national Depression. Fifty-two in a year. Sandy tired of them as fast as they came and passed them on to Lola, who felt them gold. She would bury them under her bed. She would cover the walls with an ever-changing parade of faces—except for the original picture of Lupe Velez that never lost its place of honor high above her bedroom door—each image calling out to her, speaking in a tongue she could not fully grasp but knew she'd one day understand.

That day had come. As Sandy and Lorrie began to wilt in the afternoon sun on the steps of the Norwalk train station, Lola's spirits only rose higher.

"I think I've had it," Sandy said.

Lola looked at her in disbelief.

"Don't give me that look, kiddo," Sandy said. "I'm tired. Let's go get an ice cream."

Lola shook her head no, for she knew her moment was at hand. Sandy dropped her arm and walked toward the drugstore.

"Don't leave me, Sandy. You might miss the call," Lola cried, but Sandy was already gone, and Lola knew that if Sandy could look at the train station and see only the train station as it had always been, the promise had never been Sandy's at all. Only hers. It was her name alone that would be called.

And there, in the sun atop the platform in front of the train station with Sandy still in sight but cut off from the dream—it happened.

As Lola rose to call one last time to Sandy, she heard someone shout, "You!"

Lola looked and saw a man standing near the camera that had been the centerpiece of all the morning's activity.

"With the spit curls. *You!* Come here."

She'd gone. Chosen. As she'd known all along she'd be.

Three men stood looking her over.

"A looker," one said.

"Great dress," said another.

The third man—toward whom the other two immediately turned—said, "She would stand out."

The first man said, "But, chief, you want us to improvise? We got no time for improvisation."

"I say what we got time for," the one the other had called "chief" said. "Anyway, it's just reworking what we got set—padding the scene—giving it power. This little lady could be just the punch we need—what do we have? Dottie and Evelyn—how I ever thought I'd pull it off with just the two of them." His voice trailed off as he shaded his eyes and looked out over the crowd milling at the foot of the station steps. "Mark, the place is jumpin' with broads—find me ten or twelve others. Blondes. Big beefy blondes. That'll give Dot and Evie just the company they need." He dropped his hand and turned his eyes on Lola. "Then, we'll put this dark little lady in the middle of them. Just the contrast we need in that rush toward the train." He looked at the man he'd called Mark and slapped him hard on the shoulder. "Big is always better. Remember that, Markie," he said and turned away, dismissing all of them.

Mark, the man who had chosen Lola from the crowd, asked, "What's your name?"

"Lola Escalante."

"Elegante?" he asked. "Italian?" But he didn't wait for an answer, instead taking her arm and pulling her toward the train car around which the day's filming had taken place. "What's a good-looking little wop like you doing out here in the middle of all this cowshit?"

"Waiting to be discovered," she said, feeling promise descend, certified at last.

"You been done, honey," he whispered in her ear.

Mark carted her to a section of platform in the shade where makeup people rushed around her. "Need something darker. This pink-toned crap won't work for her," one of the hovering men said. Another man with delicate hands that fluttered in the air pointed to a far box. "In that box. See the container of that darker foundation the color of Oberon's skin."

Lola closed her eyes, heaven descending, and when she opened them again, the entire platform was awash in a pink glow that for all her blinking wouldn't fade.

"Don't fuck up the eyes," her makeup man ordered when he saw her blinking.

Suddenly she was rushed toward the train car in a sea of blondes. Then, she found herself standing next to Jane Withers. Their eyes met, and Lola's heart raced as Jane Withers nodded—at her—and smiled almost as if they were already friends.

The man who'd been examining the camera earlier came over and began shouting directions to the group of extras, Lola at the front. "You're just a crowd rushing for a train. We're gonna have that whistle blowing, steam rolling, and you all are late, desperate to get on this train car."

"Now you, Janie," he said to Withers, whose eyes widened, suddenly overflowing with life, "you're going to be lost, looking desperately for Jake. This crowd is going to come 'round, buffeting you from side to side, scaring you, and this one—the dark one here, honey," he said, taking hold of Lola's arm and pulling her forward, lifting her from the crowd, "is going to come by and pull you out of the rush. Got that? Simple, no?"

Then, he shouted, *"Action!"* and everything retreated save for the platform, swirling billows of steam, the sound of an engine chugging, and train whistles screaming—all of which filled Lola's heart with an urgency that made this the only world that mattered. She saw the train and felt that her life depended on making the car, but she stopped, a sea of blondes spilling, rushing by, for there in the distance was a child, shrinking back against the train, half lost in billowing steam and terrified. The fear naked in the child's eyes struck Lola's heart. A louder whistle blew, and the child shrank visibly, eyes opening to moons, as she was buffeted by bodies pressing into the train and unaware of the terrified child. Angry now, Lola lifted her hand and saw the child's eyes wash over her, a plea for help that called to Lola, who answered, charging through the unfeeling press of people and pulling the child into the shelter of her arm and then, forcing the others back, clearing a space before the open train car door and easing the child up and into the safety of the train.

The simple scene took all afternoon.

Over and over, they rushed the train car. Over and over Lola saw Jane come to life, panic in her eyes, the tears so real Lola's heart ached every time she reached out for Jane, pulling her to safety from the crowd.

At first, Lola feared she was doing something wrong, for they did the scene again and again. But after the fifteenth time, Mark, the man who had chosen her originally, pulled her aside and said, "I ain't ever seen anyone take to it like you. A duck to water, baby."

It was as if Lola saw him for the first time. Like no boy's in Carmelas, his face quickened something in her belly.

Some of the extras were beginning to groan at doing the scene so many times, but to Lola, it remained magical and more real than the world beyond the lights. Each mad dash to the train car, each encounter with Jane Withers's terrified eyes struck the same chord in Lola's heart, causing her to reach for the young girl as if her arms alone could save Jane from being trampled. The time flew, and she wanted it never to end.

Between takes, she'd watched everything, the lights spilling diamonds, pink diamonds that made Lola drunk with happiness. Every so often, she was led back to makeup, treated like the prize her mama had always said she was as they fussed about her face.

It was after dark while she was sitting in a chair being redone yet again with powder when in the now-thinning crowd at the foot of the station platform, she saw Sandy in a circle of girls. Lola rose from the chair. "I'll be right back."

"Honey," the makeup man said sharply, "you mess up my face and it'll be your ass on the block."

"I just need a minute," Lola said.

"Yeah, Rudy," another voice said, "even extras have to piddle sometime."

Lola pushed through to Sandy and took her arm. "I did it!" When Sandy turned to her, there was no warmth. "I touched Jane Withers," Lola said, trying again for a smile.

"Goody for you" was what she got. "We were supposed to be in this together."

"But you went to get ice cream when—"

"You stabbed me in the back," Sandy said, cutting her off. "Forget it, Lola. Forget everything. Enjoy yourself. See how long it lasts." She turned her back on Lola, something Lola couldn't remember her ever having done before.

A loud whistle cut the air. Lola turned and saw her makeup man waving at her frantically. She turned from Sandy's back and went up the steps.

"Find your own way home."

Lola turned her head and saw Sandy's face, a stranger's. She nodded and went to where her makeup man was waiting.

"Rudy, you're a genius," Lola heard as large hands clamped onto her shoulders. It was Mark again. "You've taken a looker and made her into a star!"

"If she doesn't wipe that frown off, she'll ruin it all," Rudy chided.

"Unhappy, little lady?" Mark asked, kneeling in front of her, looking up through the bluest eyes Lola had ever seen.

"I've lost my ride home."

"Then slap a smile back on that face, kitten," Mark said rising. "We take care of our stars. We'll get you home. Ain't never heard of limousines?"

Lola straightened in her chair, smiling again, not even able to imagine her mama's face as that limousine raising dust on Pontlavoy pulled up in front of their tiny wooden house.

"That's better," Mark said, touching her face.

"*Places!*" A voice boomed from up high on the platform.

"Knock 'em dead, honey," Mark said, pulling her up. "Last take of the day."

Lola moved with the rest of the extras, doing what she'd done before, but feeling again as if it were all for the first time, moving through the rushed scene as if she were being carried, watched over, forgetting just as she had every time before that none of it was real.

And then it was done.

Lola stood on the platform, the sea of blonde extras emptying like water from a broken glass. Jane Withers was gone, too. She hadn't even said goodbye. But it didn't matter. Lola felt more alive than ever before—ready to dance. She looked down at her legs, amazed that there was no tiredness at all. She saw the run in her beautiful silk hose. Bending, she ran a finger along the run.

"Don't fret over silk, honey. There's more where that came from," Mark said, rushing up to her. She smiled at the man who had chosen her darkness from the crowd. "Wait here a minute, would you?" he asked.

She saw him go off to a table set up at the base of the platform. The girls who'd been extras with her in the scene were gathered around Mark and another man. She saw them signing papers, cash exchanging hands.

When Mark came back, he passed her a cup of coffee. "Go sit over there, honey."

"Lola," she said. "I'm Lola."

"Sure. Go wait over there for me. I gotta make sure these lights are going where they're supposed to."

"Do I need to—"

"Sign papers, honey—and we'll get to that, " Mark said, smiling broadly. "You did great work today."

Her heart skipped. She sat with the coffee in the only chair left on the platform. It had "Director" printed across the back. She sipped the coffee, and it tasted strange—nothing like her mama's coffee. When she was finished, Mark was back and he brought her another coffee. "Like that?"

"Uhm. What's different?"

"French coffee, Lola," he said and winked conspiratorially, pulling a tiny silver flask partway out of his pants pocket.

The last of the movie people left the platform. One man who'd been working lights all day called, "Be good, Markie."

"Ain't I always?" He turned back to Lola. "Now we gotta talk, honey."

"About what?"

"Movies, baby. You and movies. You sure you ain't done this before—I mean you were smooth out there. Made the rest look like amateurs. Even Janie was impressed."

"Jane Withers?"

"Who else. Said you could work with her anytime."

Lola was in the street by the time she was aware of moving. Her heart was full.

Mark said, "I got some papers for you to sign."

"Contracts?" Lola asked and laughed.

Mark looked at her. Then he winked. "You in school still?"

She shook her head. "I'm eighteen."

"Yeah—beyond school," he said and then asked, "How far'd you go?"

"Eighth."

"Me, too," he said and took her arm, propelling her up Front Street. "Who needs school when we got the movies?" She knew he was right, but she remembered in a rush when school had been almost all she wanted; as she was being pulled up Front Street, her mind went to the time she'd first realized how little of her life was in her own hands.

"Tu papá says no," was what her mother had told her at the end of her eighth grade, when she had been talking about entering Excelsior High the next September with Sandy.

"Porqué no?" Lola asked, disbelief so large she slipped into Spanish as she rarely did anymore.

"Eres una muchacha, no necesitan school las girls," her papa said.

Lola had cried. That had always worked on Papa.

"No más educación. No es necessary," he'd said that time, almost the first no he'd ever given her.

So, she had gone to Sandy. "Tell your daddy to make my papa let me go."

"No problemo," Sandy had said, confident as always.

Mr. Hinton had come over and talked to Papa the very next night on the porch. But he'd walked away too soon. "Can I go?" she'd finally asked her silent father, who'd remained in the dark of the porch smoking after Mr. Hinton had gone.

"No!"

She had sat on the porch and stared into the night over the flower fields beyond. There was no moon, but the stars were thick. She felt what she always felt, something . . . out there, calling her.

Lola. Looolaaaa. *Lola.*

Angrier than she had ever been that Papa could turn her promise into lie, she had turned to him and demanded, "What will I do then, Papa?"

He rose, putting out his cigarette. "Pick flowers, como all of us en Carmelas." He came to her and touched her cheek. "Mi angelita," he said, softly, lovingly again, "it would be a lie to make you believe there could be anything else."

But he'd been wrong, for the promise had remained.

"Pick it up, honey. Don't dawdle," Mark said, yanking on her hand and pulling her memory back to Front Street. They were at the Eagle Hotel and inside the lobby before she knew they'd left the street. For a moment the lights robbed her of vision, and then, when she could see the finery of the lobby, glimpsed before only from outside on the street, she wondered what it would be like to stay in a place like this. "Mark?"

"Uhm?" he asked.

"Does Lupe Velez stay in hotels all the time when she works?"

"She do indeed, Lola." He pulled her to the stairs. "When Gary Cooper lets her out of his sight, that is."

"Where are we going?" she asked, alarmed for the first time today.

"My office," he said, stopping on the stairs.

"Office?"

"Well, honey, any movie on location needs a work space. Most of the time it's in hotels."

She pulled back her arm. "I don't know," she said, sounding for the first time since rising that morning just like the girl from Carmelas she had been.

"But I got to pay you and get your John Henry on those contracts. Remember?"

Pay. Money for making a movie.

So, she followed him up the stairs. Inside the room, she saw only a large bed and a table with two chairs by the window looking over Front Street, and she didn't move from the closed door.

"My desk, honey," he said slapping the table. "Relax. You're in Hollywood now. Remember?" He laughed and went into a bathroom, reappearing with a bottle and two glasses. "To your contract." He passed her a glass.

She touched her tongue to the liquid. It burned.

"In Hollywood, nothing is signed without a drink."

"I don't drink."

"That's what Joan Crawford said. Drink up." She drank. He pulled a paper from his back pocket and sat on the bed. He spread the paper out over his thigh. Pulling out a pen, he extended it in her direction. "You have to sign here." He slapped the paper resting on his thigh with his free hand.

She stepped from the door deeper into the room. "What is it?"

"Contract," he said fast, his blue eyes fixed on her. "You want your money, honey, you sign."

She stepped to where he sat on the bed and took the pen. She signed and felt him pull her onto the bed. They were both sitting on the edge of the bed, and she saw him get out his wallet and extract a twenty.

She took it.

With a flourish, he pulled out another ten. "You did good work, Lola."

So much money. Lola's head felt odd. The room was warm. It was a moment before she realized his hand was on her hair. "Goddamned beautiful hair. I love wop hair."

Suddenly she was on her back staring at the ceiling and she felt his mouth at her neck, his breath hot. Then his head was over hers. "You're beautiful, honey—goddamned beautiful." He ran a finger over her lips and his touch was delicate, very like the fluttering of her heart. "Your eyes. They're forever black . . . forever."

He put his face close to hers. "Imagine eyes like these on the screen. I wish you could see from here, baby, the way they suck the light out of the room, pulling it all in, me with it, in, baby . . . ," and his lips brushed hers, his eyes open as wide as her own, but his were blue.

Then she felt his hand at the hem of her dress.

She pushed him off and sat up. Her head swam with the exertion, the rush of movement. She was going to rise, but a sudden absence in the room startled her.

She looked around, as if seeking in the shadowy corners near the ceiling the presence that had always been near, calling. But now, there was nothing. The promise that had trailed her like perfume for as long as she could remember was gone. The sense that someone—something—was calling to her . . . for her . . . no more. In a rush, she pushed herself up and went to the window, opening it and leaning out, far over Front Street, eyes fixed on the sky above the houses facing the street. Searching, scanning the darkness, she tried to find what she had always found looming in the distance, the sense that something out there was approaching, full of sweet promise. She found nothing out there—not anymore.

"Lola?"

She turned, and Mark was at the edge of the bed. He was still handsome—his eyes cuttingly blue—but he suddenly looked so young, no older than she. She saw it now. His suit, she could see in the harsh overhead light, was shiny in places, too short in the cuffs—bought secondhand or maybe borrowed. Her eyes fell to his shoes, scuffed, the heel turned. "You're no director," she finally said.

He hesitated and then shook his head no.

"That wasn't a contract."

He shook his head again.

"The money?"

"That was legit—that's what we pay the extras," he said too eagerly, his face a contrast in disappointment.

"I did well?"

"You did good, honey," he said, smiling, and suddenly he looked hopeful again, like one of the card players at Papa's poker games—a loser for whom an unexpected winning hand meant he was back in the game.

She watched him rise from the bed and go to the bottle. Despite the thinness in his neck, he held his head high again. He refilled a glass and offered it to her. She took it and swallowed the contents in a gulp. She lifted the empty glass in his direction. He refilled the glass. She drank again. Fast.

"Italians sure can drink," he said and slipped his arms about her waist, pulling her close.

But she drew away from him and stepped back to the open window. She held the empty glass and looked one last time into the night sky and found nothing waiting there at all.

Suddenly, she was not surprised. It had been named. The call, always there but distant, had fallen into place. The magic that had long been promised had simply come. This had been it, this entire day—only this.

She smiled, joy rising anew in her throat. She had been chosen as she'd always known she'd one day be. This day—all of it—had been her day of days. All of it golden. All of it! She thought of the whirring film capturing her, over and over all afternoon. She turned back to Mark and asked, "I will be in the movie?"

He smiled broadly, lighting up. "Right smack next to Jane Withers."

"When?"

"Christmas next."

And she thought of herself captured forever—young, golden, forever twenty feet high, an image spilling into theaters everywhere. She realized that if this was what had been awaiting her, it was enough—enough to hold onto, savor, remember for all her days, and she thought of La Luna and wondered if this had been the gift she was to get that would stay with her forever, a prized memory to make bearable a life lived out in Carmelas.

She turned back to Mark and saw—despite his youth—a man more handsome than she'd ever have again, who'd chosen her, if only for a day. "I'm not Italian," she finally said to his expectant face.

He lifted his hand, extending it to her; it hung in the air.

The invitation was so clear Lola felt fear bubble instinctively in her belly. This man wanted only what her mama said all men wanted—something Carmelas girls giggled about, the something her mama only hinted at in whispers meant to terrify as she spoke of what happened to girls who foolishly gave men that something they wanted too soon. Lola was an innocent, but no girl grew up in Carmelas surrounded by chickens, goats, and pigs without knowing exactly what the something was. No girl in Carmelas grew up in a tiny house filled with too many people in too few rooms without hearing the sounds of people making love—the sounds spilling from her own mama's room, and Mama had sounded no more terrified than the chickens, than the goats. Lola knew, too, that for Carmelas girls, there was never any doubt that it was the only gift they had to give—the only question over which there was any control at all was when to give it.

She looked again at Mark's eyes, blue like heaven, and saw his hand extended, still hanging, and her fear drained, leaving only expectation. She reached out and took his hand, feeling the palm, damp against her own, a palm smooth as only a gentleman's hand could be—nothing like the horny, clumsy, calloused palms of Carmelas boys.

So, she closed her fingers around his hand tightly, confirming her choice, seeing that this choosing of him must have been part of what the promise held all along, part of the blanket of memory she would wrap about the rest of her life.

Only then did she let him pull her back to the bed, where he eased her down as if she were a prize. She felt his lips move to her ear.

"Mexican," she said in a rush. "I'm Mexican," she said again as his tongue caressed her ear.

He lifted his head, his blue eyes washing over her, kissing her with their yearning. "You think I care, honey? Not a prejudiced bone in my body."

As his hands moved over her body, sparking sensation, she had a fleeting thought of her mama, the fury waiting there—growing with the lateness of the hour—that would explode at sight of a wild daughter's shorn head and move like fire through their little house. But that would come later. Now, she felt only Mark's tongue moving along her throat. Soon, it pushed all thought of her mama away. She embraced him—a man with dreams bigger than her own, with eyes like no others she would ever hold so close again—and Lola chose to dance before returning, as she knew now she would, to Carmelas, carrying back a piece of this day, this man to make bearable not only her mama's fury but the rest of her days.

Chapter 5

Mi Casa - 1947

Rosa Galvan walked along Firestone Boulevard in the August heat. It was the middle of the day and the road was empty, as it had been since she'd crossed Rosecrans a half mile back. Every so often she'd look back over her shoulder to check on Frankie.

"Apurate, mijo," she'd call and wouldn't turn back until she saw the husky boy she adored lift his black eyes from a tiny book in his hands and speed up. "Read when we get home."

To her left were the Anselmo beanfields, the low leafy greens shimmering in the sun against the earth in ordered rows that ran all the way to Rosecrans. She saw cars moving there, light traffic, but otherwise there was no sign of people. She and Frankie might have been alone in the world.

To her right, across Firestone, which here was little more than a service road, high yellow weeds hugged the roadbed. The slaughterhouse rose in the distance beyond the weeds, its odors so constant that the smell grabbing her nose always meant she was nearing home.

"Ay mamita," her sandy-haired brother Beto had cried, swinging Mama in his arms when he'd come home from the war two years before, "the pinche smell when I got off the bus at Harvester's Market—I'd forgotten. Como perfuma. I knew I was home!"

Rosa stopped in the road, wrapped in the heat and the smells of slaughtered meat, made even grittier by the hint of manure carried from the Norwalk Dairy way over on Rosecrans, but sweetened by the scent of green beans and baked earth. She shifted the four books she was carrying to her other arm. As she waited for her Frankie to catch up, she thought of how, not quite two years before, after Beto came back whole from the war, followed a week later by her own Rudy—his skin's chocolate hues baked into gleaming mahogany by South Sea suns she could only imagine—she'd sworn that she could ask no more of God.

It hadn't been until late that night—the day of Rudy's arrival—that she'd finally gotten him to herself. They were in the small house behind Rudy's mama's house, one large room, filled with their bed, the covers on the floor, the white sheets a gleaming tangle, made whiter by the night and Rudy's body, naked on the sheets. She had sat beside him, the sheet bunched at her breasts, her heart bursting with joy.

"We are not strangers," she'd finally said, and her heart had leapt, for she could still remember the fear she had felt earlier that same day when she'd first seen her husband turn from Rosecrans onto Pontlavoy, the September morning already boiling, the dry dirt-paved street raising clouds in the hot wind. They had not touched in three years, and that morning of his arrival home, she'd squinted to make his face clearer, and in the distance, he'd looked the boy he'd been when he'd left her and baby Frankie to go to a war that had never seemed completely real to her except for the empty space in her life when it had taken Rudy.

By the time her returning Rudy had climbed the rickety front steps of his mama's house, she'd pulled back behind his mama, for her fear had grown so great. But when he'd pulled her to him and his mouth had found hers, it had been the mouth she'd known, the kiss the same.

And that first night home, when finally they'd been left alone, their union had been as easy, light, as it had ever been. She could still see him, stretched naked before her in their crumpled bed and remember how she felt tears rise in her eyes.

"Let me see you," he whispered in the dark.

She hesitated, for she knew she'd thickened—her waist, her hips. She knew her breasts were fuller, lower.

He smiled, his teeth pearls in an inky sea.

She dropped the sheet and heard his breath sucked in. She saw his penis tremble on his thigh and fill and lift until it bowed over him.

He who'd been spent was resurrected—at sight of her.

And the heat of the day as she waited for little Frankie to catch up mingled with the heat of memory, and in her head, she could see herself dancing, astride Rudy's hips, and feel her joy rising from her middle, flowering as she had never known it to do before, the ecstasy a stranger she would hunger after evermore, erupting into screams she buried in her Rudy's neck as she told God she would ask for nothing more than this.

But she'd been wrong.

"Estoy cansado, Mama," Frankie whined, finally catching up to her and pulling her back to now.

"We're almost home, mijo. Da me tu book."

He passed up the thin child's volume, his prize for the long walk to the tiny library on San Antonio in Norwalk. "I'm thirsty."

"Callate. Do you see any agua?"

He shook his head, his cheeks round, loose—enough to make her smile. She took his sweaty hand in hers. "Look." Her heart quickened.

They were nearing Shoemaker, where, one year before, out of the last of Hinton's flower fields sold after the war, had risen the thorn thrust into her life.

Looming like a mirage on the desert was a row of the most beautiful houses Rosa had ever seen. After her lifetime in Carmelas, the streets of dirt, the houses scattered haphazardly up and down the dusty lanes, roofs sagging, the best of them a riot of colors that screamed of pinks too hot to touch and blues that would put to shame the eyelids of a whore, this row of houses, each painted in colors soft as Frankie's flesh, seemed like paradise. And Shoemaker was just the first of ten more streets, filled with houses, that rose from the earth like rows of corn.

She had watched it all, a tract of houses rising from a former flower field. First, there had been the skeletons, naked against the blue of heaven, then the weeks of maturation as the frames had grown flesh, becoming, finally, finished jewels—houses, empty, waiting for people to fill with children.

"Look, mijo. All the pretty casas."

"Quiero mi house, Ma. Estoy tired."

His house. Rosa moved purposefully, almost dragging Frankie along as she thought of that shack—behind a bigger shack. One room, and four of them now with baby Estela. She remembered the day she decided there'd be no more babies.

"I don't want any more," she said. They were in bed. The sheets were pulled up to her chin. Rudy was hovering over her, closing in.

"Como?"

"No more babies, Rudy."

"That's en los manos de Dios," he said, his hand easing by her clenched thighs, covering her.

She pushed his hand from between her legs and sat up. "I want you to use something—"

"Condones?" he said, his voice rising as if she were asking for the moon.

Estela whimpered in her basket beside the bed. Rosa's hand found its way to the baby, caressing her, stilling the cry. "Shh, I want you to use them," she whispered, not wanting to disturb the baby.

"Y sí I don't?"

Rosa picked up Estela and brought her to her breast, the mouth even in sleep opening hungrily, the lips closing on the nipple, the movement of the gums causing it to rise. "There's no room for more babies."

"We'll move in con Mama. Su casa es bigger."

And that was just when Rosa's head had filled with the images of the streets of houses going up right next to Carmelas, beautiful houses—big enough for many babies. Her cheeks flushed now as she remembered telling him to buy her a house; his hips had begun thrusting, and this threw his rhythm off. The thought of the houses had fired her own hips as she'd promised there could then be babies, a line of babies, but Rudy had cooled.

He'd bought the rubbers, which had done nothing to push the new houses out of her head. When the tract was finished, she would walk the empty streets, nothing like Carmelas streets. Paved roads. No dust. In front of each casa a huge place for grass. In Carmelas no one had heard of grass. People moved into the houses. She saw them sell. Street by street, until she found she couldn't walk up and down any longer, for she looked strange in streets where children walked and women stayed hidden inside houses she dreamed were hers.

"Mama!"

Rosa looked down. Frankie was sitting on the curb. Every street here had curbs. "Vamos, Mama. Let's go."

She extended her hand and pulled him up.

As they passed the streets of no-longer-empty houses, she knew it wouldn't be long before they were all sold, for as they moved deeper into the new development, she saw signs everywhere that the end was near. House after house was sporting grass now. New. Vulnerable. Taking root, fenced in by posts and string to keep children playing in the streets and off the grass.

At the last street of the development, called Dinard, she turned left. She saw the new school taking shape across the street, and knew this was the street she wanted to live on, for she could imagine sitting in her living room and seeing across the road the school where Frankie would go. But as she moved up the block, she knew her dream was fading fast. Two empty houses remained. Two.

She passed the house that was the development office, flags dancing gaily on the path up to the door. A tall sign stood in the middle of the wide green front yard. "Park Place Homes."

Rosa stopped. Imagine, living in a place where every house had a park in front and back.

"Un parque?" Rudy asked, sipping a beer under his mama's chinaberry tree. Behind him the Pontiac he'd bought six months before was sitting, its hood open.

"Oh, Rudy. You've gotta see it."

"Okay."

Rosa had been at the line, hanging whites. As she'd draped the sheets, she'd talked to him. He'd been unreachable all morning, his head lost in the front of his car. "Mande?" she asked, not believing she'd heard.

"Let's go look," he repeated.

Rosa ran her hand through her thick black hair, the ends loose, blowing. "I've got to clean up. Tu tambien."

He looked down at himself. "Que es wrong conmigo? I said we drive by. We look."

And as they'd driven, she pressed up against him, her chin on his shoulder, feeling in love like she hadn't since the night he'd come home from the war and shown her that her body could sing. She was talking, pointing out the features of each house.

"Each one es exactamente como the next. Un drunk would have trouble at night."

"No, Rudy. Look," she said, her hand caressing the inside of his thigh, bothered not at all that he was getting hard. Maybe hard, he would see what she saw. "La differencia es in the shutters. See, white ones—red ones there. Each house is turned in un poco different way."

"Gavachos," he said after a moment.

"Como?" she said, not getting him. She saw him indicate his head. In the driveway of one house, a group of men, all white, stared at them as they drove slowly by. She felt Rudy stiffen and the stiffening wasn't in his pants. "So? Gavachos are everywhere."

"See any brown faces in your houses con yardas como parks?"

As they drove, she looked. The streets were teeming with kids. All ages. All white. Rudy laughed.

"They all look like they got brooms up their butts. Even the niños. Give me Carmelas." And Rudy turned at Maryton and headed back, three short blocks to where the pavement ended and the dirt began. He came to Pontlavoy and turned left.

Rosa's eyes were to the right, averted. She didn't want him to see her crying. She saw the twin mulberry trees and behind them the old Ramona schoolhouse where all of them in Carmelas had gone. "Mr. Trujillo is going to the new school," she said, to say something.

"Si hay justicia—porque shouldn't he?" Rudy asked.

"He should. I wanted you to know. I saw him. Yesterday in Chata's store. He told me. He's excited about the new school."

Rudy snickered. "They build those gavacho houses and suddenly we get a new school. Que rico!"

"It's still going to be called Ramona School."

"And full of gringos con casas with yards como parks."

Rosa, still staring up at the model home, was shaken from her reverie when she heard someone call, "Yoo hoo!" She saw a man, suited and red-faced in the heat, standing on the porch of the model house that was the office of the housing development. "Can I help you?"

Rosa felt herself redden. "No. Thank you." She hurried on, pulling Frankie. Suddenly she turned back and called, "How many houses left?"

"Three. Including this one. Better hurry, honey, if you want one. They won't last forever."

"If I want one," Rosa said to herself over and over as she moved down the street toward Maryton and her right turn back into Carmelas. As she neared the corner in front of one of the new houses, she saw a woman bending over a flower bed of raised brick, filled with new soil. She was planting flowers. On a blanket spread out on the new lawn was a baby. Rosa stopped when she saw how black the baby's hair was. The baby rolled over and she saw the brown skin. The black eyes. When she lifted her eyes, the woman at the flower bed was standing, staring at her.

"Hablas espanol?" Rosa asked.

The woman hesitated and then shook her head. "Un poco."

"Está bien," Rosa said smiling broadly. "I speak English. Mi Frankie tambien. Eres mexicana?"

"Sí," the woman said.

"Me llamo Rosa. Rosa Galvan."

"I'm Carla. Carla Abrigo."

"You have a beautiful house."

The woman smiled. "Thank you."

Rosa, suddenly walking on a cloud of hope, yanked Frankie to his feet and hurried home. As she moved up Pontlavoy, she saw Rudy's mama sitting on the straw chair that graced one end of her sloping porch. From here, Rosa could see that the bottom of the chair was ready to give. She laughed and waved.

When she got to the porch, she was singing. Frankie ran up and onto his abuelita Chona's lap. The old woman hugged him tight as she crooned and kissed his head. Rosa sat on the stoop and rested her chin in her hands. In the yard next door, she saw Señora Lucita watering her desperate roses with a can.

"Como estás, Señora Lucita?" Rosa shouted, happiness bubbling.

Señora Lucita waved, the movement shaking her hips, which seemed to float under her voluminous dress. She had black, wool stockings rolled at mid calf, and even from next door, Rosa could see the veins, purple webs fanning up towards Señora Lucita's hem. "Cuantos babies did Señora Lucita have?"

"Diez—que lived," Rudy's mama said. "Tú pareces happy hoy, mija. My Rudy—he is being nice contigo?"

"Claro, mamita. Claro."

"Tell me if he gets out of the line—puedo still take a belt to him."

"Mama Chona," Rosa asked, her eyes still on Señora Lucita. "You and Señora Lucita were girls together?"

"Claro. Como hermanas—more closer than sisters. We came from Mazatlán together when our fathers sent for us here in Carmelas. Lucita was at mi lado cuando I almost lost Rudy at his birth. Without Lucita and La Luna, I would not . . ."

Rosa turned as the voice of her mother-in-law died and saw her holding Frankie as if he were treasure she might have missed. Her hair was wrapped in a wiry ball, so thick, a silver sheen that still held traces of deep black at the nape of her neck. She was round, her face especially, with a beak of nose, the end of which drooped close to her full lips. "Sabes donde are tus teeth?" Rosa asked.

She nodded. "In my glass—on the sink," she said, her mouth falling to Frankie's neck where he giggled richly.

She was brown like Rudy. The first time Rudy had brought Rosa home to meet his mama formally, the woman had been speechless. Rosa had thought his mama hadn't liked her. Only later had his mama explained her dismay, saying, "You were too beautiful, mija, demasiado blanquisima por mi Rudy—más huero even than his papi."

And at their wedding in St. John's, just before Rosa had slipped into the front door for her walk down the aisle, Rudy's mama had found her and slipped a silken white rose into Rosa's hand, and said, "Como tu, preciosa, una rosa blanca por mi Rudy. How lucky we are to get you."

And the old woman ever since had treated Rosa with special tenderness. She turned to her mother-in-law and asked, "Who was the prettiest? Tú o la Señora Lucita?"

Rosa's suegra lifted her head. "Es difícil—we were both tan lindas. The most in Carmelas that year—"

"What year?"

"The year we flowered."

Rosa's eyes filled, feelings like hunger stabbing. She looked back at Señora Lucita, bent over a tired rose bush.

Their flowering. That single year. A blink of an eye. Rosa's hand absently fell to her waist, knowing it would never be tiny again. Did all women burn so bright, then die, or only brown women on dirt streets in barrios como Carmelas?

She thought of the young woman she'd seen digging in the flower bed before the new house on Dinard—Carla Abrigo. That woman would never look like Rudy's mama Chona. Carla's skin was light—though nowhere near as light as Rosa's own. And hadn't the salesman called to her, saying, "You'd better hurry, honey," speaking to her for all the world as if she could walk in and buy any one of the three houses left for sale?

In a rush of desire, Rosa stood up on the porch and said, "Mama? Podrías watch mi Frankie por una hora."

"Claro, mija. Mi pleasure."

"I'm going up to Chata's store."

Rudy's mama reached into her apron pocket. "Get me un dulce, you know the leche quemada that I love."

"I don't need any money. I'll get the candy. Anything else? We have enough tortillas?"

Rudy's mama nodded.

Inside the house, Rosa pulled her navy blue dress from the closet. It was the one she'd worn the day Rudy had come from the war. It had a sailor collar, white and wide, that made her light skin shine. She zipped it up her waist, feeling the work it took for the zipper to close over her spreading hips. She thanked God for the elastic prison of girdles and long-line bras. In the tiny bathroom, she brushed back her hair, the black brilliant in the light spilling from the small window. She washed her face and applied her perfume, finishing with the lipstick, bright and red. She slipped out the back door, not wanting questions from Mama about the way she was dressed.

When she passed Carla Abrigo's house this time, the woman, her baby on her lap, was sitting on her porch—a tiny block of cement, Rosa noted, that would never sag or fall. Carla raised her hand and waved—almost as if they were already neighbors.

Rosa walked up the cement path, curving like lace where it cut through the lawn leading up to the model home. She opened the door as if it were already her house. The man who'd called out to her earlier rose from a desk, but she couldn't talk—she was made speechless by the hardwood floors shining through the house and singing to her in a voice only she could hear.

"Madam?"

Rosa turned and put out her hand. "Rose," she said. "Rose Galvan," she said, flattening her "a"and making sure her "v" stayed a "v." "I want to buy a house."

"Usually couples come together."

"My husband will come later. To sign the papers. How much is this house?"

"Fifty-two hundred dollars."

Her heart sank.

"Payable over twenty years."

Her heart leapt. "Twenty years?" she asked, feeling all dreams possible.

"In monthly payments that depend on your down payment."

Her heart sank. "How much down?"

"Was your husband in the war?"

"Navy. Three years I didn't see him."

He smiled broadly. "I was navy myself. For vets like us, a dollar moves you in. Think you can swing that, pretty lady?"

Rosa's heart would never falter again. She nodded her head, her eyes filling.

"Payments will be somewhere around forty-five dollars a month. Want to see what that gets you?" She nodded. The tour moved through two of the most magnificent bedrooms she'd ever seen, each with floors like mirrors and windows large enough to invite sun. In the bathroom, her breath caught at sight of the tub that was big enough for both her and Rudy. She felt herself go red.

The tour ended in the kitchen, where a refrigerator, a Kelvinator, sparkled on a linoleum floor as blue as heaven that curved at the edges of the room and climbed the wall. Next to the refrigerator was a stove with silver burners and a stainless steel grill on which she swore she could already hear her carnitas sizzling. But the capper—after an expanse of blue linoleum-covered countertop—was a washer that held a door of glass through which Rosa would be able to watch her clothes tumble as they cleaned. She closed her eyes, for she could bear no more.

She found out the man would be in the office until seven o'clock tonight, the same tomorrow. She said goodbye, that she'd be back, and walked in her spectator pumps all the way up Dinard to Rosecrans, preferring the pavement even if it meant a longer trip.

Before entering Chata's store, Productos Mexicanos, she went to the pay phone outside. She looked around to make sure no one was near, for this phone was Carmelas's link to the world. She picked up the phone, dropped in the change, dialed her brother Beto's number, and listened to the phone ring.

"Licha?" she called when she heard her sister-in-law's voice. "Está mi Beto en casa?"

When Beto got on the phone, she told him in a rush about the yards like parks, the floors like mirrors—and about the washing machine with a window through which she could watch her clothes come clean. She told him about the gavachos everywhere.

"But, Rosa, que quieres—what do you want of me?"

"I want you to be my husband."

"Como?"

"Pretend—es la only way, la unica chanza que lo tengo para mi casa, la casa de mis dreams."

"You want me to go in and pretend I'm Rudy? Use Rudy's name? Sign his papers?"

"Por mi, Beto, por favor, please—for me. I've never asked anything of you."

"Rudy knows about this?"

"No."

"Entonces—es imposible. Rudy would never forgive you."

"He would," Rosa said, crying now as she felt all of her hope slipping away. "I am his rosa, su rosa blanca. His mama told me—I am his treasure. He will forgive me."

"Rosa. What would I accomplish—"

"You know, Beto. As well as I. They don't care what we are. They only care what we look like. Help me. My Rudy is too brown."

"Rudy is my friend."

"I am your sister."

"Rudy will be furious."

"Más que furioso."

"What if he hurts you?"

"His mother will take the belt to him."

He fell silent on the phone, and the silence seemed forever before her brother—paler even than herself—asked, "When?"

"Today. Tonight."

"Mañana. I can't tonight. Tomorrow."

"On Mama's soul, Beto, en la alma de nuestra santa Mama, promise me you'll come."

"But they'll know when you move in and they see Rudy."

"Then it will be too late for them to do anything at all."

"What if they hate you?"

"You think I want the house for *them*? Estás loco? Es la casa, Beto. La casa de mis sueños, la casa perfecto por mi Frankie."

"What if they hate Frankie?"

"Who could hate Frankie?"

"All right," he said.

Rosa squealed at the phone, not caring if everyone in Carmelas overheard, for in her brother Beto's sigh, she finally heard his promise and commitment. "Hasta mañana, Beto mio," she cried into the phone and hung up.

Rosa floated into Chata's store—the smells embracing as they fell about her from the high ceiling heavy with hanging chilis reddening in the light spilling from the small high windows at the top of the wall. She found Chata propped on a stool behind the low counter, the top heaped in bagged tortillas and a tray of leche quemada, golden logs of sweetness piled high.

Chata's eyes popped wide at the sight of Rosa in her pretty dress. "Rosita," she called, dragging out the name teasingly, "ooooh la la! You must have planes especiales por tu Rudy tonight!"

Rosa laughed and the laugh was loud and free—like when she'd laughed with Chata when they'd been girls and flowering. "Beyond his wildest dreams. Dame leche quemada para mi Rudy's mama." As Chata's hand closed on a piece of candy, Rosa said, "No, not that hard one. The fresh ones at the bottom. Soft. The softest. Ella no tienes teeth anymore."

"You look beautiful," Chata said, passing the sweet wrapped in wax paper. "Like when we were girls."

Rosa reached across the counter and curled a tendril of Chata's spilling hair. "Chica, tu hair is tu best feature. Treat it como la treasure it is."

Chata looked up and into a mirror positioned at the end of the counter to catch thieves. She ran her hand through her thick curly hair. "Henry always loved my hair."

"I remember," she said, recalling the summer Chata stepped from her sister Lola's lovely shadow and captured Carmelas's and Henry Lucero's attention. Behind the counter a tiny wail rose to a shriek.

Chata climbed down and lifted her new baby, saying, "Not that he notices anymore." Casually, she lifted her loose blouse and the small pale baby closed pink lips around her mother's rose-colored nipple.

"Ay que linda," Rosa said, reaching over to stroke the girl's rosy cheeks, "tu Aurora es." Chata smiled at the compliment, the baby's sucking rising about them. "Como the mama, the baby is. Remember the summer you drove Henry más que loco?"

"I remember," Chata said. "He's the one who has forgotten how hungry he was."

"Make him remember, girl," Rosa said, "you managed once." She poked Chata's shoulder. "Take matters in your own hands," which made Chata blush at the innuendo. Rosa laughed as she turned to leave, calling back, "Otherwise we wait forever." She left the store, almost skipping, thinking of the years ahead in a kitchen with a floor blue as heaven, a sparkling stove with a black pot of beans bubbling eternally on a back burner, herself on her haunches watching her clothes tumble forever in a washer with a window, and Rudy standing in their park that would stretch green from their door to the street, a kingdom, ruled by a king—mahogany brown.

Chapter 6

El Bobo Bruto - 1951

Air, hot, damp, and heavy, wrapped about Ozzie Gallo's body as he leaned back against the trunk of the huge old mulberry tree in the August darkness. He was sucking on a Camel he'd bummed from Emilio earlier and saved. They sat in a circle under the heavy overhang of the trees, the leaves hiding the moon and the stars. He looked up Marvilla and saw all the houses were dark, no window lit. It was late. They should all be home, but the heat made moving difficult. "Any beer left?" Ozzie asked.

"Pinche Gilbert drank it all," Emilio said from where he lay sprawled. "I'm sick of spending Saturdays under these chinga trees. Two more months and I'll have money for my Chevy. Then see me move."

Ozzie laughed. "The girls'd even talk to you, Gilbert, if you had a car."

"I do all right," Gilbert protested.

Emilio made wet sounds in the darkness and moved his hand up and down through the air. "Like the rest of us—but wait 'til I get my car." He stood up and brushed down his khakis. "I'm goin' home—you chingones are puttin' me to sleep. Hasta later." He turned to walk away, but stopped. "How much you bettin' on that pinche gallo of your pop's in the cockfight tomorrow?"

Ozzie closed his eyes and groaned. "I've had it up to here with gallos," he said, disgusted with the way his pop's craziness was infecting everyone in Carmelas.

"I'm puttin' five on that gallo's ass," Gilbert said. "All my savings."

Emilio laughed. "If he scares those other birds half as much as he scares me, he's bound to win. Maybe I'll put a couple of dollars of my Chevy money in. See you vatos later." He walked off into the darkness.

Gilbert pushed himself up from the ground. "I'm goin' too . . . so fuckin' hot."

"Hotter in the house," Ozzie said.

"I got pinche *Gents* at home," he said, "and light to see those naked nenas by."

Ozzie watched his fat friend move up Mapledale toward Pontlavoy and home. Tossing his cigarette away, he saw headlights turn from Carmenita onto Mapledale cutting paths of light that rolled over him before the car—Hector Mosqueda's yellow Pontiac—turned left onto Marvilla, the taillights trailing redness. Ozzie leaned forward and watched the car pull up in front of Norma's house. The headlights went out, but he could hear the car running, the taillights beacons. He started up the middle of the dirt street. The passenger side door opened, and a dark shadow stepped out into the dirt. Norma. She slammed the door and the headlights switched on and the car pulled away, tires spinning, raising dust around Norma standing in the dark.

"He doesn't even wait to see you in?" Ozzie said, startling her.

"Am I in danger?" She turned to him. "In front of my own house? In Carmelas?"

"You were afraid to come out at night a few years back," he said, laughing, "you thought La Llorona stalked Carmelas streets—"

"Malinche," she said, "a myth to keep little brown girls in line." She laughed. "I'm not a little girl anymore."

"Who keeps you in line now?" he asked. She didn't answer, her smile disappearing. He changed tracks. "Common decency—I would think—for Hector to see you in." Her skin glistened, the dampness catching the moonlight.

"You've been drinking. I can smell the beer," she said.

"Popcorn," he said, sounding light again; he wiggled his nose in her direction. "I can smell the butter. That must mean the La Mirada Drive-In. Movie good?"

"All right." She ran a hand through her thick hair, which hung loose down her back, and looked up at her tiny house. "I can't bear the thought of climbing into that bed with my sisters."

Ozzie looked up at the house, the night making the wooden walls dark and colorless. Her father worked in a paint store and brought home paint—lots of paint. He had his sons painting his house every other month—green this time, too dark to compete with the night. Everybody in Carmelas thought him a little off and had ever since he'd arrived in Carmelas during the Depression and snapped up Pepe Escalante's Delia, his most beautiful daughter—next to La Lola anyway—a month after getting here. They'd been having kids ever since—more in that little house than anyone in Carmelas. He understood Norma's reluctance to go in. "Want to go sit under the mulberries?"

"It's late," she said.

"So hot," he said and put out his hand. She took it and they walked together to the trees, sitting against the largest trunk, side by side, she hugging her knees. They said nothing. So, he lay back and looked up at the sky through the leaves. "See that? Shooting star."

She looked up . . . too late. Then, she turned back to him. "Do you miss school?"

"No."

"I do. I dream about school sometimes."

"I dream about cow shit—then I wake up to it."

She laughed. But Ozzie didn't hear her laughter, her question dragging up memories of graduation night. Just two months ago, he and Norma Reyes had been stars—in Carmelas anyway. A handful of Carmelas kids had started as freshmen together at Excelsior High School, but this year he and Norma had finished—the first time anyone in Carmelas had. They'd ridden back from the ceremony in Norma's father's pickup truck, he and Norma riding close together in the bed, his mama and pop with Norma's dad in the cab, her mama backing out at the last minute because she had no teeth and would have been afraid to smile.

The air rushing over the cab whipped around them, and he felt as if he were flying—free for the first time in his life—with everything before him. Then, he'd felt Norma tremble, her shaking shoulder reaching through the starched stiffness of his new white Penney's dress shirt. He'd thought at first she might be cold with the whipping wind and all, but when he looked, her face was turned away. He knew she was crying. She wouldn't look at him, but she said anyway, "It's all over," her voice almost stolen by the air swirling about them.

And he'd known she hadn't meant the ceremony, but her words spoke of places he didn't want to go—not tonight what with all the chaos at home and in Carmelas over Pop and his goddamned gallo and his mama's yawning want in the face of it—to add Norma's yearning would be unbearable, so he retreated. He'd taken her hand, refusing to do more with her sadness than that, feeling in his fingertips the roughness of her palm.

He shook his head to clear it of that memory. Looking at her face now, he saw that her smile didn't go with her eyes, which seemed instead a match for her voice in the bed of the pickup two months past. "What do you miss?"

She shrugged. "It's done."

"No," he said, sitting up, "tell me."

"Every day being different—always something up ahead. It's August," she said, "summer's gone. Tell me you don't feel that old pull of September." She giggled. "And in its place, Oswaldo Gallo?"

"Manure. Mountains of shit I shovel into bags at Norwalk Dairy," and he didn't laugh, seeing no September end in sight, knee deep in shit for the rest of his life.

"And eggs," she said. "Hiroshima's egg farm. I collect. I gather." She pushed herself up and stood over him. "Five A.M. comes awfully early."

"Tomorrow's Sunday."

She laughed. "Chickens stop laying eggs? Only men have the luxury of Sundays."

Sunday. Ozzie's day of rest and then—slipping like an enemy through his defenses—a thought grabbed hold that spoke of a life—his life—lived out on Sundays. He stood up. They were standing eye to eye, and Norma was tall, her eyes even with his own, and in her face he saw what he'd heard naked in her voice that night in the pickup and knew it had to be staring out from his own eyes, too. Their faces were so close that kissing her took but a tiny incline of his head. Their lips touched, and hers, full, soft under his own, gave, but didn't flatten. Like his feather pillow—her lips—but this pillow opened. Her tongue snaked through, moving between his lips, causing his own to open, allowing entry as she found his tongue, touching it tentatively and bringing it to life, causing it, him, to need no other prodding.

He pulled her to his chest, his pelvis thrusting into her hips that he felt moving toward him. He eased her back against the tree trunk, his body over hers, his mouth fused to her own, but her eyes were open and staring into his own as they filled. He broke the kiss and pulled back. "What's wrong?"

She shook her head, and he felt her take his hand and move

it to her breast. Instead of jutting points, he found a mound so soft and round. On his own, he moved his hand beneath her blouse, her skin so warm and damp beneath his palm. He moved up to the bra, touching the coarse cotton before slipping his fingers under the cloth to the flesh he'd dreamed of touching. He felt her knee moving up the inside of his leg, caressing him where he pressed against his pants. If he just would have closed his eyes—but he didn't and found her eyes full of the same hunger that spoke of death—his. His hips stilled, his hand retreated, finding the coarse bark of the tree trunk from which he pushed himself back and off. Standing before her, he extended his hand, knowing at this distance she could not pull him under. She took his hand and let herself be pulled from the tree.

"It's Sunday morning," he said. They walked up the dirt street, hand in hand, and he refused to pull his hand away, though hers holding his seemed a chain. "Good night," he said at the foot of the slanting wooden steps leading to the door of her dark night-green house and watched her slip inside.

He headed home, trying to push all thoughts away, all thoughts of breasts dreamed of for years at last in reaching distance, all thoughts of a knee that could stroke him like a hand. His head empty, he walked through his hot house into the bedroom in which he'd lived his seventeen years and closed the door, pulling off his clothes, his penis still aroused, unspent. He lay on the bed and thought—not of Norma but of safer images pulled from Gilbert's *Gents*—and stroked himself.

A rush of movement past his door stopped his hand. Lifting his head, he heard movement in the kitchen, a distant sound of drawers being pulled open, and the fainter sounds of someone—his mother—digging through them. The fact that she was rummaging through her kitchen cupboards in the middle of the night reminded him of how nothing had been ordinary since August hit. Pop had come home higher than a kite from a rare Sunday in Santa Ana where he'd seen his first cockfight in over twenty years, and nothing had been the same since.

The noises down the hall died, and Ozzie, still upright in bed, thought of how it would have passed Pop—all of them—by if Uncle Joey hadn't chosen that Sunday to drive up in a brand new red Plymouth, with tail wings that flared so high they threatened to lift the car into the air, bribing Mama and even Pop in for a drive to Ozzie's sister, Lulu, and her sandy-headed Huero in their barrio Colonia Juarez in Santa Ana. Even that trip could have been safe if it hadn't gotten so hot Uncle Joey had needed something stiffer than Huero's warm beer and driven Pop and Huero off to find it.

They'd found it and more at the edge of Colonia Juarez where a band of Mexicans—real Mexicans like Pop—had set up camp. To anyone outside the barrio—especially the chinga cops—it would have looked like any collection of itinerant ragtag Mexicans, though these were smaller and browner, being indios from way down in Merida, looking for work and selling the chickens crammed into cages on the back of a truck that didn't look like it could have covered the frontera from Texas to California, much less up from the Yucatán. These mexicanos weren't looking for work, they were making work, selling pulque—the real stuff Uncle Joey had gotten a taste for traveling through Mexico after the war. The pulque had just been the appetizer, for those weren't chickens crammed into those cages after all, but roosters—cocks itching to fight—and the band of galleros had been traveling from barrio to barrio looking for audiences of tired men, like Pop, who would leap at the possibility of easy money won on bets placed on dueling cocks in arenas outside the law.

Before that Sunday had ended, Pop had been fifteen dollars richer and had arranged for the gang of indio cocksmen to arrive in Carmelas the last Sunday in August—tomorrow—by challenging them and the best of their gallos to a battle with the toughest bird that had ever walked the earth, Pop's own El Bobo

Bruto—the terror of Carmelas and the last in Pop's line of the meanest goddamned roosters anyone in Carmelas had ever seen. But, in making the arrangement, Pop had broken a solemn promise to Mama and thrown the Gallo house into a chaos thought settled long ago that Mama swore would never settle again if the fight went on as planned.

Sitting on his bed in the sticky heat, Ozzie wondered how anything could fight in weather like this, and Ozzie knew something about fighting. He was a fighter—lean and wiry with arms that contradicted the slimness of his body but fueled his hands, large, hard, and dangerous when coiled into fists. He knew what fighting was among boys, and he'd seen how savage it could turn when grown men indulged, too quickly abandoning fists for knives that flashed like razors. He knew, too, about the fighting between men and women, for he had witnessed battles in his own house and in the houses scattered around him that were always vicious with words in ways that fists could never be. About cockfighting, he knew only what his father had told him. That hadn't been much because Pop's talk of birds and feathers and razored talons had been the only real threat inside the house Ozzie had ever feared, threat somehow tied up with Mama's eyes.

His mother was not a pretty woman—despite her father, Paco Valdez, being the most handsome of the men who'd originally settled Carmelas, and her brothers, each better looking than the one before, but few people noticed because of her eyes—a green so cut with yellow that they seemed lit against the darkness of her skin. Few people got beyond them, the fire there, to see the sharpness of her features, the gauntness that spoke of despair. The only thing that could chase the fire out of Mama's eyes—the only part of her really left alive—was Pop's talk of cocks and cockfights. No wonder then, that Ozzie had never let Pop suck him in, the lines in their house clearly drawn, with Pop and El Bobo Bruto pushed outside.

Since Pop's fateful trip to Colonia Juarez, he had seemed almost a stranger, and if it hadn't been for loyalties already laid, Ozzie might have welcomed it, for his pop was electric all of a sudden—a different man than Ozzie had ever seen before.

The faraway slam of the screen door in the kitchen startled Ozzie, still on his bed. What was his mama up to now? Suddenly he heard a commotion in the backyard, and the alarmed crowing of El Bruto was center stage—long before dawn. Rising, he heard his father run by his bedroom door shouting, *"María Lourdes!,"* the name he never called Ozzie's mama unless he was furious or frightened or sad. This was enough to send Ozzie into his boxers, into the hall, on through the kitchen and out the back door.

There in the hardpacked backyard—swept clean by his mother as often as her kitchen floor—was his mother swinging an ax in the moonlight, his father roaring about her, pulling at her swinging arm, and grabbing for the ax. Around her feet, billowing dust, was El Bobo Bruto—Pop's only remaining rooster—as he leapt into the air, avoiding Mama's swinging ax.

Ozzie stopped short, for the bird—afraid of nothing—was not fleeing. Never one to run, the ugly cock was darting in and out of Mama's legs, his beak a knife stabbing at her bare feet, a piston, rising, falling, hitting home, raising blood. Mama screamed, her legs dancing as she stepped back, and the bird abandoned her feet, leaping from the earth, talons clawing air and going for Mama's eyes. Ozzie bent and found a broken piece of one of Mama's pots and aimed at the rooster's head, hitting El Bruto's neck a glancing blow that sent the squawking bird back to the ground.

Pop took the opportunity to swoop down over his prized rooster, but the animal struck at him, bloodying his cheek before it turned and ran, scattering the dust. It wasn't over, for Mama—ax still held high—chased the bird from backyard to front, Ozzie and Pop following.

The bird, for whom all Carmelas was home, took off down the middle of the dirt street with Mama screaming after. Lights up and down the street were going on, people were spilling onto sagging porches and into dusty yards as Carmelas watched Ozzie's mama run like a madwoman kicking dirt after the rooster that all of them hated.

Pop's friend Carlos Martin appeared like the cavalry, cutting in front of Mama and the bird, scooping the bird up in a flour sack, as Pop, ten paces behind, cheered his friend's maneuver. Carlos, holding the twitching flour sack, raced across the street into the gathering crowd in Pepe Torres's front yard and on into Pepe's shack.

"Carlos!" Mama screamed, watching him flee with the bird she'd hoped to cut to pieces. "When I get mis manos en tu scrawny cuello, I'll wring it lifeless like I will that bird!" She shouted and everyone heard.

Mama dropped her ax and turned, looking stricken. Ozzie watched her walk down the street, the dirt so dry it seemed like sand through which she moved her naked feet, back to the house, her hair loose and wild—as black as a girl's—hanging down her back over the soft cotton of her old nightgown.

Ozzie spoke to none of his neighbors—thick in their yards and the street—as he followed his mother into his own yard and watched her climb the wooden steps and go inside. At his stoop, he turned and saw his pop nowhere in sight, knowing he was wherever Carlos had taken El Bruto. He looked back up at the door through which his mother had disappeared and wished he had a house full of brothers and sisters like the twelve tucked into Norma's house. Someone to share his load. His only living sister, Lulu, was all the way in Santa Ana—as useful to him now as the three that had died as little girls before he'd ever been born. Mama was his alone to deal with.

He sat on the steps and leaned back against the porch pole.

He looked up Marvilla to where Mapledale crossed and into the tall dark mulberry trees and wished it were June, so he could hold in his chest again the joy of that time as he had danced with Norma amid the lanterns hanging from the trees at their graduation party. He ran his palm over his naked torso, the perspiration running, the air a wet wall enclosing him. How could two short months change everything? His mother—a spectacle in the streets.

Ozzie climbed up into the dark house, the heat reaching up to him from the walls. He moved toward his mother's room, stopping in the tiny bathroom, grabbing a cloth, which he put under the faucet until the water ran warm. Then he moved, cloth in hand, to her doorway. He saw her form humped on the bed. He saw that her eyes were open, staring at the ceiling. From his angle and with the dark he could not see them, but he knew if he could, they would be cold, dead, leaving only her face and all it held. "You all right, Ma?" She shook her head no.

He moved to the side of her bed. "Are you afraid he'll go back to jail?" Ozzie watched the sharp angles of her face, the beak of her nose, thankful for the darkness that made it almost as blank as her eyes. In this house they never spoke of Pop's seven years in jail. "Is that what this craziness is all about?"

She didn't move.

"They don't send people to prison for fighting cocks anymore." He cleared his throat, but her eyes never wavered from the ceiling. He moved to her feet, the blood hardened into muddy streaks. Gently, he picked up each foot and ran the warm wet cloth over the flesh, then marveled at the softness of skin that was on her hands, her arms so rough and hard. "Anyway, he won't get caught. It'll all be over tomorrow night." He wiped away the dried blood, the dirt from the street, and noticed her fingers moving along the rosary clasped at her chest. He knew the Aves filled her head. "Imagine how much better Carmelas will be. El

Bruto dead and Señora Rosaura free to hang her wash without fear of attack." His mama's face didn't move. He finished cleaning her and walked away, dropping the cloth on her scarred bureau. Before he reached the door, she spoke.

"He promised me, mijo—but more, he promised God. If he breaks his promise again . . . who knows what God will do this time?"

He left the room. The house was unbearable. He moved back out to the porch, unbearable, too. At least, outside he had the moon to watch as he stretched out on the porch.

CO CO ROOO! CO CO ROO! CO CO ROOOOOOOOOO-OOOOOOO!

Ozzie opened his eyes. The moon was gone. El Bruto crowed again, long, loud . . . but far away. He sat up. He'd slept, for the edges of the sky were flames above the mulberry trees at the top of the street.

CO CO ROO—CO CO ROOOOOOOOOOOO!

He stood and looked toward Rosecrans. El Bruto was nowhere in sight and his favorite place to greet the morning was from the top of Pepe Torres's front porch. The crowing was coming from up near Rosecrans. Pop must have him already tucked away at Henry's where people said everything was set for the cockfight tonight.

Four houses up, he saw Norma step outside and walk in his direction. His face rushed with heat. He wondered if she'd walk right by; she didn't. She stopped in front of him. "You're up with the chickens," she said, sounding anything but tired. "I'm going to have my dad put ten I've saved on El Bruto tonight. I figure either way I win. If El Bruto can do half as much damage tonight as he did to Señora Rosaura's sheets last week, you're looking at one rich woman."

"Y con tus ganas," he asked. "What would you do?"

"Mis winnings?" She smiled. "Secretos," she said and walked on.

"Secrets you'd share with Hector Mosqueda?" he called after her.

She stopped and spun in the street, her eyes on fire. "Who's talking about me and Hector?"

"Everybody. Chisme has you practically married. You go to the La Mirada Drive-In with him."

"I'll never marry Hector." She turned and walked away.

"You have to marry somebody," Ozzie called. "You can't gather eggs all your life!" She was almost running as she rounded the corner. He went in the house and put on a T-shirt and loose pants. Then, he went into the kitchen and threw some of Mama's flour tortillas into a dishtowel. In the ice box, he found a wheel of Señora Rosaura's homemade Mexican cheese, cut off a sizable hunk, and put it with the tortillas. Carrying the bundle, he left the house and started up the street toward Henry Lucero's bar where the cockfight would be—Pop might be hungry.

He walked up the center of Marvilla, enjoying the stillness of a Sunday morning, the only day the barrio slept in. Norma's mangy dog, Raton, was poking at the edge of the street, something unusual even on a Sunday, for Marvilla was El Bruto's turf from dawn until seven or so, and cats and dogs knew better than to venture out, but El Bruto was nowhere near and Marvilla must have seemed a different place. As Ozzie neared Norma's dog, he reached down and touched the poor animal's haunch. It leapt back, howling in terror, running halfway to Norma's house before seeing from its one remaining eye that it was only Ozzie, and not El Bruto back to pluck the other out.

There had been a string of roosters since Ozzie was a little boy, and his pop had done to them exactly as he'd done to El Bruto. He'd driven them mad. In premeditated moves, his pop would tease, irritate, aggravate, and torture the birds. He called it training, and who was Ozzie to argue. Pop had learned from his father, who'd learned from his, back into time.

"In every hundred gallos there is one, mijo," Pop had told him when El Bruto was young and one cock among many in the yard, "and I think this is it!" Ozzie had been fourteen or so and standing with his father watching the young Bobo Bruto dance at the end of a tether as it tore at raw meat Pop had suspended from the end of a fishing pole. Ozzie had been there watching only to prove to Pop that his refusal to have anything to do with El Bruto or any of the other cocks beyond feeding them had nothing really to do with Pop. "The others," Pop said, throwing a hand behind in the direction of the other caged cocks, "can be made to fight . . . pero es un diablo . . . este gallo."

Within one year, every other one of Pop's roosters was dead. Then, El Bobo Bruto claimed all Carmelas for his own. People from as far over as Pontlavoy would come, protesting the slaughter of their cocks—because El Bruto would not tolerate another rooster, and El Bruto won, for though chickens wandered everywhere in Carmelas, El Bobo Bruto was the only cock who walked Carmelas streets.

Not six months ago, Ozzie had gone out to the henhouse to gather eggs for Mama, and he'd come upon Pop down on his haunches and staring into the cage to which El Bruto was periodically sentenced. This punishment was the result of tearing Señora Rosaura's sheets to tatters while they were hanging on her lines. "She should take washing lessons from tu mamita," Pop said, looking up at Ozzie as he fished a Camel from his pocket. "Señora Rosaura's sheets are too white. They bring out the beast in my Brutito. If they were grey like Mama's sheets, he'd leave them alone." Then, he fell silent, and after Ozzie had gathered a dozen eggs, his pop was still staring intently at the caged animal that leapt at the bars, grasping them in long yellow claws that shook the entire cage as its ugly red comb flew back and forth, beak stabbing at its prison. "Nunca," his father said only to himself, "en mi vida has there been such a bird." With his hand suspended in midair—the Camel burned down almost to his brown tobacco-stained fingers—his eyes locked on the bird in such a way that Ozzie wondered who was in the cage.

Now, as Ozzie turned onto Rosecrans and walked up to Henry's bar, he couldn't shake the thought. Pop in a cage. Until today, Mama had seemed the only one locked away. Henry and Chata Lucero had turned half their Mexican store into a cantina. Both were closed. Just as Ozzie was about to circle around to the back, Uncle Joey pulled up to the curb in his apple-red Plymouth with wings. The windows were down. Ozzie went up to the car, Joey Valdez's calling card in Carmelas. The best-looking vato of all the Valdez boys, he was Carmelas's favorite, their war hero, his missing leg visible evidence.

"Too early for a beer, mijo. You should be sleeping. What's goin' on?"

"Mama went loca last night."

"My sister's been crazy for as long as I've known her."

"Really crazy, tío. Ran through the street with an ax."

"Mary Lou?" he asked, falling into the diminutiva by which María Lourdes had always been known in Carmelas, disbelief in his voice. "Dios mio. Tu papá—he's still alive?"

"She wasn't chasing him. El Bruto."

"Tell me she got him."

Ozzie shook his head no. "I gotta go around and see if Pop's in the back. I got his breakfast." He moved between Henry's bar and Chata's Mexican store to the six-foot redwood fence at the back. He jumped up and grabbed the top of the fence with one arm, balancing the towel of tortillas with his free hand, pulling himself up until he could lift a leg over the top. When he did, he saw into the yard and stopped moving. Pop had been after him for days to come and see his arena—which had been strange because Pop had long ago given up even trying to get Ozzie into cocks. But now, he felt his heart bubble at what Pop had made in the dusty emptiness behind Henry's bar as he saw spread before him the duplicate of all the tales his pop once told him of the cockfights of his youth, his dreams. His eyes ran around the boxy space, the dirt swept so clean there was no dust, and his eyes climbed to the Christmas tree lights—burning now—strung around the trees that grew so thick at each corner of the small yard. Finally, there was the fighting ring itself, the strings taut as bows strung post to post, a mountain of sand heaped within, creating an arena in which roosters would fight to death, the prospect reigniting Pop's old dreams.

Then he saw his pop, stretched out on a serape laid before an alcove to the right of the yard. He was lying on his back, his Mexican cowboy hat set over his face. Behind his father's compact body, he saw a large cage, and inside, still for maybe the first time Ozzie could ever remember, stood El Bruto, his beady eyes on Ozzie hanging on the fence.

"Pop?"

His father sat up, his hat falling away, and the man was not a pretty sight in the morning. He had a tiny head, disguised by the thickest coarsest hair. His skin was brown leather and in the morning the lines that had made his face seem like a map when Ozzie had been a little boy were thicker, broader, the eyes never large, falling almost in upon themselves. "Mijo?" his pop asked, surprise and something else firing his eyes. "Why are you hanging on the fence?"

"I brought you breakfast," Ozzie said and dropped his bundled offering to the ground. His father said nothing, his eyes growing small again. "And I came to see your ring," Ozzie said, wanting back his father's pleased surprise, stepping finally to his side of the line that had divided them for as long as he could remember. The new man his father seemed was back—his smile dazzling. He sprang up, no sign of stiffness in his wiry body. He went to the fence and helped Ozzie over, ignoring the tortillas in the towel. Soon, Pop was dancing, dragging him from here to there, pointing out the touches that only a real gallero would have known essential to a cockfight deserving of the name.

"Estas Carmelas people," his pop said, lighting a Camel, disdain heavy in his voice, "estos pochos—men sin cultura—they know about as much of anything really Mexican as tu mamacita. What would any of them—even Carlos Martin—know of gallos and fighting them if not for me—un mexicano verdadero?" Then Pop pulled him to the ring. "Mira, mijo, sand—pura y clean—ni un piece of dirt, only sand." He saw his father pull at the tautness of the string he'd strung around the soft white sand. "Los dimensiones—exactamente como the arenas in Mexico." He looked up at Ozzie. "Didn't I promise you long ago you'd see a real cockfight one day?" Then he laughed and pulled his son close. "I just thought I'd have to take you all the way to Mexico because this place bleeds the Mexican out of all of us, leaving only the brown. But God is good and instead," he said, releasing Ozzie and spreading his arms wide under the green umbrella of the trees, "I bring the real Mexico they've forgotten to you and all our friends in Carmelas." His pop's black eyes grew rounder. "I even got musica, mijo." He ran to a little table on which sat a record player. With a flourish, Pop lifted the arm to the record in place, and Mexico fell about them. Norteño music that made even Ozzie's feet want to move.

His father was dancing as if with an imaginary woman. "In Mexico, mijo—between fights—*always*—singers accompanied by mariachis." His father stopped moving as if caught in memory. "Las mujeres, mijo—the most beautiful women I have ever seen." Then he laughed. "Imagine what the singing did to the roosters' blood if those songs made my own so willing to bleed!"

"It's perfect, Pop," Ozzie said, meaning it.

Pop's fingers went to his lips where he kissed them. "*Sí!*" Then he turned and bowed low to the caged bird. "Y el gallo perfecto tambien. One in a million." He stood and moved toward the cage. El Bruto backed up, its claws tapping nervously on the cage's bottom. "A gift. What is the point of a gift if it is never used?"

And Ozzie was for a moment popped back to last night under the mulberries, his fingers creeping under Norma's bra as her knee made musica with his huevos—and clearly saw that Norma's offer last night in the trees was not the kind of gift his father was reminding him of now in the patio of Henry's cantina. That caliber of gift wasted—never used—was what Norma had realized the night of their graduation when on that ride home in the back of the pickup, she'd said, "It's over," referring not only to school, but to the dreams school had put into her head that she knew would never come true—for either of them.

In his mind's eye he saw a huge map of the world that had hung spread out over the wall of his Senior Problems classroom, a large red circle drawn around the Korean Peninsula, a tiny country at the map's western edge. Instead of listening to Mr. Gandolfo's lecture about the progress of the war, Ozzie—who'd been nowhere farther away than Santa Ana—had spent his time looking at the map, wondering what was out there. Carmelas suddenly seemed a cage that held them all. Wanting to spoil none of Pop's joy but unable to stop his words, he said, "But you promised Mama," and saw at last the lock that secured all cages—promises.

"Claro," Pop said softly, his black eyes shining. "That's what happens when you marry a foreigner, mijo. Your mama—all the familia Valdez—look like real mexicanos, and your mama, even with those eyes, estaba muy mexicana. Her Spanish is all right, better than most here in Carmelas, so in her way she talks like a Mexican. Your mama," he said, as if speaking of a glorious mystery, "es muy católica—like my own mama she is with her rosary. But underneath, mijo—she is something else, not so mexicana after all. She makes me swear to God that I will never fight with gallos again ever—and I make the promise . . . I do . . . because she was so afraid and she had this idea, mijo—this crazy idea no real Mexican would ever hold that my little girls—her little girls, the three who died while I was—"

"In jail?" Ozzie asked, finishing for him, feeling good at speaking the forbidden words out loud directly to his father, breaking one promise made long ago.

He nodded. "Boom, boom, boom," he said softly. "Three—en tres meses—three girls dead, and your mama tells me God is punishing us for my sins by taking mis hijitas inocentes. I could not believe my ears. That a woman brown as Mama who looks so muy mexicana could think so different to anything I've ever known. So seeing she was pocha after all—I promised to stop the pain leaking from her, mijo, threatening to drown us all." He lowered himself to his haunches before El Bruto's cage and pulled another Camel from his pocket, sticking it into his mouth unlit. "But God dumps this gallo . . . a rooster like none I have ever seen on me." He turned and looked at Ozzie. "Un gallo como El Bruto comes once in a lifetime—to throw that away."

"But why start all this now, Pop—after so many years?"

"You think I planned to go to Santa Ana con Joey that Sunday?" He jumped up and came to Ozzie, poking at his chest. "Did I seek those galleros from Merida? They dropped into my lap as if from heaven, mijo. What can I do?"

"Mama said you promised God."

He nodded. "But I am Mexican—muy mexicano—y I know, mijo, that God could only forgive a man breaking such a promise—"

"But will Mama?"

Pop shrugged. Then he reached into his Levi's front pocket and pulled out a dirty felt box. He opened it and inside lay two silver spurs. "Never used, mijo. Why would I have saved them? Gifts from mi papá as he lay dying and his words, mijo, 'I have never found a bird worthy of these little knives,' he told me, 'may you be better blessed,' and I have been, mijo." He held out his hand in El Bobo Bruto's direction, and, as if on cue, El Bruto screamed and leapt against the bars that caged him in. "Don't you see?"

Ozzie did.

Later, when Ozzie walked around to the front of Henry's, Uncle Joey was asleep in the front seat of his car. He went around to the driver's side. "Wake up, tío. Scoot over. I'll drive you home. Maybe you can talk some sense into Mama."

Uncle Joey scooted over. "You know how to drive, muchacho?"

"How hard could it be?"

Joey laughed. "See those buttons. Automatic, hijale. Buttons. Push the one with the D."

"Then?"

"Step on the gas and steer, man."

"Where's your leg, tío?" He nodded in the direction of Joey's empty pants leg as they glided from the curb, his artificial nowhere in sight.

"Left it standing all alone against Mirna's wall in Lincoln Heights. Imagine waking up to that!" Joey leaned forward as they picked up speed. "Smooth," his uncle complimented. "You like that with the chicas?"

Ozzie laughed and turned right at Carmenita.

"Isn't that fat ass coming up the street tu buddy Gilbert?" Joey leaned across and honked the horn. Gilbert looked up as they glided by in Joey's Plymouth, which was the exact color of the lips of all the girls in Gilbert's *Gents* magazine. "Slide down, mijo, like the low riders in East L.A. Make like she's yours."

Ozzie slid low in the seat and nodded at Gilbert, dumbstruck on the pavement. Joey reached down and punched on the radio. "Mona Lisa" spilled out around them. "Smooth," Ozzie said.

"Does your uncle Joey know how to live, vato?"

And Ozzie suddenly saw it all, as plain as day. Real life lay beyond these four dirt streets. In his head, he could see the map of the world spread over Gandolfo's wall in Senior Problems—Gandolfo's red circle around Korea, a gift waiting to be grabbed and used. "I'm going to enlist, tío."

Uncle Joey whistled. "Korea. You'd better hurry, mijo; they say it's wrapping up."

"Tomorrow, Joey. Take me down tomorrow. Show me what to do."

"You sure?" His uncle's eyes stared at him so hard. "Once out, there ain't no coming back." Joey sucked his lower lip. "Four fucking streets—Carmelas—never seemed small, but after the war, the smallness drove me loco." He punched Ozzie's shoulder. "Remember that, vato." He laughed. "You want the marines like your uncle Joey—Mexicans do best in the marines, mijo."

"What else!" Ozzie answered, choosing, and in his head, he saw himself—pushing off of Norma—saying no to an endless string of other promises before even realizing why—saying no even though his chorizo, so hard in his pants, had been offered what it had dreamed of wetly for too long. Still, he had said no—to his body, to Normita's hunger, to Mama's bleeding feet. He had said no.

Ozzie looked at his uncle—like no other man in Carmelas, navigating a world really neither this nor that. The vato wore suits—this one rumpled—but it was silk; the shirt was white—like no cotton that had ever come out of Penney's—startling against the black jacket, the black hair, the eyes so black they disappeared in his very dark face. The delicate chain that looped from belt almost to his ankle back up into his pocket was pure gold. No stamp of Carmelas left on the man. "Women like you, Joey?"

He nodded.

"The missing leg—that doesn't get in the way?"

"Hombre, that ain't the leg they're worried about."

In a rush, Ozzie asked, "Could you find me a woman, tío? No una nena from Carmelas—a woman."

His uncle winked. "It could be arranged, hombre."

"Hijole!" Ozzie said, hitting the steering wheel. "I'm betting the bank on Bruto tonight, tío. After he mows down those other cocks, money for the woman won't be no object!"

His uncle's eyes grew wide. "Then we had better get our nalgas over to Mary Lou's. We're going to need some of her chorizo and a little sleep if we've got cockfights and whores lined up for tonight, vato!"

Laughing, Ozzie turned on Mapledale heading for Marvilla and home, but thinking of Korea waiting like a woman just for him at the edge of the world. "You saw the world, tío?"

"I *saw* the world, mijo."

"Was it worth the leg?"

Uncle Joey slapped Ozzie's thigh. "Small price to pay."

Chapter 7

Contemplación ~ 1953

It was fall, end-of-September hot. Contemplación and her niña Luna were just getting back from their two-night trek through the once open country that people were beginning to call La Mirada. "Always a bad sign," Luna told her, "when they name a piece of the earth, mija." Which was probably why her niña had been unusually silent this trip, for two days and two nights had resulted in a harvest so pitiful that niña had hardly filled her bag, a sure sign the world was changing. They had been coming off Rosecrans down Pontlavoy—not the way they'd normally have walked home—but niña had let Contemplación stop at Chata's Mexican store and trade some of the wild mushrooms they'd gathered for a block of leche quemada. They passed Don Vicente's house, the only one in Carmelas then with a fence all the way around—but not a fence, niña said, like in Mexico, used to keep other eyes from looking in; this fence was wire and invited eyes.

The other thing different about Don Vicente's house was that it had flowers and so many trees. True there was no grass, but roses bloomed, especially the yellow ones his wife loved well. Don Vicente lived in a garden, but then that was understandable because he was the richest man in Carmelas and owned the nursery up on Firestone near Carmenita Road—proof, Luna said, of how lucky a man she'd known he was the first day he and his pale Alicia had arrived in Carmelas—signed over to him when Prohibition ended by the gringo bootlegger who'd used the nursery and Don Vicente to front his real enterprise, booze. He hadn't thought it legal until Arnulfo Carmelas had had Señor Hinton's lawyer look over the transfer of title. It was, and the rest was Carmelas history, proof un hombre as brown as Don Vicente could not only claim a gauchupin como his Alicia for his bride, but also become rich in the USA. Gil's Horticulture Heaven he called it, acknowledging, Luna said, the role Jesus played in all good luck. But to Contemplación, the heaven was here, in Don Vicente's yard where trees crowded his house, as plain as his neighbors—only larger—and the trees bore fruit of every kind imaginable and cast perfume everywhere that blended with the smell of manure from the dairy or softened the bitter scent of blood from the slaughterhouse depending on the time of day.

As they passed his house, she saw Don Vicente on a ladder placed against the trunk of a tree. He was near the top of the ladder and pulling plums, purple and succulent, from the branches so heavy with fruit that they fell towards his reaching hands.

He saw her, too, and waved hello. Then she heard him call. "Ven pa'ca. Tengo fruta para La Luna."

She stopped in the middle of Pontlavoy. " Niña, Don Vicente is calling."

Niña stopped, too, and looked back. "Cómo estás, Don Vicente?" she called loudly, no more happiness in her voice than Contemplación had heard in days.

"Mis trees son ricos, Doña Luna," he called back proudly.

"The world is dying," Niña whispered to Contemplación, "and his trees are rich." To him she shouted, "Tu eres un hombre suerte." To Contemplación, she said, "Go gather some of the richness he offers, seeing as the world is offering us so little else. I will go on ahead. My head aches y mis feet feel like strangers."

Before turning away she shouted, "Mil gracias, Don Vicente, da mis felicitaciones a tu wife."

Inside the yard, Contemplación stood at the base of the tree, holding a bag into which Don Vicente was dropping purple plums, making her mouth water in anticipation. The skin of each falling plum was cloudy, but with the wipe of a cloth, she knew, they would become brilliantly purple, and now, still hard from the tree—just the way she loved them—they would resist her teeth, revealing yellow flesh when finally bitten. Niña would save hers until they were soft and squishy and cloyingly sweet, waiting until she could gum her way through a nearly rotten plum.

When the bag was full, she helped Don Vicente down from his ladder. He took her hand and led her through the cool shade of all his trees toward the back of his house where he had another porch. There were chairs on the porch positioned to allow whoever sat there the vista of Don Vicente's yard, testimony to his green thumb. Tomato plants abounded, not left to grow chaotically as in her papa's yard but wrapped in wire cones and directed into orderly ascent. On the porch, he sat her down and called, "Alicia, tea para la Señorita Contemplación."

Don Vicente, his hair a thick grey bush, his skin as dark as niña's, his eyes as Indian and black, sat down beside her. He patted her hand. "Alicia!" he called, but to Contemplación he said, "Te gusta tu tea muy frio?"

"Very cold, señor, I like my tea."

"Contemplación," he said softly, making the name sound beautiful as he stared out at his garden. "Que nombre lindo. De donde viene un nombre like this?"

"Mi niña, señor, named me."

"La Luna?"

Alicia, thin, delicate, and pinkly pale, came out of the back door with a tray, a pitcher of cold tea and glasses. "Cómo estás, hija?"

"Bien, señora, y usted?" she asked politely in return.

"Su name is Contemplación, Licha mia," Don Vicente said, "as you well know, and she was telling me how came she by this name."

She stared up at him and waited as his golden wife poured tea, the two of them startling together, he short, thick, and Indian, she a contrast in pale elegance that Contemplación had read of in her biographies at the Norwalk Library. Doña Licha was like a queen, the only queen in Carmelas, one who stole the tongue of most Carmelas people, though she was always warm; it wasn't Doña Licha, however, who slowed her response now. It was the shaping of the tale she'd tell. Her name—she knew her mother had waited three days to name her. She knew it had taken that long for her mama to be able to look at her. She knew that with each passing day the stain on her new face had darkened into deeper shades of wine. She knew that finally there had been nothing to do but accept that she would live. So three days old she'd been before her mother finally had taken her from La Luna's arms, which had been keeping her alive with chupones dipped into sugared goat's milk to suck on and finally offered her own swollen breast to the baby who sucked—harder, her mother told her, than any of her other children had ever suckled. Her mother—in tears, La Luna had told her—had then asked, "Doña Luna, whatever will we name her?"

When the tension on Don Vicente's porch reached its peak, she blinked and saw Don Vicente and his lovely Licha staring, waiting. So she said, "They said I would need a strong name. The strength of mountains I would need, my mother told mi niña Luna." She saw something come into Señora Alicia's eyes that flowed into most people's eyes whenever they looked at her marked face, and so she shifted her gaze to Don Vicente, for his eyes held none of that. To him she said, "But mi niña told mi mamá, no, that it was no the strength of mountains I would need, but la paciencia of mountains to find my place in the world. So mi niña Luna named me Contemplación."

"Bueno," Don Vicente shouted. "Bravo. You tell a story well, mija!"

She smiled, pleased with her telling—up to now content to tell her tales only to Luna, never imagining others might listen as Don Vicente had. She sipped her tea that bore the kiss of lemons and was so cold upon her tongue. "And when the priest came to Carmelas two months later, he added Maria de Piedad and called my mark God's palm print," she said, smiling at this flourish, putting Luna's words into the priest's mouth as if another person besides Luna could have seen blessing in her stain, "while dousing me with holy water bringing me into Christ's body."

"Cuantos anos tienes ya?" Don Vicente asked.

"Seventeen."

"Y que haces con tus dias?"

"My days, señor, why, I spend them tending mi niña Luna."

"Tienes planes para andar en su camino?"

The question startled her. She saw his eyes probing, and she wondered if he could see the battle she had been waging over this very question. "My dream is to be a curandera like my Luna." She noticed his eyes cloud over.

"Que dijo tu papá sobre tus planes?"

"My father tells me to do what I can with the life I'm given."

Don Vicente rose very quickly. "Licha, donde está la maquina que escribe?"

"The typewriter?" Alicia asked, rising too, uncertainty filling her face. "The portable Rosa used in school?"

"Claro. Bring it to me."

In a moment, Alicia was back, a scarred brown case dangling from her hand. It looked bulky, heavy. Don Vicente took the case and opened it on the porch before Contemplación. He straightened. Looking at her, he said, "Señorita Contemplación, a woman necesita un esposo—"

"A husband?" she asked.

"And life may well give her just what she needs," his Alicia said, quickly stepping beside him, trying to soften his words.

"I hope," he agreed, "pero hacen mas que esperan smart people—"

"What more than hope, señor, can I do?" she asked.

"I hear you are a very bright child," Alicia said, and this time Contemplación did not see pity so heavy in the woman's blue eyes. "I hear you can use herbs as well as she."

"The world has doctors now—even for poor people," Don Vicente said. "Who seeks out barefoot women chasing weeds?"

Contemplación set her iced tea down and rose stiffly. "Señor, mi niña Luna es una curandera magnifica."

"Did I say otherwise?" he asked, his eyes going narrow. "Who but La Luna can make me salve to ease the ache that lives inside my back? No one. But am I enough—the few like me who cling to ways as old as La Luna's—for her or others like her to keep tortillas en la mesa, un centavo in a pocket? Trujillo he told me it broke his heart—you leaving school so early. Is it un crimen to suggest a curandera today might just need some skill upon which to fall back?" He squatted and slammed the cover of the typewriter closed. He straightened, lifting the machine that wrote. He extended it toward Contemplación.

"Para mi?" she asked, surprised.

"Claro. Learn to write with it. Then come to me again, and if you are bright like Trujillo says, and you can show me proof you have learned well the machine, I will put you to work typing orders and records I need to keep down at the nursery. I will pay you money you can count on to meet your and La Luna's needs."

She saw him look up at his wife and add, she knew, to please her, "Hasta viene un man para amarla y cuidarla—"

She rose, taking the offered case in hand. "Mil gracias," she said, realizing the chance of a man ever choosing her to care for had as much likelihood of happening as she had of becoming the curandera of Luna's dreams.

Bagged plums in one hand, the heavy typewriter case in the other, Contemplación trudged through the dusty street to her home, where she hid the cased machine under her bed before delivering the bag of plums to Luna.

The machine sat in its case for months under her bed, taken out now and then and touched. Then, in the new library on San Antonio one day, she'd asked the librarian if there were books that taught someone how to type. She'd carried it home, and then, typing book in one hand, cased typewriter heavy in the other, she'd gone out back in the farthest corner of her papa's yard, where she'd set up a folding table. Opening the Smith-Corona there, she'd begun her lessons. Every day.

As her fingers learned to find their way, she yearned for something other than the boring drills to play upon the keys. She thought of how she'd told the story of her name to Don Vicente and suddenly wanted to tell it yet again, this time on paper.

And she did. Every day after that, she did the lessons faithfully, but always, before daylight fled from the yard, she told a story on the page, conjuring up worlds she'd only seen through Luna's eyes, making the stories more solid by putting them on a page. She painted pictures with words day after day, her fingers getting faster and faster on the keys. Finally, she even began to type out how she felt, writing things never said out loud, realizing how, despite her love for Luna, she just did not want to walk the old woman's path except in company. She applied herself with ever more effort, and one day came when her fingers flew so fast they jammed the keys. She knew the time had come to test the skill honed in a dusty corner of her papa's yard. At the library, the lady who had led her to the typing book suggested she might get a typing test from a teacher at Excelsior High School.

This night as she sat at Luna's wobbly kitchen table, the typewriter resting in its open case in the middle of the table, the green card of proficiency next to it, all bathed in the harsh light falling from the naked bulb hanging from a wire above the table, she realized her godmother's reaction to her news was no real surprise as she watched the old woman move around the table staring at the machine. Luna made no noise as she moved over her fading, yellow, patched linoleum on naked brown feet that had seldom worn shoes, never taking her eyes off what lay on her kitchen table. Her Indian face was as blank as a mask, but the extreme roundness of her black eyes told Contemplación all she needed to know of niña Luna's growing agitation.

"For this," niña Luna asked and raised her head so fast to glare at Contemplación that the old woman's braids, still black as night near the rubber-banded tips, swung like heavy ropes. "For this Smith-Corona machine that writes—*for this*, mi Contemplación preciosa, you will turn your back on me?"

Contemplación lifted a hand toward Luna. "It is just a way to make a living, niña. Don Vicente made learning a condition of working for pay in his nursery." She lowered her hand under her old niña's hard stare and said, "It is not a matter of me turning—"

"No, mija?"

The question hung in the air, cutting, for Contemplación was the nearest to a daughter niña Luna would ever have and the old woman more mother than her own.

"I have given you all the secrets that I own," Luna said.

Contemplación felt the weight of Luna's terrible words, for in them were the ashes of the old woman's hopes—heaped high on Contemplación's shoulders for as long as she could remember—increasing Contemplación's pain.

"Gifts as old as time and more I have given you," niña Luna said, staring down at the typewriter.

Contemplación rose on her side of the table. "You've loved me," she said, naming the gift that mattered most to her.

In a sudden rush of movement, niña Luna lifted her hand, fisted it, and brought it crashing down on the keyboard, causing the keys to fly and jam. Then, she said, "When your fingers dance and make it write doing Don Vicente's bidding for the money he will throw your way—what will this ever give you to compare?" The old woman pulled back her shoulders, lifting her chin high.

Long past seventy—even Luna was never sure—the old woman's face in the harsh kitchen light was a pitted canvas, cratered scars of varying size and depth waffling her flesh and making her to everyone but Contemplación ugly and at first sight more than a little frightening. She had often tried to look at it as others in their barrio did. To them, Luna was simply curandera—the trusted one who delivered babies and sometimes healed their pains. Some whispered bruja—always behind her back—and added a darker tone to the chisme that had been trailing the old woman longer than most of them could remember. She was La Luna, a presence so long here that she had become something like the two tall mulberry trees sitting at the top of the barrio called Carmelas, floating always at the periphery. She was of Carmelas but apart, and Contemplación knew it was the face, pitted like the moon, the magic in her fingers, the talent to pull from common flowers and weeds healing medicines and salves, her voices, evil or divine—all of it and more that set her apart and built a wall that kept the world at bay and Luna so alone—except for Contemplación.

Niña Luna's defiant jutting chin had just begun to tremble when the old woman turned and left the tiny kitchen.

Alone, Contemplación stood staring down at the typewriter, one hand reaching out and unjamming the tangled keys that fell obediently back into place. Then, she closed the case, snapping it shut before placing it behind the refrigerator by the back door, amazed at how a small machine could change the world. For a moment, she was ready to forget it all. She hurried to the kitchen doorway through which Luna had disappeared and stepped up into the small cramped room that had once been the entire house. If her Luna had been sitting there, she would have taken all of it back—forgotten the typewriter, Don Vicente's offer. But the room was empty, except for the multitude of crucifixes, each Christ manifesting agony differently from its cross. The front door was open. She went to it and out onto the dark porch in the November chill. Luna wasn't there. She stepped down the wooden steps into the yard, her arms reaching up to hug her shoulders, and looked toward the mulberry trees, wondering if the old woman was hiding in the shadows.

She moved to the edge of the trees but could see nothing. From memory, however, she heard Luna say, "Un bebe especial—un gift for tus padres who were beyond babies—but most of all un gift para mi." Though she could hear Luna's words, she could see no particular place or time, for the story had been told everywhere and often, the same whether told in Luna's cramped kitchen—when it had been newly built after she'd delivered twins for Abel Gutierrez up on Marvilla and in the flush of fatherhood he had told her he would give her the moon but she'd wanted only a kitchen—or in the open fields of flowers and weeds that used to stretch far all around Carmelas as they walked hour after summer hour filling niña's bag with the riches of the earth, a flower, the nut or berry from some strange bush or tree, or simply a weed.

"No weed, mija. Yerba buena," niña Luna would say, pulling the weed from the earth and laughing teasingly. "I will dry it into dust and when your food runs straight from your mouth out your nalgas like water, it will be la cosa exacta that we need to dry you up."

"But, niña," Contemplación would ask, trailing after through fields in grasses up to their hips, "how did you know my specialness?"

And her niña never tired of telling her, "Besides your face, preciosa—you wore la vela," and she would stop and pass a dry caked palm over Contemplación's upturned face. "A veil put over this fine brown face—already kissed by God—to tell us doubly that tus ojos would see what other eyes could never see."

The words remembered made the woman Contemplación was now laugh softly in the dark under the trees, for she could not see even into the darkness of these trees. She turned and looked up Claresa to where it joined Rosecrans, seeing no sign of the old woman. She looked back up at Luna's house, the first at the Mapledale corner leaning toward these trees. La Luna's barraca was what everyone called it. A shack. One room for years, slowly added onto, the additions sorry appendages that looked grafted on. Yet nowhere in the world did Contemplación feel the ease she felt inside that sorry shack.

Luna had pulled Contemplación from her mother's body and claimed her. She could see herself at six in front of the chipped mirror in Luna's kitchen as the old woman standing behind her pulled back her hair, brushing the thickness over and over before braiding it—hurting her with her grip as she pulled the hair back, revealing Contemplación's face and the large purple stain that covered almost her entire face naked in sunlight spilling from a window.

"A perfect face," her niña said and smiled. "In every way."

Contemplación, staring not at her face in the mirror but into Luna's eyes above her, had looked for even a trace of the lie never absent from her own mother's eyes, and saw none of it in niña's face, but said anyway, "Everyone else says—"

"Just the words of fools too blind to see, preciosa, that God's plan is always perfect." Niña Luna let the hair fall, then, and pushed Contemplación's head upright so she was staring into the cracked mirror at her face covered by the imprint of a palm—blood-red, her niña said, at birth—the fingers like tendrils losing themselves in her thick black curls and obscuring her features unless one struggled hard to look beneath the stain. She stared at her image, struggling to look behind the mark God had slapped indelibly there.

"See," niña demanded.

And the stain in the mirror faded, revealing in the glass a beauty only niña in all the world could see. And that had been enough for years. Even later when Contemplación began to realize most clearly that no one else saw what Luna saw in her flawed face—that few if any eyes turned in her direction without filling to overflowing with something it took her years to name, something that had at first to her seemed like sadness, but finally knew was simply pity—causing her to avoid eyes, moving through life looking at the ground. The fact that Luna saw only beauty in her face and promise made her freer with the woman than anyone else and with the passing years they were more and more inseparable. In Carmelas where children were expected to keep their eyes averted when talking to adults, she knew her habit of keeping her eyes on the ground in conversation was not that unusual, and even among the other children, she was sure it was simply another of the oddities that had always made her different.

Only in school—after Mr. Trujillo had come to teach their one-room school when she'd been ten—did someone refuse to let her go on hiding. He'd kept her after school one day and when he'd finally come to where she sat always at the very back of the room, she wouldn't lift her eyes from her battered desktop.

"Do you know why we go to school?" he had asked.

From the corners of her eyes she'd seen him squat beside her desk. She shook her head.

"La Luna tells me you know every flower of the field—a girl so smart as that must have some idea why she sits here every day."

"To learn," she finally said when she realized that, like Luna, he would wait out her silence.

"Exactly . . . to learn to see that the world is bigger than we think. But you—how will you ever learn if you never lift your eyes from off the ground?"

Then, she'd felt his hand find her chin and lift it until their eyes were touching. "Do you remember when Chuy had the ringworm?" he asked.

"His papa shaved his head," she said.

"And Chuy," Mr. Trujillo reminded, "wore that silly woolen cap pulled down to his nose."

"He was afraid," she said, "we'd laugh at him."

"I made him take it off."

"And everyone laughed."

"Once, mija," Mr. Trujillo said. "Once, and then everyone forgot Chuy's bald head."

"But his hair grew back."

"It did."

"My mark is forever." She felt his eyes moving over her face.

"It is large and purple, and, like my hooked nose, it probably is forever," he said, his eyes on hers. "I will never lie to you."

"People stare."

"At anything different, people stare—for a while." His voice softened and he said, "And because you hide your face, the birthmark remains always new and different." Then he rose from his squat, not removing his eyes from hers. Upright, he said, "I will no longer permit your hiding here."

She had stopped looking at the ground—in school and everywhere, and Mr. Trujillo had been right and wrong. People looked, eyes always filling with the pity that she hated, and then looked away, never returning their eyes in any conversation to her face—like Trujillo had said, but she knew that they never forgot her mark was there—but what had kept her from retreating once again was that—upright—she discovered something else. No one reached a point of seeing through it, but people's avoidance of her face gave her a kind of freedom. Turning back to the trees, she wondered for a moment what her life would have been if Mr. Trujillo had never led her to this discovery that made her freer. She remembered climbing those huge trees—long after the other girls had stopped such boyish games. She recalled how for years even the boys envied her prowess, for she could climb higher than any of them. In the company of boys, higher up than anyone else where the branches thinned and became brittle, and almost hidden by the leaves, she felt one of them like nowhere else. Luna would often call her down from the treetop as night began to fall, never screaming as her mama did for all the world to hear. Instead, Luna would call up to her a birdsong Contemplación had never heard before that Luna said meant only fortune in Mexico. And the child she'd been—so high in the tree she couldn't see through the leaves to the ground—would call back the same cry.

"How high are you, mija?"

"I can see the world, niña."

"What do you see?"

"Fields that run to mountains. There is snow."

"Snow? It's summer, mija."

"But there is snow, worn like a hat, as white as your dresses—under all the embroidery."

"And colors? Come down, mija, and tell your niña what colors do you see, for night is falling, and we can over chocolate plan our summer walk into those fields. My stores are down."

Contemplación would shimmy down the tree so fast, the promise of three nights, maybe more, out walking with her niña, sleeping beneath stars. She remembered how one day she'd asked, "Will I carry my own collection bag this time?"

"How else does a curandera collect her stores?"

A curandera—and that had been the first time niña Luna had spoken aloud her plans for Contemplación's life. Contemplación had believed. Then. Now, she knew better.

"Como yo," niña Luna had said to her that first time mention had ever been made of what she would do with her life. She had been twelve that summer, and they'd been exploring the open field they knew, the section near where the new slaughterhouse had opened.

"Like you?" Contemplación had asked. "But you are magic, niña."

Niña stopped in the high yellow grass, her basket overflowing flowers plucked amid the weeds, and she brought her finger to her lips. "Don't ever use that word except to me. I know what you mean by magic, but other people misunderstand, not seeing that magic is simply another name for God's gift of being marked to use the riches of the world to ease the pain of others." Then, niña Luna set her basket down and squatted in the weeds, holding out her arms. Contemplación ran into them and was enfolded, loving the smell rising from her niña's body, smells of weeds and earth and must that mingled with the blood hanging in the air from the slaughterhouse. In Luna's arms, she felt none of the heaviness that always dripped from her mama's arms when holding her—so full of sorrow, sadness, tears—but only the joy of Niña Luna's celebration at Contemplación's being there at all.

Contemplación—no longer a child wrapped tight in Luna's arms—was a woman at a crossroads standing alone in the dirt of Mapledale at the top of Claresa.

"Communing with the spirits?"

She looked up, startled to see Mark de los Rios y Valles standing just feet away. Even in the darkness, the extreme lightness of his skin drew her eyes as it always did. He was taller than anyone in Carmelas. His hair was a sandy brown, flecked with gold and red in sunlight, and he could have been mistaken for any of the gringos seen in Harvester's Market shopping on a Saturday, which was why he'd been called Gringo all his life in Carmelas. His lightness was the source of all the chisme about the plausibility of his ever having come from Benito, the smallest, darkest man in the barrio—chisme only whispered, for Benito, much loved for years, had never come back from the war, his legend building over time, as his lovely Lola mourned him forever. None of the whispers about Mark's dubious connection to the dark dwarf-like man he'd loved as a father had ever been lost on him, she knew.

"Or talking to yourself?" Mark asked.

She smiled, seeing how tall and straight he looked, a book bag thrown over one shoulder. "Maybe a little of both." She laughed. "I'm looking for my Luna."

"La Luna," he said and looked up at the house, the open door. "She often walks at night."

"I upset her tonight." She turned back to the porch, and Gringo followed her. "You just getting home from your night school?" She sat on the stoop.

"An hour ago—just took my time walking home." He sat down next to her. "It's hard to unwind after class. The walk's good for that at least. Mind if I have a cigarette?" She shook her head no. "My mom told me you delivered the Acosta baby last week!" He struck a match.

"Luna did most of it. I helped."

"I couldn't believe people are still having babies at home—if anyone would it'd be that tight-assed Manuel—wouldn't spend a dime more than necessary. What'd he pay you?"

"Twenty—and he promised to fix Luna's toilet—"

"When he gets around to it. Thank God she didn't tear down the outhouse."

"First baby she's been asked to do in three years, a dying art, I think," she said.

"So where's that leave you?"

"I don't get you," she said.

"She's scratched out a living"—he looked over his shoulder at the house—"if you can call it that. Is this what you want?" His voice had an edge.

"Gringo—" she started, never letting anyone speak badly of Luna.

He stood up and tossed his cigarette into the night, cutting her off. "Don't call me that. I hate it," he said, staring out into the street, and for the first time in her life she wondered if his light skin, his pale face, his golden hair had marked him in a way somehow similar to how she had been affected by the stain slapped across her face.

"I hated it," he finally said, "since I was a kid. I'm not a kid anymore." He turned back to her. "Call me Mark. That's my name." After a moment, he asked, "How old are you now? I'm eighteen, so you've got to be right around there." Without waiting for an answer, he said, "I saw Gina Morales at school tonight. She said you were at Excelsior today. Thinking about going back to school?"

"No. I was there to take a typing test."

"Where'd you learn to type?" he asked, sounding surprised.

"A book—from the library. I've been practicing all year."

"No fooling. You spend a lot of time at the library for a chica who quit la escuela back in primaria!"

"I like to read."

"Did you pass?"

She slipped her hand into her skirt pocket and extracted the small green proficiency card. She held it up. "Sixty words per minute."

He took it, lit a match, and ran the flame near the card. He whistled. "That's great." He dropped the match and passed the card back. "Why did you leave school so early?"

She shrugged. "No one cared if I didn't go—and I didn't want to go to Carmenita with all those strangers—I didn't want to leave Carmelas."

After a long silence, he said, "It's getting smaller and smaller though—Carmelas." He lit another cigarette and sat back down on the steps beside her. "Won't be a place fit to hide in long—but then, I guess you know that, or you wouldn't have learned to type." He sucked deeply on his cigarette and exhaled loudly before he said, "I'm glad you did. Now don't get mad, but it isn't good for you to always be hanging around with La Luna."

"I love her," she replied.

"Fine," he said, "love her. But people around here think you've got to be just like her—like there's nothing else for you. Shit, they already think of you and her in the same breath." Beside her, he turned his head and looked straight into her eyes. "Is that what you want?"

She didn't answer but didn't move her eyes from his.

"I'm out of line—I know," he said and looked out at the night. "That can't be what you want or you wouldn't . . . have taken up typing." When it was clear that she was going to say nothing, he turned back to her.

She saw that his pale eyes held only softness.

"It's just that you've got years ahead of you, girl. You've got to do something."

"I will," she said. "I already got a job. Don Vicente's putting me to work tomorrow typing at his nursery."

He turned his eyes away and said, "Well, that'll do—at least until you get married . . . like every other woman, I imagine." In the heavy silence, he threw his burning cigarette out into the yard.

She cleared her throat and said, "But I'm not like other women, Mark," using his name for the first time she could remember, feeling it foreign on her tongue.

Looking at her again, he said, "No—but not so different either as you make yourself out to be—you ain't no curiosidad in some shop of—" before his voice died.

She peered into his eyes and saw no pity, so she went on, asking, "Remember when we climbed the mulberry trees?"

He nodded.

"Who was always at the top?"

"You."

"Me. Alone, Mark. I knew even then any bacon in my house would be bought by me—and as I tried to tell Luna—that takes real money." She saw his eyes fixed on hers as if he were seeking to find something there.

After a moment, he looked away. "It's late—goddamned dairy waiting in the morning." He rose, turned back to her, nodded and then walked off.

She watched his back, feeling suddenly a kinship for pale Mark, who had striven for years to be more Mexican than any of them. She'd heard the chisme of his loving María Felicia Fuentes who lived over on Carmenita—the loveliest of a band of Indians that had invaded Carmelas after the war, setting up camp like gypsies over on Carmenita before tents became shabby houses. She was the darkest of the bunch, hair like a mane hanging to the earth, but she was the most beautiful girl in Carmelas and every boy of their generation wanted her despite the dark wildness of her family. Totally unbidden, words—from nowhere—just fell out of her mouth. "She loves you!"

He stopped and turned. "What?"

"María Felicia," she said, certainty filling her words. "She loves you."

He came back to the porch. "Who told you?"

"No one."

"Then, how do you know?"

"I just know," she said and smiled, for in her heart she felt the truth of her words rise and float out to him.

He leaned close to where she sat and Contemplación saw hope fill his eyes. "But everyone wants María Felicia—"

"She loves only *you*."

He straightened before her. "Will I—will she—"

"Only you," she said, more certain of this than anything she'd felt in life outside of Luna's love. She felt his happiness fall in waves, washing over her, and the rest just came forth. "You will love her and care for her for all her days," and for no reason at all her eyes filled, and she had no idea why, in the face of all his joy to come, such prediction might make her want to cry for him.

He smiled broadly. "Maybe you are a bruja just like La Luna." He laughed. "Why should I believe you?"

"Because you want to. Because I have ojos that see what other eyes can never see," she said, echoing Luna's words. Then, she laughed. "And can type sixty words a minute."

He whistled. "Now that combination could buy lots of bacon, kid." He was standing before her again, close. "All her days?"

"As long as she lives," Contemplación said softly as he bent down fast and kissed her cheek right in the middle of her purple stain. "Buena noche," he said and walked away.

She saw that his step was jaunty as he hoisted his bookbag over his shoulder, tiredness gone despite the prospect of the cows he'd milk in the morning. She watched him until he disappeared.

A loud banging pulled her back to where she sat on Luna's porch in the dark. The sound was coming from behind her through the open door, and she recognized it as the banging of a pot in Luna's kitchen. Pushing herself up, she entered the house, walked through the cramped front room—the crucifixes as plentiful as before, but the Jesus hanging from each one seemed now to have averted eyes. As her Luna had taught her, she crossed herself as she passed the corner of the room La Luna devoted to the Virgin, noting the smell of hyacinth rising from the recesses. She would never be what Luna was, but Contemplación did know her flowers. She thought for a moment about telling Mark on the porch that María Felicia, whom she hardly knew, was already his. From where had the words come? She'd had no vision in her head like those that plagued or pleased her niña Luna. She'd heard no voice sending the message to her alone, like the flood of voices Luna said pursued her. She had simply looked into Mark's pale eyes and the words had fallen from her mouth—and as they'd fallen she'd been certain of their truth.

She stepped into the kitchen. The harshness of the naked bulb suspended from a wire in the middle of the ceiling was jarring. She saw Luna at the stove. Standing before a pot, she was stirring and whistling softly. "Chocolate, mija," she finally said without turning, "sweet and muy mexicano like you've always liked."

Staring at the old woman's back, Contemplación said, "I've wanted always to be like you. But my hands"—she held them up—"they do not heal."

Very softly, Luna, still at the stove, said, "They've healed my heart."

"Nor do my eyes see as yours do."

"They see beyond my scars into mi alma, mija—alone of all eyes in the world."

When Luna still did not turn, Contemplación opened a drawer, loose in its slot, and pulled out niña's wooden chocolate stirrer, very old and very Mexican. She extended it toward Luna. "Here."

Luna finally turned, and Contemplación saw the redness marring the usual brilliant white of each eye. The old woman took the stirrer and returned to the chocolate in the pot. Watching the woman's back, Contemplación felt such a hunger for the past, when all that mattered was this day and no one worried about bacon or who was ever to bring it home. She longed for the certainty of childhood when, running home from school in rain, she knew niña Luna would be waiting on her porch to pull her in for hot chocolate. She would sit at this very table, buckets placed strategically here and there about the room catching water that dripped musically from her Luna's ceiling.

But that past was gone. Luna now was bent, gray, and almost out of work entirely. She had given Contemplación all she had to give, leaving the old woman, Contemplación knew, fearful now of where she'd spent her gifts.

"Niña?" she asked softly.

"Si, mija?"

"Are you afraid?"

"I am indeed," she said, whirring the spindle between her palms, frothing chocolate.

"Of what?"

She saw Luna's body still. "That you will forget . . . as I am forgetting even now—with no one to remember after."

"Then fear no more, mi niña Luna." Luna turned at the stove, water spilling from her eyes. Contemplación lifted her hands and moved her fingers in the air. "My machine that writes? These fingers can make it sing, niña, and after working in the day for Don Vicente, every night you and I together will put it down—all of it—on paper, memories pulled from inside your heart, your head—all your secrets, Carmelas's too—"

"But I don't write—"

"I do, and as you talk, I'll type your words—sixty to the minute—on paper," she said, coming close and this time pulling the old woman into her arms, "so they will last and be remembered."

Chapter 8

The Whole Enchilada - 1958

Nora de los Rios y Valles had never really known what hunger was until after her television came, even though getting it had been Zapi's idea.

Zapi was her husband—had been since she'd turned sixteen. Getting him had not been easy, and she'd promised herself nothing would ever come between them. Now, just seven years later, something had.

Before the TV, she couldn't remember really wanting anything but Zapi. Zapata de los Rios y Valles, whose papa had named every one of his six sons—but the first one that everybody whispered was not his at all—after some hero in the Mexican Revolution. Not that she'd ever heard of any Zapata, but she'd loved her Zapi forever, long before Zapi had figured it out. It had taken until the summer of 1951 to get him into such a fever that he finally asked her to marry him—the only thing she'd ever worked for.

That summer she'd picked flowers in the fields across Carmenita Road, getting brown from labor in the sun—browner almost than Zapi. Her breasts had risen out of nowhere at the beginning of July. She had never felt so beautiful before, but Zapi was only talking about Korea. He wanted to join up like his carnales were doing before it all ended.

Nora and Zapi had been dancing under the mulberry trees at Ozzie Gallo's going-away-to-the-army party, and Zapi had been telling her how he was counting the days until he turned eighteen so he could join up—because his mama Lola would never sign for him, seeing how his papa had never come home from World War II. Nora had panicked, then, because she was already sixteen. If she had to wait until he came back from a war, she'd be too old for him to want. That night in the dark under Señora Rosaura's jacaranda, she'd let him touch her breasts for the first time. Only over her shirt, but he'd gone crazy, begging her to love him.

When she'd told Lupe, her closest friend, Lupe had told her she could only salvage such a stupid move *if* she never let him touch her again. "A taste, Norita—never more than a taste, chica," Lupe warned. Nora never let his hand get close to her breast again, and he went wild.

"Te necesito," he would moan in the dark, his hand caressing her leg—never allowed above her knee. She let him touch her hair, her face, in the dark under the mulberries, his body pressed against hers, his face a picture of agony, never again letting him any closer to her breasts than her shoulders. Lupe had been right.

"Mis huevos son blue de love para ti," he'd moan in the moonlight, but still, he didn't ask her.

At his cumpleaños, his mama Lola had a party in their front yarda with a piñata, shaped like a donkey, hanging from the porch post, for there was no tree in the yard. His mother pointed at it, saying, "A burro, mijo," in front of everyone, "como tú. An ass," for he had turned eighteen and was leaving in a month for the army and Korea. Then, his mama Lola started crying. Gringo, her oldest boy—the one Zapi always said his papa had loved best—slipped his pale arm around her and all the old people crowded round her too, people talking in a rush of the fat little Indian that had worked magic in Carmelas for everyone. Beer appeared and Zapi's mama, drinking beer after beer on the porch, cried in her sister Delia's arms, complaining now of Zapi's father, who had gone away to war and not come home. "Un tonto if I ever saw one," Zapi's mama cried between sips on her beer. "Six sons and he goes off to war—who wanted him? They told him go home, but he insisted, mi Benito who dreamed of being a soldier. Tontos—todos los hombres—tontos. Piensan que it comes with the huevos? Now mi Zapito—following his papi."

Until then, Nora had never imagined that Zapi might die. She knew there was a war in Korea, but she didn't even know where Korea was and had no idea about war at all except for the movies. She hadn't seen many of them before taking up with Zapi, and his movie-crazy mama Lola started carting her with them all to the Norwalk Theater on San Antonio for Saturday matinees.

Unable to think of Zapi dying before he was hers, she'd run off toward the distraction of the piñata where all their banda of friends were gathered in a circle, shouting and screaming as blindfolded vato after vato swung at the rainbow-colored ass hanging in the air—always missing, which might have been due to all the beer. Zapi grabbed her, and Chuco blindfolded her. Someone put the bat in her hands, the boys teasing that it was Zapi's chorizo she was holding. She swung the bat at the piñata, and her blow struck gold as sweets rained like promises into the earthen yard. The promise in the scattered sweets never turned into proposal, so before summer was completely gone she went to see La Luna.

Nora had heard stories about the old bruja all her life—enough to make her keep her distance. She was always polite when she encountered the old lady, who had once delivered babies and was known for potions that could heal the sick or steal a reluctant heart—but kept a wide berth around the woman's shack that sat up at the top of Claresa near the mulberry trees. Her fear that Zapi might never come back steeled her. After picking in the flower fields, she arrived at Luna's shack in the dark. She was halfway up the steps when she saw the old woman watching from the darkness of the porch. "Señora?" Nora called.

"En que puedo servirle, señorita?" The voice was low and gravelly.

Nora strained to see her. "Mi novio—" she started.

"Zapata de los Rios y Valles," the old woman said—it was not a question.

"Claro, señora. He is going to the war." Suddenly, more than potions of love, Nora wanted knowledge. "Por favor—tell me—volverá alive mi novio to Carmelas after the war?"

The old woman laughed, lightening the dark. "El soldado his fat brown papa was. This one will miss his war."

"I want him to marry me," Nora said in a rush of relief.

"I feel your desire." After a long silence, she asked, "And he? Que quiere él?"

"He wants me—but he just doesn't know to ask."

The old woman laughed again. "Bring me a piece of cloth that he wears close to his body, y una pieza de su hair."

Two days later she found Zapi's mama hanging clothes, and Nora offered to finish hanging them. After protesting, Lola left Nora with the clothes to hang. There were six sons, and she could not be sure which clothes were Zapi's until she lifted the white boxers from the bottom of the basket. They were covered in red diamonds. She'd seen them when he'd opened his pants to show her how she made him suffer. Before closing her eyes, she'd seen the red diamonds on his chones. She slipped the boxers into her loose blouse.That night she'd returned to La Luna's with a diamond cut from Zapi's boxers.

"Su cabello?" the old woman asked, accepting the cloth.

Extracting pieces of his hair—held in a bobby pin—from her

pocket, Nora passed it too. That had been even easier to get. He'd had her pinned against one of the massive mulberry trees last night, his hips doing the only talking. He hadn't even felt her pull the hairs.

"Then, he is yours," the bruja said.

And Zapi had asked—not two nights later. Desperate, in the dark, his pants undone so his espada could breathe, he had pulled away from her lips and demanded, "When will you give me peace?"

"When I'm your wife."

"Then be mi mujer."

"Cuando?" she'd asked, her heart leaping.

"Soon or I will die."

She had wrapped her arms around his neck and shouted, "Nothing will ever come between us, mi amor."

She just hadn't counted on Zapi discovering Gorgeous George and wrestling when he finally got out of the army in '54, having never been farther away than Fort Ord. They bought Señora Lucero's place when she died. It wasn't much, but it was cheap and it kept Zapi busy, and, with the house, the babies coming so fast, and work, he'd had no time for anything until his friends had taken him one Friday to a bar with a TV. After that, wrestling was nothing for Zapi on the radio.

By 1956, he was positively losing sleep over the thought that Gorgeous George would be dead and gone before Zapi ever got the chance to see him wrestle in the privacy of his own house. He'd driven her crazy. Morning, noon, and night, the man bitched and moaned about how TV could change his life. He could think of nothing else. Nothing.

Even in bed. He couldn't sleep. He wouldn't let her sleep. One night he was going on as usual, she lying beside him, her head on his hairless chest, her hand rubbing circles on his hard dark belly, the sheet bunched low on his hips covering his huevos. She could see the mound of him there, looking soft and sleeping. If she wasn't going to sleep, nothing was. She moved her mouth to Zapi's and whispered, "But we got no money, honey," as her lips fell and her tongue moved over the surface of his lips, which shut him up about the television. While her tongue played with his lips, her fingers slid beneath the sheet and found his inky salchichon lying across his thigh, caressing it, wanting him to moan for her like he was lusting after a goddamned television. But the piece of flesh under her fingers moved not at all. She moved her lips from his mouth to his ear and whispered Spanish words that usually did the trick, but his verga refused to climb. Finally, she said, "Maybe we could take some money from your next check—" and his goddamned pinga bared its head and reached toward heaven.

Payday—the next Saturday night—Zapi came in late from work, struggling up the porch under the weight of the biggest box she had ever seen. She saw over Zapi's head, as he slid through the door, the neighbors hanging from their porches staring, having read the ZENITH in giant letters on Zapi's box.

"You got a TV?" Mirta from across the street shouted to her. Mirta and one-legged Joey Valdez came first—her landing a war hero and getting him to settle down in Carmelas was still the gossip on everybody's lips until the arrival of TV. When others saw Nora letting them in, everybody on Marvilla who could squeeze in overflowed Nora's tiny house. The men set the TV up, which turned out to be much more than just plugging it in. None of them could get any kind of a picture. Zapi had to go all the way back to McMahan's at Norwalk Square because they'd forgotten to have him buy an antenna, which they'd never have realized at all if Zapi's tía Chata from the Mexican store hadn't come over loaded down with bags of pan dulce when she'd heard TV had arrived in Carmelas at her nephew's house and told them TVs needed antennas to get clear pictures. Even with the antenna, it took Gringo, Zapi's oldest brother Mark, to finally get a picture at all by nailing the wires up the wall above the set. By the time the picture finally cleared, the wrestling was almost over, but they all got to see Gorgeous George, curls dancing, pounding somebody's head into the mat. There was beer being passed by this point. Most of the women on the block picked up their kids when they fell asleep, left their husbands, and went home. Those remaining retreated with Nora to the kitchen for coffee and the remains of the pan dulce Tía Chata had brought.

When Nora finally got Zapi alone, she was in bed. He wasn't complaining anymore. He was strutting naked around that bedroom acting like a king, trying to make sure she could see his lanza was feeling as lively as he was. He came to her side of the bed and sat close, smelling of beer and thinking he was the funniest vato that had ever come out of Carmelas. One of his hands closed around her breast and he said, "Nena, scoot over," as his other hand pulled back the sheet. "Zapi quiere dulces."

"Where'd you get the money?" she demanded.

His hand fell from her breast. "I used my check like you said—"

"Zapi, you make fifty-five dollars a week. That TV is twenty-four inches."

"Es un portable," he said softly.

"How much?"

"A hundred eighty-eight dollars. Es un sale, vieja. I got four weeks more to pay it off. Think of it like layaway—like you do at Christmas."

"Layaway you pay before you take the shit home," she said, her voice growing hard and loud as she threw back the covers.

"You're going to wake up the kids, shut up!"

"How much you got left from your check?"

Zapi turned his big brown body away from her and went to the battered dresser like he was looking for his cigarettes. "Ten dollars," he said sheepishly.

Nora leaped from the bed. "What kind of a moroncito have I married?"

He turned to face her, holding his chin up.

Faster than he could move, she grabbed his loose huevos and roared, "Do you think with these?" She squeezed and pulled hard—all in one move.

Zapi leapt away, racing to the open window and slamming it closed. "You told me I could use my chinga check," he said, one hand shielding his privates, the other searching for his boxers.

"I said you could save part of it—save, until you had enough—"

"Five bucks a week," he shouted back. "I'd be too old to want to watch anything by then."

"What are we going to eat?" She moved toward him, her face twisted hard, and she thrust it close to his. "While you're sitting around on your ass watching that goddamned maricón Gorgeous Jorge—"

"He's no queer," Zapi roared back, thrusting out his chest until it was touching hers. "And you, ten cuidado con tu boca!"

"You watch my mouth," she said. "You are one selfish bastard. You got three kids—"

"And *they* got the only TV in Carmelas."

"Tell 'em that when they got no beans to eat," she said, grabbing the bedspread and storming out of the room.

Definitely, in the beginning, it had been Zapi's TV—an intrusion she neither wanted nor needed.

"What was wrong with the way things were?" she said to Zapi not long after the TV arrived. He was scooping chocolate ice cream for himself and the boys while she washed dinner dishes.

Looking up from the ice cream, he licked a finger and then

dropped the spoon in the soapy dishwater. Sliding behind her, he pressed against her nalgas, his hands cupping her breasts. "Get with the times, nena."

"Papi!" The boys called loudly from the front room. "It's starting!"

Dropping her breasts, Zapi gathered up all three bowls and scurried from the kitchen.

After the novelty wore off, the neighbors drifted back to their own houses—more and more finding the means to buy their own TVs—so nights at home became almost like they were before. There wasn't as much talk anymore. Zapi had never been the gabbiest vato anyway—but the boys had been chatterboxes. Zapi wouldn't put up with any noise while the TV was on, so they learned to keep pretty quiet. A pattern descended. As soon as dinner was over, Zapi and the boys piled up on the sofa watching TV. Sometimes, seeing the four of them lying all over each other, Zapi's hand playing with one's hair or stroking another one's leg, she almost warmed to TV. Then, she would realize that since TV, they never even went to the movies anymore.

"Who needs the movies," Zapi asked, "when we got TV?" He even tried to get his mama Lola to come over on Saturday nights instead of going to the movies. She did. Two times. "Not the same thing at all," Mama Lola said, going back to the movies—at least until Mark's wife, María Felicia, got sick and started to die. Mama Lola gave up movies for Lent the year María Felicia died—as if that sacrifice would fix her favorite son's wife's cancer.

It was only at the end of the TV's first year, just after María Felicia died, leaving Mark with three babies, that Nora began to get really angry about the TV. She was always exhausted—her Lalito still not sleeping through the night. Things were worse with María Felicia dead—Mark still had one baby in diapers and, with his grief so raw, he wasn't interested in taking much care of any of them. So it was up to Mama Lola and Nora. That anger exploded one night just after she came home from Mark's place on Pontlavoy. After working like a mule all day at her own place, with dinner barely on her own table, she had to go over to Mark's and do it all over there. When she finally got Mark's babies down, she walked home, only to find Zapi sacked out on the sofa, the TV blaring, her two older boys perched asleep on the back of the sofa, and the baby, Lalo, naked and sprawled on the floor covered in shit, his diaper where he'd thrown it after getting it off.

Furious, she clenched her teeth and entered her kitchen, which was not much under the best of circumstances. Tonight it was a nightmare—dishes stacked in the sink, the table still cluttered with the remains of dinner the bastard Zapi had promised to clear. Spinning, she went back to the doorway into the front room and saw the disaster there from a whole different angle—the centerpiece her Zapi, passed out and oblivious. She let out a roar so full of rage that Zapi sat up, his brown face as close to pale as it would ever get. The boys woke mid-roar and fell from the sofa back. Baby Lalo began to wail. She darted back into the kitchen, grabbing dirty plates from the table, which she threw across the front room, aiming for Zapi's head. The boys crawled on their bellies for the hall and as they slithered by, she struck out at them blindly, slapping their legs, their behinds. "You son of a bitch," she yelled before running back into the kitchen. She was just reaching for her black frying pan, caked with carne asada from dinner, when he entered the kitchen. She lifted the dirty pan high over her head, taking aim. He thrust out his arm and grabbed her wrist, the pan held high in the air. She kicked at his shins and screamed.

"You crazy bitch," he said, his face close to hers, "throw one more thing and your ass is out of this house!"

"You don't have the energía to switch channels, you fat ass—"

He twisted her wrist until she dropped the pan. As Zapi bent to get it, she lifted her leg and kicked him square in the butt, the blow unexpected and sending him sprawling. Looking for more ammunition—anything—she took the pot of cold sopa de fideo from the stovetop and hurled it, the pot hitting Zapi's shoulder just as he rolled over, the contents spraying in an arc over his face and the wall, and then it was as if Nora heard her baby Lalo crying for the first time—he sounded hurt and terrified. Jumping over Zapi, she ran into the front room and scooped up Lalo, smeared in dried shit, carrying him down the hall to the bathroom. Thrusting him into the tub, sobbing a duet with the baby, she turned on the shower, kicked off her shoes and climbed into the tub, pulling the curtain. She sank to the porcelain, holding her screaming baby to her breasts as the warm spray soaked them both.

The next day she went to see La Luna for the second time in her life, no longer afraid of the old lady. The old bruja held Nora's hands and stared into her eyes. "You must find a mirror," La Luna said finally. "Look into it deeply. Find there the woman you want to become." Disappointed, Nora had risen, thanked the old woman, and pushed three rolled dollar bills into her rough hands, thinking the transaction close to robbery.

Not a week later, coming out of Zapi's aunt Chata's Mexican store with a bag of tortillas, still warm, she came upon Rosa Galvan, who lived with the gringos over on Dinard. They stopped and shot the chisme like when Rosa had lived with them in Carmelas. At one point Rosa reached over, touched Nora's face and laughed. "Girl, you know who you are the spitting image of? On TV, I mean." Nora shook her head no. "That woman on the new show where her husband is a doctor—Donna Reed. Have you seen it? You gotta see it. She looks like you, just más flaca."

So that week she turned it on and stepped into a house like none other she'd ever seen. She found that the woman who lived there—a strand of pearls around her neck—did have a face something like her own. The husband was a doctor, but he had the blackest hair and a look rather like Emilio Mosqueda's over on Carmenita. When the woman's face next filled the screen, something called to Nora, reaching out of the screen and grabbing her, forcing her from the sofa onto her knees where she felt like she was looking into a mirror. That night, slipping into bed, she crawled close to Zapi, laying her head on his chest. She told him of the show, saying nothing of the newfound hunger in her heart, and speaking only of how the doctor looked as Mexican as Emilio.

"Like Emilio. On TV? I gotta see this."

"A doctor," Nora said.

Zapi laughed. "Yeah, a Mexican doctor. Tell me another."

"You think there are no doctors in Mexico?" Nora demanded.

"I know from nothing about Mexico," he said, easing her off his chest and over onto her back where she hardly felt his lips on her skin as she lay staring up at the ceiling, turning it into a giant TV screen from which Donna Reed smiled serenely, the brilliant pearls becoming little mirrors reflecting all of Nora's possibilities.

She never missed another show, being observant, faithful in ways she'd never been to the church, to school, or anything but Zapi, looking forward to the final moments when Donna Reed waved goodbye—one hand rising to touch the strand of pearls at her neck as if it were magical, like one of La Luna's good luck charms.

Nora found *her* pearls in Sav-ons at the Norwalk Square, not three months after. Zapi was waiting in the car with their two smallest boys while she went in for nickel cones. She had six-year-old Chacho along to help her carry the four cones. On the way to the ice cream counter, she passed the jewelry stand, and the strand of pearls hanging from a headless neck stopped her cold. She—who never wore jewelry, had never wanted any adornment save for the earrings placed at birth and the band of gold Zapi had put on her finger at marriage—was drawn to the pearls, for they were the ones she'd been watching for weeks on TV, the ones that circled Donna Reed's neck, the very pearls that Donna's fingers stroked whenever crisis fell on the Stone household, and it seemed to Nora that from the pearls, Donna pulled peace. Nora wanted no more than that, the ability to quiet her storms before they erupted into ugly screams and raining blows, with thought going to her targets only when it was too late, the blow already struck. So, no matter that the pearls were $2.99, something she had never wanted, never needed until now, she bought them, leaving her change enough for only three cones.

Her pearls bagged and in her pocket, she waited at the ice cream counter while her three cones were scooped, and she ran her palms over her hips, feeling them already smaller from her month-long diet and glad now she'd lacked the nickel to buy herself a cone. Making her way with Chacho back to the car, she imagined herself thin and tiny-waisted like Donna Reed, and pictured how the pearls would look hanging around her own neck, gleaming against skin much darker than Donna's own.

At home, she hid them in her dresser drawer under her cotton panties, never quite finding courage to put them on until she realized their power to change her. It was an ordinary morning, as rushed as ever. She had been hurrying since rising, packing Zapi's lunch, sending him off, whipping up breakfast for the boys, washing dishes while gathering clothes, getting baby Lalo down for his nap, making beds and starting wash. Out in the backyard where Zapi had placed the old washer with its electric wringer, she was putting baby Lalo's load of diapers through the whirring wringer, one hand guiding the cloth into the sucking rollers, the other pulling the diaper through to the other side. Chacho, home from school with a runny nose that slowed him down not at all, had been her shadow all morning long, tagging around at her heels, tripping her from underfoot. Pulling at her blouse, he whined, "Mama, mama, mama, *mamá*!" a litany that was a constant irritation she was expert at ignoring. As she was pushing cotton through the wringer, his little hand pushed hard at her elbow, and her hand went into the wringer, the rollers gobbling her hand wrist deep.

Screaming, she reached for, found, and pulled the plug. She bellowed in pain as she twisted the hand crank backwards to free her burning fingers. Chacho ran off through the dust howling as if he'd already been beaten. Cursing, Nora went into the house, swearing that after she soothed her hand she'd find Zapi's black belt and beat her boy's butt. Baby Lalo was screaming in his crib, his chupón lost somewhere in the room. Running to her bedroom and her battered dresser drawer, she searched under her panties for the extra pacifier she always kept in reserve and saw the bagged pearls.

Taking them out, she wrapped them around her bruised fingers, and her anger dissolved. She closed her eyes and saw Donna Reed at her sink in her huge kitchen, into which Donna's television son, Jeff, stormed, wanting attention. Donna Reed just dried her hands, left piled dishes, and took her boy to the table where she calmed him by listening to him as if she had no other demand on her time and his words were gold.

Opening her eyes, Nora returned the pearls to their place, and she went out into the front yard. In her sweetest voice, she called, "Chacho!" No answer. "Mijo," she called again and saw her oldest rise from behind the ruin of a Chevy coupe Zapi was trying to resurrect. She saw the terror in his face, and her eyes filled. She sat on the front stoop and patted the porch. "Ven, mijo," she called softly.

He came slowly. He sat beside her. She lifted her arm to embrace him, but he shrank back, expecting to be hit. Ashamed, she pulled him to her. "What did you want, mijo?" He shrugged and leaned into her. She caressed him, unable to say what she wanted to say, wondering where Donna Reed found the words.

The pearls had begun to work magic with her children. She wondered why she couldn't use the pearls to change the way she reacted to Zapi—who knew every button of Nora's to push and did regularly, especially after he began to drift from watching the TV into baseball, playing Wednesdays, Friday nights, and Saturday afternoons in Norwalk Park. Friday and Saturday games usually turned into victory drinks at Henry's over on Rosecrans with his Carmelas teammates. Could they win all the time?

At first, the drinking caused Friday night riots when he came home late sticking his drunken face in Nora's while she tried to watch Jack Paar. Only when he'd start grabbing at her, did she blow—fighting like a street cat with him, until finally she tried to use the pearls with him as she did with the kids. She started putting them on on Friday afternoon. When he'd get home, she had only to touch the pearls to imagine how Donna Reed would react—though God knew, Donna's husband, Dr. Stone, would never have come home drunk on a Friday night and tried to put his hands up Donna's dress. But if he had, Nora knew Donna would react with stillness. Donna never let anger win. She always wrapped herself in stillness. With the help of her pearls, Nora found that stillness the next time he came in, fists cocked, ready for battle. She bit her lip and stroked her pearls, falling into stillness. Zapi was thrown. He goaded her, even kneeling in front of her, blocking the TV—his beery breath usually enough to make her scream—teasing her to fight. She simply smiled, said nothing and concentrated on Jack Paar and Betty White. Finally, giving up, Zapi went to bed.

One night—Zapi out again—she shut off the TV as Donna waved goodbye. Nora looked around her front room and wondered why the walls suddenly looked so naked. She ran her hand over the worn fabric on the sofa and imagined the doilies on the arms of Donna Reed's sofas, and wondered why her house couldn't be pretty like Donna Reed's. For the first time in her life, she questioned why things were the way they were. Standing in the middle of her small living room, she saw that the house was old. The walls had been papered over so many times by Señora Lucero that it looked in places like an old woman's legs. When they'd bought the place, Zapi had painted everything a pale brown, right over the paper. The floors were hardwood, but marred and dull and always dusty. She ran her eyes over the worn sofa, the best sofa she'd ever had, but secondhand, a gift from her cousin Petra. There was a table of sorts at each end of the sofa, one maple, the other a darker brown. Lamps that didn't match. One shade tall and square, the other short and round. Why had it never seemed so ugly before?

She started with doilies. She got a long runner at Woolworth's that she spread over the back of the sofa and matching doilies for the arms. The doilies covered the most worn spots. She got bigger doilies for the tables.

One payday she went to Sears and in the floor samples being sold found two matching lamp shades. The lamps looked hardly different anymore.

She started dusting every day and Tía Chata up at the Mexican store told her about a paste polish she could use on the wood. She was in the middle of polishing the living room floor when Zapi stepped into the house after work, saying, "What are you doing?"

Nora had towels wrapped around both feet, and she was skating about the living room, furniture pushed to the side, polishing, the kids trailing her. She burst out laughing, realizing how ridiculous she looked. Zapi didn't laugh, but went on into the kitchen demanding dinner, which she'd forgotten about. Later, when she'd gotten something on the table, they sat around it without talking.

"I want to see you when we sit at the table," Zapi said and picked up the bowl of plastic flowers she had set in the middle of the table. Nora rose, taking it from him fast.

"I just want the table pretty for you after working hard all day."

Zapi examined the red plastic place mat under his plate, matching those sitting under the other plates. "Where you getting the money for all this?"

"All this?" She laughed, scooping beans into his plate. "Tencent store."

"What do you need 'em for?"

Her hand went to her neck. She said, "Covers up the nicks in the table. Eat, mi amor."

The next Saturday Zapi never came home from his baseball game, staying out later even than usual. When TV went off the air, Nora walked into the kitchen, washed out her cup and placed it neatly in the new white drying rack she'd bought at Newberry's. Turning, she noticed that the tired linoleum in the cramped kitchen was dull. She'd always cleaned it regularly, but it had never been shined until Nora noticed how Donna's kitchen floor shone like glass and that when she mopped or waxed, it seemed like no chore at all. So, she'd started waxing, weekly, and even her faded linoleum lit up—not quite like Donna's though.

Tonight, not in the least tired, her babies all asleep, Nora decided to mop her kitchen floor. She went into her bedroom to get her shiny patent high heels she'd bought the week before at a Penney's sale. Pulling them from the closet, she slipped into them. Before leaving the room, she glanced in her dresser's mirror, her reflection wavy in the cheap glass, but sufficient to check her appearance. Turning, she put her hands to her waist, loving the way the belt of her new shirt dress pulled tight—helped by the skirt of the dress flaring wide over her hips—made her waist seem tinier than it was.

When she'd come upon the dress in Lerner's, she hadn't even known she wanted it, but on the mannequin it looked like the same style that Donna Reed wore every week. When she saw the fifteen-dollar price tag, she walked away, but outside on the sidewalk after she'd dug again into her purse, she saw the twenty-dollar bill that was for food. She tallied up the store of goods still in her cupboard, allotted the three dollars for rice and beans, and marched right back into the store and bought it. Now, before her mirror, she lifted her hands and turned the high collar up in back as Donna did. The light from the overhead fixture caught the strand of pearls at her neck, highlighting them like stars.

Whistling, she left the room, and, in the kitchen, she filled her bucket at the tap, adding just the right amount of liquid wax, found the mop outside the back door, and was in the middle of applying the coat of wax, feeling beautiful and almost as if she were dancing when Zapi stepped through the back door. "Mi floor—ten te cuidado!" she said, her voice rising to shrillness like it used to do, sounding sharp and hard—nothing like Donna's. Catching herself, she smiled up at Zapi and said much more softly, "Por favor, mi amor," imagining that would have been what Donna would have said to her Dr. Stone.

Zapi opened his eyes wide, the reddened whites a stark contrast to his chocolate skin. He started laughing, tracking dirt-smudged footprints across her waxed floor as he howled, grabbing the sink for support, his teeth flashing brilliant and white and beautiful like pearls. His laughter—ugly in the ugly kitchen—made her anger rise up her throat and press at her clenched teeth. She dropped her mop, and one hand found her pearls. She felt anger sink as she smiled and waited for him to stop laughing.

When he did, he said, "Estas loca?"

Nora felt her smile stiffen, but she held on to it.

Zapi's smile disappeared. His face went flat, and when he spoke, Nora swore he sounded like his voice would break. For a moment, she was afraid he was going to cry, and she couldn't imagine a world where Zapi would let his tears fall right in front of her. Her smile faltered.

"Who are you?" he finally asked.

Her smile fell.

"I feel like Mark," he said in the face of her silence, naming the brother, pale as a gringo, who still refused to live since his María Felicia had died. "But this is worse," Zapi said softly, "his wife is dead. You're here—walking, breathing—but just as gone." He lifted his eyes and looked around the kitchen. "All this shit you've started hanging on our walls," he said and swept his hand over the table's surface, knocking Nora's red plastic place mats onto the floor. "I like the pinche nicks, the scars. I hate your thinking you have to cover them up."

She bent and picked up a mat from the wet floor.

He bellowed and slapped the mat from her hand. "It's cold, Norita—plastic and cold."

"It's pretty," she said, her voice rising against her attempts to keep it still. "What's wrong with pretty?"

"I love pretty," he said, coming close, causing her to back a step away. "I loved pretty—tu—soft, round, fleshy, mi amor. Where is your flesh? What is left to hold on to—flaca eres tú. If I had wanted skin and bones, why would I have chased la gordita morenita Nora Peña through the dirt streets of Carmelas?"

"I chased you," she said softly.

"When have you chased me last?"

She imagined Donna Reed at her sink and Dr. Stone stepping into the kitchen, his eyes cool but desire burning behind them—and Donna, in the face of such desire, turning her head, blinking her eyes, and looking back at the dishwater, making him come to her. "A lady," Nora said, hanging on to the image in her head, "doesn't run after her man."

"Norita, when were you a lady?"

"I want to be," she said and the hunger dripping from her voice bounced round the room.

He felt it, too, she knew, for he took time before he asked, "Why?"

And her mouth opened, closed, but she couldn't find words to explain how she'd never known what pretty was because there had been no prettiness anywhere around her. So she had been satisfied, content, and wanting nothing more than Zapi, but now *she knew*, and everything around her seemed suddenly ugly, hard, nicked, scarred, and brutal. How could she find words to tell him she wanted him to talk to her like Dr. Stone talked to Donna Reed week after week, show after show? How could she make him see she wanted him to look at her as if she were a prize, hard won? She wanted the world clean and free of dirt; she wanted air that wasn't laced with the smell of cowshit from Norwalk Dairy or blood from the slaughterhouse. She wanted to listen to her children, to put them first despite the hours of work and diapers, clothes to wash, to hang and iron. She wanted to feel beautiful and kind and good. She wanted grass and roses. She longed for gentleness and hands that didn't strike without first thinking, mouths that didn't wield words that cut like knives and could never say aloud how full of sorrow such remarks spat at those most loved could leave her. But she didn't have the words. Shaking her head, she simply said, "I want it to be like on TV."

"*What?*" His eyes grew wide and round. "Estás really loca—you think any of that shit is real?"

Her head snapped up. "You thought it was real when Gorgeous George threw his enemies to the mat."

"That was wrestling. This *crap* you watch night after night—it's bullshit, Nora, bullshit." Pushing off from the sink, he ran out of the room. She could hear him screaming from the front room, "Did you learn this chinga crap from TV?"

She went into the living room and saw him tearing her doilies from the worn arms of the green sofa, the nearest to new she'd ever had. Then, he went to the big calendar she'd hung over the back of the couch. She'd torn off the calendar part, leaving the picture, a river, lush mountains in the background, trees huddled thickly about a sparkling river—something like what Donna hung above her sofa. He ripped it from the wall and tore it into pieces. Then, he advanced on the TV and grabbed the plastic roses she'd arranged on top of the cabinet and threw them against the wall. "You want goddamned flowers? Get real ones!"

"There are no flowers in Carmelas," and as she said the words, she realized she'd never even missed them until she'd seen how living rooms on television overflowed with roses and what they did for the people who lived in those rooms. "You're an animal," she said softly.

At the TV, Zapi spun and laughed. "We're all animales, Norita, y lo sabes la veracidad de mis words. We eat and shit, Nora. We live and sweat, Norita mia. We wash away the dirt, but it comes back and it smells, Nora, it smells like the air in Carmelas. We fight—with hands and hearts and mouths, Nora. All of us! We lie, we cheat, and we seldom show our sorrow. We leak, Nora, our eyes, our hearts, our penises. You bleed, Nora, every month you bleed and all of it is to remind us we are animales. We live, we die, and the only thing that gives it any sense is heat, the heat we make, we share, we spend. Where is your heat? Where is the Norita who burned for me under the mulberry trees? "

"There's more, Zapi. I know there's more."

"How do you know?"

"TV."

He roared as he spun and grabbed the television from its stand like Gorgeous George used to lift his opponents into the air. Gasping, he crouched and hoisted the set higher in his arms and moved past her into the kitchen.

"What are you doing?" she screamed, following him and sounding again like Nora Peña, the terror of Carmelas, who, with her sister Ramona, could take any vato in Carmelas.

"Watch me, Nora."

She didn't really know what he was going to do until he moved through the open back door onto the porch. "No!" she screamed, and somewhere in the back of the house she heard her baby Lalo cry, but she raced after Zapi anyway, and in the door she saw him heave and the TV left his arms and hung in midair for what seemed an impossible time before it fell and collided with the earth, the screen, all twenty-four inches, shattering like a broken glass. He straightened and when he was upright, she leapt. Her legs went around his waist, her hands tearing at his hair. He tried to spin to free himself, but only fell from the porch, dragging her with him into the dirt, where they rolled—a pair of wrestlers.

She sounded like a stricken animal baying under the moon, as she flailed him with her fists, digging at his face, his eyes. Suddenly she was flipped and on her back, Zapi over her, his hands grabbing her wrists and holding them down in the dirt, straddling her and pinning her to the earth.

"Mi amor," he said softly, "mi amor," over and over until she stopped struggling. Finally, he climbed off her and walked around the side of the house, away in the darkness, leaving her in the dirt.

After he was gone, she rose, standing stiffly and dusting off her shirt dress. She saw one high heel on the far side of the yard. The other was who knew where. She retreated to the porch where she sat through the hours before morning, running all of it by, trying to figure it out, until she saw the night becoming morning. She lowered her eyes to the ruins of the TV, want rushing over her, hunger and desire. She looked at her hands, clasped in her lap, the dust from where she'd rolled with her husband in the dirt still clinging to her dress, her skin.

She lifted her hand to her neck to touch the pearls that were no longer there—torn off in the battle in the yard. For a moment, she wanted to go out into the yard to look for them in the dust. She stopped herself.

Chapter 9

La Región de las Ilusiones ~ 1960

Rafael Trujillo was down on one knee at the end of a Thursday school day, his voluminous handkerchief spilling from his hand, its ends catching on the wind as he wiped Lupe Gallardo's running nose. They were in the open breezeway that ran outside the classrooms at Ramona School.

"Mejor, mija?" he asked of the eight-year-old, after coaxing her to blow loudly into the starched linen, startlingly white in contrast to the red-brown tones of his long fingers held against the darker browns of Lupe's turned-up nose.

She nodded, pulling back from the handkerchief and running her forearm across the just-blown nose.

Rafael laughed and tousled her blue-black hair, tendrils flying everywhere, fallen loose from the pigtails in back, only one still held with a blue ribbon. "Be well, Lupita," he said, rising from the ground. "Tienes tarea?"

"Mucho homework, Señor Trujillo," she moaned. "Multiplicación—dos por dos son cuatro."

"Bravo," he said clapping. "Estudias bien, mija. Hasta mañana."

Lupe turned and skipped down the breezeway, a thin math booklet hanging from one hand. Farther down the breezeway, Rafael saw Les Hutchins lounging in the open door of his sixth-grade classroom, watching. His face, all twenty-four years of it, was full of censure.

"Ralph, how in the hell are any of them going to learn decent English if you speak to them in Spanish all the time?"

Rafael smiled. "From gringos like you, my friend."

"I'm not kidding, Ralph. That's why we have the rule about no Spanish. If you were in my class, I'd have fined you a nickel."

Rafael pulled a nickel from his pocket and walked up to the young teacher, his green eyes red-rimmed and heavy and so grave behind his glasses. Rafael held his hand out, palm up, the nickel naked in the center of his smooth hand.

"Funny," Les said.

"I didn't make the rule," Rafael said. "I break it often—so I'll pay my fine." He turned his hand over, the nickel falling, caught by Les as it fell. Rafael smiled again. "Well worth a nickel to make a little girl whose head is full of cotton feel better. Best nickel I've spent in a day or so." He laughed, but he noticed the clouds didn't lift from Les's eyes, and Rafael liked this new teacher fresh out of L.A. State and his enthusiasm that came with being new. "What's eating you . . . besides the fact that Eisenhower's man is out and a Democrat—a Catholic to boot—is back in the White House?"

"Don't remind me," Les said sourly. Then he sneezed. "A cold—that's what's eating me. That was Lupe Gallardo you were with. I've got her brother, Rudy. His nose is worse than hers. But, shit, if it wasn't Rudy, it'd be another one." He sneezed again, more loudly. "Never had so many damned colds. What's with all you Mexicans and colds?"

Rafael slapped his shoulder. "What's the fine for swearing, Les?"

"Kids are gone for the day. So report me."

"Now why would I do that?" Rafael asked and turned away. He moved back towards his own now-empty classroom. As an afterthought, he looked back and called, "But we do have to do something about that cold of yours. I'll bring you some menudo tomorrow—nothing like menudo for a cold."

"I thought it was for hangovers."

"Whatever ails you, Mr. Hutchins. Magic stuff, that menudo." Rafael stepped back into the coolness of his classroom and looked at the papers he would grade for another hour before going home, chuckling as he sat down at his cluttered desk, enjoying the stillness now as much as he'd enjoyed the bustle of the children all day long.

He was no longer chuckling, however, the next afternoon when he found himself in his principal's office in response to a summons delivered by Mary, the school secretary, at the end of the school day.

Mr. Harden, Jules to the staff but never to Rafael, who liked the formality of last names—and the distance—fell silent behind his desk, after he'd spoken his piece. He was a man of few words, and Rafael liked that about him, almost as much as he liked his hands-off approach to running the school. He left the teaching to the teachers—usually. He'd always treated Rafael with the respect due him as senior teacher, his tenure running back to before the new school was built, when Ramona, at the edge of Carmelas, had been one room fronted by the two tall mulberry trees and he the only teacher.

"And who, may I ask, complained about my use of Spanish?"

"Now, Ralph—you know that's not important. The only thing that's important is what's good for the children. I thought we'd all agreed. The children must learn English."

"I agree. They must learn English."

Mr. Harden smiled, looking relieved, as if the feared confrontation wasn't going to happen after all. He started to rise saying, "Then this matter is settled—"

"No, Mr. Harden," Rafael said, refusing to rise, causing the principal to stop in mid-ascent. "I teach in English all day long. But the Mexican children—I live with them, you know, right next door—and they know me in Spanish before they ever come to school. Sometimes, Mr. Harden," he said, his voice rising, "they need me in Spanish."

Mr. Harden sat back down with a sigh. "I trust your experience, Ralph—"

"Then trust my use of it, Mr. Harden." Rafael rose, feeling suddenly very powerful. "I am on your team, Mr. Harden—but my first responsibility is to all the children, their needs—"

"It is a difficult world out there, Ralph—"

"Indeed," Rafael agreed.

"These Spanish-speaking children are outside it—"

"They must be brought in—"

"Exactly," Mr. Harden said.

"And my Spanish—my use of it with them—is proof that crossing over need not mean erasing everything—"

Mr. Harden grimaced and said, "Now you're going political on me, Ralph."

Rafael laughed, realizing he might finally be facing the battle he'd been expecting for years. "But everything is politics, Mr. Harden. That's the American Way."

"Learning English is the American Way."

"Claro que sí!" Rafael said emphatically, feeling suddenly up to fighting, if this were to be the day.

Ignoring the Spanish, Mr. Harden, a bit redder than at the beginning of their meeting said, "I wouldn't have said anything, Ralph."

"But?"

"The person complaining said he was going to go to the school board if I didn't speak to you."

"I would love an invitation from the school board," Rafael said.

"We don't want them poking around here."

"I do not fear a confrontation, Mr. Harden."

He smiled. "That's why I'm principal. I do." He cleared his throat. "Then we understand each other?"

Rafael lifted his eyebrows in question.

"No Spanish in the classroom," Mr. Harden said, looking very uncomfortable.

But Rafael cared nothing for Harden's discomfort and was about to say more when something in Harden's face collapsed, and the white flag went up with his concession. "Except for soothing over some unavoidable rough spots."

Rafael hesitated, even when he saw the pleading in his principal's eyes. He was not certain he was ready to end it.

"Or in certain social situations—outside the classrooms," Mr. Harden added, "when it can ease their crossing over." The principal smiled sheepishly.

Rafael finally nodded, but could not help adding defiantly, "Which is all I've ever done."

"Agreed," Mr. Harden said. "We've merely formalized our arrangement."

Rafael rose and wordlessly extended his hand.

Outside the office, he did not feel so victorious. He moved through the breezeway, his nose catching the familiar traces of blood and butchered beef carried on the air. He sucked in the scent, the stamp of home, a blind unintentional gift of the meat packing plant that went with this corner of Norwalk and employed half the men in Carmelas. To him it had become over his years in Carmelas the marker that defined his life, his purpose, his place, a constant reminder that from blood and offal he had risen, proof in flesh that others could, too.

Moments later, back inside his classroom, he felt the nag of paranoia as he ran faculty names through his head, wondering who would have betrayed him. He could recall no incident with any of them—except for the encounter with Les Hutchins the day before. Les Hutchins. Surely not Les. First-year teacher. A threat from him to Mr. Harden would have been meaningless. No. It could not have been Les. It had to have been one of the others, teachers with whom he'd worked for years. The thought made his heart heavy. He looked at the stacked papers lying on his desk in wait of his attention. He had no heart for that this afternoon. Instead, he grabbed his leather briefcase, and the minute his hand gripped the handle of the bulky leather box, a Fuller Brush man's sample case, old already when it had been presented him, he smiled. He could do nothing about whoever had reported him, so he pushed his doubts away, for he was not one to let anger linger long. His hand grasped the handle of the case without lifting it. He remembered the first day he'd carried it to school.

One teacher—gone now—had said, "What drunk salesman did you steal that from?" And Rafael remembered how those few words from a gringo he'd admired could make him feel ashamed of the case and cause him to say, "A gift from friends," as if that would excuse it.

The man had laughed and said, "With friends like that, Ralph, you don't need enemies."

The insult—even dressed in laughter and cliché—had wiped away Rafael's embarrassment and clarified who he was and where he stood. So, he had corrected himself and said, "My finest friends," meaning every word.

After that day, he'd carried the briefcase always—conspicuously—even though more than a few had laughed at a fifth-grade teacher's need for such a case. Even now, through his clenched fingers, he could feel the power of the briefcase rise up through his hand into his arm and into his body, strengthening his heart. He was alone in his empty classroom, but the briefcase in his hand carried him back to the night it had been given, when he'd first realized that none of them in Carmelas was alone and had first seen in the realization that which empowered and hobbled all of them.

The night of the gift had been a hot June night, the last graduation ceremony the old Ramona schoolhouse would know, for in September, the new school already taking shape would open. Rafael had postponed the usual late afternoon ceremony until after dark, for the week had been so hot, and he had known the coolness of dark would be appreciated by his neighbors and his children as they gathered in their graduation finery in the rows of folding chairs, some benches made with two-by-fours laid across chairs, all placed by the lower grades, from first through fifth, the graduating sixth graders having no obligations this day but signing autograph books while picnicking and playing in the lunch area and waiting for the night. There had been ten sixth graders that June, all graduating—two with honors—and all due to go to Carmenita School in the fall for seventh and eighth grades. But this graduation carried so much more meaning, too, for it marked an ending—the closing of the only school most of them in Carmelas had ever known. One little room, in which most of them had spent some time . . . to be replaced in September with the opening of the new Ramona School.

So, that night the school yard beneath the towering mulberry trees was especially festive, streamers hanging from the old trees' branches, oil lanterns placed strategically to brighten the area, aided by the moon. By the time the ceremony was due to begin, the chairs were full, people standing in the back—old, young, all ages in between—to honor the ten who'd arrived at this jumping-off spot and to honor also the old school that was closing down. For after this night, the graduating ten—and all of them in Carmelas really—would be pushed into a world wider than Carmelas.

Dressed as always for graduation night in his signature black suit, white shirt, and black tie, Rafael Trujillo looked over at his wife, Martha, heavy and warm in her new turquoise dress, sitting next to where he stood on the raised platform they'd made into a stage. Then, Rafael began to call out the names of his neighbors' graduating children, and this year he called out his own boy's name, Cruz—at the bottom of the class, but there. As each one came forward, Rafael said a few personal remarks to note the child's specialness.

"Armando Pimental, a reader if there ever was one! One hundred books en los dos años pasados, all checked out from the Norwalk Library, all of them read! Un hijo que un family can be proud of, a young man who will give honor to nuestro barrio, una voz that will be heard beyond Carmelas."

Specialness was remarked on for even the slowest of them—his own blood this year, Cruz Trujillo—"who one day will prove la veracidad en el dicho that waters still run deep."

The audience applauded wildly, as if Armando were their own, Cruz, too—all of these children. As Rafael thanked his guests—neighbors all from a barrio of four unpaved streets they called Carmelas—for coming and invited them to his own yard across the road for a fiesta and his wife's carne asada to finish off the night, Chata Lopez stood in the audience.

"Una palabra, maestro," she said.

"Only one word?" Rafael asked and the throng broke into loud laughter, for Chata was the chismeada of the barrio and her Mexican store the springboard for barrio news. She was never at a loss for words or friendly gossip.

As she moved her pink-satined voluptuous hips up through the crowd, carrying a bulky package it took both her arms to hold, the crowd grew still with expectation. She came up the central aisle and stepped up onto the makeshift stage next to Rafael.

"Para usted, Señor Trujillo, un regalo—too little—to say gracias for todas de sus efforts para our niños," Chata said, before passing him the brown grocery-bag-wrapped gift. "Un hombre de importancia in our barrio necesita un badge de su posición. Muchisimas gracias, profesor, from all of us."

The people gathered under the two tall mulberry trees broke into wild applause. Rafael tore off the brown wrapper and found the salesman's used sample case.

"Es real leather," Chata said, as if to excuse its scuff-marked edges.

"Claro," Rafael said, holding it up for the gathering to see, wondering only for a moment where Chata had found it. "Magnifico," he shouted. A small lie.

"Almost new," Chata whispered, her rouged cheeks too pink for her brown skin.

And for Rafael at that moment with Chata's whisper clearly an attempt to make the used case something finer, the lie became true. The salesman's used case became what it was intended to be, a beautiful, rich thank you, and for the first time he saw how they were one people—that all the children of Carmelas were theirs regardless of whose bodies had brought them into the world. Suddenly, he could say no more, for all the words he wanted to speak stuck in his throat as he was overcome with the power in the crowd, their strength he'd never completely seen before. He nodded, blinking his black eyes, the moisture there catching the lantern light and the moon. He pulled the case to his thin chest. He sucked in air, and his nose filled with sky touched by the scent of blood and flesh; he was surrounded by people who were his own, most of whom had never gone to sixth grade in school, yet knew—*knew*—that a teacher, a real teacher, carried a leather bag to hold his books, his papers, his life, and that such a teacher walking through the world carried them with him, for he held their children in his hands.

Lola de los Rios y Valles—still wearing beauty that had once gotten her into movies, whose voice was famous, too, in Carmelas for being even prettier than her face, her skin—rose in the center of the crowd and spontaneously began to sing "La Golondrina," a song that always cut the hearts of Mexicans separated from a home most of them could not remember, and her voice, layered in sadness that had never lifted, he'd been told, since her husband had been lost in the world war, made the pain of longing central to the song naked in the school yard. "De donde irás," she sang, her voice a piercing vibrato that rolled across the night, beginning the words sung to someone moving on—who knew not where—but only on. "En la región perdida," she crooned, the notes building to crescendo, a song of the movement from a region lost toward somewhere else. "La Golondrina," she sang, her voice a cry that spoke of doves, white and pure, rising on the wind, taking flight. The crowd began to join her, their voices blending into one. But Rafael Trujillo could sing nothing at all, was able only to hang on to the used leather gift that would hold his books until it fell apart.

That June night was years gone.

A memory to be called back whenever Rafael felt as alone as he did now, standing in his classroom feeling surrounded by gringos—teachers, principal—to whom there was no real connection. He blinked his eyes, fighting back tears triggered by the memory of the gift and of the offense this afternoon that had made him see again how wide the gulf remained between them. He tightened his hold on the handle of his leather case, more battered now, more scarred, and more beautiful than ever—which tied him to Carmelas, the very place he'd spent years trying to push his children to see beyond. His certainties all suddenly seemed up for grabs. Into what was he really pushing them?

He looked around the classroom, new desks gleaming, blackboards shining, wiped clean, walls covered artfully to attract young eyes, young minds, and he saw not this new classroom, but the wooden room of the old Carmelas schoolhouse where construction paper—any paper—had been like gold and he had taught for fourteen years—cast-off desks, clouded windows that hadn't ever opened—and he felt a longing he couldn't name.

He'd won with Mr. Harden this afternoon. They both knew Rafael would go on doing as he pleased—no, as he thought best, and that was an important difference Mr. Harden had probably missed. But the victory somehow seemed hollow. He tightened his grip on his case and picked it up. Ignoring the papers to grade, he strode from the room, locking the door.

After locking up his room, he moved down the breezeway, but stopped at Les Hutchins's open door. He looked at the other classrooms, locked at ten minutes after three. At least Mr. Hutchins stuck around. Always.

A thunderous sneeze rang out inside. Rafael stuck his head in and saw Les Hutchins at his desk, bent over a book, his head almost touching Rudy Gallardo's, the boy round and sturdy as a young bull, and the sight of the heads close together—one yellow-haired, the other black as night—made Rafael tremble as if someone had shown him his dreams made flesh. "Salud, Señor Hutchins," Rafael said.

Les Hutchins looked up, Rudy, too. Les didn't smile. Rudy did—despite his runny nose.

"Staying late today," Rafael said.

"Every day," Les Hutchins groaned, wiping his red, swollen nose with the back of his hand. Rudy sniffled, sucking up a nose full of congestion with a hawking sound.

Rafael saw Hutchins grimace as he said, "Rudy, how many times do I have to tell you, blow your nose."

Rafael pulled out a crisp linen handkerchief and walked to the pair. "Aqui," he said, offering the handkerchief to Rudy. "Todo el tiempo, un caballero usa un pañuelo."

Rudy took it. "Graciás," he said and blew his nose in the white cloth.

"What'd you say?" Mr. Hutchins asked of the exchange.

"I told him gentlemen use handkerchiefs, Mr. Hutchins. Always."

Reddening at what must have been the realization of his own oversight, Mr. Hutchins said, "We'll remember. Won't we, Rudy?"

Rudy snorted. Smiling, he said, "Señor Hutchins esta ensenandome."

"And he's not going anywhere until he gets it," Mr. Hutchins said.

"Ah," Rafael said in surprise at Mr. Hutchins's understanding. "Tu hablas some espanol after all, Señor Hutchins."

"We'll all be speaking Spanish one day is my guess," Les Hutchins said. "I might as well get a head start."

Rafael felt new, felt almost as he had the night Carmelas had given him the case, felt as he always did when his eyes seemed to clear and he could glimpse a truth not seen before. The joy rushed up his throat and made him laugh, deep and loud. He went to the door. "Vayan con Dios, mis amigos."

"We'd all better walk a little more closely with God, Mr. Trujillo, what with your Kennedy in the White House," Mr. Hutchins said, breathing loudly through his mouth. "Now get out of here, señor, so Rudy can figure out what's going on with his long division."

"A smart boy like Rudy will get it in no time," Rafael said.

"Let's hope so," Hutchins said and took Rudy's neck in his hand, shaking it playfully. Rudy laughed, and Rafael walked out of the room, the sound of a brown boy's laughter following.

Rafael walked on down the breezeway. At the last classroom, he stopped and suddenly reached out and touched the bricks, the coarseness there pricking. He turned his head and looked down the breezeway to where it opened onto the playing field; in the distance he could see the two old mulberry trees, silent sentinels, marking where the old schoolhouse—a single room—had stood.

A wave of nostalgia rushed over him like wind, the longing to turn back clocks. He ran his palm over the rough surface of the bricks as he glanced backward to where his old school had stood. Maybe it was the scraping of his flesh on the brick wall battling with the longing in his heart that set Rafael back on course and made him know the longing was wrong. He turned back his head, scanning the classrooms on the breezeway until he focused on his own hand caressing the brick wall of the new Ramona School. This was better.

The new school, its classrooms—gringos all around him. This was better. His students, brown and white together. Carmelas children with gringo teachers except for him and Miss Urrea, whom he'd insisted so powerfully on hiring that the others had acquiesced. The two of them with their brown faces and Spanish words softened his children's movement out.

This was better, for this was the world—full of gringos, the only world they'd ever have unless Mexico marched back across the border to reclaim the land. He laughed aloud at the very outlandishness of the idea. His laughter died. How would the gringos ever know who Rafael and all his children were if they—he—hung back in brown pockets like Carmelas that held a beauty only they could see—a safety only they could feel—but which would defeat them in the end?

Rafael left the breezeway, cutting across the grass at the front of the school. He walked up Dinard to Mapledale, pavement and tract houses to his left, dirt roads and Carmelas to his right. He turned right towards home, his shiny black loafers raising dust in the hot May afternoon, dimming the luster of their shine. He could see his own house in the distance down Mapledale, little different from the others on the outside, better tended maybe, a newer paint job, but that was all. He sniffed the air, the scent of blood gone, the earthier smell of manure carried on the light wind from Norwalk Dairy across Rosecrans heavy in its place. Carmelas streets were empty, but as he passed Claresa, he saw Señora Rosaura down the block hanging whites in her front yard, the wind too light to raise much dust this time of day. Watching the old woman at her clothesline, he felt all his agitation drain away, a sense of peace descending. Though he knew it all illusion—something doomed—he saw all of Carmelas—her earthen streets, her houses scattered along them haphazardly as if by God, and her Señora Rosaura waving at him from amid her sheets—as buffer, a borderland that might—like family—nurture children until they could walk away.

Chapter 10

Penney's from Heaven - 1961

Bobby Valdez drank. He played cards. He bet the horses.

But Bobby worked.

It was just that the work never quite covered all the bases.

Like home base.

Which was where Nadia was sitting now—December 16—on her front porch at three o'clock in the morning. The night was chill, and she could have gone inside where it was warmer—but she wanted the cold, for it kept her fury alive.

"Como una bomba—Nadia."

She was alone on the porch. And the words were only echoes of Bobby's words. She was like a bomb. But like a bomb, she'd go off, and then the anger would be gone. Tonight she wanted the fury to last.

She looked out across the grassless yard to where Camenita Road's pavement began. The street was middle-of-the-night empty. Across the wide road, fields disappeared into darkness.

Forty years old. She was. Bobby two years older. Her fingers gripped the loose flesh of her upper arms that mirrored the spreading, the softening of her body.

"My fingers almost touch around your waist."

Bobby had said that. Years ago.

What waist could endure four children? Healthy children. A small price.

She looked up the dark street toward where Rosecrans crossed Carmenita Road, the corner Bobby would have to round. "Goddamn you, Bobby," she said softly.

Not that he did this every payday.

It might have been better if he had. Then she'd know what to do with him. Bobby's way was worse. He gave them time in between bouts to believe again. To hope.

It had been a month and a half this time. So long, that this morning when she'd followed him out to the car, ducking in and kissing him fast even though they were in the street, and had said, "Remember, Bobby. Tonight you take me shopping for Christmas. Only eight days and this is the last payday," she'd never even doubted.

And here she was. On the front porch at three o'clock in the morning in the same dress she'd slipped into at five o'clock, Bobby's favorite—a green that matched her eyes.

"Like no other eyes in Carmelas."

That's what Bobby had said the first time they'd danced. Well, the color was the same.

She pushed herself up from the wooden steps. She placed her arm around the porch support and rested her face against the peeling paint.

"He's not coming, Ma. You know it."

That was what Junior—just sixteen—had said from where he'd been sitting on the sofa at six o'clock. She'd begun to feel the same thing from where she sat in the big green overstuffed chair, but she'd told him anyway, "It's early yet."

Manny, six and trying hard not to squirm, sat next to Junior. "He's too coming."

"It's only six," Judy, fourteen, protested from her end of the sofa, sounding doubtful.

All of them fools. Even Daisy, twelve, gone to Rosie's for the night—but not before she'd left her list of Christmas wishes, as if wishes put into writing had more chance of coming true.

Nadia, hours later now, looked up into the night sky. From this side of Carmelas, the stars had no competition at all. She looked for the brightest star and found no single star that stood out. Where was the Christmas star?

"It comes, mija. Cada año at Christmas, La estrella de Cristo comes."

Her auntie's words. Old memories. "I'm forty," Nadia said aloud, counting backwards in her head. Twenty-five years since they'd buried the tiny woman in Calvary Cemetery in Boyle Heights. And if she hadn't died—there'd have been no Bobby.

"You can't live here alone," her tía's son Jorge had told her after the funeral. "Quince años tienes."

"Fifteen's old enough," she'd argued. But he'd brought her here to Carmelas anyway, where he'd ended up after meeting Magdalena Fuentes, one of a Carmelas band of indios famous for their gypsy ways and black-eyed daughters, who tía swore had cast a spell pulling her only boy from civilization in Lincoln Heights to Carmelas, a barrio with dirt streets. For Nadia, it *had* been like going to another world when he'd forced her to move in with him and Magdalena.

"La estrella de Cristo," Nadia said, shaking her head this lifetime later. A dreamer—tía—just like Nadia—a fool. She thought of this past September, when, moving through Penney's, she had felt drunk with the riches around her, clothes in a hundred textures, colors. School clothes, plenty enough to make her ache. Instead of mannequins, pale and thin, perched around the store, she saw her own brown children, draped in the clothes that would make them the princes she knew they were. It had been the rustling of her Penney's bag that reminded her none of it could be hers beyond the pair of jeans she'd managed for Junior, the two flannel shirts—sale flannel—and a single dress for each of the girls in sensible colors that could go with anything. Suddenly, she felt almost too tired to go on. She leaned back against a shelf and looked up as if to heaven, and in the air, suspended from the ceiling hung a giant blue card—"JCPenney" stenciled in brown letters. "Open Your JCPenney Charge Today!" another sign suspended below the first commanded.

And so she'd gone. She. Like a soldier, she'd marched to credit. "I'd like a credit card," she said, sounding like a general. A woman passed her papers. She filled them out despite the flooding doubt. "When will I know?" she'd asked, passing the papers back to the woman behind the glass.

Three weeks later, the answer came. No.

Standing on her porch now—Christmas just around the corner—waiting for Bobby and staring at the sky in search of tía's Christmas star, Nadia saw the fool she was—and that's when she found the brightest star, which now seemed to outshine all the other stars in heaven. Tía would have sworn it was Christ's star. Tired of being such a fool, Nadia knew if she had a gun, she'd have shot that star from heaven.

Her stomach spasmed. Letting the porch pole go, she ran a hand across her belly. As it had for fifteen years, her stomach danced through December, becoming a wild Mexican polka by Christmas Eve.

"When have we had an empty tree?"

Bobby again. And he was right—but there had never been a Christmas when that fear wasn't the biggest thing in the house.

"How many times have I had to borrow from my goddamn cousin Jorge?"

"And he always gets paid back," Bobby said before walking out of the kitchen, fighting as always in retreat.

She hated Christmas.

"Why can't you just shut up about it, Nadia. You want everybody in the house to hate it, too? Things work out."

This from a man who could blow a whole goddamned paycheck at the races. She felt her face settle into a comfortable frown.

"You think your pinche cara will break if it ever smiles?"

Bobby again. Where had her smiles gone?

The bastard stole her smiles. She glanced at her wristwatch. The bars shut down at two. Her heart sank, knowing it meant Bobby was playing cards. Poker. He always lost, but the chingado never even knew how bad until the sun came up and the cash was gone.

"Don't talk like that. You want to sound like a puta? I don't like you talking like a pig."

"*Bastardo!*" she screamed. They'd been standing in the kitchen that day and her voice could carry.

"Callate!"

She walked to the back door and leaned far out before screaming for all the neighbors to hear. "*You goddamn shit bastard!*" She roared curses—all in English, for they didn't sound so ugly as in Spanish—knowing she was making no sense but loving the fact that friends on both sides and in back would hear.

And now—tonight, alone in the dark of Carmelas, the neighbors all asleep, she gave a final look at the stars, wishing it were summer. Not September summer—that was as bad as December for Nadia. School. Clothes. Christmas with another name. She wanted June. Her niños home. No worries at all but the manageable kind. In June, her stomach disappeared—not the stomach, for each year since Manny its roundness grew—but the pains, they disappeared. Surely in June, she even smiled.

"Úlceras," Rosie over on Pontlavoy had diagnosed just the week before.

"No," Nadia said, in Rosie's kitchen, sipping coffee. "Christmas."

"You doing tamales this year?" Rosie asked, sitting on the other side of her pretty new formica table.

"Not 'til my Christmas is done. Bobby can sing for tamales if he don't take me shopping soon."

"Why not join la Christmas Club?"

Nadia, standing on her sloping porch in the dark, almost laughed at the memory. She had done the Christmas Club.

"Just think it's a loan."

Bobby's words. It had been June. A Saturday night. She and Bobby had danced all night. Lupita's wedding from over on Claresa. Nadia had had too many beers, but how many weddings came with mariachis, live music, and dancing. At home after the reception had finally ended, he'd pulled her into bed before she'd slipped her cotton nightgown over her head. She had been laughing, trying to cover her breasts as his hands teased her flesh. She felt the sheets cool beneath her back as he flattened her on the bed. She sucked in the air, her breathing fast, and she was filled with the smell of summer clinging to sheets she'd hung just this afternoon in summer sun. His hands, his tongue played upon her flesh and she felt herself melting into the sheets beneath her. She felt his body ease over onto hers, the weight familiar, welcome. She felt his knee ease her thighs apart and wondered how a knee pressed between her own could seem a kiss.

And when it was done, and his lips moved up her neck to her ear where he whispered, "Te quiero," in a rhythm matching breath, she lifted eyes up toward her window to the moon beyond the glass and thanked God for taking auntie and bringing Bobby in her place.

"Come to the races with me tomorrow," he'd said when his breathing had cooled. In the circle of his arms, she heard him say, "Don't worry, I got money set aside. All the bills will get paid."

He'd promised. "There's this horse, Nadia. It's named Green Eyes." He rose over her and looked down into her eyes. "Fate. No? Like your eyes. Like God was whispering in my ear, 'She'll win, she'll win.' You know what ten dollars could get us?"

Nothing.

"You said two races. Green Eyes already lost," she'd said, the day in ashes around them at Hollywood Park.

"Goddamn it, Nadia, don't jinx me." They stayed all nine races. He hadn't had enough left to buy either of them a hot dog on the way out.

"I won't touch it," she'd screamed later in the week.

"I'll pay it back. Friday."

"*Noooo,*" she screamed. "That money's for Christmas, so we can finally have a Christmas without any worries—"

"You want the lights shut off? You want the kids to eat?"

She'd given him the money. She'd emptied out the Christmas Club. He hadn't paid it back.

But he worked.

And he drank. And he gambled.

But not all the time.

But enough for things always to be short. And she knew it would be this way forever. Pain shot through her stomach. How would she bear twenty more Christmases like this? And with Manny only six, that meant twelve more miserable Septembers before he was even out of school. Her worries would surely eat through her stomach and push her into the earth before then. If God were good. She crossed herself. Her children. Where would they be if she were gone? Her kids'd have only Bobby and his crazy familia Valdez if she were to be blessed and die. So, she took it back.

She heard the door open behind her. "Mama?" Turning, she saw Manny, her littlest. Brown as a nut. Round as a barrel. Manny. Sweet as a block of leche quemada. "Que te pasas, sweetie?"

"What're you doing?"

"Waiting."

"For Santa?" Manny asked, excitement filling his voice.

She shook her head.

"Papa? You waiting for Papa?"

She nodded.

"Will he get here before Santa?"

She went to the door, opened it, and lifted Manny, wearing only baggy underwear. "Where are your pajamas?"

"Papa and Junior don't sleep in pajamas."

She carried him to his bed, setting him down, pulling the cover up to his chin. She kissed his cheek, loving as always the smell of this baby she hadn't really even wanted when he'd come.

"I hope you're happy, you big macho," she'd thrown at Bobby when she was sure another baby was coming. "How many times have I begged you to do to yourself what Tonio over on Pontlavoy did."

"Tonio's crazy, letting someone take a knife to his huevos."

"He's the same as ever. Better, Martha says."

"What are you crying for? I love babies. We'll manage."

"We hardly manage now."

"A little late to cry over it now."

And Nadia heard herself echo Bobby's words, "It's late, baby," as she buried her nose in the velvet folds of Manny's neck and wondered what the house would be without him. "Tomorrow we'll make candy—leche quemada," she promised, pulling away.

At the door, Manny asked, "You hate Christmas, like Junior says?"

"Not my favorite time of year," she said. She ran her eyes over the other kids and left.

In her bedroom, she had just slipped her nightgown over her head when she heard the front door open and then close. She waited for footsteps in the hall. They didn't come, so she walked down the hall and found Bobby in the overstuffed chair. One foot shoed, the other naked where he'd pulled off shoe and sock.

He was sprawled, head back, mouth ajar. His teeth, straight—brilliantly white—were beautiful.

She wanted to hit him. Then, she realized that his getting home before dawn meant he hadn't been playing poker after all. She rummaged and pulled out his wallet. Breathless, she opened it and found one goddamned twenty-dollar bill. She threw the wallet at him. This was the last payday before Christmas. She stepped on his naked foot—hard. He didn't move. "I don't care if we eat only beans for the rest of the week, this," she shouted, waving the twenty-dollar bill before his sleeping face, "is Christmas!" Then, she marched off to bed.

As she drifted to sleep, she divvied up the twenty dollars. They had to have a tree. Manny would be easy. The Woolworth's made him happy. Junior, Judy, and Daisy would be harder. But she'd manage. Her stomach tightened, the pain causing her to roll on her side. She'd manage.

The next morning Bobby was gone by the time she woke at eight o'clock.

In the bathroom she washed her face, then brushed her teeth and hair. In the mirror, she saw the puffiness in her face, the pull of time.

Bobby worked. He didn't beat her. Ever. Never raised a hand. No matter how she yelled.

He didn't talk.

"What men do?" That's what Rosie Perez—the last of the Fuentes girls, and Nadia's first friend after moving in with cousin Jorge and his wife, Rosie's sister Magdalena—said when she complained and reminded, "He touches you still."

Like he means it. His hands were the gentlest things about him. She fell in love with his hands. She'd been in Carmelas a month. There had been a wedding under the huge mulberry trees by the old school. Lights had been strung. Mariachis played.

Bobby had passed the table where Nadia was pouring the punch. As she'd filled his glass, he said, "I've never seen eyes like yours. Not in Carmelas." And they had danced, and the feel of his hands on her waist, the way he guided her about the hard-packed earthen dance floor had been so gentle that she had felt carried.

Twenty dollars, she reminded her image in the mirror, trying to pull back the anger of last night. He'd gone to work. Hung over. She hoped his head felt filled with knives.

Rosie stopped by just after noon telling Nadia her Daisy had gone with Rosie's Licha to help Señora Rosaura with her tamales. "We got our tree," she said, sitting at Nadia's kitchen table. "It makes me cry to sit and watch the lights in the dark."

"Why?" Nadia asked, pouring coffee for her friend.

"They remind me of how beautiful things can be."

Nadia said nothing, pulling a pan from the cupboard, and then, from the tiny Kelvinator, she took the can of sweet milk she'd hidden at the back.

"What you making?" Rosie asked, lighting up a cigarette.

"Leche quemada. Mi Manny loves it. Manny!"

"Takes forever," Rosie said. "Too sweet."

"Not for me," Manny said, barging into the kitchen.

Nadia adjusted the fire under the canned milk. "Watch the fire doesn't go out, Manny. When it starts to thicken, call me." She grabbed her mug and she and Rosie went out onto the front porch. "So I guess you're all ready for Christmas?"

"Tamales still to do. Get your tree at Harvester's. We got a real pretty one. Four dollars."

"I want a small one."

"'Cause you hate Christmas."

Nadia nodded. "And because I'm broke. As usual."

Manny stepped onto the porch. "Mama. My arm's tired."

"Be un hombre," she answered. "Keep stirring."

"You believe in Santa, Rosie?" Manny asked.

"I've seen him," Rosie said.

Nadia slapped her friend's thigh.

"Was he like the pictures?" Manny said. "Did he have a white beard?"

"He had a beard but his eyes were black and his skin, Manuelito, was as brown as yours and mine, un verdadero indio mi Santa was!" Manny spun, laughing, and ran back into the house. "Here comes the mailman," Rosie said.

Nadia looked up and saw the skinny little gringo dressed in blue with a hat that looked like a jungle hat. "Think he's afraid of getting sunstroke in December?"

"Gringos," Rosie said. "Who can figure?"

"You think gringos ever worry about Christmas?"

"That or something else. It's life, Nadia, worry." Rosie put out her cigarette. "Bobby taking you shopping today?"

"I waited last night. I'm going to walk to Norwalk Square this afternoon. Not like I'll have much to carry back." She sighed. "You got big dreams, Rosie?"

"Little dreams. Like my new Formica table. They're safer."

"I look ahead and see nothing different."

"Maybe there'll be some surprises, girl."

"I want to dance," Nadia said fiercely.

"Turn on the radio. I'll dance with you," Rosie said.

"It's gettin' thick, Ma!" Manny hollered from inside the house.

"Keep stirring," Nadia shouted back, as the mailman came across the dirt yard.

"Morning, ladies. Merry Christmas."

"Same to you, Mr. Baker," Nadia said as she took the letters he passed to her.

"What's that you got from Penney's?" Rosie asked.

Nadia passed over the electric bill and held up the Penney's envelope. "Probably another rejection—didn't I tell you how I applied a couple of months back? Bobby said they'd turn me down. They did. Nice of them to tell me twice." She tore it open and pulled out a three-fold sheet of paper. She opened it, and tucked inside was a JCPenney credit card.

"Nadia, that's a credit card," Rosie said in wonder.

"It's a mistake—I told you they wrote me a letter a couple of—"

"Nadia, believe me, that's a credit card. I know. My sister Plata has one."

Nadia took the card, passing the letter to Rosie, who lifted it and read.

"This isn't no mistake . . . it says you got a two-hundred-dollar limit. See," Rosie said, pointing at the page.

Nadia read the words. Suddenly, she jumped up, grabbing Rosie's hand, and they ran through the yard to Señora Del Valle's, scattering chickens as they went next door to the wooden shack that listed to the right. "Señora, señora," Nadia called at the door.

The door opened and Señora Del Valle, bent and aproned, broke into a smile, wide and toothless. "Como están, chicas. Entran. En que puedo servirles?"

"Bien, bien," Nadia said, pulling Rosie inside. "Your phone, señora? I need your phone." Nadia moved through the tiny room to a second room in back where she knew the phone was by the old lady's single bed. She sat and scanned the Penney's letter for a number. Finding it, she dialed, thanking God he'd given the old woman who had nothing else in the world a son who never visited but had installed a telephone so he could talk to his mamita once a week.

When a soft female voice answered, Nadia said in a rush, "I need to speak—" and she realized she didn't know who to ask for or what to say.

"This is credit. How can I help you?"

"I've got a credit card," she said awkwardly, "and . . . I was thinking of using it . . . and I wanted to know . . . if I can."

"You want your outstanding balance?" the woman asked. "I'll need your name."

"Nadia Valdez," she said in a rush, lengthening the first syllable like the gringos did.

After a moment the woman's voice returned. "Your account has a zero balance, Mrs. Valdez."

"Oh," Nadia said, instantly angry at her rush to believe. "So, it's no good."

"No good? It's never been used," the woman said.

"I can use it?"

"Like money, Mrs. Valdez. Merry Christmas," the woman said before hanging up, and she sounded like she meant it.

Shivers danced down Nadia's spine. She found Rosie in the kitchen slapping dough between her palms helping the señora make her tortillas amid the old lady's chatter. "It's mine," she said and pulled Rosie from the kitchen. "We have to go, señora. Thanks for the phone. I'll bring you some leche quemada later."

Outside, Nadia said, "It's gotta be a mistake. They just turned me down." She pulled Rosie close and said, "Do you know what it would mean to get my Christmases back? I know they'll find out and take it back. I know it as well as I know my goddamned Bobby is never going to change."

"Then, use it," Rosie said, "until they do."

"What?"

"It's a sign, Nadia. A Christmas sign, like in all the movies. It's *Miracle on 34th Street* all over again—you know the movie where Santa *really* does come to town. He's come to Carmelas. God knows, he's overdue."

Nadia held up the blue credit card that shimmered in the December sun. "And Santa is a gringo mailman."

"Yes!" Rosie said.

"But it's a mistake."

"So? They'll find out next week or next month or maybe never. You can enjoy, Nadia, enjoy for one goddamn Christmas. Use it!"

"What could they do?"

"Just take it back," Rosie said. "By then, Christmas would be over."

Nadia knew it was just this kind of thinking that had branded all the Fuentes family, even Rosie, the angel of the bunch, as larcenous and of questionable honor. She looked up at heaven and decided. "I swear, I'll hide the card after—never think of using it again—until September, but only then . . . and I won't tell Bobby." Then she looked at her friend and let out a whoop. "Felíz Navidad, Rosita." She trusted Rosie with her secretos even if she had come out of Fabiano Fuentes's house.

Rosie grabbed her and the two began to spin.

"Que pasó, Mama?"

As Nadia spun, laughing, she saw her Judy running up, and she shouted, "Santa's come."

"Sure," Judy said.

"What's the matter, girl? Don't you believe?" Nadia called out as she danced.

"You're smiling, Ma," Manny called out in wonder after stepping onto the porch to see what all the commotion was.

Nadia, spinning still, saw him on the porch, one hand lost in the pan of candy. "It's Christmas, Manny!"

He laughed, the laughter rising to heaven. Nadia joined him, hanging her head back as she and her girlfriend of so many years spun like girls at the edge of Carmenita Road. The sky seemed to rise forever and she was filled with a yearning as deep as the blue void above her that her days—free of worry—would go on and on and she would live to grow old, longing always for another Christmas.

Chapter 11

Stakes ~ 1962

Ready to do battle, Sammy Archuleta stood under the spreading leaves of Señora Rosaura's jacaranda, facing the street that had been his own and would become something different tomorrow—unless he acted. Wrapped in darkness, he looked up through the dripping leaves blackened by night and turned into lace, bringing to mind his dead mother's inky mantilla, worn only on Sundays in church. There was only a sliver of moon, so the sky, seen through the leaves, was dark. There were no stars.

Hands thrust deeply into the pockets of his baggy khakis, head bent far back, he stared up through the tree, running his plan through his mind until the stiffness in his neck caused him to lower his head and look out into the street.

Claresa.

He said the name aloud, its sounds soft and delicate. In his head he saw the child with huge brilliant black eyes in a sunken face, an image that had appeared there years before when he was first seized by the desire to know why the street, dry and dusty all the year—where little grew along its edges that was not colorless and hard—would have a name that sang Claresa.

"How would I know, mijo?" his mother asked impatiently around a clothespin still sticking in her mouth as she hung the last of his father's blue work shirts out in the sun. "Un caminito has to have a nombre, no?" She took the clothespin from her mouth. "Preguntas! Todo el tiempo, questions. Go play."

"Who would know?" Sammy asked, knowing even then that the answers to the questions that always filled his head were found with other people.

His mother had bent and grabbed the empty clothes basket. "One of the viejas, mijo. Go ask Doña Matilde. She's as old as the hills and been here forever."

So he had.

"Mi mama me dijo que usted are older than the cerros—" he'd said, holding onto the chain links of Doña Matilde's new fence encircling her tired house, his bare feet burrowing in the street's dusty surface.

The woman was among the oldest in the barrio and her age enough for all who crossed her path to call her doña. She was sitting on her sagging front steps, her face a picture of sourness. He'd known her all his life, which is why he stood safe outside her fence, for she struck terror in the hearts of the muchachos in the barrio because she could roar and did often and thought any child in Carmelas hers to command—to smack if smacking were in order. Out of the blue, she, who rarely laughed, cackled loudly, but her laughter did nothing to alter the severity of her face. "No me digas—como los hills I am old, eh? I will thank tu mamacita mañana for the complimento. Why should mi age interest you?"

"Porqúe you have been here forever and would know the answer to mi question."

She said nothing, not even lifting a shaggy eyebrow in question.

Despite her scowl, he asked, "Why is the street Claresa?"

She rose on the step, covered to her ankles in heavy brown cotton. "And you, Sammy Archuleta, are the smartest boy in Carmelas? *Hah!* Long ago someone decided it needed a name, that's why."

"But why Claresa?" he demanded, sure she'd never tell him even though he was the smartest boy in the barrio and needed so desperately to know.

She turned and went to her tattered screen door. Pulling it open, she hesitated and then turned back. "Once there was a little girl—before mis hijos were even born. Se murío. Even La Luna couldn't save her."

"And when she died?"

"Her papa . . ." she said, pausing as if struggling to remember. "Rogelio—sí!" she said loudly as if grabbing the name from some faraway place, sounding as if she'd won a prize. "Sí! La familia Sanchez," she said, seeming very certain now. "They could not let her go. We named the street Claresa—so they could keep her name upon their tongues." She paused, making no move to go into her house. "Hay que curiosidad, niño."

"What?" Sammy asked, wanting always to know other people's stories. "What is odd?"

"I can no longer see her face."

And at that moment a child's face had exploded in his head and remained to this day. The dying face of a child he had never known which from that day had turned his dusty lane Claresa into something feminine and beautiful that, unlike the lost child, would go on forever.

Or so he'd thought. Then.

Now looking at the street and all they'd done to it in preparation for the final insult that would come tomorrow, he realized how really like the girl the street was turning out to be. Doomed—unless he stopped them.

He'd found out about the city's plans for Carmelas like everybody else, when he'd seen the orange signs tacked to the spindly trees scattered along Claresa. He'd just rounded the corner from Mapledale onto Claresa, school books heavy in his arms, when he saw the circle of people gathered around Señora Rosaura's jacaranda, the only flowering tree on the street. The circle was mostly women, old women, for it was barely three-thirty and the men wouldn't drag back into the barrio until dusk or later from their jobs. He saw Don Vicente's shock of white hair nearest the tree trunk and its orange sign. The old man, the richest in the barrio, lived over on Pontlavoy, but since his stroke five years before, he'd seldom left the barrio, his sons running the nursery that had made him rich but no longer necessary—except for here in Carmelas where on most days he was the only man around. As Sammy neared the excited circle, he saw Jesus Mata leaning against Doña Matilde's old cockeyed chain link fence, a paper bag clutched in his brown hand disguising not at all the open beer can inside. Jesus was around most days, too—but he was useless, and no one in their right mind would go to him for anything. So in the daytime, anything that came up fell to Don Vicente.

"It keeps him alive, mijo," his mother said when he'd asked her why everyone depended so on an old crippled man. "And don't you underestimate Don Vicente. He has lived. He walked all the way from Mexico, you know, un indio who married his patron's pale daughter to save her from guerilleros—que romantico, no? And his head is high—"

Señora Rosaura, whose jacaranda held the sign, saw him first as he approached. "Sammy," she called to him, "vente pa'ca." She ordered him to come close. "Don Vicente, nuestro Sammy is here. He will know the words."

Don Vicente turned his head, his eyes brilliant coals beneath white eyebrows that had always reminded Sammy of wiggling worms. He held up his enormous hand and waved Sammy in.

As he pushed through the old women, they touched him as he passed. At Don Vicente's side, he felt the old man grip his shoulder. "Niño, the city esta yendo do something to the streets, but for the life of me—"

Sammy looked at the sign.

Civic Improvement Notice:

(1) Surfacing treatment will begin 10/20/62 in preparation for asphalting beginning on 10/23/62. Residents are asked to arrange alternate parking until surfacing procedures are completed.

(2) Wiring crews will simultaneously establish electrical conduit poles and lighting implements.

In carrying out these municipal improvements, the city of Norwalk regrets any inconvenience occasioned.

After reading the notice, Sammy looked at the old man and said, "Gavachos at city hall have decided necesitamos caminos asfaltados y luces."

"Lights? En los caminos?" Don Vicente asked.

"Claro."

"Who asked us?" Doña Matilde demanded, stepping through her drooping gate to push Jesus off her fence.

"Hay signos como este en Pontlavoy tambien," Don Vicente said.

"On all the streets, Marvilla, too," Chata Lucero—who ran the Mexican store up on Rosecrans—said.

"Paved streets estarán buenos," Señora Rosaura said, a gummy smile breaking her lined yellow face.

"Sí," Don Vicente said, "the streets get bad when la lluvia comes."

"Three days of rain in January, Don Vicente?" Sammy reminded softly.

"It will end the dust," the old man said, a pronouncement.

"Imaginan!" Señora Rosaura said, clapping her hands. "We can hang las ropas—las whites even—without waiting for the wind to die to stop the dust."

The women began to drift away, except for Doña Matilde standing guard at her gate.

"They could have asked us," Sammy said, echoing Doña Matilde as he stared at the sign.

"Callate, hijo," Don Vicente said, tapping his cane hard on the earth, raising dust, as if to pull Sammy's attention. "The world doesn't work that way." He turned and moved down Claresa toward Rosecrans, shuffling down the middle of the dirt street as he headed for Henry's cantina at the corner where Sammy knew he would sit in the coolness, drink beer, and think.

"Luces," Doña Matilde spat contemptuously.

Sammy looked up and the bitterness in her face made him feel better.

"Quienes necesitan luces—we have the moon for light. Only these crazy gavachos need to competir con la luna."

And Sammy was amazed that the day had finally come when he and this vieja agria were standing on the same side of an issue.

"The moon softens—hides the world's warts," she said and her gaze settled on Jesus Mata drinking cerveza from his bag. "Who needs lights to see the likes of this borracho hanging on my good fence," she said, her voice rising, as she lifted her hand to swing again at Jesus Mata, who jumped gingerly out of her reach, "dirtying up the world."

Jesus laughed, safe beyond her reach, and bowed gravely. "A sus ordenes, Señora Guggisberg."

She spat at him before turning back into her yard.

"Can't fight city hall, schoolboy," Jesus said to Sammy, showing the disdain some of the boys in the barrio had for Sammy's love of books.

"Don't think so, vato?" Sammy asked acidly as he walked by him toward home, leaving Jesus with a defiant "This schoolboy can try" in his wake. But it had been Jesus' taunt that had propelled him to his plan.

And so here he was days later, lost in the dark under Señora Rosaura's jacaranda determined to put his plan into action, the details of which he'd been working out for days. It had just been the Friday before that he'd finally figured out the way.

He'd been in his auto shop class up to his elbows in finishing the tune-up on his English teacher Mr. Crachiola's new Impala when his shop teacher had slapped the shiny front fender.

"She's a beauty, isn't she?" Mr. Leeds said, bending over the big V-8. "All that power and yet so fragile."

"Fragile?" Sammy asked, smiling at the way Leeds could check up on his work without making it appear he was doing so.

"Remove the distributor cap and the power is illusion—gone." He laughed. "Let that be a lesson to you, Sammy boy."

"And what might that be, maestro?"

"The real secret of power lies in the tiniest cogs of any mighty machine. The man who knows machines thus understands the world."

"A poet," Sammy teased.

"And don't you forget it, Archuleta," Leeds had said and moved on.

Sammy smiled as he remembered Leeds's gift of the plan, and he stepped from the overhang of jacaranda out farther into the street, the surface rolled flat, hard, planed as the street had never been. He stamped his foot on the hard, dry earth that felt already as if it were covered in asphalt. From the middle of the street, he turned back to look at the side of the road, and he saw the heavy twine suspended between thick wooden stakes placed at intervals the length of Claresa. Pieces of yellow cloth were tied to the twine that marked what would be the new boundaries of the refigured street. No wind blew in the darkness, so the yellow rags hung limply. He saw where the twine ran behind Señora Rosaura's prized jacaranda, loved like a child by a woman who was unable to make any other living planta or flor rise from the earth. Solidly behind the tree, the twine ran in two directions to points in the darkness where twine and rags disappeared. Señora Rosaura's jacaranda had taken root long ago in the roadbed itself and thrived—not too far out in the road to have ever bothered anyone in the barrio, for its purple blooms more than made up for any inconvenience of location in a roadway that had never been sure of its edges anyway. But city hall and the road crew had different ideas as they'd drawn clear straight lines to mark the edges of the new paved road that made Señora Rosaura's jacaranda a trespasser not to be tolerated on the new Claresa.

"Mi jacaranda!" Señora Rosaura had screamed the Friday afternoon before, causing Sammy to leap from the kitchen table where he was doing algebra and run out into the yard, for the woman, his neighbor, had sounded wounded, and to come to her aid was as natural as putting on his pantalones in the morning.

Outside, he saw Señora Rosaura at the tree, ripping the remains of a new poster that had been tacked to the tree. "Si tú tocas mi tree con un finger de tu mano, voy a cut it off, bruto!"

"Can't have a tree in the middle of the street, lady."

"Mi jacaranda," she screamed at him. "Es mi jaca—"

"Hacka what?" the sun-browned gringo demanded.

Señora Rosaura saw Sammy. "Samuelito, este malcriado quiere destroy mi—"

Sammy put his arm around her shoulder, quieting her before looking at the gringo. "What are you going to do to her tree?"

"Cut it down."

"Why?"

"What's the matter with you people? To pave the fuckin' road that's why."

"She loves the tree."

"It's got to go," he said and walked away.

Sammy turned back to Señora Rosaura, who had her hands to her lips as she stared at the tree. He said, "I'll call city hall."

She shook her head. "Es imposible, hijo." Her hand touched the tree. "Que lástima—inexplicable," she said softly, "the ways of God."

"God had nothing to do with this, señora," he had tried to

argue, but his voice lost words, for he saw that to Señora Rosaura, the tree was already dead.

And the senselessness of it—city hall's decisions and their acceptance of them—rushed over him as he stood now in the middle of Claresa in the night.

He'd even mentioned it the night before when Mr. Trujillo had stopped by his house as if the only reason for his appearance was to see if Sammy had any questions about his algebra. Both of them knew the real reason. Ever since his tía had to go on night shift at Burke's Cafe, 7 P.M. to 7 A.M. four nights a week—the only job she could get after his mama died and his pop's social security couldn't even feed them—Trujillo'd been coming by regularly to ease the auntie's mind that her favorite sister's hijo would be all right alone at night in their little house and not turn to the streets as his brother Arturo had and end up like him—in prison or worse.

Trujillo would never stay long, guaranteeing only that Sammy was home. But when he'd told Mr. Trujillo about the city's plans for Señora Rosaura's flowering tree, the teacher had only shrugged and pointed out that of more immediate concern was the fact that three of Sammy's fourteen algebra problems had been answered incorrectly.

And Trujillo's lack of concern had surprised him, for Trujillo was concerned about everything in the barrio; he was an intruding presence poking into everyone's lives, especially Sammy's since he'd been Sammy's fifth-grade teacher years before.

"The boy has talent, special talent, Lupe," Trujillo had said to Sammy's mother after he'd graduated from sixth grade and was ready to move on to Carmenita School for junior high.

"He asks a million questions," his mother had said. "I'm too old—his preguntas make me crazy."

"That is his talento, Lupe. He asks questions. No one can shut him up. We must together let no one try."

We. Mr. Trujillo's words. So, ever since, Mr. Trujillo had been around, advising, directing, pushing—as if Sammy were his own to worry over.

And Sammy had seldom really minded, for Trujillo was a man to talk to, and there hadn't been a man in the house since his father died and Arturo got locked up the last time. True, he was different from Papa or any of the other men in the barrio. Trujillo's house over on Mapledale was filled with books—in Spanish and English. He used words Sammy had never heard in other men's mouths. His voice was soft and fine. He never yelled as if volume alone could make one right. And he talked to his fat wife in a way different from how Sammy had ever heard a man deal with a woman—as if her words were as important as his own. Trujillo seemed to stand apart from the other men, yet everyone respected him. He was their children's teacher and had been for years. That's why when this man, who seemed to hear and care about whatever Sammy had to say, had shown no concern at all for Señora Rosaura's tall flowering tree—showing he was no different from Señora Rosaura, any of them—and was as ready to accept the killing of the tree, the street, without a lifted hand, Sammy had grown so angry.

The anger rushing over him now in the dark was as intense and still as much directed at his maestro Trujillo as at any of them, for his acceptance was so unexpected.

Well, it was their acceptance. Not Sammy's own.

He looked up toward Mapledale, and he could see the outline of the street-making machines lying there in wait of morning—big yellow trucks, dimmed to hulking shadows, some with enormous rollers that would follow others with tanks to dump asfalto, hot, bubbling liquid to drown Claresa. Calmness fell, for he knew they would move on the morrow over his dead body.

He walked up the dark street to where the trucks waited. Claresa was no wider than it had ever been, but it seemed so now.

The houses that lined the street seemed far away, scattered unevenly up and down the block, some far back, others close to the street, giving the lane a naturalness that matched the haphazardness of the world. The muted lights spilling from the curtained windows made little dent in the night.

And darkness was what he wanted. It spoke of nights he'd always known here, darkness that held no fears at all. Each house he passed was fronted by hardpacked uneven patches of dirt, a car in a yard here and there no interference to the chickens that would begin their scratching with the sun, nor to the people who used their yardas as extensions of too-tiny living rooms when heat drove them into the night to sit and smoke and drink with neighbors on summer nights. He knew their stories—even those never talked about except in whispers—as he knew his own.

He passed Remi's house, feeling safe in the knowledge that Remi was in the hospital again with a new bleeding and not parked at his bedroom window keeping an eye out for Sammy's every move. He moved by his own house, the lights on behind curtains he'd closed tight so that anyone who happened by would think him tucked away inside where he was supposed to be as his tía ordered every night.

But tonight he was in the street.

He'd waited until eight-thirty to leave, long after Mr. Trujillo would have come by if he were coming. His leaving was a lie to his tía. He knew that, and it hurt, for his auntie always said, "I must work, mijo, but I can only do it so long as you and I work as a team—so long as you don't break my trust in you. Without mi confianza en tú honesty, I would be lost." He knew it was not the first lie, for he'd been leaving many nights lately for moments with Lucita in the dark—but never without his schoolwork done, and he'd always been in bed by ten o'clock.

Tonight he would be later.

He looked a final time up at his house, its yarda as still and empty as the others, for summer was gone, his mama's cement

Virgin that Arturo had tucked into a niche staring out at him, offering benediction. It was October now, the nights gone cool, and the emptiness of the street made it seem almost like a gringo street where front yards were grassy spaces for people to look at and never walk or sit upon.

He remembered one summer night when his mother had dragged him from his play in the street. He had been only six or seven, and she held his hand tightly as if to do otherwise was to risk losing him as they crossed from Carmelas over into the gringo tract, its straight paved streets a different world, to visit Rosa Galvan, his mother's dearest girlhood friend. Usually the visits were in the other direction, Rosa trekking back into Carmelas, arriving to warm welcome as if she had come some great distance. But that night, they'd been crossing over, for Rosa's husband, Rudy, was working late, providing an opportunity, infrequent now, for the two women to visit and seem like girls again. He and his mama walked up Dinard toward Rosa's house.

"A jewel," his mother said, referring to the house, the stuff of dreams, "and it's no longer even new."

But to Sammy, dragging on her arm, Rosa's house was cold, from its blue, so pale the moonlight bleached it white, to its lawn, so chilly and sharp against his naked feet, to its smells, which were so faint as to be no smells at all, at least none of the smells he knew. As they walked across Rosa's grass, Sammy could not get over how silent the world had become here. He looked up the block, house after house a perfect copy of its neighbor, fronted by an enormous, empty yard, so different from the noisy life he'd just been pulled away from.

"Donde están everyone, Mama?"

"En sus casas."

"Where do they play?"

"In their *back* yardas, mijo," she said, pulling on his arm.

"How do they find each other?"

Mama laughed loud. "I don't think they want to. Apurate, hijo, Rosa tiene cookies para ti."

He'd wanted only to go home.

Claresa. Then and now—a world apart.

Color. Smells. Dust. Noise, which blended with the scent of blood and manure forever hanging in the air—carried from the slaughterhouse in one direction, the dairy in the other—creating a grittiness that hung heavy over Carmelas and touched his nose and tongue and layered him as it layered the others and made them one.

No longer a child in need of a mother's hand in the dark, he reached the row of trucks waiting like an army in the night. Enemies. All. Powerless until gringo hands would ignite them into violence in the morning.

He approached the first truck in the line and moved close, bending over the high front fender, peering into the engine compartment open at the sides. He glanced back over his shoulder and then around him. He was alone. His hand reached into the engine compartment, its darkness blinding his eyes but not his fingers as they ran over metal, cooled from inaction, bundled wires, his fingers recognizing parts and knowing just where they were going as they moved deeper to the engine's heart. He felt the distributor he was seeking in his palm as he closed around its cap and pulled it out, the act reminding him of the picture he'd long ago discovered in the Norwalk Library of an Aztec priest atop a gleaming pyramid holding in his palms a bleeding heart. His own heart raced, for he knew now he felt like that Aztec priest as he straightened and stared at his hand, the fingers unfolding and baring the distributor cap, larger than in Cracchiola's Chevy Impala in auto shop, but the same in function and intent. He looked up at the dark sky and raised his hand and what it held toward heaven, feeling in his heart a power that could indeed build pyramids and more.

He lowered his hand, knowing that in no time at all he'd have a small mountain of distributor caps, each marking a disabled truck. He moved to the next truck in line and bent forward. His hand was just reaching into the dark when he heard a throat cleared.

His hand pulled back as if burned. His heart racing, he looked up over the engine compartment and saw a shadow, the outline of a man leaning against the side of the next truck in line. Sammy squinted, trying to identify the face lost in the night, wondering for a moment if the city could have had the foresight to place a gringo to guard the trucks. As if on cue, the shadow bent forward, arms rising, a flash of flame lighting the face when the match fired a cigarette suspended from its mouth. Sammy realized he'd have preferred a gringo guard, for the face revealed sank his heart—a face familiar and unwanted, now.

The face was an Indian's, reddish even in the dim light of a flame that flickered and died. But the flash had been enough to identify the lean, angular face, brown-red skin stretched taut over a skull-like face that always brought to mind the days of the dead when October's end would fill the barrio with paper skeletons. He knew the face, its leathered hardness, lines cut like fault lines in the earth, so deep and dark he'd wondered as a boy if they'd taken special time for this much-admired man to clean.

Sammy said nothing. The shadow across the way leaned back and he saw the burning cherry of the cigarette's end suspended. The face behind the cigarette remained silent, and Sammy knew Trujillo would say nothing, for he'd always been a man who knew one never spoke too soon with children if it were really the child's words one wanted.

"Cómo está, Mr. Trujillo?" Sammy finally asked of the man he'd thought he'd escaped this night.

There was silence and then, "Cómo estás *tú*, hijo?" floated deeply in the dark to him.

"I'm *fine.*"

"Are you?"

After a stillness that must have told the shadow Sammy would say no more, Mr. Trujillo said, "You have school in the morning. It's Sunday night—too late for you to be playing," not even reminding Sammy of this betrayal of his auntie's trust.

"I'm not playing."

"Malinche's moon," Trujillo said.

Sammy looked up and saw a thread of moon shedding no light at all; he hadn't heard anyone refer to this last remnant of moonlight before it went completely dark as Malinche's since before his mother died. When he drove her to distraction, she would lift her old sealed Mexican pot, threatening to uncork it the next time the moon shrank to a sliver, freeing Malinche to chase him through Carmelas under a moon that gave no light at all. "Mexico's whore," he said, the word sounding ugly in the dark robbed of moon, "reminding me of how not to walk."

Trujillo laughed now, and the laugh wasn't the usual one a grown hombre threw at children. "Like una mosca eres tú."

"A fly?" Sammy said, surprised, thrown as always by this difficult man.

"Fighting against a fly swatter."

And still Sammy didn't feel the man was laughing at him. "How did you know to find me here?" he finally asked.

"I know nothing, my friend." Sammy laughed now. Trujillo laughed, too. "Except what I hear when I lay my ear against the dirt streets of Carmelas. Did you think there were any secretos here?" Sammy laughed, not really wanting to. "Some tales we speak of softly—but no secrets are allowed." Trujillo cleared his throat. "I know for instance you linger too long in the dark with Hector Reyes's girl Lucita."

Sammy was startled. Had the man been standing here all evening watching him and Lucy huddled together against the trunk of Señora Rosaura's jacaranda until her mother, screaming her name in the dark of Claresa, had ordered her home out of his arms not an hour before?

"I thought you wiser than the others," his old teacher said, "saving the pleasure of women until your life would not be threatened by distraction."

Sammy could see Lucita's breasts, his palms alive with the feel of them suspended under her loosened bra, his nose filling with their scent, a distant smell of roses. "I have not known real pleasure, Mr. Trujillo," he said.

"Good. You have things to do."

Sammy saw the cigarette arc through the night, thrown.

"There are many trucks left," Trujillo said. "What are you doing to them?"

"Taking away their power."

"How do you do that?"

Sammy extended his hand, palm up, even though he knew Trujillo could not see what lay there. "I collect these, the source of all their power."

He laughed. "So you will have won?"

Sammy nodded.

"Until when? You think, niño, no more exist?"

"I know. But gringos are so stupid sometimes. It will take them half the morning to figure out the problem. Then, you will see, two days or three to get the parts, excuses to sit on their nalgas and do nothing."

"But in the end?"

"Claresa will be paved," Sammy said softly and saw he'd known it all along. He'd planned a string of other insults to be done to the trucks in a long line of guerrilla attacks, each more damaging than the next, but even while he'd planned he must have known that there were only delays, no victory really possible. Of course he'd known. Sammy Archuleta was no fool. "But not without someone speaking out," he said.

"You?"

"There's only me with the courage to stop them"—the direction of his accusation clear.

"And I suppose Carmelas is filled with cowards? Es Don Vicente un cobarde, mijo? He walked a thousand miles on bare feet from Mexico bringing his Alicia out of madness. That must take some courage. Or Señora Rosaura—who has never had two centavitos to rub together and can still thank God for *her* blessings? Or Remedios Camisa—lying bleeding in the hospital as we speak? Surely there is courage there."

"You're twisting my words."

"Then explain to me, mijo. What did you mean?"

"They accept having no say at all."

"But you don't?"

"*No*. I wouldn't be here if—"

"Pulling wires from trucks in the darkness of an almost moonless night?" Mr. Trujillo's voice got sharper as he asked, "Where did you learn this trick you're playing?"

"In my shop class. Auto," Sammy said, too fast, realizing too late he'd never told Trujillo he had enrolled in the class at all.

"You have a car?"

"No."

"Your tía has a car?"

"No."

"Then why are you learning to take cars apart?"

"They put me in the class. It's just an elective."

"They?"

"Counselors. Said it couldn't hurt, Mr. Trujillo."

"They told me, too," he said softly. "Years ago. They lied. Such advice was a road they wanted to chase me down. And you took the advice?"

"Why not? What's wrong with learning about cars?"

"Nothing is wrong with learning anything, niño—if it takes you somewhere. Is this where this learning has taken you—to pull wires from trucks in the darkness?"

"It gave me the means—yes—to say no to what I cannot accept."

"A 'no' no one will hear even comes from you. A 'no' that won't last beyond tomorrow? And what is this crime you can't accept?"

"They're going to pave Claresa."

"All the barrio," Mr. Trujillo said.

"Yes. And put up lights—"

"Which will keep you from the darkness and Lucita."

"And everything will change, Mr. Trujillo."

"How can anything stay unchanged? You think you will go forever with Lucita pressed up against a tree—wanting nothing more—nothing changed?" Mr. Trujillo moved around the truck and joined Sammy. He pulled out a cigarette, extending the packet to Sammy, who shook his head at the offer.

"Good," his teacher said.

Sammy watched the face as it sucked on the cigarette, hollowing the cheeks.

"You know I am from Texas?"

"I heard."

He smiled. "No secrets. Heh? Colonia Ladrón. *My* barrio. You know the meaning of 'ladrón'?"

"Thief."

"My barrio. Outside San Antonio. Far outside. Not wrapped round with gringos like Carmelas. A world apart."

"Just like Carmelas," Sammy argued.

"Maybe," Trujillo conceded. "My father. He was a lucky man. He worked not in the fields con los otros hombres de Colonia Ladrón. He worked in San Antonio in a factory. In the barrio we had a small school that went to eighth grade. No one needed more than that."

"Said who?"

"The gavachos in San Antonio—but most of us thought so, too."

"My point, Mr. Trujillo—"

"My point you haven't heard. I wanted to go to high school, so mi papá went to the school and they found a place for me in San Antonio and I would drive every day with my papá and come back with him in the evenings. The school was at the edge of town where Mexicans, some Mexicans, could go. I lasted until eleventh grade."

"Why?"

"Too many shop classes." He laughed. "But the war came and I got drafted and was ripped from Colonia Ladrón and thrown into a world where the streets were paved—"

"And straight, so goddamned straight," Sammy said.

"As if the straightness can remove danger from the world," Mr. Trujillo said.

"But why are they doing this to us?" Sammy asked. "Paving us over?"

"Carmelas frightens them."

"Sure," Sammy said and laughed.

"It is a savage wild place," Mr. Trujillo said, laughing in the dark. "To them, niño. They see our houses, thrown here and there as if by God and painted in colors that scream and make them nervous. They see our dusty streets, the lines of which can change like the course of rivers. They see our yards, spilling with chickens, decaying cars, and too many children—and in all the color, the noise, they see chaos threatening their belief that they can control the world. So they will pave the streets and light the night."

"I know," Sammy said as if to a brother who understood his anguish.

"And why should this break your heart?"

"They didn't ask."

"And that would be a reason I could buy," Trujillo said and fell silent. He tossed his cigarette away and then said, "Do you think anyone asked Malinche before her own people threw *her* into a camp of woman-hungry Spaniards? If I believed that was your motivation, I would be pulling wires from those trucks along with you. But your despair comes not just from this."

Not wanting to look at his despair, Sammy asked instead—suddenly wanting very much to know—"How did you become a teacher?"

"The war," Trujillo said. "Five years in Europe. We were the first in Rome. Yankees." He laughed. "That's what they shouted at us as we rolled into Rome. From rooftops, niño. 'Viva Yanquis.' The brownest of us—the black ones, too—were yankees. And the women, hijale. Gavacha women—so hungry for a piece of chocolate."

"You were distracted?"

He nodded. "But never did I use chocolate to buy distraction. Chocolate I gave, niño. And after the war, I was put on a ship that circled the world—"

"El mundo total?"

"All the way around, and I ended up in Long Beach with money in my pocket and a yearning for brown girls who spoke Spanish and had black brilliant eyes. We got on a bus. We went to East L.A. and it was like wallowing in a brown river after a drought."

"Women?" Sammy asked eagerly.

"No. The place. East L.A. Its smells. The beans, niño—gringo cooks in the army have no idea of what to do with beans. Arroz. Enchiladas. My heart ached so for Colonia Ladrón that I couldn't dance that night in the Knights of Columbus Hall—until one girl, braver than the rest, called me an indio in uniform and winked. I never went back to Colonia Ladrón."

"Mrs. Trujillo?" Sammy asked in disbelief that her heaviness could ever have glided on a dance floor.

"You find that hard to believe?" He laughed. "She could dance, niño, and I found my home inside her arms. So I married her. I read of GI bills and went to school, deciding to become a teacher. And I did—despite all their kind advice."

"But how did you get here—to Ramona School from East L.A.?"

"No one would hire me in L.A. I heard of this little school in a barrio called Carmelas. I got that job. One room, niño." He pointed his arm. "The school used to be over there, next to that mulberry tree. First grade through sixth. My esposa," he said, laughing, "you'd have thought I was taking her to the moon. But she came. She went where I did—muy mexicana she is. And so I was back in a barrio. And it fit like a glove. I loved my school from the first day." He paused and then said, "But I was still glad when they tore it down."

"Why?"

"We got the new Ramona School."

"Only because the gringos came in their new houses and demanded a new school. The gringos got Ramona School."

"We got it, too. So what did it matter? The new school kept the old name. I went along with the name. Un Trujillo on the staff. And I got Miss Urrea the second year. How many schools, niño, have two brown people teaching? Two steps forward, mijo. So, pardon me if I don't cry over you losing your dirt streets."

"But Carmelas will change."

"High time, niño. We could use a little light."

"I don't want it to change."

"You didn't want to leave the womb either, I would imagine."

"They could have asked us."

"Now, that is a horse of a different color. We are Malinche's children—remember that. Like her we are invisible to those who use us unless we find a voice—as she did—big enough for the world to hear."

"Which is what I was doing—"

"Pulling wires in the dark? Where is there a voice in that? Voices that are heard aren't afraid to name themselves. Voices that change things venture out into the world. It's a big world, niño—I've been around it. Remember?"

Sammy looked up Claresa and in the dimness could see Señora Rosaura's jacaranda where it stood beyond the pale. "They're going to cut down Señora Rosaura's jacaranda."

"That is a shame."

And Sammy's heart leapt, for Trujillo cared after all. "When the solution would be so simple," Sammy said. He pointed down the street at the twine marking the sides of the new roadbed. "They need only move the stakes and twine three feet on each side of the street and the tree wouldn't be in the road."

"You make it sound so easy, niño."

"It would be. I could do it myself."

Mr. Trujillo laughed. "The gringos will be back tomorrow, so hung over from their weekend that they would probably never even notice—"

"Until it was too late!" Sammy said loudly. "Then what could they do, Mr. Trujillo?"

"Nothing, niño. You would have saved the tree."

"Como un hijo that tree es to Señora Rosaura."

"Her prize, niño. I know."

"And I would only have to pull up the stakes and put them back into the earth on the other side of señora's jacaranda."

"The other side too, mijo, to create balance, los gringos love balance, you know."

"Yes! Then I would smooth the earth where the stakes had been—no one would know."

"But me," Mr. Trujillo said.

"And me," Sammy echoed.

"And you know how we keep secrets," Mr. Trujillo said.

"It would be my way of saying 'no'—"

"To what? To lights? To asphalt?"

"No," Sammy said softly. "To their not even asking."

"A voice, mijo. A statement."

"Señora Rosaura's jacaranda!" Sammy said loudly, getting Mr. Trujillo's point. "That 'no' would last beyond tomorrow."

"As long as sap flows in the tree."

"But I would still lose the street," Sammy said, his joy evaporating.

"Its dirt. Its dust. The houses would still line the pavement. The same people, mijo." Sammy saw there was truth in that. "Life is a deal, niño. We give a little—"

"And get what?"

"Señora Rosaura's flowering jacaranda."

"But it's midnight already," Sammy said.

"That gives us until morning, no?"

Sammy's heart danced. "But what about school?"

"This is all school's ever been about." Mr. Trujillo pushed off from the truck and moved down Claresa, pulling stakes as he went and laying them neatly three feet over. Sammy ran to follow, trailing him on the other side of the road, matching Mr. Trujillo stake for stake as they set out to redefine Claresa to save an old woman's flowering tree.

Chapter 12

El Grito de Socorro ~ 1963

He hit her.

The first time hadn't been with his fist. It had been the back of his hand, thrown over his shoulder as if to bat away a mosca, but it hadn't been a fly, it had been Socorro Collado—her face, her cheek. His hand collided with one of her cheekbones, its height the only thing that had protected the rest of her face that first time.

There had been no blood that time. Just a drunken blow, hard but thrown blindly, no real target then in mind. With the blow had come a hard, cracking sound that had echoed in their tiny kitchen and echoed still in her memory to this day. There had been no real pain, just numb surprise that changed her life.

She was thrown backwards by the blow, and her sharp intake of breath had caused him to turn from their chipped sink, cold water running out of the stained faucet from which he'd been drinking like the animal she'd called him. As he turned, his eyes—glazed since he'd staggered into the kitchen from outside—opened wide, and the drunkenness drained out of them. His hand had reached out, not to strike again, but to touch, and his black eyes, made into diamonds by the ceiling fluorescent light spilling into them from above, filled with what she saw was horror that, if he'd turned into words then, might have changed the course of their lives. But he said nothing, pulled back his hand, and ran out of the kitchen into the night.

After he'd gone, she stood in the center of the tiny kitchen, the ancient cracked linoleum paled by time to a whispered blue, and tried to figure out what she had done.

She continued doing that for years until finally she realized it didn't matter at all what she did or did not do.

She remembered talking to Serafina across the street over coffee about the sometime violence of men. Serafina's husband, Chacho, had been working with Cesar at the meat packing plant in those days, and she was like an older sister, wiser—the only one to whom Socorro would have said anything at all, for Serafina could keep secrets, which, she always said, was not a virtue, but only the fact of being the last of old Paco Valdez's kids, born years after one-legged Joey with no one at home to get in the habit of sharing secrets with. "Mija," Serafina said, rising from the table to go to the old stove and the coffee pot there. "Who are they going to punch?" She brought the pot and refilled Socorro's cup. "Their jefes at the slaughterhouse?" She laughed, the sound raucous in the kitchen. "Better me. I need his cheque."

That of course had been before Cesar had lost that job cutting up cows because of drink. But that conversation with Serafina had helped, for it had pointed to something else as the reason Cesar would go off from time to time.

She had stopped blaming herself years ago, but it had taken her until last night to see there would be no end to it unless she stopped it.

In her bathroom, she saw her face in the medicine cabinet mirror, the morning sun washing the room through the window over the tub she could not get clean. Her reflection wavered in the flaking mirror, but years of experience with this dilapidated mirror in her closet-sized bathroom had taught her to look through the distortion to her face.

But this morning, she tried to ignore the reflected whole of her face as she applied her lipstick carefully, for one side of her mouth was swollen and painful to touch. She could not even roll her lips together to even the color. She never wore much makeup. Cesar had never liked it—except for lipstick, hot and red, that caused her brown skin to catch traces of its color and black liner around her eyes.

Her eyes. She looked at them, both almost swollen shut, and saw that the bridge of her nose, normally so high, seemed flat—even now with her bulging eyes. The blue-black circle under her right eye fanned out over her cheek. She saw the glint of gold at her right ear, the emptiness on her left lobe testimony to the torn hole too sore to hold a ring this morning.

She ran a nervous hand over her thick black hair, noting the swirl of grey rising from her forehead. She was no longer young. But her hair was long like a young girl's. Cesar had liked long hair.

She would have Aurora cut it—to her neck.

She lifted the heavy hair, baring her neck, and saw the laceration rising from the collar of her dress up her neck. She let the hair fall, turning from the mirror and the mark made last night when Cesar had pulled her from their bed and dragged her across their bedroom.

That mark and what came after had led to her decision.

Drunk, he'd stumbled into the bedroom the night before. When she'd first heard him enter the house and trip over the hassock she'd placed before the front door, she'd rolled to the wall, pulling up her legs, making sure her cotton gown was down in back. There had been a time when she'd been unable to sleep until he dragged in on paydays. But that was long ago. Now, she needed tricks like the hassock to wake and warn her.

She pretended sleep as he entered the darkness of their room. She heard him swear as he stumbled about in the dark, struggling out of his clothes. The smell of stale beer gagged her. She felt him get into the bed, not even moving when his naked leg touched against her. Minutes passed before she let herself believe Cesar was choosing sleep.

Then, she felt him turn and press against her. She felt his thing, hard and big against the base of her spine. She waited, praying he would sleep, but then she felt him move his hips, sliding himself up and down against her cotton-covered spine. She didn't move. Then his fingers were at her gown, pulling it up.

She sat up in the bed, scooting away, her back against the wall. "Borracho!" she hissed, knowing she should say nothing, unable to stop, making sure only that the name was thrown as a muted roar, for her children were across the hall.

He laughed.

Once she had loved Cesar's laugh, as deep as the brown color of his face.

"Come on, Sokie," he said, his words slurred. He reached for her.

She slapped at his grasping hands, thick, coarsened by years of hard labor in the dairy, in the slaughterhouse, and finally spreading cement, laying foundations for other people's new houses. "No me molestas!" she said.

"Bother you, vieja? You love it!" he said and lunged for her. He rose over her, pushing her down, lowering his face, his mouth pressing against hers, his tongue forcing itself into her mouth, pressing at her clenched teeth, the sour beer smells rising up her nose. His hand was pulling up her nightgown as her own hands fought to keep it down. He won. Worming his hand up her naked body, he grasped her breast, his calloused palm hurting.

She opened her teeth, his tongue marching forward. She felt it in her mouth and fury rose like never before as his tongue bored into her mouth—claiming it—an insult that drove her to do the unbelievable—she bit the offending flesh, bit hard. He reared up, pulling back, tearing his tongue on her teeth. As he escaped, his blood left salty traces on her tongue.

There was no victory, for he hit her.

No flattened hand this time—a balled-up fist crashed against her mouth, throwing her head back against the scarred headboard. Stunned—as much at her unthinkable behavior as his blow—she fell still.

Then his hands were at her gown, hiking it up, pulling at her cotton underwear. He forced her down and threw her legs wide, slithering between them as he climbed up and into her. He tried to kiss her—as if to prove he knew all her bite was gone—but she turned her head, his mouth falling to her neck.

Frozen, she didn't move. How could she have bitten him? She pushed the thought away and tried, instead, to do what she always did when he came to her unwanted. She tried to remember when she'd loved lying with him in twisted sheets, summer outside a window. But this time, the images wouldn't come. She tried harder and forced her mind to wander farther back to thoughts of nights before they'd married when her passion had been so strong for Cesar Collado she thought she'd die.

Suddenly, images leapt into her head. She saw the two of them in his Chevy under the overhang of Señora Rosaura's jacaranda, the night there darker than elsewhere, sweeter for the perfume of purple flowers nearby. She would let him take his clothes off—but never hers. He would lie with his head in her lap, the back of his head rubbing, grinding at the juncture of her thighs, his nakedness stretched against the black leather seats, his body thick and solid—brown from head to toe—his penis high and hard—darker even than the rest of him—her hand caressing, as she dreamed of the day she would replace her hand with her body to swallow him as wives were allowed to do. And he, staring up at her eyes, would whisper sweetness.

"Amante mia."

Smiling down, she felt his love, though she loved him only with her hands.

"Mi tesoro—tú," Cesar Collado sighed between clenched teeth.

She closed her eyes—the girl she'd been—feeling every bit Cesar Collado's treasure, her value in Carmelas evident in her selection by this dark, most desirable of the Collado brothers famed in and beyond Carmelas for their physical prowess and perfection.

"Mi corazón," he'd moan as she slipped her palm over the top of his exploding penis, his essence arcing through her fingers in the darkness, drops hitting his chest where his heart lay. She placed her damp hand flat against his chest, feeling his love beating wildly against her skin.

"No, mi amor," she whispered back, "eres tú, *mi* corazón," as she'd known the first time she'd bumped into him in Chata's store in the back by the huge barrels of beans where he'd been hiding among the chiles hanging in clusters from the ceiling, firing the air, its blend of must and earth raining heat reflected in Cesar's eyes as he'd taken her shoulders in the shadowy recesses of the store. One of a huge band that had invaded Carmelas the year before—strangers from Colonia Juarez—buying the Loreto shack on Marvilla and filling it with sons, each handsomer than the last, culminating in Cesar, the brownest, mas guapo Collado of the bunch. As she stood close to him in the summer damp of Chata's store, her heart had banged behind her breasts, giving itself to him then at his first touch, simply pulling the rest of her along, with all of Carmelas cheering them on wondering what beauty two such perfect and admired people could bring into the world.

"Mi only corazón," she heard him say—a memory of hearts, his, hers, the way they'd been, that stabbed as it collided with the ruins left entwined in these sheets now, destroying the memory, the images, the strategy that had allowed her to be wise and safe.

Safe?

She felt the blood flowing from her nose, a line running into her mouth. Horrified, she heard herself cry, "Weakling!" The words were loud, a curse, her venom amazing, for her love had once been as intense. "Cobarde," she spat at him, wanting to hurt him. "Coward!" she screamed, all the while knowing she would only hurt herself, but unable to do anything less. "You come to me only when you're drunk."

"Puta!" he roared as she felt him pull out of her struggling body, his eyes even in the dark holding something she hadn't seen before. Suddenly afraid, she found strength and pushed against him, kicking, flailing, screaming, forgetting children across the hall, knowing only that she was in real danger now.

Freed, she scurried away, over him—out of the bed. "You treat me like a whore," she said, telling herself to be still, knowing stillness was the only way to stop the madness.

He roared again, leaping up, and grabbed her neck to pull her back into the bed. "Que tu deserve," he yelled, "un holster for mi bicho—es toda que tú eres." He rose above her, standing in the bed, his hands pulling on her neck, trying to lift her by her neck. "You want out of my bed, puta, I'll put you out—desnuda into the streets."

He dragged her from the bed, pulling on her nightgown, which rose over her body, becoming a noose tightening about her neck as he dragged her from the bedroom and into the short hall. She struggled to rise, cursing her stupidity, but he slapped her down, roaring.

In the hallway, she heard a *"no!"*—a scream that wasn't Cesar's—and felt the nightgown noose about her neck loosen as she was released and allowed to breathe. Looking up, she saw Cesar stuggling with a brown monkey on his back that was her boy Juan Pablo, thirteen, his eyes as big as summer moons flailing her naked Cesar. *"No más!"* the boy shouted.

She scooted away, rising, and before running, she saw the other two, Lydia and Junior, cowering in their doorway, and their eyes were her decision.

Escaping, she ran into the living room to the phone and called the police, the number a memory held in reserve as if she'd always known she'd one day do this. She screamed her address into the phone and cried, "My husband—he will kill me!," just as Cesar, a bull with a tiny matador, Juan Pablo, in pursuit, ran to her bellowing and tore the phone out of the wall.

"Mamá!" Juan Pablo cried as he leapt at his father's legs and hung on. "Va te—correte—run to abuelita's—"

Her mother's house. Yes! A haven. So, she ran out into Claresa at three o'clock in the morning. The street was empty, the streetlights painting the pavement with warm circles of light that made Claresa a different place. Barefoot, she cut across her dusty yarda to the blacktop, the surface still warm on her naked soles from the sun that day.

"Mamá," Juan Pablo cried, his voice piercing in the empty street. She turned around and, to her horror, she saw Cesar run naked from the house holding the receiver of their phone like a weapon. Even drunk, the man could run.

She looked around at the dark houses of Carmelas she'd known all her life, and broke its second rule. She screamed, as if she were dying, in the middle of Carmelas, and let her secrets spill into the street.

That she would scream startled even her, and it stopped Cesar in his tracks. She saw the disbelief in his face as he froze at the curb. She lowered to her haunches, sucking in air, and screamed, *"Ayudame!,"* her grito de liberación, and her husband, Cesar, became, like Adam in the garden, suddenly aware of his nakedness.

Lights went on along Claresa, doors opened, people's voices filled the night.

"Que pasó?"

"Esta Socorro screaming in the street?"

"Y él—the naked one," a male voice cried, breaking into laughter. "Es Cesar!"

Socorro screamed a final time. As she saw Cesar run back into the house, the women on the block gathered her up.

"Mira, su cara," one woman said to another as Socorro turned her face to the lamplight.

"Que pasó, preciosa?" Señora Rosaura asked, lifting her up, like the mother she was to everyone in Carmelas.

Socorro told it all, saying, "Mi Cesar—he tried to kill me." She lifted her neck, showing the welt like a badge. The circle of women sucked in air, horrified as much at the public revelation as the sight.

Chacho, Serafina's husband and Cesar's friend, came up.

"Está borracho," Socorro said to him.

"Estas tú bien?" he asked, concerned for her.

"He tried to kill me."

Chacho shrugged. "He's drunk, Sokie."

"Go check on my kids, Chacho," she asked as a siren filled the distance, lights flashing as the screaming cop car turned from Rosecrans onto Claresa.

"You called them?" Chacho asked in disbelief.

She nodded.

"You could have come to me," he accused. "I would never have allowed this! Instead, you call the chinga cops." He rose and looked at the advancing lights. He spat. "I'll handle this," he said, "as you should have known." He loped across the street to find Cesar.

The police were kind to her. They sat her in their car.

"You want to press charges, ma'am?"

"Yes."

Serafina, standing guard by the open police car door, bent forward, her hair in huge rollers. "Chica, piensate—he'll go to jail."

"Good."

And he went.

But that was last night.

She glanced at her battered face in the old mirror. She had much to do this morning, and, heart unrepentant, she left the bathroom, the damage to her face unrepaired, her decision made.

"Will they keep Papi forever?" Lydia had asked the night before when Socorro had gotten her back to bed after Cesar, neighbors, and police were gone.

"No, mija."

"When will he come home?"

"He's not coming home, mija." She said the words aloud for the first time, terror filling her heart at the thought of a woman—herself—without a man.

Juan Pablo, looking very much a little boy, stood in the doorway. When their eyes connected, he said, "Good," and she fought the urge to demand he speak no ill of Cesar.

In her living room now, as she picked up her purse and checked inside for bus money, she thought of her son and wondered for a moment what kind of man he would become. She left the house and walked up Claresa. She tried to calm her jumping stomach by reminding herself that Juan Pablo was safe in school. Lydia and Junior were at her mother's for the day. Little children were already in the street, playing as they did every day. As she walked in the street, they smiled and said hello, but she knew their mothers were surely watching from behind the curtains.

She passed her mother's house, the house she'd grown up in, knowing her mother would keep her little ones inside today.

Her mother.

The old woman had been the last to arrive on the scene the night before and she'd been still sitting at Socorro's kitchen table when the sun had finally risen. They'd talked the night away. As dawn lightened the streets, her mother said, "But to call the policia, mija—to tell them to take him to jail."

She searched her mother's face, the eyes collapsing in upon themselves from age, the mouth a colorless line without her teeth, and saw only an old woman afraid, and the fear was catching. "You know it's not the first time he's beaten me," but as she said it, she realized she'd kept so much back—even from her own mama—always minimizing bruises and excusing Cesar's ways.

"Los hombres se enojan," her mother started.

"My papa got mad," Socorro said, "and never did he hit you."

"No," her mother agreed. "He was not like other men."

Socorro lifted her head, pulled back her hair and bared her neck. "Look at my pesquecho, Mama. My face. You want me dead?"

The old woman crossed herself. "No, mija. Don't talk foolish."

Rubbing the welt already darkening into bruise, she said, "This is more than simple anger, Mama."

Her mother rose from the table, saying, "But what did you do, mija—for him to almost—"

"Mama!" Socorro said incredulously.

Her mother took her empty mug to the sink. "I'm old. What do I know? If Papa were alive—if you'd have had hermanos, they would have never allowed this—"

"But I have none."

Her mother shrugged. "What do I know? What did I ever know," Mama said, sounding so tired, "except that you are my only blessing. Maybe a night in jail will teach him—"

"I won't let him come back."

"Mija!" her mother said. "This is his house."

"Then I'll come to you—until I can—"

"Callate, mija. Estas upset. Say nothing now. Think. The world may look different in the morning."

But as Socorro reached Rosecrans, she knew morning had changed nothing. At the corner she was waiting for the street to clear so she could run across to the bus stop when Aurora Mendez pulled up in her husband's big LTD. He worked the nightshift at the meat packing house, so Aurora—alone among Carmelas women—had a car to use all day.

"Amiga," she called out.

Socorro went to the car and saw her friend—plump and pretty with her brown hair lightened to a sandy blond to maximize the lightness of the skin she prized—sitting inside gripping the wheel.

"Cómo estás, sweetie?" Aurora asked, concern everywhere in her voice.

"Mejor."

"I heard you caused a ruckus," Aurora whispered.

"From way over on Pontlavoy you heard my scream?" Socorro asked, smiling.

"We heard nothing 'til the chisme started this morning—but, girl, from what I heard it was some grito!" Then she laughed teasingly and asked, "Where you going? Running away?"

"To church. Can you drop me?"

"Claro, get in." Aurora laughed again. "But do you think this is the time to pray?"

The big Ford LTD moved like a boat and Aurora was an able pilot, gabbing away, eyes more on Socorro than the road. "I'm on your side, honey. Let ol' Cesar cool his nalgas in the can for a while. Maybe teach a few of these chingados a lesson. Make him pay!" Aurora looked at her. "Tu nariz—you sure it isn't broken?"

Socorro felt her nose. "I hope not."

"He'll think twice before he tries this otra vez."

"No más," Socorro said. "I'm through. He won't get another chance—never."

Aurora looked at her so long Socorro wondered if she'd ever turn back to the road. She finally did, straightening the car. "But what will you do?" Aurora asked—Aurora who always had an answer for anything and courage enough to even bleach her hair despite anything the Carmelas viejas might say.

Socorro felt a chill, for she had no idea but to say, "I'll get a job."

"What can you do, honey?" Aurora asked.

Aurora left her in front of St. John's next to Norwalk Square. "I'm going shopping," Aurora said. "I'll be in Penney's. Walk over when you're through talking with God. We'll get a strawberry sundae and get you thinking straight."

Scororro skirted the church and went into the rectory. A secretary ushered her into Father Gomez's study. It was a small room, lined with books, Christ hanging everywhere. Father Gomez was assistant pastor at St. John's—there only because of the barrios in Norwalk that required a Spanish-speaking priest—and the only priest she'd every really been comfortable with.

From the day of his first Mass, she'd been struck by his gentleness. Only later did she recognize the strength behind his soft words and easy smile. Over time, he'd proven himself the friend of barrio people, speaking for them in their schools, at city hall. She trusted him to understand her.

"Like all priests, he's got no cojones" is what Cesar said of him, after she'd come home late from volunteering at church, which she'd never done before Father Gomez came.

"Estas seloso," she'd countered, "of his fineness."

"Jealous," Cesar said sarcastically. "He is a woman—which is why I don't care if you play with him."

When Father Gomez entered the study, she saw his pale face drain of its little color as he took in her face. "Que te pasaste?"

"Mi esposo."

"Porque hizo Cesar esta obscenidad?"

"Why?" she asked, surprised. "He was drunk."

"He must be sorry to have hurt you."

"He's in jail, Father."

Father Gomez paused. "Do you need a doctor?"

She shook her head. Then in a rush, she said, "I'm leaving him. I will live like this no more."

"Calma te, Socorro."

"I am calm. I need only one thing."

His eyebrows rose.

"A job, Father. Let me work at the church. I will do anything."

"You work with us now."

"For pay, Father. I will need money."

"Why do you think we have volunteers? There's no money to pay for anything."

She said nothing.

"Your marriage is forever," he said after a heavy silence.

"I said nothing about a divorce," she whispered, the very word more shocking in this tiny room.

"A woman without a man—"

"Better than a dead woman," she said and bared her bruised neck.

"Your children," he said, ignoring her neck, her fear, and, to her sorrow, she saw him planting his feet, standing strong as she'd admired, but on the wrong side of the line she'd drawn. "What will people say? In Carmelas?" he asked.

"They will no longer say that it is all right for a man to beat his wife."

"But what will they see?" Father Gomez demanded, anger creeping into his voice.

She shook her head as if to clear it. None of this was right.

"A family without a father," he said, answering his own question.

And she saw suddenly that Cesar had been wrong; Father Gomez had cojones after all and like all men could not see beyond them. Father Gomez said, "What would this world be if all women walked away?"

She felt despair and something close to defeat.

"Anger is a terrible thing," he said finally, his voice softening. "But a woman obeys her husband. She accepts—he is your husband. For better or worse—your vows." When she said nothing, he held out a carrot. "I'll speak to Cesar."

Socorro still said nothing.

"I'll speak to your neighbors. We will not allow this to happen again."

But even if Cesar would not hurt her like this again, she saw an endless line of smaller hurts, insults that would go on, secrets tolerated as part of life. Her life. The thought of such a life turned her stomach; she rose, left the room and walked out into the sun.

"Socorro." She heard her name called, felt her shoulder touched, turned. Father Gomez, looking miserable, said, "Lo siento—I will talk to Father MacGregor to see if we could find some little work to see you through until you come to your senses. We will talk to him—Cesar is a reasonable man."

"No," she said and wondered where the no came from, for she felt defeated.

"No?" Father Gomez asked, surprised. "Think on this. Go into the church. Pray for wisdom. Think of your mother—her shame. Think of Carmelas."

"Carmelas?" she asked. "What has the barrio to do—"

"The only thing it has is its families. The only strength is that no one is alone. If you do this, what might you be beginning?"

"And if I stay?"

"You will be an example."

She laughed to keep from crying over the example she would be—especially to her children. She turned and walked away. She didn't go looking for Aurora in Penney's. She wanted time alone to think. The four miles home—a straight path up Rosecrans—would be a journey with time for that. She slipped off her flats, hearing in her head her mother say what she'd said a thousand times, "Damas—real ladies, mija—don't walk down the street with naked feet." So be it.

Shoes in hand and barefoot, she began to walk. She saw again her Juan Pablo's eyes, as he hung from his father's neck—Lydia's, too, as she cowered in her bedroom doorway with Junior pressed against her, his four-year-old face an open-mouthed horror—all their eyes filled with fear, and she felt a cry rise in her own throat, for she was terrified, terrified of being alone, unsure she could be anything but what she was.

And yet, compared to the fear naked in her children's faces—who could learn of love only from what they saw—*her* fear was nothing. She felt her rebellion surge anew.

"People will whisper, mija," her mother had warned this morning when Socorro had taken Lydia and Junior to the house in which her mother had never been afraid. "Behind your back, but always so you can hear. La divorciada, la divorciada. Your life will be yours alone."

And Socorro Collado, trudging through July sun back towards Carmelas, vowed to make that enough.

Chapter 13

Desertions ~ 1965

"Dickie!" Mona's hand hit the table hard. "Dickie. What's wrong?"

He gripped the table so hard it began to shake. He had the sense, for a moment, of not knowing where he was—feeling like he'd been fighting, struck in the head, left reeling. He looked down at his hands, rough brown slabs, clenching the table so hard the knuckles of his fingers paled of brown. He shook his head to clear it, the booze dancing crazily with her news.

"Are you drunk?" his wife asked, her voice shrill and loud.

He nodded his head. He was drunk, but this reaction—the wave of memory that cut his heart—wasn't from the booze. It was the news that flooded Dickie's unsuspecting soul with a glimpse of what wants might really lie within him.

Mona's words had done this. She was good with using them as weapons. She could throw words like Dickie had once used a knife. These words had not been like that. He'd stayed out much later tonight than ever before—in fact, he'd contemplated for the first time just staying put where he'd been, seeing it through to morning. He hadn't been able to, after all. So he'd come home, hoping to find Mona already long asleep, but she'd been standing in the kitchen, by the stove, sipping coffee from her favorite mug. Still feeling the booze in his legs, he'd sat at the kitchen table, watching Mona's face, waiting for the battle that might cleanse.

Instead, without even looking at him, she'd simply said, "Chata closed the Mexican store today for good," the words striking him a blow like none other ever received. "No warnings," she said, "nada—she just closed up shop."

Mona's voice was distant—he awash in images, sights, smells—the textures of Chata's Mexican store swirling behind his eyes. Amid it all, he saw Chata propped behind her counter, her tiny nose lifted in scorn, her unpainted lips, full as the rest of her, curled. "Productos Mexicanos," he could hear her saying, correcting him when he called it the Mexican store—though she never did the gringo kids who'd begun coming for her candy—and, wanting to understand her insistence, he saw himself a boy, saying, "Pero, Señora Chata, el signo outside—" and she had pulled him by his arm outside, Rosecrans humming traffic behind them, and pointed upward at the sign, painted long before Dickie had ever been born, in white that had seen brighter days. "Productos Mexicanos," she said, but Dickie could remember looking up and seeing only the few remaining letters—**Prod tos Mex can s**—and saying, "Señora, hay letras lost." He could still hear her reply. "So? Use your imagination."

"Are you crying?" Mona's words stilled the rush of images and memory, bringing him back to his stark kitchen.

He could feel the water at his eyes, its spill—the traces moving down his cheeks. He glanced across at Mona, who seemed to be backing toward the sink, her face strange at what she must have seen in his trembling, his tears. Had she ever seen him cry?

Then, whatever had chased her anger away was gone, the anger back, her eyes running from fear to more comfortable fury. "I'm fed up, Dickie." Her voice began to rise. "You out running around. When do I get a Saturday, Dickie? Where the hell *are* you Saturday nights, Dickie? I know you don't drink at

Henry's anymore! So where the hell are you?" She gave him no chance to answer. "I sit home. Me and the kids. You know how many damned kids you got, Dickie?"

He nodded, sinking lower onto the chair, one hand freeing itself from the table and wiping his eye.

"*Your* mama came for dinner—I told you this morning, she was coming from next door for dinner. I sit here all night and listen to that old lady go on and on about Chata's Mexican store closing as if you Collados were really Carmelas people . . ." She sighed. "I look at her and I see me, Dickie."

He pushed up from the table and shivered when he saw her stiffen and crouch back, her hands closing into fists, preparing. His size cast shadows across the small kitchen, but he only wanted air. When he was at the front door, Mona's courage returned. "Where are you going now? It's after three in the morning."

"Air." The moon was up, but clouds were thick and their movement across the sky made him dizzier. He lowered his eyes to the street, Carmenita Road, black and empty in the night. Beyond the pavement, a field lost itself in darkness. As a boy, Dickie could escape into the field. Now there was a fence. Wire. Surely barbed—escape so much harder now. He heard the screen door open behind him.

"Come to bed," Mona said softly from the doorway, her fight put away for now.

"You don't remember?" he asked his wife.

"Remember what?"

"The Mexican store."

"Of course I remember, mi abuelito was Arnulfo Carmelas, from the beginning my people were here. You and your mama—like you're the only ones with memory." She ran out of steam. More softly, she said, "It's been there forever. But who goes anymore—couldn't find anything on the shelves. That's why Chata closed it down. Remember her canned goods?"

In memory, he saw them. Latas—rows and rows of canned goods—half of them naked of labels. He remembered once trying to find the sardines Mama wanted for Papi's breakfast. "Más bajo, jovencito," he could hear Chata instructing from her perch behind her long counter. "No puedes see? Las latas square ones—con la llave en el lado?" Dickie saw the square skinny can with the key at the side to pull back the lid. He could see himself carrying it to her and asking, "Como sabe, Chata, que it holds?" She took his coin, bit it, and, laughing, said, "Ni un centavo if what I say no está inside."

"She knew what every can held," he said to Mona years later, as he sat on their wooden steps at the edge of a cliff over which they could fall.

"But who wants cans without labels these days? It's closed—" she said as if finishing it—"and what the hell does Chata closing the store have to do with you never home—"

"Everything," Dickie said softly, feeling close to something important. He heard the screen open and close as she stepped onto the porch. He felt her body lower, press against his as she sat on the steps. He heard a match struck, saw fire out of the corner of his eye, and smelled smoke. He laughed. "Remember Chata's chocolate cigarettes?" He watched her face in profile, exhaling only when he saw her face soften, the lips move toward smile.

She nodded. "Those you could eat." She held up her cigarette. "These keep me from eating."

Dickie looked at her face. She was resting her chin in the palm of one hand, her elbow resting on her knee. Exhaled smoke swirled in a funnel skyward. Her skin was very dark, but lighter than the night, creating a profile etched, sharp, beautiful, her neck softening under her jutting chin. "I like you with meat," he said.

"How would you know—one way or the other?"

"I'm sorry," Dickie whispered, knowing how dangerously full his words were.

She looked back into his eyes; he knew she'd heard his despair.

She pursued it and asked, "What's wrong?," the fight gone from her lovely eyes, fear in its place.

All Dickie could say was, "My mother used to make me leche quemada."

Both were struck silent by the oddness of the remark. He remembered how his mama would make leche quemada every Friday night when he'd been little, the last of a long line of the most handsome brothers Carmelas had ever seen—for what good it had ever done any of them. He'd always been his mama's prize and every Friday she'd make leche quemada because he wanted it and she'd shape the candy into cows like the ones his papi milked at the dairy or roosters that were spitting images of Carmelas's famous fighting cock El Bobo Bruto. In his head, he could hear his mama saying, "But ours, mijo," as she popped a golden brown rooster, soft as fudge, into the mouth of the boy he'd been, "we eat!" Unlike El Bobo Bruto—who'd seemed invincible then—his mama's candy roosters melted in his mouth, drowning him in sweetness that lasted long after they had disappeared, long after leche quemada had become old-fashioned and deserted.

That thought fell out of time but dropped him back hard on his wooden porch.

"Leche quemada," Mona, beside him, said. She looked him straight in the eye and asked, "If I make you leche quemada, hombre, will you touch me again?" She held his eyes.

The blackness in her eyes invited confession, but he said only, "She'd shape them into animals. Roosters. El Bobo Bruto."

Mona's eyes drained of expectation, and she turned back to the empty street, scanning the horizon across Carmenita. "I'm still waiting for that goddamned bird to come back out of time." She extended a bare foot, pulling up her robe and showing a scar, puckered skin lighter than the rest. "Got me coming out of Lupe's house over on Pontlavoy. I must have been ten. I haven't been able to get near a live chicken since."

"Rooster," Dickie corrected.

She was silent for a space. "Too sweet for my taste. Leche quemada. Always was. I preferred those candies—the orange ones shaped like peanuts."

"Chata's gringo candies," he said, realization dawning. "You deserted, too."

"Did I?"

"The Mexican dulces for Chata's penny candies she loaded up on when the Mexican store first began to—"

"—fade," she said sadly, nodding.

"That counter," he said, "longer than any I ever saw."

"Covered," she said, "in candies. Stuff of dreams, hombre."

"Tootsie Rolls," he said, his voice rising. "Ay! Those paper straws—"

"Striped," she said, turning toward him, her voice warming, "ties at both ends—"

"Filled with that sugary powder shit—took the pinche breath away," he said.

She hit his shoulder playfully. "What about the sour balls, amor, so big—one almost choked me once." She laughed. "God, I can feel the sourness on my tongue." She shouted. "I can smell it, now."

"A pinche trail of sweetness," he said.

She put her arm around him and leaned her mouth to his ear. "Mi vato loco Dickie—a poet. Imagine!"

He laughed, finding her arm around him comforting. "Brought all the gringo kids—that candy."

"For a while," she said softly, "most of 'em too chickenshit to walk through this barrio—like we were going to beat their paddy asses."

"Like you never did, mija?"

She leaned her head against his shoulder. "I could fight."

"Could? What you mean 'could,' chica?"

"I'm sick of fighting, Dickie." She pulled away from him.

"Age," he said, "hurts too much when we get old—"

"Don't talk about getting old." She paused and then asked, "Remember the chocolate Chata used to sell—for hot chocolate?" He heard the youth spilling from her words."The real Mexican stuff—the stuff that came in cakes?"

"Ten to a pack," he said, enthusiasm catching, "each wrapped like a coin. You'd take it apart and dump it into hot milk and stir—"

"Not with a spoon, at least in my house. Mama used one of those wooden sticks, what the hell were they called—"

"I've forgotten," he said, adding it to a list only getting longer.

"Until it would foam," she said wistfully. "God, I haven't seen that stuff in years."

"Chata stopped selling it," he said.

"I wanted Nestle's Quick," she said quietly.

"Me, too," Dickie said. "And I badgered my mama until—"

"She bought it—at the Mayfair," she said, finishing his thought.

"The Mayfair grocery store sure as hell never smelled like Chata's Mexican store."

"No." Mona tossed her cigarette. He swore her words were wrapped in the scent of red chiles that used to hang from the ceiling of the Mexican store in clusters, spilling on him.

"When I was little," she said, "just stepping inside Chata's made my nose dance. I'd almost forgotten the smells. Alive, Dickie—like a garden almost—even with all the dust, the must, the cobwebs everywhere."

Dickie moved closer to her face. "A tangy smell is what I remember—the chiles—"

"My god," Mona said, "she had a forest hanging from the ceiling—some of those pinche chiles as big as bananas."

"Touched the air inside with fire," he said, the smell heavy now on the porch.

"Dickie," Mona said, longing so heavy it competed with the

remembered scent of chiles, "is that why Chata's shutting down the Mexican store makes you cry?"

He said nothing. She pushed herself up from the steps and went to the screen door, opening it. In the doorway, she said, "That *is* why, you know."

He looked up at her in the darkness of the porch and her white chenille bathrobe made her dark face disappear in the night save for a sparkling where her eyes were. He said, "I don't get you," and it was the truth.

"Gringo candies instead of tu mama's leche quemada? Nestle's Quick en vez de Mexican chocolate? Mayfair Market instead of the Mexican store. A string of desertions long enough to make you cry. What other desertions tienes tu in store?" She stepped inside.

Dickie stared at the door long after it closed. Then, he turned back to Carmenita Road, as dark in the night as Mona. He lowered his head to his knees and wrapped his arms about his face, the flannel of his shirtsleeves soft and leaking scent, a perfume too quiet to have been Mona's, too pale to have ever been sold from Chata's dusty shelves.

Chapter 14

Price Tags - 1966

"Mr. Archuleta!" Sammy's head snapped up in attention. "You do understand English—don't you?" the English teacher demanded.

Sammy felt all eyes in the class upon him—the only brown face in the room— as he stared into the steely fixed gaze of Mr. Tucker, his English teacher. He tried to hold his teacher's stare, swearing he wouldn't lower his eyes even as he looked down at his desk top. "I didn't hear the question."

"No," Mr. Tucker said.

The silence after caused Sammy to raise his head.

"You have to be awake to hear questions asked. We sleep at home—"

"I wasn't sleeping."

"You have a talent for simulation, then, Archuleta, for you fooled me."

Sammy could only watch the thin, black-suited man pace back and forth, a stack of papers in his arms to be returned, and think of an undertaker preparing a burial.

"Then, answer my question."

"Your question? I missed it, remember?" Sammy said, hearing the edge in his voice.

"What is Maggie's problem with Brick?"

"She's a cat, Mr. Tucker—dancing on a hot, hot roof—wanting only hard relief."

A guy Sammy didn't know snickered on the far side of the room.

"And Brick?" Mr. Tucker demanded, his voice going louder.

Sarcastically, Sammy said, "He ain't the brick he used to be—he's lost his hard edge."

The entire class laughed and Sammy eased back in his chair as he saw red creeping up from Mr. Tucker's tightly bound collar. "That, class," he said looking at the clock, "would require development for which we are today, out of time," and ended discussion. He moved up and down the rows, passing out papers. "This first paper was a grand disappointment." He passed near Sammy's desk and tossed him his paper.

Sammy sat frozen, looking down at his paper, the F huge and red, scrawled across the whole first page. When he could move, he pushed himself up to go.

"Archuleta, I'd like a few words with you," Mr. Tucker said as he sat at a teacher's table at the front of the room. Sammy went to him. The man said nothing until they were alone, the table wide between them. "I like to be honest with students." Sammy averted his eyes."When I talk to you, look at me." Sammy looked up. "I have serious doubts about your ability to finish this course. This paper is a mess."

"It's the first paper—"

"I don't believe in setting students up for failure. It's the first paper, but I can already see there are too many problems—"

"You said all the papers were bad."

"Yours," Mr. Tucker said, ignoring the interruption, "has fundamental problems I can't take the time to deal with. It wouldn't be fair . . . to the others. I won't take the time."

Sammy felt his earlier anger returning, preferring it to numbness. "I've done well in English classes before—"

"This isn't high school." He took the paper hanging from Sammy's hand and set it on the table, his bony forefinger stabbing the page. "Look at the English. You're code switching. You're using half English, half Spanish."

"I was showing you how Carmelas people talk—"

"That wasn't the assignment—"

"Your assignment," Sammy argued, "was to find someone in the world whose behavior is like Camus's doctor quarantined in that plague city—somebody who keeps plugging away, keeps going when there's no point at all. That's what I was showing you with Remi, my neighbor who does the same thing, wanting the world when he can't get much beyond his room or the barrio we live in—"

"Where do you prepare me for that in your thesis?" His voice was rising. "This is just a story that whirls off the page—spinning here, there, connected to nothing—dragging me along, no rhyme, no reason. You don't know what a period is. What's all this talk about blood—"

"Remi—he's a bleeder."

"A hemophiliac? Then why don't you say so—you want your reader guessing? This isn't a creative writing class." He tossed the paper across the table. "I don't have time for this." He stood up stiffly. "I didn't start doing this yesterday. I know work that can be salvaged." Sammy picked up his paper and went to the door. "I know it might seem harsh, but a review of the basics can't hurt. Maybe it's just interference—from Spanish, I mean."

Sammy turned at the door and stared into Tucker's eyes. "I don't speak Spanish for shit!"

Sammy had gone home after his encounter with Tucker even though he had a history class later in the day. No one was home, his auntie at work, Arturo, too, at his new job at the dairy, and the house was small and oppressive. He decided to go out into the sun, not into the front yard, but out back. On his way through the kitchen, he thought of all the beer his brother Arturo had bought yesterday to celebrate his new job at the dairy, and Sammy wanted some if any was left. He opened the fridge and found three remaining bottles of beer at the back behind the milk. From the way Arturo had come home last night from Julio's across the street, Sammy knew he wouldn't be able to remember how many had been left anyway, so he took one. He popped off the cap and after pulling a paper bag out from under the sink—his tía saved every goddamn bag she ever got—he placed the bottle inside, gripping it at the neck. Outside, he sat in the sun on the steps facing his backyard where he could drink in peace away from anyone's watching eyes. In Carmelas, their barrio of four little streets, the only world that mattered was out front in the yards facing the blacktopped streets. Carmelas people lived their public lives in the front yardas where there were no secrets. In the backyard where he sat on his flimsy two-stepped stoop, there were just the chickens pecking in the dirt. Out front, Señora Rosaura would be sweeping and watching, having nothing better to do than snoop into his business. That was the only reason his aunt Carmen had taken her job at Metropolitan State Hospital—a step up from doing dishes at Burke's Coffee Shop—she'd known Sammy wouldn't really be alone because Señora Rosaura or some other chismeada in Carmelas would keep him in line. He couldn't get away with anything, what with his auntie's watchdogs trusted to keep an eye and to announce—*loudly*—his slightest transgression.

Today he just wanted to be alone in the warm October sun, still summery. He breathed deeply, pulling in air that carried the hint of cows and soothed him. He lifted the paper bag and drank deeply from the bottle inside. Then, he closed his eyes and tried to figure out what had happened—and not just with Tucker this morning, though it was the capper. College just wasn't like high school. He was so alone at Cerritos. Hardly anyone he knew had gone on, and those who did had schedules that didn't match his. No one from Carmelas had gone on to school—except Remi, and he'd already dropped out because of a fall on the stairs three days after school started. Remi. Why had he ever chosen him to write that paper about—but Remi was just like Camus's asshole doctor, couldn't see the ocean for the goddamned sand and still dreaming about walking to the other side. Remi would never finish college—who was he kidding? He never stopped talking about Las Vegas like it was some goddamned Oz, and both of them knew he'd never see it, anymore than he'd ever ride the Cyclone Racer at the Long Beach Pike, and yet the fool kept on planning, trying, dreaming, and sucking Sammy in as he had forever, planting himself in Sammy's brain waiting to leap even into a fucking English composition he had no place in. How could Sammy explain Remi to anybody else when Sammy hadn't even figured him out? No wonder fucker Tucker didn't know what in hell Sammy was talking about. Tucker didn't even remember that Remi had sat in his class for the first three days of the semester asking so many fucking questions Sammy didn't see how anybody could have forgotten he'd been there, way at the back by the door so he could leave early to miss the rush on the stairs. But it had happened anyway—for all the planning, Remi had still been caught on the stairs, a snail lost in a rush of stampeding buffalo—and the asshole was still talking about trying again next semester. Now, if that wasn't *just* like Camus's silly-ass doctor, Sammy didn't know what was.

When Remi was gone, there'd been no one else. The worst part was having to eat lunch alone, and making any connections was hard. He was a fish out of water. The cliché made him wonder if maybe Tucker was right.

Like a Mexican out of Carmelas.

Now that was more like it—fresher and still true—which was

probably why nobody from Carmelas ever landed very far away. Maybe college wasn't for him either. He could go to work. Chuy's father worked at Ford over in Pico Rivera and when he'd gotten Chuy a job, he'd told Sammy he could do the same for him. Why not? He'd have done it for Arturo, too, except his prison record and tattoos fucked that up. So why not just go see Big Chuy and to hell with all the college crap?

A shadow moved before his closed eyes, and, opening them, he saw not a cloud moving before the face of the sun, but Remi—the most able of his aunt's watchdogs—standing before him now, more unwanted than ever and blocking the sunlight. Remi was standing because he couldn't manage the sitting what with his bad knee. Not that Sammy was in any mood to be inviting him to sit.

Remedios Camisa lived next door. He was probably standing here now because his bedroom window looked out into Sammy's grassless backyard, a fact Sammy shouldn't have overlooked, for Remi spent more time at that window than anywhere else since he'd been in bed so much of his life. And when in bed, he was always propped up so he could look out. "So what do you want?" Sammy asked, making clear he didn't want any company.

"Why are you home? I saw you sitting here. Something's wrong. I know you got a class now. History with Singer."

"Fuck Singer," Sammy said, irritation rising at the thought that Remi knew Sammy's schedule probably better than he did himself; the irritation now seemed to point his anger in Remi's direction, and he felt better with a target in sight.

Remi sighed, censorship in motion.

To which Sammy said, "Fuck Cerritos. Fuck college. Fuck you, too," feeling like he was flinging stones at Remi.

"Something's wrong. You never talk like this."

"What do you know about me—but what I choose to show you?" Sammy asked, his voice louder.

"I know you. I know you're smart enough not to have to resort to gutter talk. I know you value school."

Sammy lifted the brown-bagged beer bottle to his mouth and drank. Lowering it, he said, "Get out of my chinga hair," and he was surprised at the sudden rush of anger, the desire to punch Remi's round yellow face intruding forever into Sammy's life—unasked. But people couldn't go around punching Remi. He'd learned that long ago, having heard—from everyone and Remi's mother—that Remi bleeds and bleeds and can hardly stop once started. But today, he allowed himself to imagine punching Remi's nose—low in the bridge, flaring at the nostrils, a bird's beak—and blood flying, an endless river of blood that would turn the dirt in the yard to red mud.

How in hell could Remi know anything about school—real school? He'd never gotten through a single year of school in his life and wouldn't have had any education at all if it hadn't been for the string of home teachers provided by the school district every time a bleeding forced him out of school and home again. Shit, Remi wouldn't have had any idea about the world at all if it hadn't been for his books and for Sammy, who Remi had chosen—without asking—long ago to be his bridge to a world too dangerous to navigate on his own, and today, Sammy was tired of it all, especially Remi waiting on his porch or at his goddamned window like a vulture—every day—for Sammy to come home after school in order to suck him dry by prying real school—real life—vicariously out of him. And it had only gotten worse when high school had finally ended, for the home teachers ended, too, and Remi was left adrift, more dependent than ever on Sammy until he'd fallen—three stairs—crashing to his knees, slide rule mangled with his knees. Two months later, he was just getting out of bed.

Sammy felt his anger falter as he remembered the horrible rush of relief that had filled his heart after he'd realized the accident had freed him from a responsibility he'd never wanted but had gotten when Remi had registered for every class Sammy had signed up for at college.

"So we can ride together—every day!" had been Remi's jubilant explanation when Sammy had demanded to know why Remi was in all his classes except P.E.

But Sammy didn't want to think of Remi's loss or his own relief. He wanted the release of the anger that had been pumping through him moments before.

"Am I bothering you, Sammy?"

"Yeah, Remi. You're bothering me."

"I'm sorry."

Guilt rushed back in waves. "Oh shit. Don't be sorry, Remi. Just be gone."

Remi started to turn away, but stopped. "That beer in the bag?"

"Yeah," Sammy said, holding the bag up. "Want some?" he asked, taunting him.

Remi glanced quickly toward his house and then back. He nodded. His hand closed around the proffered bag and he brought it to his mouth. He drank and grimaced. "Awful stuff," he said, passing it back.

"Why drink it then?"

"So you won't drink it all."

Sammy brought the bottle to his mouth and gulped down the beer.

"You'll fall, Sammy. Lips that touch—"

"Go home, Remi."

"Look at Arturo—no offense, but isn't beer what got your brother started?"

Sammy drank again from the bottle. Then he rose.

"Where you going?" Remi asked.

Wanting to sting Remi by reminding him of everything he

couldn't do in life, Sammy said, "I'm going to the Pike," and he would have said Las Vegas—Remi's most burning desire—but he knew that was too far away to be believed, so he'd chosen Remi's second dream, just as impossible. "I'm going to ride the Cyclone Racer until I'm screamed out," he said, choosing the very ride Remi could never take but had dreamed of since Sammy had told him of his first wild ride.

"Take me," Remi said in a rush and looked back nervously toward his house.

"Yeah, sure," Sammy said, jumping up and going into the house, grabbing the keys to the old VW Bug Arturo had acquired on his way home from prison and been letting Sammy use ever since, so long as he was going to school and not fucking up. He stepped through the little hall into the tiny bathroom, telling himself Remi deserved even worse than Sammy was giving him. He took a leak and then combed his thick hair, admiring the way it fell over his collar. He pulled black curls back, wondering how long before he could tie it back into a pony tail—feeling anger bubble again at the thought of the ration of shit he'd be getting for that from his aunt, Mr. Trujillo, and even Arturo—who had no right to ride anybody's ass about anything after his track record. It was his fucking hair. He spun from the mirror and ran through the living room outside. He was inside Arturo's Bug before he noticed Remi already sitting in the passenger seat, staring straight ahead.

"Get out."

"I'm going with you."

"You want me to pull you out?"

"You want me to tell your tía that you were drinking beer and cutting school?"

Sammy stared at Remi's face. "I was kidding—about the Cyclone Racer."

"I wasn't—about telling," Remi said, staring back. "Tu auntie told my mama if she caught you drinking beer one more time she'd have Arturo take back the Bug."

"You wouldn't."

Remi held his hand over his heart. "I would."

"You'll get hurt. What about your knees?"

Remi shrugged and then said, "They get hurt anyway." He turned his head away and looked out the window toward his house. "All I ever wanted to do was go to school, go to Vegas, and ride the Cyclone Racer. School's a wash. Vegas might as well be across the world. That leaves the Cyclone Racer." He turned back to Sammy. "One out of three would be something. I've been so blue, Sammy, and it was like destiny me coming over when I saw you sitting on the stoop where you shouldn't have been and you up and mentioning the Pike—it was like God whispering in my ear, 'Do it, do it!'"

"Your ma—"

"She thinks we're going to the library."

"You'd really fink on me?" Sammy asked, starting up the car.

Remi smiled. "Only for something worthwhile. Drive."

Sammy shifted into reverse, but before popping his clutch he looked at Remi. As always, he was wearing his suit—a Mexican from Carmelas going to the Pike in Long Beach to finally ride the Cyclone Racer for the first time in his life in a black suit with a goddamned white cotton shirt buttoned all the way to the top. No tie. "You forgot your tie."

"I thought casual would be more fitting."

They stood at the foot of the Cyclone Racer, both staring up, heads bent far back, eyes scanning the enormous white skeleton that seemed to hang precariously at the edge of the harbor. The pile of peeling lumber appeared too fragile to hold up the string of peaks and valleys that cut the brilliant October sky.

Sammy Archuleta felt the wind rushing off the water slice

across his face, through his hair, stinging his eyes. He felt fear roll in his stomach and he was amazed, for he'd ridden the roller coaster a hundred times. More. His eyes moved from the Cyclone Racer to the sky where wind was chasing billowing white clouds across the heavens at dizzying speed. He dug his hands deeper into his Levi's pockets, wondering if this would be the day the tired mountain of wood would finally fall. He lowered his eyes and looked at Remi standing beside him. He saw the mouth hanging open, the eyes so wide and round the whites made circles around the black irises. Looking back at the towering frame of the roller coaster, he saw the tiny line of cars making the first ascent—the only one that really mattered, so steep, so slow the rise. His eyes narrowed and he saw there were no people, the cars all empty; it was a weekday and early to boot. He heard the intake of Remi's breath—sharp—as the first car reached the top. Sammy's heart began to race as he watched the first car edge over, seeming to hang for a terrible moment in the air before falling, swift and fast, into the abyss. He turned and looked at Remi's staring eyes and felt like he was looking through them, amazed that something old and familiar could become new again when seen through another's virgin eyes.

The slow clack of the ascending roller coaster cars had been replaced by the crashing clang of the descent, distant, jarring in the stillness all around them, and the sound pulled Sammy's gaze back to the roller coaster. The beer he'd drunk this morning was no longer warm in his belly or his head. The humiliation that had fueled the need for the beer seemed distant, too, and his anger at Remi had flown, so that he wondered now how to talk Remi out of riding the roller coaster. As he watched the cars careen over the rickety track, he felt fear he'd never felt and said, "You don't have to do this."

"I want to," Remi said and began to move forward toward the entrance to the ride. Sammy saw Remi's dark hair, thin, fine and delicate as a girl's, standing in the wind. Sammy stood still for a moment just watching Remi move. Penguins came to mind. And it wasn't just because of the black suit and the crisp white shirt. At eighteen, Remi was what he would be. A barrel of a man. He should have been tall, but his legs had been stunted, his knees twisted out of shape by countless bleedings that explained the slowness of his movements, the stagger in his step, and the unnatural shortness of his legs.

Sammy watched Remi slide the dollar bill through the barred window of the Cyclone Racer's ticket cage. He saw the bruise, dark and purple, that spread from Remi's knuckles across the top of his entire hand before it lost itself beneath the cuff of his jacket sleeve and suddenly thought of Remi's mother who trusted Sammy and had told him so forever. "What if you get hurt?" he asked in a rush.

But Remi didn't answer and moved through the revolving turnstile.

They were alone in the cars. Sammy had wanted to ride a car in the middle of the line, but Remi had chosen the first car, normally Sammy's favorite position. Sammy climbed in first while Remi took his time getting in, having to lift his own right leg into the narrow car, his knee still stiffer than usual from the fall he'd taken in September. The lap bar stood in the air in front of them. Sammy closed his fingers on the handgrip and pulled it down, hands shaking. A skinny gringo appeared out of nowhere to check the guard and lock it in place. Remi's hands clamped on the handrail; he stared straight ahead.

"Thank you, Sammy," he said softly. "I will remember this forever."

The car lurched, throwing them back hard against the seat, jarring them as it began to move. Instead of looking ahead, Sammy could not take his eyes off the bruise marring Remi's hand. What were they doing? Fine time to be asking, was all

Sammy could think as he lifted his eyes from the hemophiliac beside him to the ascent.

The incline got steeper, the clacking wheels grew louder, and the blue sky full of whipped-cream clouds filled the horizon, the only thing visible save for the line of track climbing up beyond them toward a point where all track seemed to disappear. The muscles in Sammy's neck grew taut as he struggled to keep his head forward. Tension built, pressure climbed as the car struggled up toward the summit. He felt ready to explode.

"Ahhhhhhhhhh!" Remi screamed in triumph, hands held high above his head as they arrived at the top of the first ascent in imitation of the way Sammy had told him men with huevos rode roller coasters. "Hold on!" Sammy yelled as the car balanced at the edge of the world, forgetting his own huevos bunching as they climbed in his pants seeking protection, for he was thinking only of all the blood Remi could spill. The ocean invisible in the ascent filled his eyes, extending to the horizon where it became sky. Then, they fell, the descent so sharp, so steep that it seemed no car could cling to the tracks. Sammy's stomach rose to his throat as his ass lifted from the seat under him, his entire body flying forward, all his strength rising to push back against the fall. The ocean rushed up at him, his head bobbing wildly. He looked sideways at Remi and saw his head banging back and forth, looking just like one of those bouncing heads on a stick gringos put in the back windows of their cars.

Hitting bottom, the car careened back up toward heaven, moving faster in this climb, which was neither as steep nor as terrifying as the first. At the next summit, the car did not fall, but careened instead sideways, spinning around a curve. Sammy's body, thrown toward the right, slammed against Remi, whose body slammed against the metal side of the tiny car. Sammy heard a thudding bang and, looking down saw Remi's knee, swollen and huge under his dark slacks, slapping against the bar that held them in.

Racing, the car careened along a track that darted to the right, then the left, making hairpin turns that seemed so sharp no car could make them. A straight piece of track had them hurling toward the ocean again, and Sammy roared as he always did just here when the car seemed ready to leap from the tracks and fly out over the sea. But at the last minute, when salvation was nowhere in sight, the track, invisible beneath them in the first car of the line, spun right and they were swirled not out to sea but back toward the shore. Sammy glanced at Remi, who was bug-eyed.

"Ayudame!!!!!!!!!!!!!!!!" Remi roared in the rushing air, screaming for help at the top of his lungs, and the fear seemed naked, Sammy's own.

"I'm falling!!!" Remi yelled, and Sammy knew they'd settled into the roller coaster's last descent. He looked at Remi and saw those eyes, so wide and round, then looked down at Remi's bad knee slapping against the hard steel of the car.

"AHHHHHHHHH!!!!!!!" Sammy roared and held his hands aloft, realizing it was too late for changing anything.

Despite the terror marring his face, Remi roared, "AHHHHHHHHHHHHHH!," too, and lifted his arms, holding his hands high, where, bruised, they danced with wind.

The afternoon sun was low in the sky as they drove over the Shoemaker Bridge. The wind was blowing still, but scent of sea was gone, replaced by the smell of cows. "Home," Sammy said as they turned left onto Firestone and drove toward Dinard, the smell of cow shit, of earth, of life growing heavier in the air whipping through the open windows of the car.

Turning right onto Mapledale, they entered Carmelas and the sinking feeling that had been so heavy in Sammy's stomach all during the wild ride at the edge of the ocean in Long Beach returned. "You all right?" Remi nodded. "I think we did something stupid," Sammy said.

"I think we did something grand," Remi said, before adding, "pal o' mine."

Remi talked like that—like people didn't, at least no one in Carmelas. He dressed like every day was First Communion, a wedding. Like no one in Carmelas—like no one in the world. At the corner, they turned onto Claresa and there was Señora Rosaura taking down her sheets.

"Cómo está, señora?" Remi called out, waving. Sammy waved, too, and the old lady left her sheets and shuffled across the street, making Sammy squirm. He turned to Remi and asked, "What if you got hurt?" as he pulled Arturo's car into Sammy's yard—right up to the wooden front steps.

Remi shrugged, saying, "I'm always getting hurt," as Señora Rosaura reached the driver's side.

"Samuelito, mijo," she said, "hay una cartita que viene para ti."

He watched her reaching deep into her apron pocket, pulling out a long envelope. She was always intercepting the mail, and she couldn't even read. "Para mi, señora?" he asked. She nodded and passed him the letter. He looked at the return—University of the Seven Seas—feeling the old woman's eyes on him. He looked up; the whites of her eyes were yellow. "It's nothing." She was already looking past him at Remi, concern filling her eyes.

"Remedios," she said, pursing her lips, "pareces palido hoy. Todavía estas enferma?"

"Si, señora," he answered. "Mi rodilla."

"La cruz de Cristo fue heavy, too, mijo," she said. He nodded solemnly. She slapped the car door, stepping back, her finger in the air. "Ten cuidado, muchacho." She glanced again at Sammy. "Y tu, mijo, pon tus ojos en your friend—always." She turned back to the street, her sheets hanging on her lines, blindingly white, daily advertisement for her homemade laundry soap that his tía said had been keeping la vieja señora in rice and beans for years.

Sammy watched her move slowly away. "Are you going to tell your mother?"

Remi shook his head no as Sammy turned back to him. Then, Remi said, "I'm no informer."

Sammy looked back at señora bent over her basket overflowing with whites. "Informers are in movies, finks overflow Carmelas."

Remi, sounding sad, said, "I wouldn't have told your aunt either—about the beer." They were silent until Remi asked, "What's the letter?"

Sammy shrugged. "Remember the week you were at school senior year when you dragged me to that talk somebody from the floating campus was giving—"

Remi's eyes went big. "You filled out those scholarship papers—"

"To shut you up."

"They turned you down—"

"I turned them down. I would've still needed a thousand dollars. You got a thousand dollars, ese?"

"Open it," Remi said, not sounding down anymore.

"Why? I wouldn't go if they gave me the boat—"

"Open it."

He did. He looked up. "They're offering me a free ride."

"Around the world?"

Sammy nodded, reading it again. "Even books. Spending money's all I'd need."

"A miracle," Remi said.

"Yeah," Sammy said, thinking it more like a joke what with him flunking out of college before he even really started. He looked at Remi. "You going to keep me in spending money?" He stuffed the letter back in the envelope and stuck it under the ratty visor. "I got auntie, Arturo, and no fucking prospects—"

"Arturo's working, acting right—"

"Callate," Sammy ordered, getting out of the car. "You never saw that letter."

Sammy didn't go to school the next day, more convinced than ever school was behind him for good, but not quite ready to tell Arturo or his auntie about his plans to go to Chuy's father for a job at Ford. He stayed in the house lying low because outside people on the block would have asked questions.

In the afternoon when he'd have been home from school anyway, he went outside and walked next door toward Remi's. Señora Rosaura was coming down the middle of Claresa, a bag in her arms, back from the long walk to the Mayfair now that Chata's Mexican store up on Rosecrans had closed down forever. "Señora," he said, "what're you walking for. I told you I'd take you to the Mayfair." He took her bag.

"How could I ask con tú so sick today, mijo?"

"I'm not sick, señora," Sammy said, sounding as polite as always, though he knew exactly what she was getting at.

"Pero—tu auto—nunca left the yarda today. You walk a la eschool?"

"Just today," he said, stumbling on the words, knowing she was on to him.

"You must leave muy temprano," she said as she passed, and he knew she'd find some way to tell his aunt.

After helping her in with her bags, he crossed the dirt yard to Remi's house. He climbed up the cement steps. Remi's house was the only one on the block with a cement porch. The railing too was white, all white, painted by his father every spring. The house was simple, frame like all the others, but there were shutters on the windows facing the street. He knocked on the screen door, probably the only one in Carmelas with the screen intact.

Remi's mother, Ruth, appeared at the door. "Sammy, cómo estás?" she asked, pushing the screen open. "Pasas, mijo."

"Remi?" Sammy asked, loving the sound of the woman's Spanish, different from Carmelas people—like Trujillo's, Texas at its edges, where they'd come from after the war and been in no more hurry to return to than a flood of other Texas Mexicans.

"In his bed. His knee. A new bleeding." She seemed preoccupied and added, "It's just so soon after we got the last finally stopped." Sammy thanked God for the deep brown of his face, for he felt heat rise that would have turned a light face red and revealed his shame at having taken Remi on the roller coaster. "Esperate," Remi's mama said, "un momento. I'll see if he sleeps."

In the now-empty living room, Sammy looked around. Pictures were hung on the brown walls. One an ocean scene. Another of Christ with a bleeding heart visible in his chest. Still another displayed a pair of hands, brown and veined, clasped in prayer. He looked away from the pictures down to the floor, the carpet there. Probably the only house in Carmelas that had carpet wall to wall, a necessity in Remi's house since when he was a baby.

"The wood might cut my Remi's skin," was what Remi's mother had told Sammy when as a little boy he'd asked in wonder why she had rugs from wall to wall like the gringos on the television.

"Then he would bleed?" Sammy had asked long ago.

She nodded.

"All over your carpet?"

"Alfombras can be replaced, mijo. Las rodillas de mi Remi are harder to fix."

Even then, his knees.

"He's awake, Sammy. Make him smile," she said when she came back. Sammy passed into the hall, marveling at the softness of Remi's mother's voice.

"Then go live with Remi," his own mother had roared on

more than one occasion before she died when he'd dared to speak of the sweetness in Remi's mother's voice, "if you cannot stand mi voz."

Stepping into Remi's room was as it had always been, like stepping into a world wrapped thick with cotton. The world beyond the open window was just Sammy's own grassless back yard. Everything in the room was soft, corners of furniture rounded, softened with cloth.

"In case I bump," Remi had explained long ago.

His friend was on his bed. His bad knee was propped, a pillow underneath. Buckets of ice were propped against his leg, the naked knee swollen large and purple. His eyes were closed, his hands folded over his chest. "Remi?" Sammy asked louder than he'd intended, holding his breath, horrified at the thought Remi was dead. Remi finally opened his eyes. "You're bleeding?"

"A little."

"How do you feel?"

"Wonderful."

"Did you tell?" Sammy asked, his voice a tight whisper.

"I never would."

"I should never have . . . ," Sammy started, awash in regret.

"I'm glad. I've done it. What I have wanted to do ever since you told me about the first time you rode it." He smiled. "I rode the Cyclone Racer. How about you? Are you feeling better?"

Sammy shrugged.

"You didn't go to school."

Sammy shook his head no. "I'm going to quit."

"Like me."

Sammy nodded.

"But I'd have never quit except for this," Remi said, touching his knee. "What could make you quit?"

"Maybe I'm bleeding, too."

"I know how that can hurt."

"I'm sorry."

"I'm not."

Sammy turned and moved to the door, wanting out of the room, out of the house.

"You know what my bleeding has given me?" Remi asked. "Not just this one—all of them?"

Sammy turned at the door and wondered what gift there could be in blood that won't stop flowing, in knees that swell into balloons and cripple walking. He lifted his eyes in question.

"Stillness. I can sink into it. Patience . . . a fine gift. Maybe your bleeding could give you enough to play a mediocre game of chess."

It was dark; there was a pounding on the front door, movement past Sammy's bedroom. He got out of bed, wearing only boxers, and opened the door to his room. He heard voices in the living room. He moved down the hall and stepped into the room, one lamp lit, and saw Remi's mother, dressed, standing just inside the door.

"What's wrong?" Sammy asked.

"Mi Remi," Remi's mother said, "his bleeding just won't stop. We're taking him to the hospital. We'll need blood, I was hoping your tía could help us like before."

"Claro que sí," Sammy's sleepy aunt said. "I'll wake Arturo and he'll carry me down in his car."

"Me, too," Sammy said.

"No es necesario, Sammy," Remi's mother said softly. "You have college in the morning."

"I want to give my blood, too."

Arturo dropped Sammy and tía off in front of Orthopedic Hospital in downtown L.A., driving off to park. The hospital waiting room was crowded—all Carmelas people, ten or twelve—neighbors all. They might have been gathered under the mulberry trees in Carmelas, voices rising loudly in camaraderie Sammy didn't need now. These people saw each other every day—all of them acting like they had something new to say to each other. The room seemed to shrink around him, stealing his air. Across the room sat Lola, head back against the wall, one delicate hand thrown across her eyes. The woman made everything into a movie. Next to her sat Mark, her oldest, but his pale arm was thrown around his new wife, Contemplación, her face in shadow, the birthmark that had always fascinated Sammy hardly visible. He'd been a little miffed that he'd been caught by as much surprise as anyone else when she and Mark de Los Rios y Valles had run off to Las Vegas to marry alone in front of some gringo justice of the peace—he'd always felt a closeness to her that he thought might have warranted her dropping some clue. Everyone had thought all Mark's attention to Luna's old shack and overgrown yard was to repay her the attention she'd poured on María Felicia when the gringo doctors had sent her home to die. Luna hadn't cured her, but Mark and Lola swore the old bruja had eased her end. All along it was Contemplación he'd been sniffing after. No one in Carmelas had been able to believe Mark would've ever chosen Contemplación to replace his María Felicia; Sammy's surprise had been that anyone in Carmelas had the sense to see what he'd always seen in tiny Contemplación. Sammy looked at her, her face in shadow, the birthmark hardly visible. She stood, the light revealing the purple palmprint darker than her skin laid over her face. She called tía's name and walked to them, embracing her as if she hadn't seen her yesterday. "Come sit with us. Lola's here." As she eased tía away, she reached out and touched Sammy's cheek. "Cómo estás?"

"Bien," he said, looking down as he said, "I'm happy para ti." He glanced up and she nodded before taking tía away. Sammy eased back to lean against a wall when Socorro Collado stepped into the room and went right to him.

"Mijo," she said, "my Juan Pablo told me tonight he and Ana Maria are getting married." She grasped his arm. "Tell me the truth. Is she pregnant?"

Sammy held up both hands. "I know nothing."

"Talk to him for me?" She moved close. "Find out what's going on." She smiled. "Come see me at the dairy tomorrow and I'll give you a box of Big Sticks for tu tía Carmen."

Sammy relaxed when someone pulled Socorro away. A box of Big Sticks—for what—to tell her she's lucky it was only Ana Maria pregnant the way her Juan Pablo was chasing everything. He wouldn't be caught dead in the dairy where Socorro had talked herself into a counter job after she'd run off her husband, Cesar, a few years ago, acting now like she owned the place. He could be home in bed. He closed his eyes and felt a hand on his arm.

"Mijo," his tía Carmen said, back again and bending close. "Señora Rosaura's feeling a little dizzy, help me."

He pushed up and took the old woman's free arm and helped her to a space cleared for her, anger rising that they'd take blood from such an old woman.

As she dropped to the sofa, she looked up at him and smiled. "Muchisimas grácias, mijo—the blood," she said, pressing a cotton ball to the bend of her arm.

"What are they taking blood from an old lady for?" he demanded of his tía.

"I insisted, mijo," Señora Rosaura said from behind closed eyes. "I made them—compensación for Remi's loss."

They were all crazy. He made his way back to a dark corner near the door and had hardly settled in when Arturo grabbed him from behind, shaking him.

"What is this, vato?"

Sam saw him holding the envelope from the floating campus. "Nothing—crap."

"I can read, ese," Arturo said, squeezing his bicep hard enough to make him squirm. "You never said nothin' about applying for this—"

"A joke, Tootie. I was just checking it out to make Remi happy—never intended—"

"Cabrón," Arturo said, sounding mean, "it says they will pay for everything—"

"I'm already in school—"

"Fuckin' Cerritos won't be there when you come back in a year?" Arturo let his arm go, pushing up the sleeves of his own shirt and baring the biggest arms in Carmelas, muscles dancing, signaling agitation, the tattoos solid from wrist to shoulder, becoming a rush of images hiding holes he'd punched with needles into his arms for years. "Oportunidades como this vienen nunca to anyone in Carmelas. Only an asshole—"

Sammy spun in his grip. "You got me pegged, hermano, I am one certified asshole."

"Don't fuck with me," Arturo threatened, his voice a growl he was trying to keep under control so others in the room—already looking—wouldn't hear.

Sammy, feeling safe for a while in the crowded waiting room, pulled back his arm hard, turned away and bumped into Mr. Trujillo just entering the waiting room.

"How are you, Sam?" He waved to his Carmelas friends already there.

Sammy's lucky night, from Arturo to Mr. Trujillo—a fixture in Carmelas, their teacher, who lived among them and had for as long as Sammy could remember, Sammy's mentor, with whom he'd conspired and saved Señora Rosaura's jacaranda when the city had paved Claresa. Sammy would rather have Arturo beating his brown ass than this red-brown hombre who brought television Indians to mind. Mr. Trujillo had retired the year before and talk in the barrio was that he was moving soon to San Diego and his boy Cruz's avocado farm. Cruz had been as badass a vato as Arturo, the two, Mr. Trujillo said, had been headed for the same jail cell, but after Arturo's last arrest, Cruz had left the barrio, ending up in San Diego growing avocados and making something of himself, just not the something Trujillo had dreamed of. At least Trujillo's more frequent visits to Cruz's farm had finally gotten the old man off Sammy's ass, but the look in Trujillo's eye now made that questionable. "I'm fine," Sammy managed to say and took the extended hand. Trujillo's fingers closed around his own and squeezed tightly. Sammy squeezed back as men were supposed to do. The man did not release his hand.

"They just told me they won't take my blood. Imagine. My pressure is too high." He lowered his face near Sammy's. "So I am especially glad to see you. Your blood will replace mine." He loosened his grip. "Science. A wonderful thing. Can you believe there is a bank of blood? We give ours, build Remi's account, giving him just what he needs, saving his father the need to pay. A wonder." Sammy extracted his hand. "You," Trujillo said, looking at him sharply, "are in college."

He looked into Trujillo's eyes, finding him the hardest man in the world to lie to. "I'm quitting," Sammy said.

Trujillo's smile disappeared. He took Sammy's arm and pushed him back out to the bank of closed elevators, his eagle's beak of a nose almost touching Sammy's. Sammy glanced back at Arturo still pinning him with his eyes in the waiting room's open door. "Why?" Trujillo asked him.

Sammy told him. Told it all, about the humiliation in front of a class of gringos, the teacher's crack about Sammy not understanding English and with him the only Mexican in the room, and the baseless comments about the paper, all leading to his decision to leave.

Trujillo listened. Then he laughed. "As well you should," he said after a long moment. "Un cobarde does not deserve an education."

"Why am I a coward?"

"Because you bend—you crawl."

"I'm simply leaving."

"You crawl away." He stood and looked down his long high nose. "The direction of one's crawl makes no difference at all." He walked to the elevators and hit the "down" button hard.

Sammy followed him to the bank of elevators. "My teacher told me I should leave—that I didn't belong."

Mr. Trujillo turned back. "No. You said he told you his was not a creative writing class, as it is not. You said he said your writing had no plan, no organization."

"He said he had no time for me. That's telling me to go."

"And like all brave men, you do exactly as you're told," Trujillo said, as the elevator doors opened. Trujillo stepped inside. "I thought you different," he said, holding open the doors.

"He thinks I can't—do it."

"You prove him right? You think any gift—your education the finest one—comes without price tags?" He stared into Sammy's eyes; Sammy refused to look away. "Do you know, mijo, your mother's maiden name?"

"Gallardo," Sammy said, not moving his eyes away.

"You know what it means in English?" Sammy said nothing. Trujillo smiled. "Gallant. Imagine, mijo." He lifted his hand from the doors and they closed.

Sammy turned to find Arturo bearing down. He barked, "You're going to answer this, ese—"

"My ass," Sammy said defiantly as another elevator opened. Arturo straight-armed him, the flat of his hand landing on Sammy's pecho. He flew backwards into the open elevator. "Your ass, mijo, I own, 'til you got the balls to reclaim it." He looked over his shoulder and stepped into the elevator, his hands reaching down and hoisting Sammy up as the elevator doors closed.

A week later, Sammy took the bus down to Remi's Orthopedic Hospital in downtown Los Angeles. He was whistling as he stepped off the elevator on Remi's floor, happy still from this morning's English class when he'd given Tucker the rewrite of the failed paper he'd done over on the weekend and even carried to Trujillo's house on Mapledale where the man had read and marked and sent him home to write again before late Sunday night giving, finally, his approval. And Tucker hadn't wanted to read it, telling him, "I told you I don't have time for this," to which Sammy had said, "Read it, and if after reading it you tell me to go, I'll go." Tucker had read and his face had shown nothing when he looked up from the paper and said, "This is acceptable." He passed the paper back, saying, "The F remains, of course, and I'm making no promises. Salvage may be possible, but I assure you I'm not a man whose positions often change." In his mind's eye, Sammy had seen the price tag dangling from Tucker's tentative gift, realizing Trujillo was right there, too. He'd wanted to tell Tucker to go fuck himself, but he hadn't. He thanked him as Trujillo had insisted he do. Then, he'd left the room and gone to admissions and dropped all his classes. He was leaving for New York in a week—the University of the Seven Seas sailing at the end of October. He was going to be on board whether he wanted to be or not—fuckin' Arturo taking Sammy's letter over to Trujillo—there was *no* winning after that. His ass, like Tootie said, more theirs than his. Well, Chuy's father's job would be waiting in Pico Rivera at Ford when he got back.

He knew there was ambivalence—how was that for a schoolboy word—excitement about the idea of going round the world like Trujillo had, but Sammy was scared shitless, too. If he was alone at Cerritos, what would life be on a boat filled with rich gringos? He'd not think about it.

Now, it was hours after his triumph over Mr. Tucker at Cerritos, his managing to save the day on his terms—well, sort of. Arturo and Trujillo were breathing over each shoulder, but he'd rewritten the paper, willing to pay whatever the price tag called for. He glided by the nurses' station, still whistling and attracting their attention, for Sammy could whistle. He breezed into Remi's room, and Remi was sitting on the edge of the bed, his gown high above his knees, the bad one still twice the size of the left.

"The bleeding?"

"Stopped," Remi said and his eyes were wide, the whites visible all the way around. "You just missed it."

"What?"

"Un milagro, amigo mio, un verdadero miracle."

"Tell me."

"Dr. Post came in here with a needle and a bottle and he shot me . . . in my hand. Not thirty minutes ago, and it stopped . . . the bleeding in my knee." He snapped his fingers. "That fast, and this time they hadn't been able to get the bleeding to stop. Even with the transfusions. But this shot did it." Remi got up and gave a shuffle that abler feet would have turned into a dance. "I'll ride it again. The Cyclone Racer."

"You'll bleed."

"And I'll shoot myself, in my hand, right here—with this new miracle," he said, extending his hand. "This vein. The doctor said whenever I bleed, wherever, I inject this—"

"What?"

"Concentrate. That's what they call it. They aren't going to need whole blood anymore. Concentrate—made, he said, from plasma pulled from hundreds of people—all mixed together, so you can't even know who the blood came from . . . just for me—people like me. Concentrate. That's what it's called. I bleed. I inject my hand with concentrate and my blood becomes like yours. It stops bleeding."

Sammy bent on one knee and ran a hand over Remi's purple swollen knee. "It still looks bad."

"That's normal for my knee. But nobody else will have to get knees like mine—not anymore. No little kid has to lie in bed, fighting the pain, trying to hold off long enough for it to stop before the trip to the doctor because the blood is so expensive. This is cheap, Sammy. Cheap. And it's going to get cheaper. And nobody's knees'll ever have to swell and ruin and cripple."

"A miracle," Sammy agreed.

"Las Vegas," Remi said, his face a beaming moon, "a place I've dreamed of going—dreamed we'd go—together. Even across the desert—he said I'll be able to carry bottles of concentrate with me in an ice chest. I will be free."

"Free." Sammy echoed Remi's cry of liberation as he saw with a chill his own fast approaching.

"What happened to your eye?" Remi asked, touching the still-swollen bruised eye.

"Arturo—I pissed him off."

"Your quitting school?"

Sammy nodded. "He changed my mind."

Remi whooped. "We'll both be able to finish school."

"Ride roller coasters," Sammy said, laughing.

"Without any price to pay, " Remi said and clasped Sammy to his chest in an abrazo that Remi said was like his abuelito told him men in Mexico give one another.

Sammy let himself be held, deciding he'd wait to tell Remi about switching schools—enough miracles for one day, but he crossed his fingers behind his back, feeling fear somewhere deep in his soul that had nothing to do with his being forced out of Carmelas—this had to do with Trujillo's warning that night in the hospital elevator not to ever forget about price tags clinging to any gift. Wrapped now in his friend's joy, he pushed his fear out of sight, hoping that miracles, magic and divine, might prove exceptions.

Chapter 15

Taking Count ~ 1970

Mickey Escalante pulled into the parking lot of the Norwalk Dairy. He parked his '67 Ford LTD out of sight of the large glass front windows. Walking around the front of the dairy, he saw no Blanca behind the counter at the cash register ready to sell the Van Der Danders' milk. The late afternoons were always slow, his daughter said, with people not yet home from work, giving her time in the cool back room to stock the refrigerated cases. Good for her. What could be better on these hot end-of-September days?

He pushed through the double glass entry doors, not wanting the bell hanging from the door to spoil his surprise. As he stepped into the empty dairy, the cool air inside wrapped around him, brightening what had already been a joyous day. He hadn't wanted Blanca working, but she'd been determined, so when Socorro Collado, who'd been working the counter at Norwalk Dairy since she'd first convinced the Van Der Danders that a woman would be an asset, had finally gotten her high school equivalency at night school, found a good job with the county, and suggested to Blanca that she'd be the perfect replacement, Blanca had badgered until he'd agreed. At least it was close to home in a clean place where the shelves sparkled and the floor gleamed. He noted with pride the immaculate surfaces that Socorro had insisted upon and Blanca maintained, the girl always cleaning, sweeping, dusting, since she'd climbed from her crib.

"So brown," he heard his mother whisper— in his head, where his mother continued to live long after they'd lowered her into the ground. He remembered how he and his mama had pressed against the windows in the nursery at Norwalk Community Hospital where a pink blanket had covered everything except Blanca's face, round, unwrinkled, and very, very brown. His mother, sounding stricken, had said that she was almost black, and he'd told her that was the way he loved his women.

Then. Now.

He looked up at the clock—four-thirty—and then to the doorway behind the dairy counter, strips of rubber hanging in place of a door. Suddenly, it was important that he surprise his Blanca, working diligently as she always did somewhere out of sight. Those Van Der Danders had better know what they had in his little girl. He moved behind the counter, wanting to surprise; he usually dropped by on Fridays, always just after five o'clock. It was Thursday, four-thirty, and she would have no idea.

Pushing through the rubber strips into even cooler darkness, he moved down a narrow pathway created by boxes piled shoulder high on each side of him and came to a corner. He rounded it, and his life changed forever.

There, at the end of another narrow path, in dimness, stood his Blanca, her back to him. Her hair, an inky coarse cascade, danced halfway down her back. Danced. Her head, thrown back as if she were peering toward heaven, moved from side to side causing the hair to swing, to sway. Her shoulders and her back were naked, richly brown where bared by swaying hair. The darkness of her skin was more startling in contrast to the pale arms that held her. Only her holder's forearms—thick, corded—were visible, for the hands themselves were lost to sight, buried in his daughter's jeans—loose, he saw now, at the waist—cupping his Blanca's cheeks.

"Dios mio—no," Mickey said. Blanca screamed, and Mickey wanted to run as his girl saw him. She had no blouse on at all. The man—a boy—holding her lifted his head, eyes wide in terror, from wherever it had been nuzzling. The eyes, as blue as Mickey's own, swept over him and then sideways as if seeking escape.

"Pa—" Blanca started, but did not finish one single word. Her face broke, and, pushing her way through stacked boxes, one arm crossed over her naked breasts—which Mickey saw—she fled. That left the boy, whose eyes were not on Mickey but on the place to which Blanca had run.

"Mija!" Mickey roared, but heard only the distant slamming of a door at the back. He wondered if she was running blouseless towards the cows. He turned back to the boy. He was shirtless, his torso powerful, his shoulders those of a man who worked in fields with cows. His Levi's were unsnapped, but they were up, his erection covered by the flaps. He looked terrified and so very young.

"Nothing happened, Mr. Escalante," he finally said.

"Nothing," was all Mickey said, moving toward the boy—slowly. His heart raced at the fear radiating from the kid. As he closed in, he saw the boy's hands struggle to button up his fly, the erection still aiming left, making it difficult. Mickey stopped his approach, allowing the boy time to put himself together. When the boy was finally buttoned up, Mickey said, "What do you see when you look at me?"

"Look, Mr. Escalante—nothing really hap—"

"What do you see?"

The boy looked him over, not seeming so afraid anymore. Finally he said, "Blanca's pop—that's what I see."

"Beyond that."

"You're pissed."

"Beyond that." He appreciated the boy's intentness; his blue eyes moved over Mickey as if seeking to find what he demanded.

"A mailman?" the boy finally asked, uncertainly.

Mickey nodded. "Three months on the job. Lincoln Heights Post Office. You know where Lincoln Heights is—what's your name?"

"Andy. Andy Van Der Dander."

"Blanca's boss—" Mickey started.

"Oh no, Mr. Escalante—I'm nobody. My dad's her boss. I'm nobody."

"Nobody," Mickey repeated, stepping closer. He noticed the boy backing against the wall, his body tightening as if preparing. "A nobody who had his hands down my Blanca's pants."

"Nothing else," he said holding up his hands.

"I'm a mailman," Mickey said and let his words hang in the air for a moment. "I asked if you know where Lincoln Heights is."

Andy shook his head.

"Nothing but Mexicans there, Andy. You know many Mexicans? Besides Blanca, I mean?"

"Well, sure—all the people in Carmelas shop here."

"Carmelas," Mickey said, "a pocket. Four fucking streets."

He saw Andy's eyes widen at the obscenity.

"Didn't pave the streets until seven years ago. A handful of us. Hanging on, Andy—trying to do the best we can. Until I started working in Lincoln Heights, delivering mail—I'd forgotten how many of us there really are out there." Mickey stepped closer, and now they were almost nose to nose. "Since I been walking those streets, I've come to realize what I thought was true of just us Carmelas Mexicans is true of the whole breed." He fell still.

Andy swallowed. Hard. "What?"

"Venganza," Mickey hissed, the word hanging in the air.

Andy's head was pressed back against the wall. "I don't speak no Spanish."

"I know you don't, Andy. Most of us don't anymore either. But 'venganza' is a word we hold on to." In a rush of movement he grabbed hold of the boy's cojones. Mickey's palm squeezed, hard. "Vengeance, Andy. You touch my Blanca again—scratch that, Andy—get near my Blanca again, cabrón, I'll get even. I'll rip these," he said, squeezing more tightly, "off your fucking body and stuff them up your gringo ass." He let loose of the boy's balls and stepped back. "Believe me." He turned and walked away. As he reached the rubber strips hanging in the doorway, the boy called out.

"Mr. Escalante . . . I love her."

Mickey moved through the doorway and out of the dairy, unable to bear the thought of home, winding up instead at Henry's cantina, sitting at the bar, nursing his grief with beer late into the night.

"Mickey," Hector said from behind the bar, "you got time for one more beer. Then I'm closing up, man." He pulled a fresh mug from the tap, and turning, set it in front of Mickey. They were alone—Mickey the only customer in the bar. "Que has pasado, amigo?" Hector asked. "You're wrapped in this big grey cloud."

"Nothing," Mickey said too sharply, his tongue thick from all the beers.

"You look good in that uniform, hombre. Tomorrow's payday for most of the vatos in Carmelas—I got girls on. They go for men in uniforms—even pinche mailmen."

Mickey cocked his head and said, "I was a machinist, Hector. For years, you remember? I learned in the army." He drank from his beer. "The army was good to me. You know I boxed in the army?"

"You should have stayed a boxer, man. You coulda put Carmelas on the chinga map."

"Pinche featherweight—but I was good. Could take a punk Dutch gringo any day of the week." He sipped his new beer. "Now I'm a mailman."

"Carrying cartas—"

"I like being my own jefe. I'm outside. No one hanging over me. Heaven, Hector." Mickey lit his last cigarette and crumpled the Camel package. "But I was a good machinist. I had a thousand jobs."

"So good you kept getting fired?"

"Quit. Boss just looked at me funny—I'd quit. No fear. You know what it means to live sin miedo, Hector?"

"No, hombre."

"If I quit a job, I got one the next day. I'd be out lookin' by six in the morning, and I didn't stop until I got a fucking job. Never failed."

"Now you're a mailman."

"Because I got scared. Two years ago I quit this job, fucking gringo boss. You know the kind of gavacho who talks to Mexicans like—"

"Some gringos don't?"

"Three days I go without a new job—never in my life have I gone three days without a job. So, I stay at the next one a year before I quit. Getting the next one after that took a week, Hector. I'm fuckin' down to dimes, man, when I finally get something and it's good, but it ain't so good as the job before. That changed me. I got scared. Then, Chato sees this ad. They need mailmen. I take a test. I was always good in school—"

"I know, ese, you went all the way to eighth grade."

"Chingate!" Mickey said halfheartedly. "Anyway, I aced the pinche tests. Now I'm in Lincoln Heights. Surrounded by Mexicans."

"Home sweet home."

"Nothing like Carmelas, man. There—everywhere you look, Mexicans."

"With those blue ojos, they probably think you're a gringo—"

"Fuck you." Mickey stood up, scooping bills from his pocket.

He turned from the bar. "What I'm tryin' to say, Hector—goddamn it—I was happy . . . until today."

"It's the beer, Mick. Mañana, ótra vez you'll be happy."

When Mickey got to the door, Hector called out, "Mi hija told me tú boy, Indio, is a big Chicano on campus at Cerritos."

"His hair is down to his ass. You seen him lately?"

"Let him be."

"All the time we fight—you know what over? 'Cause I won't call myself a Chicano."

"Todos los kids are locos," Hector said. "What do you care what he calls himself?"

"Me, Hector, he cares what I call myself." He moved to the door. "Whoever heard of a Chicano when we were kids?" Hector said nothing and Mickey slipped outside where the night was cool as if summer was gone.

The sky was thick with clouds. No moon. At his car, he opened the door but didn't get in. Half-hidden under his seat he saw the edges of some envelopes. He grabbed them and cursed. Four census forms, addressed, that he should have delivered two weeks ago—the bigwigs had been stressing how important to get them all out on time. He crumpled the four forms and slipped them into his pants pocket. The country's going to fall apart because of four uncounted houses? Besides, he had bigger problems at the moment. He could feel his beer, so he slammed the door without getting in, deciding to walk home. The walk over to Pontlavoy in the night air would clear his head. He turned from Henry's onto Claresa, walking down the middle of this street as familiar as his name. There was no need for moon, the streetlights bathed him. The houses were dark, but he knew everyone tucked away inside and sleeping, the street lonely. He remembered when the night streets were always dark and he'd imagined Malinche lurking in the shadows to grab a child solitary, hungry, and alone. He ran his eyes to the darkest reaches between the houses, no longer afraid of fallen brown women doomed to wander the night for their transgressions. He'd welcome Malinche's appearance tonight, wanting desperately not to feel so all alone. He began to cry quietly as he walked on.

In front of Chato's house, he stopped. His compadre of a lifetime. He'd taught the chingado English after his father had brought them from Mexico before the war. Mickey was godfather to Chato's first son, Joey, and Chato had returned the honor by accepting to be Blanca's when she fell into the world brown and wrinkled. He wiped at his eyes and walked across the dirt yard to the dark house, sinking to the new cement porch they'd poured last summer. He put his head in his hands, his grief reminding him of Chato's own the day he'd run into Mickey's yard, his despair as thick as the scent of blood blowing from the slaughterhouse and hanging in the air.

"My Joey! He killed a man. My Joey. With a knife, they say."

"How do you know—"

"Joey—he called—from jail, compa'. His one call. I have no money. I've never had any money. I never cared, Mickey. Nunca did I care. What will I do now for mi Joey sin money?"

"We'll get money—somehow," Mickey promised.

"He's wild," Chato cried, "I know he's one wild vato, but Joey—to knife someone." He sat heavily on Mickey's lawn chair. "What didn't I do? I beat him—always." He looked up. "Didn't I beat him every time he did wrong?"

Mickey put his hands on his friend's shoulders, finding no words, and simply pulled his broken friend against his heart. The memory of that holding forced Mickey up from the curb in front of Chato's house and to his friend's door. He pounded.

"*Quien es¿*" Chato roared through the door.

"Mickey—el amigo de tu juventúd whose heart hurts."

The door opened. "Miquel—Marta's been calling here all night." He stepped out onto the porch, naked save for his billowing boxers. He looked at Mickey closely. "Estas borracho?"

"Not drunk enough," Mickey said, sitting on the steps and pulling Chato down beside him.

"Marta said something about Blanca—a misunderstanding between you—"

"My Blanca," he said and shook his head. "I cannot tell."

"Come in and sleep. Tomorrow things will look better."

"But it's more than just Blanca—it's mi Indio, too." He sighed. "They are so far away. Not like cuando they were babies. I thought I knew them. I don't know them at all."

"Niños. Be thankful you have only three."

"Bless God he gave you nine."

"Would you like to share my blessing?" Chato said and slipped his arm around his friend.

"I don't want jokes." He looked across at Chato, his face round like a cat, his hair shooting from his head in wild disarray. "You are my brother."

"You have six of your own. Real brothers. Go wake them up."

"You are my brother."

Chato pulled Mickey close.

The closeness opened Mickey's heart, and he said softly, "My daughter is a puta."

Chato jumped up. "Watch your mouth. My godbaby—she is an angel."

Mickey told him what he'd found in the back of the dairy this afternoon, telling it all to the only man in the world to whom he could whisper his shame.

"Did anything happen?" he asked, lifting his eyebrows.

"I almost ripped his cojones off."

"Between them. Really happen?"

"He was still in his pants. She in hers—but her blouse—"

"That is nothing. No one saw but you. You told him we would kill him if he touches her again?"

Mickey nodded. "How can I ever get it out of my head?"

"You forget—to be young, how it is, hombre—"

"Blanca is my daughter."

"Whose daughters were you chasing?" Chato slapped his shoulder again. "I remember when Mona's father, Fabiano, came gunning to your papa—but you had slipped away already to Korea."

"A false alarm," Mickey said after a moment. "God, those Fuentes were a wild bunch—the girls wilder than the brothers. I avoided that."

"You've heard about Mona?" Chato asked. "Dickie Collado's gone." He sighed. "Mona is in pieces over on Carmenita—four kids."

"Dickie'll be back."

"He's taken up with another gringa—serious this time. Mona booted him. If she put him out, any of ours could do the same."

"We are becoming just like the gringos," Mickey said softly.

"Then where's my new LTD?" Chato asked and laughed. "Mona had nice legs, eh, hombre—in her time." Chato laughed. "Hijole! She used to wear those skirts that billowed when she danced. Those legs, brown all the way to her thighs—"

"Higher," Mickey said.

Chato punched his shoulder. "Chingón, I ain't never had tú luck with the chicas—except with mi Margarita. You get them green, they don't know no better. Gracias a Dios por la inocencia."

Mickey pushed up from the sagging porch as if he'd been struck. "Is that why we want them innocent, Chato?"

Chato rose and embraced his friend. "Go home. Go to sleep. Tomorrow, you will see different."

Mickey moved back to the street, waving over his head, and walked to Vieudelieu where he turned right and walked the block to Pontlavoy. On Ponlavoy, he found his house. The house he'd lived in all his life. But it looked so different now. He stood in the street in front of it. It was frame like its neighbors, set farther back from the street. It was painted. Marta insisted. She wanted sensible colors. She chose grey, the trim white. And she was the real Mexican.

"So brown." His mother again, muttering in his head.

He smiled. So much noise from one dead old lady. She'd said that about Marta when he'd brought her over to the house the first time—a niece of Señora Rosaura's. From Mazatlán, as so many of them were in some way connected to that city by the sea.

"Marta," Mickey called loudly, swaying in front of his house. He moved from the street to the yard, dirt like all the others, just more trees, more flowers. Marta liked bright Mexican color in flowers, just not on her walls. "Marta," he called again at the base of their steps. After a time, a light went on. The door opened. She stepped out, hugging a bathrobe around her. Her face looked a nightmare.

"She's gone," Marta said and pulled out a note from the pocket of her robe. "Ellos han escapado."

"Eloped?" he asked, reaching up for it. He read the words:

> *Papi, Ma,*
> *I'm too ashamed to ever come home again. It's not like it looked to Papi. Andy loves me. We're going to Las Vegas. When you see me, I will be clean again.*

Marta came to the edge of the porch and sat. "She's marrying him, Mickey. Mi Blanca. Con un gavacho named Ban Der Donder. I no puedo even say el nombre."

His hand found her leg. "Put your front teeth on your lower lip. V, V, V, Van . . . Van . . . Van Der Dander."

"Ban Der Donder."

"That's closer, Marta." He patted her thigh and sat next to her on the porch. "We'll practice."

"I needed you tonight, hombre."

"I'm sorry." He looked out at the street. "Feel the change, Marta?"

"Toda cambía, mi amor."

"Not here. Not in Carmelas."

"Aquí tambien. Everywhere is the same."

His eyes filled. "I saw my Blanca's breasts. She was in the back, with that yellow-headed Dutch boy, and she had no blouse—"

"She is marrying him now."

"I saw her breasts, Marta—"

"She is ashamed," Marta whispered.

After a silent space, he sighed and said, "Chato me dijo que Mona Collado is alone now—she left her husband—"

"He left her—chisme is he ran off with a gavacha he works with." She paused before saying, "She was la novía de tu juventúd—no?"

"My youth," he said, nodding. "She loved me, yes."

"Y tú?" Marta demanded. "Me dijiste always que tu heart burns for morenitas. She is almost tan brown como yo."

He shook his head. "My heart burns only for morenitas black as night," he said looking up at her. "Como tú." She smiled and pushed up from the porch. "What's happening to us?" Mickey asked.

She leaned down to him. "To us—nothing." She put her arms around him and he smelled her body, clean from a shower. She kissed his hair. "Come in to bed."

"Más tarde. You go."

She looked at him. "Will you be all right?"

"My daughter is in the desert with a Van Der Dander and you can ask me that? Indio thinks I am a fool because I won't be a Chicano—"

"But Late loves you as he always has. So do I. The head of our Indio is a confusion of ideas now. Blanca will—"

"Mi Blanca," he said softly. "Will I ever feel—"

"You must. A pity to let that go—"

"My Chocolate—does he have a game tomorrow?"

She nodded. "How did a Chocolate Escalante come to gringo football?"

"Let's move to Lincoln Heights, preciosa," Mickey said in a rush.

"What?"

"Here we are a pocket wrapped tight by gringos. They steal our daughters, blind our children with dreams of footballs, baseballs—"

"Lincoln Heights there is no baseball?"

"There are Mexican-Americans everywhere."

"If you want Mexicans go to Mexico."

"Then let's go to Mexico, mi amor."

"I've had my full of there, thanks God."

"We're stuck," Mickey said.

"You're a mailman," she said with pride—as if he were a general leading armies.

"I can never quit again."

"Bosses are what made you quit. It's like you are now your own boss. Come in the house. I make you coffee. On my new grinders."

He laughed. Marta had a JCPenney card and a Sears. She bought every appliance that came on the market. Their kitchen was like Disneylandia. "My mama would not believe what you have done with her kitchen."

"Es mi cocina now," she said and moved to the door. "I'll see you? In a bit?"

Alone, he sent his eyes back out to the street. He tried to remember when it and all the streets of Carmelas had been dirt. He closed his eyes and saw instead Señora Rosaura's jacaranda. That tree—over on Claresa still—he could see as clearly as he could hear his mama's voice inside his head. And near the tree, he could see Marta standing as she'd stood that first time he'd rounded the corner and seen her. He'd been a man already, then, but still, her darkness lost in shadow had made him catch his breath; the sun had been almost gone, shadow turning her skin so dark she looked like an Indian, wild in the twilight that transformed her into the Malinche of legend that his mother had thrown at him always as proof of the danger lurking in dark Indian faces, to her almost synonymous with betrayal. Then, he'd seen it was only Señora Rosaura's niece, newly arrived in Carmelas from Mazatlán and ever since, beauty in a woman was darkness, skin, eyes, hair. His Marta. His Blanca.

"Blanca! You name a baby brown like an Indian Blanca. We will be laughed out of Carmelas."

His mother's words.

Alma Blanca Escalante. Then Indio had come, so brown, Mickey gave him the name. Then, there was Late, his baby, who was now so big he was the John Glenn varsity's steamrolling star. Short for Chocolate—not his real name. His babies. All of them brown, as brown as Marta.

"Mi Blanca!"

He shivered at the memory of his mother's voice as she lay dying, calling not for him or any of her own, but for his Blanca—browner than any in the house—to hold her close as death marched through her pale body. He closed his eyes, Thursday bleeding into Friday behind them.

The sun roused him. He was sitting, leaning against a porch post, where he had slept the night away. He looked down at his blue uniform, the pants not much worse for all the wear. He looked at his wrist, his body aching with the movement. Ten o'clock!

He jumped up, his head exploding. *"Marta!"*

She appeared at the screen. "You wake, mi amor. No worry. I called tu post office. The mail will run without you. For today."

He sat back down. His hands rose to his head. The screen door slammed. He looked up and saw Indio. "Cómo estás tú, mi principe?" he asked.

"Bien, pop. Glad to see estás usando más español."

"Where you off to?"

"Class. I'm late."

He watched the boy, tall, slender, dark, his hair, a woman's hair, hanging farther down than Blanca's. He saw feathers, turquoise feathers in the hair. "Indio! What is that shit in your pinche hair?"

The boy turned, his hand reaching for the feathers. "Like it? Michelle gave them to me. This is how los indios wore their hair in Aztlan."

"Perdoname," Mickey said. "I had forgotten."

The boy jumped into his '65 Mustang and drove off—away.

The door slammed and Marta appeared, coffee in hand. He took it. When he sipped, it tasted new on his old tongue. Over the brim of the cup he saw a man scanning the house next door.

"Need something?" he asked.

"I'm looking for Perez. Javier."

"No one's home."

"Are you Escalante?" The man came over into the yard.

He nodded. The man, short, suited, and brown as a nut, stuck out his hand. "Mucho gusto."

Mickey took the hand. "Not so loud. Mi cabeza."

"Mi cabeza de cerveza," the little man sang, white teeth flashing brightly.

"Something like that. Who are you?"

"Me llamo Manuel Picante."

"Picante?" Mickey laughed. "Are you?"

"Hot for what I'm doing, yes."

"What are you doing?"

"Census."

"We already got ours. Weeks ago."

"But you didn't mail it back—a mailman should know better," he said, looking down at Mickey's uniform.

"I've got a headache," Mickey said.

"You'll have a bigger headache if you don't do this. I'm with Somos Unidos and we're making sure all mexicanos get counted."

"Sit," Mickey ordered, wanting this Picante's loud voice still.

The man pulled out his forms. He asked questions. More questions. And more questions.

"I could die before you're done. You'd lose a count."

"Last question." Manuel lifted his paper and read: "Which box would best state your preferred label?"

"Mi label?"

"Escuchame, por favor. Latino. Mexicano. Hispano. Mexican-American . . . or Chicano?"

He had a vision of his boy, blue feathers in his hair. Blanca appeared in his mind's eye at a slot machine in Vegas, a gringo's arm, knotted, powerful, and white, around her long dark neck. She was smiling. Late—Chocolate Escalante, who wasn't quite sure where he stood, appeared before his eyes in full regalia, footballed from toe to head despite the heat. Then, he was gone like the others.

"Chicano," Mickey said, answering the census taker's question, his count finally taken, hoping it might make some difference after all.

Chapter 16

Las Adelitas - 1973

Adelita was her name.

Angel's mujer.

She'd always hated it when he introduced her like that. But she never knew how much until lately.

Angel's woman.

"If I told you once, I told you un million de times, it's not like that."

That's what Angel said when she bitched about it.

"It's in your head—your fucked-up Spanish. You know the words, but you translate them—missing the sentido—the cultura behind them." That's what Angel would say.

She remembered years ago when it first started. They were in Norwalk Park, lying in the sun. He was on his back. She was over him, one leg over his hip, her other knee in his groin, pressing against his virilidad, su fortaleza, sus cojones in her book—and they were rolling around like marbles in a sack. He was smiling to beat the band—and Angel had teeth that smiles were made for—enjoying the massage even though he knew it wasn't going anywhere, when suddenly they were surrounded by this group of vatos, some of them from Carmelas and a few she didn't know.

"Angel?" one said. "Estas occupado?" and the group roared, laughter spilling out over the grass.

Angel rose, pulling Adelita to his chest. "Not with anything I can't get out of. Que quieren? What's up?"

"We're gonna play ball. Necesitamos un shortstop."

"Give me five minutes," Angel said. Then he said to all of them, "Conocen a mi mujer?"

They were silent. Even the ones who knew her from the barrio or school.

"Adelita Rincon," her Angel said.

And maybe he was right. When he flashed those teeth he could almost convince her. It was the way gringos looked at women that made it sound so bad in English. His woman. He used to say that in Spanish, real Spanish—not like hers, poisoned by English—it showed respect to women, showed a man's effort to tell the world a woman was standing at his side. That's what Angel used to say.

Angel.

What kind of a mama would name her baby Angel? To Adelita it was like his mama Nora must've been walking out in the moonlight pregnant and daring God to prove her wrong.

Adelita could remember when Angel got sent away to juvie the first time when they were just in high school and his mamita was carrying on, crying, "Que he hecho, en nombre de Dios, que he hecho en mi vida to deserve this?"

"You named him Angel." That's what Adelita had wanted to say way back then. But brown little girls in Carmelas weren't brought up that way.

All through high school Adelita stood by her Angel. Three trips to juvie. The last for one year and it had been the camps that time. But she was there when he went in, and she was there when he got out.

"Estas loca, that's what you are . . . como un bed bug," her mother told her over and over again. Usually while she was mopping. Her ma held things in, saved them up, but God help Adelita when her mama started mopping.

"I love him."

That was what Adelita would say to her mother's Angel insults.

Sometimes that alone was enough to get her mama swinging the mop—at Adelita's head. She'd take off, running out the back into the dirt, the dust, and the chickens, heading next door for Frida's, almost hanging herself on the clothesline—her mama's big cotton chones were mas que ample to do the job—with her mama screaming after, "And look at the paraiso love for Pancho Rincon got me!"

And the old woman had a point. It just didn't mean much then to Adelita.

The last time Angel got out of juvie though—he was different. Adelita went with his mama Nora to pick him up. Her hair must have been two feet high, the way Angel liked it—and her eyes, valgame Dios—she had mascara from here to Mexico. Cleopatra had nothing on Adelita in the eye department that day.

She felt like a queen waiting for her Angel outside Los Padrinos with his screaming mama who'd maintained pretty well on the drive to Downey—she'd been driving Angel's big Chevy, an Impala, black like Adelita's eyes. That was what Angel said. But his mama hadn't had time to wash it, so the black was a bit dusty, and his mama was propped up on pillows and still her ojos could hardly see above the wheel. Adelita didn't feel safe. But thank God Angel's mama didn't start the screaming until they arrived outside the hall.

So, Adelita was standing there in the August sun, terrified her eyes would start melting, holding up Angel's mama, and the way she was leaning on Adelita, Angel's mama was forcing Adelita's underwires into her right breast—so with all that and the screaming, she was more than ready to bail when her Angel stepped into the sunshine. Angel's mama Nora was on her own. Adelita ran to him, and it was like the movies—except for the underwire cutting into her skin, but it was worth it, seeing Angel's eyes light up when he saw what those underwires could do. Adelita's mamarias were so high, she could have rested her chin on them.

Suddenly she was in his face, and just as she was about to kiss him, she saw what he'd done to his face. He had this tear, this tiny, lopsided tear, tattooed at the corner of his eye. She had to look twice because he was so brown the tiny ink-blue tear was almost invisible. Almost.

"What've you done?" she asked, her finger touching the tear.

"Put my pain into my flesh."

He said that.

Her Angel. A poet. This vato loco getting out of juvie for the third time—with what looked like only prison up ahead, and he gave her poetry. Adelita knew something about poetry even then because with all Angel's time in juvie and she being the loyal Carmelas vata that she was, the only relationship she'd had was with books and movies, keeping Angel's abuelita Lolita company on Saturdays at the Norwalk walk-in, poetry on celluloid his abuelita Lola never tired of repeating. So, it was natural La Lola's nieto Angel would have a way with words.

"Every time I look into an espejo," he said, "I will be reminded. I can never go back. Nunca—o estoy lost."

And her Angel changed.

No more khakis. No more flannel shirts with only the top button buttoned, the tails flying, baring a crisp white T-shirt underneath. And he went back to school. Got his GED in six months. Then he went to Cerritos.

"Puercos don't change sus spots," her mother said. No, she wasn't mopping; she was browning arroz at the stove.

"Puercos?" Adelita said. "You mean leopards."

"I mean pigs. Angel is a pig—I don't care how many movies his abuelita says she was in!"

Adelita started to say something, but the way her mother was swinging that wooden spoon through the sizzling rice, Adelita bit her tongue. But *she* knew. He'd changed.

Angel had been at Cerritos a year when Adelita graduated from John Glenn High School. Barely—all her reading had been poetry, after all, nothing to do with school.

"The whole world is stupid," her mama said when Adelita brought home the good news. "To give a diploma to a muchacha que runs con Angel."

Adelita's papa was more supportive.

"You listen to a drunk?" her mother screamed.

"My children will be educated," Papa shouted, rising from his dilapidated chair, knocking over his beer can.

"He's proud of me, Ma," Adelita shouted.

"Un borracho con one shoe?" her mama roared and turned back to the stove, laughing deeply.

Con one shoe? Adelita turned and saw Papa standing, one shoe on, the other who knew where.

She followed Angel to Cerritos.

By then Angel was into MEChA. He was the big Chicano on campus. She could remember the first day she walked into the MEChA office, and Angel took her in his arms and said to everyone there, "Mi mujer. Mi Adelita."

For some reason it really rubbed her wrong that day. "Your woman?" she asked.

Everyone there had laughed.

"Ha estado robado de su culture," he said to all his MEChA friends in Spanish. He was speaking it all the time in those days. "Forgive her."

That was '68. The Chicano thing was big then. People were going crazy over what they called themselves.

"Es importante," Angel would say. "La cosa mas importante que toda, what we call ourselves."

"Somos Chicanos," Adelita said, her mouth against his throat, the two of them in the backseat of that old black Impala.

"We are," he said and slid his hand under her blouse—which was as far as she let him go in those days.

"Mi Chicana," he whispered, pulling her face up with his free hand. "La Chicana de mi corazón—de mi vida," he sighed, his words hot breath on her parted lips, his eyes so black they disappeared save for the sparkle of light there, reflections of the lights at the back of the Cerritos College parking lot. "Mi morenita," he cooed as his finger rolled her brown nipple gently, causing it to climb and her to force her thighs together as if they were seeking something to hang onto.

They were Chicanos—unidos, even in the backseat of Angel's Chevy.

"Chicanos?" Mama cried as she stopped her mopping after Adelita enlightened her. "Que pasó a tus brains. We are Mexicans—"

"Americans," Papa said from the table, his voice sounding faraway and slurred.

"Tell that to the gringos, viejo, who sell you the beer we can't afford to buy!" Mama shouted.

"Mexican-Americans," Papa said.

"Chicanos," Adelita insisted.

Papa turned in his chair and looked at his Adelita, his eyes bleary but his voice clear. "Tu mama is a Mexican—a foreigner, mija. I brought her up from Mexico. From Mazatlán." He laughed. "That is one fishing trip I should have missed."

"Borracho!" Mama said, dragging the rag mop across the floor, looking menacing.

"But I am born here. A citizen—" her papa said, bowing.

"With your brown face," Mama shouted, "you better keep your birth certificado on you at all times 'cause if la migra see you, Panchon, you're a goner."

"I am a citizen," Papa said, ignoring her. "When I was a boy, I lived in Los Angeles—"

"Before he moved *up* to Carmelas," Mama said, "and got his good job scraping mierda off cows." She stopped mopping. "Gracias a Dios I never saw where he lived before."

"Nobody was a Mexican then, mija," her papa said. "You ask someone brown—what are you? They would say, 'Spanish. Soy español.' Never me, mija. That's why this Chicano crap is for the birds. We should say what we are. Mexican-American. That's me."

"Borracho—that is que eres tú," Mama said and went on mopping.

"We should use the name we were made ashamed to use," Papa roared.

Adelita tried to explain all this to Angel, but she chose the wrong time to explain. They were in the back seat of his Impala—way out at the back of the Cerritos parking lot again.

"He was saying we should use the name we —" but Angel was all over her, covering her mouth, running his tongue over her lips in that way he had that got her lost. His hand slipped into the waistband of her Levi's, and his tongue was driving her crazy, his fingers gentle on the cotton of her panties, easing down, heading south.

And his trip must have shown because no sooner was she in the kitchen when she bumped into Mama, who said, "Tell me the truth," the minute Adelita slipped through the back door. Sure it was one o'clock in the morning and Adelita was an hour late, but she hadn't expected her ma to even be up. She had work in the morning—early. But work was the last thing on Mama's mind. "Tell me the truth," she said. Her mama was standing there in her blue flannel nightgown, and she looked so tired. She worked in the kitchen at the state hospital—passing out food to the inmates and mopping floors. Adelita's Mamita just couldn't get away from mopping floors—she started at five A.M., and there she was, still up and demanding, "Tell me the truth."

"What, Ma?"

"Estas intacto?"

"Como?"

"Tu virginidad."

Adelita started to wise off—but her mama was starting to cry. "Ah, Ma."

"You stay all night out with Angel."

"All night? It's one in the morning. Hours before dawn."

"Dime. La verdad."

"Juro, Mama," Adelita said, placing her hand on her heart. "I swear. I am intact."

Her mother pushed herself up from the table as if she weighed a ton. "Tente cuidado, mija—much care, que hombre compra la vaca cuando—"

"My milk ain't going anywhere, Mama."

And so the next time Adelita was in Angel's backseat and he whispered, "Preciosa," his tongue moving down her throat, his fingers broaching the elastic around the leg of her cotton chones, it was like Mama was in the car, so Adelita sat up, pulling his hand from her pants, scooting to the safety of her side of his backseat.

"Que pasaste?" he asked, his voice low.

"This cow ain't—" and she saw how silly she sounded. So, she laughed, the laughter an echo in the car.

"Don't leave me like this," he said, and pulled her hand to his lap, pressing her palm against the tube of hard flesh tenting his slacks. "Eres mi mujer."

Adelita began to move her hand, wondering if this was what a helpmate did, if this woman at his side was there so she'd be near his pinga. A ready hand. A helping hand. Her hand moved faster, and her Angel leaned back against the seat, his eyes open and fixed, his head on the cushion. His breathing was jagged, the darkness of his skin darkening even more as his cheeks hollowed, sucking in air. His nose, an eagle's beak, an Aztec crown, kept perfect company with the lips below, open now, full, protruding in the darkness. Suddenly, he pulled his lips back, baring teeth that caught the lights of the parking lot and were so beautiful they gentled the grimace that took hold of his face as he erupted.

His woman.

For how many years.

"Let's get married," Adelita said to him before jumping out of his car one night—and Mama said she never listened.

"When we're done with school."

And Angel was right.

She, who'd barely gotten out of high school, wanting only Angel and a wedding ring, knew now there would be no Angel ring on any finger of her hand until her school was done.

Angel and Adelita got to UCLA at the same time.

"You've got nothing to do but go to school. I've got MEChA, work, and school," he said, explaining why it had taken him so long, as if she'd been complaining, and she hadn't.

"Es un sueño," her mama said when Adelita took her to UCLA the first time. "Mi hija en a place como this."

Angel stayed in Chicano studies—but Adelita drifted.

"Un abogado?" Angel said one night in his apartment as he scooped beans from the ever-present pot on the back burner of his stove. Her Angel was muy Chicano—muy macho—but the man could make frijoles that put even her mama's to shame.

"Yeah, the movement needs lawyers." That's what Adelita said—as if she needed a reason to choose law school.

Her Angel was standing at the stove, his bowl of beans hanging in the air, shaking his head. "But I see us teaching—maybe here at UCLA. We're in demand, baby. We can call our shots."

Adelita shook her own head even harder. "I'm going to be a lawyer," she said, and it wasn't a question. This woman wasn't asking.

He brought his bowl of beans to the table and sat. He didn't eat. He stared at her and then said, "We'll see." Then, he smiled, saying, "A man y su mujer—they decide things together."

But Adelita had decided. Her Angel just hadn't heard her.

Lots of things changed after that.

Angel had gotten where he hardly pressured Adelita about sex anymore. She was still in the dorms at school, because, after all, the room and board were free with her grants. Everyone laughed. A junior in the dorms. But she was happy. Angel lived out in the valley. He had an apartment in La Irrigación, a barrio in Panarama City. "Ten times the size of Carmelas," he said, "but the same underneath." He was a youth counselor, working with the vatos, knowing where they were because he'd come from the same place. And that tear at the corner of Angel's eye? He said it worked wonders with the vatos, got him mileage he'd never have gotten otherwise.

But La Irrigación didn't seem like Carmelas to Adelita, especially when she'd arrive late on a Friday night. There were bars on people's windows. No one needed bars in their barrio Carmelas. But to Angel, La Irrigación felt like home.

The Friday afternoon Adelita got the biggest news of her life, she was getting ready to drive out to Angel's as usual when it dawned on her she wasn't marrying Angel any time soon. She had years yet. So, why not give her Angel two gifts and make this a real night to remember? This cow was ready to start giving the milk away. She ran down the dorm hall to Cynthia's room. She was black, beautiful, and into liberation. She had boxes of condoms. One condom wouldn't set her back at all.

"Take a box, honey!" Cynthia said, passing her a small box of Trojans. "You're plannin' a celebration—make it memorable, baby!"

Condones in hand, she drove onto that Friday evening 405 freeway chomping at the bit. When she finally got to Angel's, he was out, so she just took off all her clothes and climbed into his bed. She lay there as the sun sank from the sky and the room went dark and then black. Sometime in the darkness, she fell asleep, and when she woke the clock next to the bed said three in the morning. She reached out across the bed. No Angel.

Well, she wasn't going anywhere. Sure, she wondered about Angel for a while. But she'd grown up in a house where Papa was always leaving them wondering. He always came home; they just could never be sure when. She'd gotten good at waiting.

There she was in the dark, naked. A Chicana bearing gifts. That was Adelita. She laughed. In the darkness the laughter sounded odd. Her gifts. She placed her hand between her thighs on one of the gifts, uncomfortable even now touching herself. Her own hand sure as hell didn't feel like Angel's hand.

Okay, they had gotten that far. In fact the only thing they hadn't done was *it*. She'd let him use his fingers. His little finger. What damage could that do? Although in the dark, who could tell one finger from another? But she was still a virgin.

And why?

She reached up and switched on the light. The first thing she saw was the poster that covered half the wall across from the bed; it had followed Angel from his Cerritos days, had been around so long she hardly even noticed it anymore. She was looking at it now. Black and white, the images were stark. Men and women, a line, arms thrown about each other. Mexican men. Mexican women at their sides. The men were holding guns and smiling at her from across the room—across sixty years or more, for they were fighting a revolution that still waged on behind them in the photo. The men held the guns, and the women, smiling as broadly, had draped across their shoulders, over their breasts, the rounds of ammunition the men needed to fire their guns.

Sus mujeres.

They were smiling.

Adelita looked down toward the bottom of the huge poster and saw that the women's feet were bare, calloused, and hardened.

The men she saw wore boots.

One woman's smile was marred, a missing tooth, a gaping hole. Adelita ran her eyes over the faces of the men, their mouths almost obscured by moustaches, but all of them in full possession of their teeth.

Her eyes moved lower and saw the title she had seen a hundred times. "Las Adelitas."

La raza.

"Que importa," she could hear her mama saying as she mopped her tired blue linoleum in her Carmelas kitchen. "La raza. Where has it gotten me?"

"It's the gringos who have stepped on you, Mama—on me," Adelita could hear herself arguing, sounding just like Angel.

"Sí," Mama said. "Los gringos. Y before them? In Mexico—was I a queen, mija? Who stepped on me then? Whose floors do you think I was mopping then—until your papa found me. Saved me, mija. Now I mop his."

Las Adelitas. Adelita ran her eyes over the poster, Angel's favorite.

And she could hear him say from inside her own head, "Eres tu, como them—comos Las Adelitas."

She looked down at her own breasts and found her nipples hard though it was almost summer and the room not cold.

"Adelita?"

She lifted her eyes and saw Angel in the doorway looking shocked at finding her naked in his bed. She smiled despite herself, for Angel was beautiful. She lifted her arms, her breasts full, high without the help of any wires. "My gift—para ti."

"Adelita," he said. "Are you sure?"

"I've been a fool."

She watched him undress in the light, loving as she always did his body, but finding it so much grander in the light. As he came to the bed, he was already pointing toward heaven. She kicked off the sheet from her waist and pulled him to her, their flesh melting into each other.

His mouth was on her breast, seeking, finding her nipple, his fingers in her body, gentling her, softening her, until she pulled at him to hurry. He entered her and she felt no resistance at all. Amazed, she wondered where her hymen had gone. His fingers in her back, against her nalgas, pressing, pulling, his verga sheathed inside her body, the contractions she would force causing him to moan, as his fingers pressed and stroked. Why had she waited?

As he came, she bit at his ear and let her remaining gift out of the bag, saying, "I've been accepted into UCLA law school." He didn't say anything, then.

Afterward, in the dark, he smoked and seemed to have pulled away. She lay against him, her hands caressing his chest, playing with the sparse hair that was as much hers as his.

"Have you applied anywhere else?" he asked, sounding miles from celebration.

His question startled. "I wanted only UCLA."

"What if I go somewhere else? I've applied to Harvard. Yale. I'm going east."

"We'll be bicoastal?" she offered lightly.

"Adelita," Angel said sitting upright in the bed. "I'm serious. Te quiero conmigo."

"But what about my—"

He got out of bed. "Look at them!" He pointed at the poster of Las Adelitas. "Those are Chicanas, ellas go where van sus hombres."

Adelita sat up stiffly. "They're not Chicanas. They're Mexicans."

"Mi punto—"

"Your point is—"

"Eres mi mujer," he said.

"Which means?" she asked.

"You go with me."

"Como ellas," she said, indicating the poster and the laughing women weighed down with bullets their men would shoot but never have to carry.

"Like them. The same goal. To keep us as we've been—together rebuilding Aztlan."

"Together?" she asked and got out of bed naked.

"Cover yourself," Angel said—sharply.

But she ignored him, walking unashamed to the dresser where she'd put her clothes. She slipped on her bra and stepped into her panties. "This Aztlan we're building," she said, slipping into her slacks. "Besides carrying the toolbag—passing you tools—what do I do?"

"Adelita," Angel said. His eyes were wet. "Mi mujer."

She shook her head, tears in her eyes at the sight of her Angel crying, his tears seeming to flow from the tiny blue tattoo beneath his eye as he stood naked in front of his favorite poster showing the sacrifice of Las Adelitas. But she said, "No."

Then she walked away.

Chapter 17

La Vida Lucky - 1976

Everybody called him Grito, and he was the luckiest vato that ever came out of Carmelas, his barrio—four invisible little streets forgotten at the edge of Norwalk.

"Tienes suerte, mijo. And don't you never forget it!"

"Lucky, 'buelita?" That was him as a kid, always asking the same question, loving to hear his granny go through it all over again.

"Jorgie Collado," she'd say, nodding her head to make her point. "Eres *tú* lo más lucky boy in the world."

And he was.

His mother and father were killed in a car wreck.

He was born there—in the wrecked car. They never got his mama to the hospital. She died in that car, but not before going into labor and delivering him, screaming but whole. That same night, he was put into his 'buelita's arms where he was held, loosely, until she died at eighty. She looked a hundred.

"Pero, I got mis marbles," was what she'd say whenever she looked in a mirror. Tapping her head, she'd turn from the mirror and say, usually to him, "It ain't beauty que counts, mijo."

He was surprised when she died.

Rico, sitting next to him at the bar, asked, "At eighty you think someone's buying long-playing records?" Rico was Grito's oldest friend; after 'buelita's funeral when all the neighbors finally left, he'd taken Grito to Henry's cantina up on Rosecrans to get him drunk. Sipping his beer, Rico shook his head and said, "Surprised. She was not the picture of health, my friend."

"But she looked like that when I was eight," Grito argued. "Tell me I'm wrong."

"Come to think of it, hombre," Rico said, "she always did look ready to drop dead." He was Grito's best friend, and Grito let him say things he would never have allowed anyone else to say.

"As long as I can remember—a wind could blow her away," Grito said, shaking his head and downing his third beer. "She never had good skin, ese."

"Like roads in Mexico, her skin," Rico agreed.

"Claro," Grito said, starting on another beer. "So, you stop paying attention to things like that—then *boom* la vida sneaks up and smacks you in the head."

"Think how she felt," Rico said and bought Grito another beer.

Lucky—that's how she felt. She had her marbles right to the end.

"Sort of."

That was Ninfa. Later that night, after Rico brought him home drunk, Grito sank onto the porch and Ninfa held him in her arms and rocked him. His face was buried in her softness, her scent wrapping around him, softening his pain. With Ninfa he could be a bull climbing between her thighs, and he could also be a little boy crying for his abuelita.

"Don't get me wrong, honey," she said into his hair between kisses. "A treasure, 'buelita was. But she was old when you went to her . . . too old to raise a little boy."

Reluctantly, Grito lifted his face from Ninfa's breasts and looked into her dark eyes. "That was her strength, vieja," he said. "Mis tiós told me. She was a different woman with me. Her own sons told me with them she was a general, a cruel commandante who beat on them as if they were drums—and never kissed them. But me, Ninfa—with me, she was too tired to slap anything around anymore but tortillas and kisses. I was blessed."

"I was," Ninfa said and moved her face closer to his. "She made you a man who can let a woman love him."

He let her hold him on their front porch—'buelita's porch, really, for they had lived with the old woman all their married life. The house would become Ninfa's own only now. For a moment there, in Ninfa's arms, he was fourteen again on the same front porch, but the arms holding him weren't brown like Ninfa's. They were yellow, wrinkled, old—his 'buelita's arms.

"Mijo, mijo," his 'buelita said and kissed the back of his neck. "Why would I be mad? It's your skin. If tu want pictures from your ass to your eyebrows, es okay conmigo. "

He pulled loose of her arms and stood. He lifted his T-shirt sleeve and showed her his tattoo, a woman, naked, but covered by hair that flowed around her like a blanket. "She dances, 'buelita." He flexed his bicep and the tatooed hips swayed.

"She don't look like no woman I want you bringing a mi house. But next time, Jorgie," his 'buelita said, standing, "take me with you. There's got to be pictures better than that to put en tu skin."

Lucky. Him. Grito Collado, the blackest vato in Carmelas, and on this night that 'buelita had been given back to the earth, he wanted Ninfa to understand the old lady's gifts. He pulled out of Ninfa's arms and stood, taking off his shirt and baring his back. "She picked that out," he said. There was silence. He turned and looked over his shoulder.

"That proves what, Grito?" Ninfa asked. "An old woman goes with her fifteen-year-old grandson to a tattoo parlor and has them put the Virgin of Guadalupe—from neck to waist—on his skin—"

"She loved me."

"Claro, sweetie. She loved you. But it don't prove she had her marbles . . . even then."

What did Ninfa know from marbles? His heart hurt too much—the echo of all the beer was too heavy on his tongue—to find words to make Ninfa see what he remembered of summers when the August heat would boil, and 'buelita would shell peas on the porch into the night, seeking cool. On nights when the moon was full she'd say, "Jorgito, show me la virgin." He'd jump off that porch, shirtless in the heat anyway, and go stand in the yard, not too far from the steps where 'buelita sat because her eyes weren't too good, and he'd turn his back to her. He'd hear a sweet intake of breath. "Más allá . . . a little more far into the moonlight, mijo." He'd move until she said, "Basta. There. Be still." After a moment, she'd say, "Move tus muscles, mijo . . . not so fast, suave, más suave. Ay, mijo. Parece como la virgin dances in the moonlight . . . for me . . . for me."

Swaying drunkenly, all he could say as Ninfa lifted her arms to him was "lucky." He sank back onto the sloping porch into Ninfa's body. He felt her arms go round as he rested his ear at her belly and wished there was a heartbeat inside there promising another baby to ease his heart.

Blessed. Him. With women and six babies—surely enough blessing for any man.

"Let's go to bed, precioso," Ninfa whispered as she helped him up.

In the dark bedroom, babies sleeping, quiet, he pulled off his clothes. Tripping on his boxers, he fell naked onto the bed. Closing his eyes, he heard Ninfa say, "I will never be small again."

He lifted his head and saw Ninfa standing in front of the full-length mirror he'd nailed to the bedroom door, her hands pressed at her waist. She was naked, and he ran his eyes up and down her form, seeing at one time the front view reflected in the glass and the back, her rounded shoulders, the body that seemed to flow in waves, expanding to hips, her nalgas high and round—still solid—her thighs, large, loose, and beautiful. "Te quiero," he said softly from the bed, loving to say he loved her in Spanish.

She turned from the glass and leaned back against it, the movement causing her heavy breasts to sway. The light from the bureau played tricks with her flesh, dark everywhere, but at the breasts, the waist, the dark was less strong, a contrast to the skin exposed to sun. Her eyes, her breasts caused him—despite his grief, the beer—to climb from between his legs.

"I was beautiful, Grito. You know I was."

He rose on his elbow, extending one arm. "You are, preciosa. You are."

She came to the bed and sat next to him, leaning back on the headboard. He sat up and pulled her against him, his hands moving over her softness, his mouth on her face, her tears, salt, spilling into his mouth.

"How can you bear what I am when you know what I was," she whispered.

He lowered his face to her neck and ran his tongue over her flesh, tasting salt there, too, his hands caressing and feeling nothing different, the flesh the same to him as the first time. He lifted his face. "Ninfa?" Her head was leaning against the headboard, her eyes closed. "You remember our first time?"

She opened her eyes."Under Señora Rosaura's jacaranda," she said and smiled.

"Hiding from the pinche streetlights the gringos put up," he whispered.

"And the moon," she said. "You had your shirt off wanting everybody to see your new tatoo."

"Only you," he said, his mouth in her hair. "Your name over my own heart, nena."

She laughed softly.

"I put your hand on my chest, remember, the heart with your

name not two weeks old. When I lifted my own, you left yours there, on my pecho—"

"Like velvet," she said, "your skin—black velvet—and me, put there forever." She turned her head, kissing his hair. "Why else do you think I let you take me beneath the mulberry trees," she said.

Grito rose to his knees, next to her on the bed. "I spread my shirt for you."

"I remember, amor mio," she whispered, her mouth on his chest, "like I was treasure, you laid me down."

Grito looked at her full breasts now as if seeing them that first night he'd unbuttoned her blouse. Now they were naked; that night they'd been encased in cones, pointed at the moon. He reached out and stroked her breast just as he'd touched the flesh that had risen above the cups of her bra then. "Ay, chica," he sighed, thinking of how her skin had felt under his hands, supple, firm, yielding, young, amazed that her body felt no different to him now.

"The me I was—forever gone," Ninfa said.

"No," he argued, "so beautiful—so lucky, me . . . to have won you, Ninfa Galvan—your mama with her yellow hair screaming of the black babies we'd have." He pulled her to him, his hands slipping down her body, over the loose beauty of her belly, down, but she pushed at his hand.

"I can't be pregnant again—I can't pay no more."

"I love you pregnant," he said. She turned away from him, and he pressed up against her back. "Do you remember," he asked, "when you were carrying the twins?" His mouth at the nape of her neck.

She nodded. "I was so huge—"

"The only way I could enter you, nena, was from behind." He smiled, his lips touching her skin. "I got to like it that way—the feel of your back against my chest, the way your nalgas moved, glove-like upon my espada—hijole," he sighed, his penis hard at the small of her back. He nuzzled his nose up under the back of her thick hair, his hips moving in rhythm to his words. He slid his arms around her as he had when she'd been so big with the twins, one hand moving up to cup her breast, the other moving down, cradling her belly that had held all his babies, and he said again, "I love you pregnant." The words once said slowed his hips.

"Why?" she asked as if he were a madman.

He had no answer, and his penis, in the darkness of their bedroom, fell, for Ninfa in his arms had cooled, tensed. Even holding her, he felt almost alone in the bed on this night he'd buried his abuelita and wanted anything but such solitude. "I will just hold you," he said. Because his pinga had retreated, she must have believed him and relaxed in his arms, falling asleep against him.

A few weeks later, he'd come home from riding bikes with the four oldest, always raising comments in Carmelas—this crazy tattooed vato riding like a gringo on a bike looking like a duck with four brown little ones trailing behind. When he'd gotten home, bikes put away, kids in front of the TV, he went looking for Ninfa and found her in the bathroom. When he peeked around the bathroom door, she was bent over in the weirdest way.

"Help me!" she said. "Close the door—I don't want the kids to see."

He closed the door behind him. Ninfa was squatting, a mirror between her legs. Grito didn't know if *he* wanted to see. "What are you doing?"

"I can't find it."

"What?"

"The goddamned string. I'm always losing it."

He got down on his knees and joined in the search. No string was found.

"No más," she said, falling into his arms as he tried to comfort her in the bathroom, his body reacting as always to her nakedness. She pulled away and pushed him out of the bathroom. Staring at the closed bathroom door, he felt fear—as if his luck might just be running out.

That night in bed, he noticed she stayed on her side of the bed. He rose on one elbow. "Ninfa," he asked, reaching for her, but she backed away—as if she were afraid of him. Startled, he lay back down, wondering how Ninfa could fear him.

"Grito," she said quietly. "Please—I don't know if the IUD's even up there anymore. I've had nothing but trouble, amor—you know the last one caused cysts. With this one, I've been bleeding like Niagara. I can't take the pill—you know I tried. It ruined my eyes."

He sat up in bed, her fear washing in waves over him. "Está bien, vieja—it's okay. You stop all this shit. I'll take care of it—rubbers from now on."

"Oh, Grito," she said rolling onto her side, "you were wearing rubbers with Janet and Ignacio."

He had been. He felt her despair at being able to trust nothing.

The next day they'd walked with the kids to Norwalk Square. Ninfa had gone into Penney's with the three older ones tucked into one stroller, and Grito took the twins in the new one, Junior walking alongside, and ended up in Sav-Ons near the pharmacy looking over the counter for the condoms. When the customer at the counter finally left, Grito leaned onto the counter close to the gringo clerk, an old guy, friendly-looking.

"What can I do for you?"

"I got a problem," Grito said, lowering his voice. "My wife has tried everything—pill, IUD, the works. Rubbers even failing—"

"You could double up."

Grito closed his eyes, giving up and asking for a double pack of Trojans.

As the clerk turned, he said, "You already got three?"

"What?"

"Kids, man."

"Six."

The man whistled. "Then, buddy, why not just get cut?"

"Cut?"

And the man laughed at the horror on Grito's face and started talking about balls and thread-like tubes. Grito bought the rubbers.

In the month after abuelita died, life moved back to normal, his ache retreating. Life with Ninfa was normal, too. She never refused him, but something was missing. It was baseball season though. He and his vatos took to playing regularly. One day he came home late from the baseball game with Rico and the guys at Ramona School—real late because they'd gone drinking after. The house was dark and he thought Ninfa in bed, but he found her in the kitchen, bent over the sink. In the harsh light, her face looked ruined. "What's wrong?"

Before she could answer, she doubled over the chipped porcelain and heaved into the sink, the retching sounding oddly like 'buelita's jagged breath as she lay dying. Horrified, he put his arms around her shoulders as they shook and heaved. The sink filled up with vileness, and when the stream of greenish bile stopped flowing, she retched on and on. He turned on the faucet and with cupped hands helped her drink. Then, she was crying, the sobs shaking her powerfully as she raised herself and moved into his arms.

He let her cry, just holding her, getting wrapped up in her smells and the feel of her pressing up against his chest like she was trying to climb in. When she finally stopped crying, she looked up and said, "I hurt so bad, Grito. "

"Why? What's wrong?"

"I went to La Luna's today."

"Why go see that old bruja?" he asked, seeing the toothless shrew who had been in Carmelas as long as anyone could remember and, people said, once delivered all the babies.

"She's no witch . . . a curandera," Ninfa said.

"But why?" he asked again.

"I'm pregnant, Grito. Lucy on the next street told me I don't have to keep havin' them. She took me to La Luna's. She's not so spooky—up close—just old." She pushed back and looked up at him. "So I tell her I can't have another baby. She took my hands and kissed them. Then she got up and got out a pan. She poured in something green from a bottle in the back of a closet. She cooked it—slow—adding lots of hierbas. Secret things she said women have forgotten—except for her. We sat and talked while it simmered. An hour, Grito. She said timing is everything. She said I'd drink it and the baby would stop."

"Stop?"

"Just stop. Go away." She looked up at him. "I drank it. She said it would hurt like hell—the price I had to pay—and, Grito, it has . . . like nothing I've ever felt before. I've been hurting and vomiting all day. " She doubled over and began to heave again, her hands rising to her mouth to hold the liquid, yellow water now, inside. It ran through her fingers, down her arms. She slid to the floor, he with her, cradling his Ninfa.

The next day when he came home from work, she had the kids off to her sister Elizabeth's on Marvilla, candles on the lopsided table, enchiladas in the oven, and smiles for Grito. He didn't ask if the baby was gone. He knew because she stood on her toes, wrapped her arms around him, and said, "Te quiero—mucho, mucho."

He just said, "Lucky," holding her, wondering what they were going to do.

The following Saturday in Henry's cantina after baseball, he thought he would run his ideas by Rico.

"You're going to cut your nuts?"

Grito wanted to put a fist in Rico's mouth. The place was busy. "Lower your fuckin' voice. An' no, I ain't gettin' my nuts cut. I'm *thinkin'* about gettin' a vasectomy. "

Rico got up from his barstool. "Don't mess with your huevos, man! The slightest slip an'—"

"Think I'd go to a butcher, ese? I'd want to be in an expert's hands."

"The only hands messin' around down there should be your own—or Ninfa's."

"I'm just thinkin' about it."

"Sure it's not Ninfa doin' your thinkin' for you?"

"Stop being such a pinche asshole. You know nothin' about nothin', ese. They cut these tubes, man, like threads that run from your balls to your—" but he couldn't remember the rest the pharmacist had told him when he went back to ask about a doctor. "That's all they do. They tie up the loose ends—Rico, cut that out!"

Rico was back down on his barstool, writhing his legs together as if in pain.

"Doesn't affect nothin'." But Grito didn't sound so sure.

"Not what I heard," Rico countered.

Grito said nothing. Sipped his beer. Lit another cigarette. After a moment, he asked, casually, "What'd you hear?"

"This guy I work with, Johnny Martinez, you remember him, the redheaded Mexican from over on the one-ways—"

"With the freckles?"

"That's him. He got it done."

Grito waited. And he waited. "So?" he finally asked.

Rico looked around to make sure no one was listening and then leaned close. "It ain't moved since."

He kept his appointment anyway, going to the urologist whose card he'd gotten from the pharmacist in Sav-Ons, but not with enthusiasm. In fact, the twenty minutes he'd been waiting in the doctor's office so far had been a battle. Bolt or stay?

"Mr. Collado?"

Grito jumped out of the stiff-backed chair in the gringo doctor's waiting room. "I'm Collado." He could still run for it—but then where would he be? So he walked to the nurse and followed her to a cubicle.

"Have a seat."

He moved by the nurse and lifted himself onto the end of the table.

"The doctor will be with you shortly. Before he comes in, I'll take your blood pressure." He turned his back and slipped off his shirt, hearing a sharp intake of breath. He saw the nurse's startled face. "That's the Virgin of Guadalupe. Isn't it? On your back?" He nodded. Regaining her composure, she said, "It's so large—beautiful—I've never seen anything like it." She wrapped the band around his bicep, his tatooed dancing woman peeking seductively over. "Blood pressure of a boy," she said, smiling, and went to the door. "Remove your clothes, Mr. Collado—a smock's on top of the table."

He stripped to his shorts—white, billowing, and long. He slipped them down past his hips and saw his naked image in the mirror at the sink as he rose, shorts in hand. Blood pressure like a boy. At twenty-seven—married eleven years—he was no boy, but the man in the glass looked young, solid, hard, the dark flesh reflecting the overhead light and years of labor framing houses. A large cross was tatooed between the rises of his chest. He flexed, the movement lifting his pechos framing the cross holding the names of his six children, causing the hearts capping each mound of chest muscle to ripple—the nipple rising like a chocolate kiss poking from the hearts. Inside the heart inked just above his own heart was Ninfa's name.

So lucky.

"Mr. Collado."

He looked up and saw the doctor enter, wondering for a moment if the way the doctor mauled his name was reason enough to walk out. Then, the doctor smiled, the mauling only ignorance. Grito said, "Call me George."

"Well, George, climb up on that table." He did. The doctor was reading his file. "You're only twenty-seven. That's very young. " No longer smiling, he lifted his grey, almost colorless eyes and looked Grito over. "You seem very fit. " He cleared his throat. "What we're going to do is very final." Chill gathered at Grito's tailbone. "Lay yourself down flat, George." His hand landed at the hem of Grito's smock. "Lift your hips." Grito did, and the doctor raised the smock, baring him. "You've tried all other options?" the doctor asked.

Grito nodded, recalling trying to slip on a third condom the other night. "Why do I get the feeling you ain't pushin' this procedure, doctor?"

The doctor, examining Grito's privates, said, "I push neither way. That's up to you. I just want you to know that when it's done it's done."

"What's done?" Grito asked, thinking of Johnny Martinez, the freckled Mexican with the penis that no longer moved.

The doctor's milky eyes smiled. "Just the paying, George. Not the playing." Grito felt the doctor's cold hand lift his scrotum and all it held. "These will never know the difference," the doctor said.

"What about their buddy?"

"He does what they tell him."

Grito nodded. "It's just . . . "

"What?" the doctor asked.

For no reason he could think of, he said, "I love my wife pregnant." There it was again. Words that suddenly seemed so important and Grito had no idea why.

The doctor laughed and released his scrotum. "Of course you do," he said, turning to a counter top where he sorted what looked like a collection of knives. "Pregnancy liberates," the doctor added. "There's no more to fear."

"Fear?"

"Neither you nor your wife need ever be afraid again," the doctor said offhandedly, moving to Grito's feet. "Spread your legs a bit—I need elbow room." The doctor swabbed his balls with something cold. "Who shaved you?" the doctor asked.

"Ninfa—my wife."

The doctor laughed. "She took everything off. All she needed to do really was around your scrotum. That's where I'll be working."

Grito remembered last night lying on the bathroom floor, naked, Ninfa leaning over him, saying, "I've always known you loved me, Grito—but *now,* I know you love me as I want to be loved." Her eyes were glistening, and he didn't think it was the reflection of the silver Gillette razor she held high. With her free hand she picked up the can of shaving cream. Bending lower, she sprayed it like whipped cream all over his bush, the only hair on his body. "Spread your legs," she said as gently as she could. He did. She reached out and cupped his huevos, lifting them.

"Careful," he said, but only to the doctor busying himself between Grito's legs.

The doctor lifted Grito's scrotum. His hands were not like Ninfa's, but they were warmer than before. He lifted a large needle in the air. "Novocain." He jabbed him. "Nothing to be afraid of now, George." He turned to the counter and his array of instruments. When he turned back, he said, "Deader than a drunk," and to prove his point, with thumb and forefinger he flicked Grito's penis. He felt nothing. He looked up to see the doctor holding a scalpel to the light. Grito closed his eyes.

And as hard as this might be to believe—considering where he was and why—he could see behind his closed eyes himself loving Ninfa. A series of scenes racing by, years of loving—arms, legs, rolling bodies, coiling tongues. His pinga was shot full of novocain, so he felt the heat of memory only in his heart. The images slowed and he saw himself on Ninfa, his face buried in her breasts, the rise of her belly pressing at his chin. She was pregnant, large with child, and she was wild, free, unafraid like at no other time. Getting it, Grito opened his eyes wide as he lay on the table in the doctor's office.

"The names in the cross?" the doctor asked. Grito lifted his head from the table, the smock bunched under his chin, and saw the doctor staring at his chest. "Whose names?"

"My babies."

He whistled. "Glad you found me before you ran out of torso. You probably hardly know her not pregnant."

Grito closed his eyes. He saw his line of children, brown like him. He would now have what he had thought could only come with babies. Ninfa. Laughing. Round. Joyous—except when she was afraid.

"I've opened you up," the doctor said. "Want to watch?" He reached for an overhead mirror. Grito closed his eyes. Unaware that his audience had fled, the doctor went to work. "My God, look at the size of this vas. Where'd the other one go?" he asked.

Grito jumped. "Other what?"

The doctor smiled. "The other vas. I think you've got only one. Now you may feel a pulling in your stomach." A truck ran through Grito's stomach and out. "All tied up. Nothin' to do but stitch you up." The doctor whistled while he worked. Then he said, "Was last year a baseball season or what?"

Grito wasn't thinking of baseballs. He was thinking only of all the years ahead with his Ninfa unafraid, feeling once again what he'd felt all the years of his life. Lucky.

Chapter 18

The Days of the Dead ~ 1989

"She's evil."

Before the doctor on the radio could say anything else, Mercedes, who had felt unable to move just moments before, reached up with a speed that belied her years and switched off the radio that perched on the shelf Danielito had placed above her stove years before so his mama would never have to be without her radio.

"Talk, talk, talk," he would say to her, sitting at the kitchen table sipping her coffee as he often did, stopping by after work, sometimes before even going home.

"It fills my house with voices," his mother would say, across the table from her youngest boy, now growing old himself.

"Musica," he'd say. "What's wrong with music? Then, we could dance."

But Mercedes liked the talk, and when the TV began to outdo the radio, she could not have been happier. She hardly listened to the radio anymore—except when cooking in the kitchen or struggling with sleep in her night-dark bed. The days were filled with talk on TV. Every year, there seemed to be more shows full of talk—

stories of other people's lives. She could practically sit before the TV from morning to night with one hour after the next filled with talk. But she had her special shows. Her friends. Oprah—la negrita—was her favorite. But she loved Sally, too. They never pushed too far, backing off and leaving people to their deepest secrets—allowing Mercedes to almost forget her own—dispensing always consolation.

Mercedes never read a newspaper. She never lingered over news beyond the chisme of her barrio. She'd had her fill of ugliness.

"And you think this parade of whiners baring themselves naked on television isn't ugly?" Felicidad, her oldest child, looking sourer than usual, had said to her just last week upon stepping into the tiny house and finding her old mother sitting, feet propped, mesmerized as Oprah cried with a guest whose husband had six other wives she'd known nothing about.

"They are trying to become clean," Mercedes protested as she flicked off the TV and turned her face up for Felicidad's descending lips, the struggle the only reason she allowed herself to watch.

"Some things can't be made right, Mama," Felicidad managed before silenced by her own kiss.

Which is just what the woman on the radio had been saying, and normally that would have been all the signal Mercedes would have needed to reach up and switch the station, but she was in the middle of browning rice—with one of her hands busy sprinkling onions and the other stirring the sizzling grains—and could do nothing . . . but listen.

A woman, somewhere, had lost her babies, two little boys. Kidnapped—that's what she'd said—days before. Lies. All of it lies. A car—not stolen at all—pulled from a lake with two little boys strapped into the back seat. The mother walking away to a man—not her husband—who wanted her but not her babies.

And the woman on the radio had said, "Imagine them . . . water rising about them. Do you doubt for a moment they were calling 'Mama'?"

The onions had fallen from Mercedes' right hand, the fork from her left. Frozen, she stood staring down into the browning . . . blackening grains—unable to move.

She tried to imagine Oprah or Sally, what they would say, but heard only the brittle woman on the radio saying something about women who sacrifice their babies for a man.

"She is evil," the radio doctor said, and the verdict allowed movement back into Mercedes' arms.

After she'd switched off the radio, she looked down at her ruined rice and then turned off the gas, the rapid movement causing her arthritis to act up. The smell of the burnt onion blending with the earthy scent of beans bubbling on the back burner sickened her. She picked up the end of her apron and covered her nose. Then, she walked from the kitchen through the tiny living room out onto the porch and into the late October sun. Grasping a porch pole, she eased herself down onto the wooden stoop. Her heart was thudding in her chest, the noise seeming a roar inside her head—like the roar of a river flooded by winter rains. The very idea caused her to yearn for the days when the street before her was dirt and the houses scattered haphazardly up and down Claresa had been filled with friends. Then, when panic threatened as it did now, she could have fled to Chata's or Señora Rosaura's, walking into their houses as if they were her own and demanding coffee and warm pan dulce and talk . . . safe talk. But new people filled the houses. The old people had gone, slowly, until she alone was left, surrounded by a new flood of mexicanos struggling to find a place with work and food to last a lifetime. She knew the struggle, but the people, these mexicanos, she didn't know at all, amazed that sixty years spent hiding in Carmelas could have changed her into someone who shared no more than language with people she would have thought her own.

Her own had become over the years the ones she'd shared a

life with here in Carmelas, who had with time become a band with bonds tighter than blood but who had fled . . . into death or worlds beyond Carmelas . . . far out of reach.

"We want you out of here!" Felicidad had said loudly, her hands on her ample hips, two weeks before.

Mercedes had been sitting on a kitchen chair that night, Felicidad confronting her, in league with Piedad, Caridad, and even Elizabeth, her sisters all lined up behind. "No," she said.

"Mama, you are impossible!" Felicidad shouted. "You've been robbed ten times in the last two years!"

"There's nothing left to steal, Mama," Elizabeth said sweetly.

"Then I'm safe."

"Poor people stealing from other poor people. It's sick," Piedad said quietly. "Carmelas was always poor, but never like this."

"Danny," Mercedes said and looked at her youngest boy standing in the kitchen doorway looking uncomfortable, "is across the street."

"Why?" Felicidad snapped. "Because *you* wouldn't leave, my baby brother has to raise his kids here!"

"I'm afraid to come visit at night, Mama," Piedad said softly.

"I come at night, Mama," Felicidad shouted, "and you know what I see? My brother's oldest boy Jerry spray-painting the walls by the Santa Ana freeway! Fifteen years old and he looks like a vato gang banger."

"I kicked his ass, sis," Danny said from the door, "when you told me."

"Maybe she could put bars up on the windows," Elizabeth said in a spirit of compromise.

Felicidad threw her youngest sister a look that shut her up.

"I won't live in a prison—" Mercedes said.

"You *are* living in a prison," Felicidad insisted.

"This is where I came to your father out of Mexico. This is where I'll stay."

"You deserve better, Mama," Elizabeth said and stepped from behind her sisters and went to her mother. She put her arm around her.

Mercedes patted her baby Elizabeth's hand,. noting the age spots, and said, "No, I don't, mija."

"Señora?"

Mercedes, on her stoop, her heart stilling, jumped. She looked up and saw a neighbor boy of eight or nine at her curb.

"Está bien usted?"

She smiled at the concern in the child's voice and said, "Bien, bien. Y tu?"

The boy seemed in no hurry to move on. After a moment, he said, "My teacher me dijo la historia de Halloween. En Mexico no hay Halloween."

Now she placed him. He was one of the twelve Acostas who'd moved in six months before up near Rosecrans in Berta Moreno's old place. Not a one of them could string a sentence in English—all of them illegal.

"It is different here," she said.

He reached into a paper bag and pulled something out. "Pan de muerto," he said and walked up to her. "You want?"

She extended her hand, palm up. The child set the piece of sweet bread shaped like a skeleton onto her open palm.

"Mi mamá . . . for mi clase she cook them."

Mercedes looked down at the sugared bread, a skeleton in her palm, and felt the past touching.

"You are early from school, no?" Mercedes asked, unable to take her eyes from the bread.

"I hate mi eschool, so I leaved."

There was something in the child's voice that pulled her. She looked up and he seemed near tears. "Mi mama me dijo que Halloween is like—exactamente like—el dia de los muertos. Pero . . . is no like it at all."

"It is fun," Mercedes protested. "Mis hijos loved it. They could dress up like skeletons—"

"I want regresar a Mexico, señora."

"Are things so good in Mexico?"

"Mi abuelito es in Mexico."

"Maybe your grandfather will come here to you."

"But how? How will he find his way? There are no cempasutchil flowers here."

Her head filled with a burst of yellow-orange, the color of the Oaxacan flower she had not seen in sixty years, and she understood the boy's fears. "How long," she asked, "has he been dead?"

"Dos años. Last year, señora, vino a mi . . . al lado de mi bed—on the day of the dead."

"You dreamed he was by your bed."

"No. He was. He said las flores helped him find his way."

She saw in her head herself as a girl throwing the orange petals along the path leading to their house next to the church in Mitla—when she had been unafraid of calling back her dead.

"Be generous with the flowers, Mercedes, so our dead will not lose their way," she heard her own mother say out of time.

"Mi mamá me dijo," the little boy said, pulling her back, "the pan de muerto and las calaveras will be enough for Papi to find his way—"

"Your mother makes the sugared skulls?"

"Claro, but there are no flowers here."

Mercedes pushed off the porch. She extended her empty hand. "Come, mijo." She led him around the back. "De que parte de Mexico are you?"

"Oaxaca."

She smiled. "I . . . tambien . . . am from Oaxaca, so I know that carnations—red ones como the corazón de Christ—y marigolds can work with the cempasutchil to guide the spirits of our muertos home."

Behind her house, she went to the last of her summer tomato bushes, the fading plants bordered by the marigolds to keep away the insects. She took her scissors from her apron and handed them to the boy.

He took the scissors. "But will they work alone, señora?"

"You have my promise," she said.

While he cut the marigolds, she went to the pots lined up against the house holding the carnations she loved. "Mijo," she called to the boy as she bent and snapped the red blooms from the tall stalks.

He was by her side. "Red ones. Just like in Oaxaca. White ones, too, you will need." The boy had removed his shirt and the marigolds were heaped inside. She laid the cut carnations. "Tienes un dog?"

He nodded.

"De que color?"

"Negro con spots blancos."

"Black. Very lucky. How could a Oaxaca boy like you not know his luck. Could tu abuelito swim?"

"He was too old to swim."

"Then he will need help crossing Nine Rivers—"

The boy smiled. "El Rio Chignahuapan."

"The place between life and death," she said, rising and placing the last carnation on the pile. "If the spirit knows how to swim, no problem . . . pero cuando one is old como tu 'buelito, he will need help." She laid the last of the carnation blooms upon the pile held in his shirt.

"Espero que—" the boy began.

"They will work," she assured. "The flowers and the dog—you are in business." She watched him move away. Before he rounded the house, she called out, "Be generous with the flowers, mijo."

She slipped her scissors into her apron and heard shouting from the front of the house. She would recognize that shouting anywhere. Felicidad had arrived. She moved through the dust of the yard around the house, feeling suddenly very tired. When she rounded the house, she saw Felicidad in the street holding the Acosta boy by his arm as he struggled to get free, dropping carnations onto the pavement.

"Mama!" Felicidad shouted when she saw her mother. "I caught him running from around the house with your flowers—"

"I gave him the flowers," Mercedes said. "Let him be."

He was picking up the last of the blooms when she stepped up. She patted his head. "Tell mi hija que you are no ganger banger." The boy shook his head. "Vayate," Mercedes said.

The boy ran off shouting, "Gracias, señora."

"They don't even learn English. You never went to school and *you* learned English."

"He's learning."

"I'm starving, Mama. I've been dreaming about your rice all morning—"

"I burned it," Mercedes said, leading the way to the stoop.

"What?"

"Callate, mija," Mercedes said, pressing her fingers to her throbbing forehead, "me duele mi cabeza."

"Speak English, Mama, or you'll forget it."

"My head hurts. There is frijoles."

In the kitchen she ladled beans into her daughter's bowl. "You should smile more often, mija."

"Not a whole hell of a lot to smile about, Mama. My Lucy's Beto lost another job. Two months before Christmas." She tasted the beans. "Sal, Mama, pass me the salt."

Mercedes passed the salt and a towel of warm tortillas. "I made them this morning, just after Leeza. She had these men who had become women—"

Felicidad held up her arm, "Please, Ma, I'm eating."

"Mija, they were pretty, más pretty que ever I was."

"What were you givin' the flowers to that little boy for?"

"Para el dia de los muertos. All Souls' . . . All Saints'."

Felicidad stopped eating. "That's right, tomorrow's Halloween. I've still got to buy candy for all the little vultures." She paused and then said, "How come you never did any of that Mexican Day of the Dead stuff for us—the paper skeletons, the candy skulls?"

"You all became Americans. Here there was Halloween."

"But what did he want with the flowers?"

"In Mexico, we believe the dead come back for two days in November . . . if we invite them . . . if we guide them back on paths of flowers."

"Superstition," Felicidad said.

"That little boy doesn't think so. He says his grandfather visits."

Felicidad fell silent. Then she said, "I wouldn't mind my pop coming back for a visit." She bent over her beans but didn't eat. Straightening, she said, "Can you remember him young, Ma?" She didn't wait for an answer. "I can't. I only remember him lying in that hospital bed we put up in the middle of the front room, sinking into himself, wanting only to be gone." She pushed back her bowl. "When they come back, Mama, do they come back old?"

"They come as they choose, mija . . . any way they choose."

"I'm almost as old as Pop was when he died. Imagine," Felicidad said and turned and looked at her mother leaning against the stove. "What's wrong?"

Mercedes held up her hands to show she was fine.

"Your face? Are you all right?" Felicidad got up and went to her mother, looking into her dark eyes. "Something about you is different. Do you hurt? Your heart?"

"Mija," Mercedes said, "stop, before you make me sick."

Felicidad touched her face. "I just can't imagine the world without you."

"Maybe you would smile."

"Mama!"

"Maybe if you stopped worrying, you'd smile."

Felicidad picked up her purse from the table. "You don't like my sour face?"

"I love your sour face."

"That's what you get, Mama, when you go and name a baby Felicidad."

And Mercedes' head filled with images of La Luna, the Carmelas curandera, placing the baby, wet and slippery, on Mercedes' belly, flat again after delivering up the child she had been so afraid the nine months long would be born dead or twisted, penance for her crime. The child wailed lustily, but Mercedes couldn't look.

"Lindisima," La Luna said, "color de oro como her papa." These words caused Mercedes to finally lift her head and look at the baby's beauty, realizing she'd been too afraid to even contemplate a name.

"What will you call her?" La Luna asked.

"Ni un idea do I have," Mercedes said, unable to take her eyes off her baby girl.

"What is it you wish for most in all the world?"

"Happiness," Mercedes whispered, "some joy."

"Felicidad!" Luna said, confirming the child, stamping wish in flesh.

The images watered and leaked away, leaving Felicidad—almost an old woman now—standing before Mercedes looking anything but happy. "My wish for you . . . for me, your name."

Mercedes sat on her stoop long after Felicidad left that day. As dusk neared, the wind picked up and she caught the scent of cow manure on the air drifting over from what was left of the dairy. It was an earthy smell—like frijoles in a pot—but cleaner somehow. She sucked the air deep into her lungs and felt an absence. Then she remembered, the blood was gone. The meat packing plant was twenty years gone—with it the biting metallic smell that had blended with the pungence of the cow manure, softening it to "Carmelas perfume," her Victor used to say, when, home from the dairy, he would sit with her on the stoop before dinner.

She closed her eyes and called him forth, something she rarely did. And he was there. Not old and torn as Felicidad remembered but young, powerful, golden, as when she'd first seen him in the market off the Zocalo in Mitla.

No indio, that stranger then. His hair had been dark, but the sun that day had painted it with reds that heightened the yellow of his skin. So used to faces as brown and Zaptoecan as her own, she had stared too long at the stranger who was two heads taller than any man in the market. He had stared back, shaming her, and causing her to leave the market without her vegetables. As she hurried toward the Zocalo and home on its far side, she glanced back, and, to her fright, he was standing staring after, looking for all the world like a gauchupin from her uncle's books that told of conquest and conquerors with faces like this stranger's.

She opened her eyes and he was gone, nothing substantial enough to grant forgiveness. She thought of the yellow-red cempasutchil, wanting to still believe a flower petal could call back the dead as more than memory. Night was near. She looked across Claresa to Danny's house up near the corner at Mapledale. It was a crazy-looking house, for it alone, among all its neighbors, was two stories high. Not five years old, it had been built on a loan of city money to redevelop the area—but Danny had been one of the few in Carmelas with a job and pay enough to even qualify, so it looked odd and out of place dressed in its beige stucco and Spanish tiled roof next to the shabby frame houses. Mercedes had loved the roof at first, for it was like tile she remembered from

Oaxaca, but the years had weathered it to a different hue and it seemed artificial and out of place. Its windows were all barred and Danny told her he had an arsenal inside to keep the thieves outside. Maybe Felicidad was right. He should have built his Spanish hacienda elsewhere. The lights were on in Danny's house. She saw his Chevrolet inside his wrought-iron fence, locked up for the night. She was so tired and thought sleep might ease the ache and lift the cloud she'd been unable to chase away.

Inside her kitchen, she boiled water for tea to invite sleep. She heard her front door open and close, then Danny calling "Mama!" loudly to let her know it was only he, coming, as he often did, to say goodnight, to check on her.

She sat him at her kitchen table. She poured their tea.

"You look tired, Ma," he said, staring into her face.

She nodded.

He sipped his tea.

"You know the Acostas up the street?" she asked.

"Wetbacks, Ma, the whole bunch."

"As was I," she said. "Your papa, too."

"A whole different breed."

She chose not to pursue the difference. Instead she said, "The littlest Acosta boy came by today and he made me think of when I was a young girl. He is Oaxacan—as I was—and he talked of a flower I haven't seen in sixty years. Cempasutchil."

"Cempasutchil," her Danny repeated.

"A perfect ear, you always had, mijo." And she saw him smile as he had smiled all his days at any compliment she threw his way. "A special flower at this time of year. What I would give to see that flower again . . . tomorrow for Halloween."

"What would you give, Mama? A smile?"

She laughed, feeling silly, rose and cleared their cups. At the front door, she kissed her Danny's cheek. Then, she went to bed—and could not sleep.

An hour passed, and she wondered if there might be moon outside her window. Rising, she went to the window across the room, pulled back the curtain and saw only blackness. She rested her face against the old glass and suddenly, beyond the window, it was raining, sheets of water, falling so thick and fast she could see nothing past it. She lifted her face and glanced back toward her bed, but there was no bed.

She was in a room, dim save for a single lamp, an oil lamp like none she'd seen in years. A naked floor, bodies humped here and there, sleeping, amid stiff-backed chairs, some with people sitting, shadows obscured in the dark room.

She felt weight in her arms and, looking down, saw her baby, Esperanza, dark and Zapotecan, small for almost two. The brown of her sleeping face seemed brushed with red, for she was hot with fever that burned through her blanket.

"They say the rain will last for days."

Mercedes turned and saw a woman, too brightly painted—still not pretty save for rich, thick, piled hair.

"Rain or no, I'm crossing in the morning," a male voice, rough and hard, said from the darkness.

"The river's in flood," the painted woman said.

The man in darkness laughed. "The Rio Bravo just gets wider, never rising higher than your lovely knees."

"Then why have you waited?" Mercedes asked.

"I am a man used to my comforts. The crossing's more comfortable in sun. But sun or rain, I've business in El Paso that cannot wait. At daylight, I am on my way." He pulled his chair, the legs scraping loudly on the wooden floor, closer to the younger woman with painted eyes. "Does business await you in the north?" he asked, his voice low, insinuating.

The woman's blood red lips laughed. "I carry my business with me."

Mercedes pulled her baby closer to her body and turned back to the window, wanting to hear nothing of their words. And outside the window, time jumped, for the night paled, becoming instantly day, though the rain had not let up.

Spinning, she saw people rising from the floor, and across the room at the door she saw the man of the night before, the woman with him, too. Mercedes went to her and said, "Please, are you crossing today?"

She nodded. "My friend, he is arranging it now."

"Take me with you." Then in a rush, Mercedes said, "My husband . . ."

"He's waiting on the other side?" the other woman asked.

Mercedes shook her head no.

"He sent for you?"

Mercedes shook her head again.

"He promised he would send for you?"

Mercedes nodded.

"They never keep their promises."

"I'll find him. I know where he is."

"And if there is another woman?"

Fear cut through Mercedes, stabbing.

"Go home. Don't be a fool."

Mercedes rummaged through her baby's blanket and found the twenty-dollar bill, part of the money Victor had been sending for a year, most of it saved. She pulled it out and pressed it into the woman's hand. "Make him take me, too. I must cross today."

The woman closed her fingers on the bill and in what seemed but a moment, Mercedes was out of the room, in falling rain, and standing at the river's edge in mud. She tried to see to the other side, but the rain was thick, the day too grey. Her rebozo was wet through, sticking to her and covering her baby bundled in the crook of her arm.

The woman, her skirts tied up high around her naked thighs, was removing her shoes. "Take off your shoes," she said. "He says naked feet can better grip the bottom."

Then, Mercedes saw the man step barefoot into the water. He strode forward. The woman, her bare hair wet and hanging now in thick ropy strands, followed into the fast-moving water. Forgetting to remove her shoes as she'd been instructed, Mercedes followed, gripping her baby to her bosom—the water cold and biting, grabbing at her legs, her trailing dress. The man was far ahead and the woman called out, "He's not lying. It's just above his knees."

And time jumped again, for Mercedes was now so far into the river that she could not see either shore. The woman, moving gingerly, was just ahead, but the man had become a hazy outline far ahead in the gray rain.

The water, brown as earth, swirled by, catching in Mercedes' skirts, slowing her down, creating distance. She heard the woman call out, "Hurry," and so she tried to move faster through the water, the earth mush under her shoes, when, without warning, her leg shot out from under her, her leather sole offering no traction, and she went down, her arms flying outward as she fell back into the rushing water. She screamed, muddy water filling her mouth, her hands sinking into mud as she pushed herself up out of the water, rising, sputtering in the rain. And only then did she feel the absence in her arms and realize.

"My baby!" A wail loosed upon the wind.

Frantic, she spun in the water, slapping at it with her hands, seeking, looking, searching, seeing only muddy swirling water. Falling back into the water, she reached for the bottom, swinging her arms in an arc, wide and hopeless, feeling, frantic, digging into mud. Rising, she saw the woman at her side, paint running blackly at her eyes filled with horror that confirmed Mercedes' loss.

Mercedes tried to run down the river with the rushing current, her eyes scanning the brown foamy surface for a speck, a sign, seeing nothing, nothing, hearing only the screaming of an animal.

And then, she was on land again, the rain still falling, but lightly now. The river, a brown, wide ribbon, still swirled by. She saw far down the river bank the man running, looking, finally stopping, turning back, and Mercedes fell into the mud, black sinking all around.

She woke up screaming.

Sitting upright in her own bed again, she was screaming, terror bouncing off the walls. Her hand found her mouth, covering it, the screams dying, becoming gasps, deep hungry gasps for air. She glanced about the room, as familiar as her body, and she felt herself return out of time. Her hands felt the mattress beneath her and it grounded her. Heart racing, she reached for the old clock by her bed and saw in its lighted face the time—four-thirty in the morning and she knew she had been dreaming dreams untouched in years.

The room was black save for the clock face, and she held her veiny hands up close to her eyes and stared at them, feeling still the water, icy and cold as death, racing, pulling, spilling over them. She lay back down and pulled the covers up to her chin and stared at the ceiling and waited for morning. The time passing seemed forever.

"She is evil."

The radio doctor's hard brittle voice passed through her head, the words a litany, interspersed with thoughts of death that made her tremble, for she could not bear what waited on the other side.

When the room was light, she rose, dressed, and tried to live her day as always, but today time hardly moved. At three o'clock she turned the TV on. Oprah—a presence dark and warm filled the screen. After Oprah went off, she tried to sit through Geraldo, but couldn't. In her kitchen, she warmed tortillas on the stove, wrapped them around slices of yellow cheese, and fled the house. She sat on her stoop looking up and down the street, wishing there was someone into whose house she could go for refuge.

But there was only Daniel's, empty she knew at this time of day, his Susana still at work, the children not yet home from school.

She leaned back against her porch post and closed her eyes. She must have slept, for when she opened her eyes, wakened by a tooting horn, she saw Daniel's Chevrolet at the curb, and dusk darkening the sky. She straightened on the stoop, seeing her Daniel coming round the car, carrying a cardboard box, a flash of yellow-orange peeking over the top.

"Ma," he said, his voice spilling excitement. "Start smiling!" He lowered the box before her face, and for the first time today her heart lifted. Three tired, drooping flowers, in green plastic pots, sat in the box. "Cempasutchiles, Ma."

"Danielito," she said. "How?"

He sat next to her on the steps, laughing. "I was telling this Paco I work with—a real Mexican like you, Ma—about how my ma was homesick for a Oaxacan flower and he knew the flower and told me I might find some down at the Central Market. So, when I got my break, I drove over—just a skip and a jump from Lincoln Heights anyway—and I found these. The last. A big demand these days, the flower guy said, for the few he can get. So I grabbed them. I know. They're tired-looking what with sitting in the car all day."

"They're beautiful, mijo," she said and lifted her hand to his cheek, bristly under her fingers. "Flores de mi juventud."

"I don't want you crying, Ma. You promised me smiles." He stood up.

She smiled.

"Better. Bet you've forgotten it's Halloween. Kids'll be coming. I've got candy in the car for you to give them. Go get a bowl."

She carried the box of flowers into her kitchen. She was reaching up into her cupboard for a big bowl when Danielito stepped into the room, a bag of candy in each hand. They filled the bowl and went back outside.

"I'll sit with you awhile just to make sure none of the little vatos get wise."

They sat on the porch and the children came, in dribbles, then in a flow, then ending in a trickle. The Acosta boy never came.

Danny stood up. "Well, Ma, I think I'll be gettin' home. You goin' in?"

"I'll sit in the moon a little longer."

Danny looked up and down the street. "Not too long now, Ma. The bigger boys start coming out to play soon." He bent and kissed her.

She watched him climb into his car, drive up the block, and finally disappear inside his house. Only then did Mercedes rise and go inside. In the kitchen she removed one of the potted cempasutchiles, leaving the remaining two in the box. She lifted it and walked outside. She moved up Claresa toward Rosecrans and stopped two doors from the corner at Berta Moreno's old house. A group of older boys were hanging out in the yard.

"Is this the Acosta house?" she asked.

"We're out of candy, lady," one of the boys in the yard said, snickering.

She hunted through the boys on the porch, looking for whoever looked more Mexican. It was not in his face, for all the boys were brown, but in the clothes, the cut of hair that was not quite American. She found the haircut. "Esta tu señora madre en casa?"

Her formalidad caused the boy to step into the yard. "Sí, señora. Hay un problema?"

"No problems. I have a gift for your little brother."

"Manolo?" He looked into the box and his eyes got wide. "Cempasutchil."

"Claro."

He jumped up the steps and called his mother. A tiny woman stepped onto the porch, pulling a sweater about her shoulders. "Señora?"

Mercedes went to the steps. "Tu boy . . . Manolo . . . un regalo . . . cempasutchil."

The woman's eyes went bigger than her son's. "Manolo!"

The boy appeared. "Did you go trick-or-treating?" Mercedes asked.

He shook his head.

She extended her arms. "Cempasutchil."

They sat together on the porch and pulled off all the petals, mixing them in a large bag already holding the petals of the flowers she'd given him the day before. "The real thing from Mexico," she said, "with a little something new from here thrown in—like you now that you're here." The boys in the yard had wandered off except for Manolo's older brother. "Your name?" she asked.

"Juan Pablo, señora."

She extended the open bag to both of them. "Be generous with the flowers."

Manolo reached in and took two handfuls. His brother, hesitant, standing at the line of age that separated boys from men, thrust his hand into the bag, choosing boyhood for one more night. He raced to the curb and joined his brother scattering the flower petals along the pathway to the door.

When Mercedes walked away from the yard, she saw the Acosta woman on the porch, an arm around each boy, a trail edged in petals winding to the street. She saw the black dog, speckled with white blotches, skipping around their feet.

At home, Mercedes waited until Johnny Carson was over. She liked his talk least of all, but it made the tiny living room seem full of people. When he was done, she took the bag of cempasutchil petals she had plucked from the remaining plant during Carson's show out onto her porch. She glanced up and down the street, empty now, dark save for the moon and pools of light beneath each streetlamp. Certain she was alone, she went out to the street and scattered flowers, creating a border from street to stoop on both sides of the cement path Danielito had laid for her two years before.

When she was done, she sat on the steps. The flowers were like bits of fire calling at the night, calling. No one came.

She pulled her sweater tight about her neck and leaned back against the porch post. She closed her eyes, leaving her ears to listen, and she felt lighter than she could remember.

A long time passed. Still, no one came. The street was empty. Night was nearly done. She pushed up from the step, pain radiating in her stiff, cold limbs, and, turning, froze. Under the eaves, far back on the sloping porch stood a woman so dark she almost disappeared into the shadows. Mercedes knew instantly who it was—never even questioning how a babe pulled to heaven could become the woman fate had never allowed to be. "Esperanza, you've come."

The woman, wrapped in a rebozo, stepped to the edge of the porch, catching the moonlight. Brown shapely arms reached up, pulling the shawl from hair that hung loose and free down past her shoulders. The body was lost in loose white cotton, flowers embroidered everywhere in turquoise, red, and yellow.

Mercedes tried to speak, but no words came. Her eyes moved up to the face, the skin so fine, so taut the bones behind were clear, and she saw *realized* in the woman's face all that had only been promise so long ago in her baby's face. The eyes were Indian, large, black, and brilliant as stars, the face, like hers, more Zapotecan than any of her other children.

"You could not swim," Mercedes said in English.

The woman turned slightly, extending an arm, and there at the edge of the porch sat a dog, black, white, and red.

"He helped you over?"

The woman nodded.

"I am evil."

The woman moved, but Mercedes saw no feet—she floated off the porch but not down the steps. She hovered in the yard and then touched down at Mercedes' side. They were the same height, their eyes fixed on each other.

"I am evil," Mercedes said again, the words often felt but spoken aloud for only the second time in her life.

The woman shook her head hard before lifting her hand, allowing a finger to graze Mercedes' lips, ordering her still. The face came close, the lips falling on Mercedes' own, lightly, almost unfelt. She felt the woman's arms embrace her and pull her close. Mercedes found the woman's ear, the scent of cempasutchil in her hair, and said, "Te quiero, hija mia, forgive me."

Mercedes felt lips at her ear, felt them move, heard air whistle through them into her own ear, but no words came. She lifted her own arms and wrapped them around the woman, holding again what she'd lost years before in the river. The dog began to bark. It jumped about their feet, howling. The woman pulled away, stepped back, the dog dancing wildly about her feet. Mercedes saw her look beyond into the street. She turned. In the street, a line of people, wavering—half here, half gone—calling. Looking up the street toward Rosecrans, she saw an old man climbing Berta Moreno's porch—the Acostas' porch now—the dog there growling fiercely. When Mercedes turned back, the woman, brown like a Zapotec—brown as Mercedes—was lifting the shawl back over her hair.

"No," Mercedes said loudly, stepping toward her daughter—who faded, growing smaller, becoming girl, then baby, before disappearing finally into air as she had once into brown muddy water.

Mercedes went to her stoop and sat. The street beyond her yard was dirt again. Where had the pavement gone? She heard herself sob, the sound a yearning tearing through her body. She sucked in air and the night was perfume, manure heavy in the air laced with blood, offal, earth. The dirt street was empty, and in the dim morning light, she saw Señora Rosaura's jacaranda in radiant bloom.

"Come."

She turned her head and Victor stood at the edge of their house, beckoning.

She rose. "Victor?"

"Preciosa," he called, extending his arms.

She moved toward him but stopped. He was young again. "You are as you were."

"We come as we choose. You said so."

"But I am old."

"I will make you young, my love."

"Can you forgive me?"

"That is all we have to give."

She looked back at her house and she saw herself—old—sitting on the stoop, head leaning back against the post. Then, she looked down at herself and saw only young brown naked toes peeking out from the hem of a Zapotecan cotton gown. She looked back a final time and saw the old woman—herself—as if asleep on the porch for all to see, her mouth hanging open. She moved to the old woman whose face was her own, and, extending an arm, skin smooth and young, she gently closed the mouth, not wanting Danny to find her ugly in the morning sun. Rising, she looked toward the street, seeing before the woman on the porch a trail of flowers, yellow-orange flame, stretching to the dirt street. Turning from the street, her breath caught, for her husband waiting at the edge of the house was younger still, looking every bit the man she had first seen in the Mitla market. "I have had such secrets."

"Gone. All gone," he said and slipped around the corner of the house.

She followed, running.

Chapter 19

Malinche's Children ~ 1994

Sammy Archuleta was home.

Sitting on the stoop looking across the dusty yard to Claresa, he tried to remember the street when it had been dirt and dark save for the light shed by a summer moon. The moon was there, but it couldn't compete now with the garish yellow streetlights that sallowed the black asphalt and made his memories of how it had been before harder to grab onto. And that was disturbing, the sudden slipperiness of memory, to a man who had made of memory a bank from which to draw during all his years of exile. In fact, memory alone had been enough to deny the exile, for in memory his past seemed always present, a shroud which could be called forth when needed and dropped around wherever he happened to find himself. But memory wasn't working now and hadn't been for some time.

He glanced across the narrow street to the houses there beyond the spill of yellow streetlight. They were the same—but not the same. Bars. There were bars on tiny windows now. The Ochoa house across the street had a heavy black security screen over the front door, making the small frame house appear to be a fortress in the shadow—proof that Manny Ochoa, who had feared nothing, had passed the house on to strangers.

Sammy's eyes, frantic now, moved up Claresa and stopped on the tree. He exhaled loudly. It was still there. Señora Rosaura's jacaranda, summer green, no purple May blooms, but there, and in a flash the street of then was back, a dusty ribbon, graced by one old lady's valiant tree. From his place on the step, he sank into the vision, so real he could see the mulberry trees standing tall at the top of the street, so real he could even hear the distant rush of voices that had once filled the summer nights. And then it was gone. Not the street. But *that* street. Claresa long ago. His eyes were still fixed on Señora Rosaura's jacaranda, but in the light of the lamps it seemed almost a different tree. What had he been expecting to find?

He knew. He wanted to come home, a yearning building over some time, made palpable this past wet April as he'd stood by Remi's dead body in the Redding hospital, Remi's blind wife beside him, Sammy's arms helpless and overflowing with a Penney's plastic bag holding slacks Remi had called about that morning—not two hours before—asking them to bring him something new to wear home. So certain Remi had been of imminent release that he'd buoyed the wife who'd called Sammy five days before in despair, telling him Remi's end was in sight—his T-cells gone, his body shutting down—that Sammy was needed, for everyone in their small Redding hospital was terrified of Remi's AIDS. Junie had begged him to come and take Remi back to his hematologist in San Francisco. He'd gone, but Remi's vital signs were too low for him to risk the five-hour drive back to San Francisco, so they'd spent the time beside his bed, watching him sink. Then, he'd rallied, sending them home to sleep, even calling them that last morning, sounding like himself, directing them to buy him his signature black pants and a bag of Oreos before coming to the hospital, insisting he was coming home. Sammy and Junie had followed his instructions, thinking Remi—who'd done it before—*might be* springing back, going another round. They'd been wrong—Remi was dead when they'd arrived. Sammy had been shaken by the death of his oldest friend as he'd never been shaken before; even his papa's—his mama's—passing had not left him so perched at the edge of solitude as losing Remi. Things hadn't been the same since and had really been named only this morning, during the eight-hour drive of the day spent getting here that had seemed like flight.

He hadn't even known he was trying to run home when he'd fled his house this morning; he'd only known his life since Remi's death had grown increasingly unbearable. A turning point had been reached this morning when he'd told Delilah he was leaving. When he'd climbed into his Regal, pulled away from the house that he'd made himself believe was home, he hadn't even been able to look back in the rearview mirror for fear Delilah would have been on the steep porch staring after him. Then, he'd been sure it was home from which he'd been running, the marriage that had begun to stifle long before Remi died, turning into stranglehold after. The feeling of flight from the chains of that house had stayed with him as he'd driven through Cow Hollow, onto the 580 inland to the 5 that had brought him all these hours later south to Norwalk—Carmelas.

All the long drive down, he'd felt that the pressing at his back had been the pull of that house—Delilah, his daughters—as he ran away. Only as he'd pulled off the Santa Ana freeway onto the long curving Rosecrans exit did his whole sense of flight turn upside down. Rounding the curve that had suddenly felt as familiar as the flesh on the inside of Delilah's thigh and wrapped in air spilling through his open window, he saw that this had never been a flight from home, but rather a desperate race to get back home before it was too late.

And now, sitting on the porch of the house in which he'd been born, staring out at the street, he wondered if he'd waited too long.

But he hadn't been wondering as the rush of August night air had swirled around him in the car when he'd left the freeway just an hour ago. The singing air had been thick with the odor of cars, but the smell filling his head then had been colored by something more—the tangy pungence of cows—manure, cow shit turned by time and sun into the rich brown scent of earth. As he moved down the off-ramp, this scent of home had been enough to make him realize the undeniability of the exile his life had been since leaving Carmelas years before. Feeling a peace descend—maybe the first in years—he'd sucked in the warm night air, only to find no trace of the smell of blood except in memory. Its absence—jarring—had changed the consistency of the night and threatened his newfound sense of peace. He'd tried to pull it back by telling himself that he'd known the meat packing plant was twenty years gone, and yet the absence of that smell from the slaughterhouse, once layered thickly across the sky, still made him feel afraid. So, he'd pushed on the gas, racing up Rosecrans, seeing as he passed that the tract houses of the gringos didn't look as fine as he remembered. Taco Joe's was still there, the dairy, too—but where were all the cows? He saw the edge of Carmelas, the line separating it from the gringo neighborhood around it harder to spot. He turned onto Claresa and thought for a moment he'd turned onto the wrong street, until he'd seen his house, the yard, familiarity reaching out to him and pulling him in.

Home now, on his own stoop, the fear was even stronger and it wasn't just the absence in the air, it was the street itself. Even the jacaranda he and Mr. Trujillo had saved when the gringos had first paved Claresa seemed a shadow of the tree it'd been. So, he gave up the street, dragging his eyes back to the earthen yard, as hard as a floor, which stretched to the paved street—his yard, not alien at all. He concentrated on the yard and hugged his knees to steady a world that seemed to be falling away. He wanted to feel what he'd felt as a boy sitting here, but he was forty-eight and terrified he'd stayed away too long.

Heart pounding, he stretched out on the old cement porch and stared up at the stuccoed underside of the house. His heart slowed, for in the night, the pale stucco seemed clean, soft as cotton. New. Not the house, for it hadn't been new when he'd been born. The stucco. He remembered when Arturo and Papa had finished stuccoing the old frame house. He'd been seven that summer—July just after the fourth and the carnival under the mulberries by the school—but before Arturo had gone to real prison.

Staring up at the stucco, it was easier to imagine he was seven again, the world small, his mother alive, his papa, too, and Arturo clean. Sammy closed his eyes, awash in memory that wrapped around him like a dream.

"Cabrón, wake up!"

Sammy felt his shoulder pulled, his hair tousled. Startled, he opened his eyes and saw Arturo bending over him, appearing as if out of nowhere. He sat up, saw Arturo's truck pulled up next to his own Buick in the yard, and wondered how much time had passed. "I must have fallen asleep," he said and saw Arturo step back, unsteady on his feet.

"A long drive, Samuelito." He laughed. "What's the matter? You look like you seen a ghost, man!"

Arturo was drunk. There was nothing new in that, for Sam had never believed Arturo's promises as Delilah had. But he saw that Arturo was also old. He was still big. But his flesh seemed softer, overflowing. His hair, as thick as Sam remembered, was white, the shocking white that comes to hair once black as an Indian's eye. He had on a cotton shirt, open at the throat, silver hair bubbling at the collar. The sleeves rolled up high revealed arms still big with power, each a canvas covered with images inked into every inch of visible flesh. "I was dreaming," Sammy said. "I fell asleep and was dreaming of the night you finished stuccoing Mama's house—do you remember?"

"Estoy borracho," Arturo said. "Too drunk to remember."

"I thought you stopped," Sammy said, giving Arturo the lie to step into if he chose.

But Arturo laughed, pushing Sammy over so he could join him on the steps. "That's what I told your Delilah. Got her off my ass, man." He stopped laughing. "What she don't know can't hurt her."

"You didn't have any of these—when you stuccoed the house," Sammy said, one finger selecting and tracing the woman's face inked into his brother's skin, half-covered by his shirt sleeve, an image that had fascinated Sammy for years.

"I was new then, 'mano. Ain't new no more." He laughed and pulled up his shirt sleeve. "She ain't either."

Sammy looked and saw that his brother's skin had become brown leather, creased, and the creases cut across the tattooed face, aging it, sagging it, turning the once lovely Chola into a shrew.

"But who ain't gettin' older." He lifted his arm and flung it around Sammy, pulling him close. "Except for ti, 'mano. Tu pareces como un baby still. Ni un gray hair in your head."

Sammy felt small next to his brother, but he always had. The hand that slapped against his thigh was a slab of thick-fingered flesh. Looking down at the inside of his brother's arm, the skin there no lighter shade of brown, the tattoos as thick, he saw the scars, hard bumps of rigid flesh no tattoo could hide where needles had pierced Arturo's flesh and Sammy's heart along with Mama's—Papa's, too.

"And hands," Arturo said, his free hand grabbing Sammy's own and turning it palm up. "The hands of a caballero if I ever seen one."

Sammy pulled his hand away as if he were ashamed of the smoothness that was testimony to a brown gentleman's years in exile. He stood up.

"Life's been good to you, Sammy," Arturo said.

"Yeah," Sam replied, knowing now it wasn't really true.

"So why you goin' an' fuckin' it up, man?" Sammy didn't want it to start like this; he avoided his brother's eyes, saying nothing. "Delilah called me today," Art said. Sammy's face tightened at the mention of his wife's ploy. From the beginning, she'd aligned tía, Arturo, too—maybe Arturo most of all—on her side. Hers—to make a front that held Sam in. He held his anger. "Said you been pulling back for some time. Remi's dying, she said, brought things to a head." He paused, waiting for a response but getting none. "Remi—poor fucker—his fate was sealed years ago." He stared up at Sammy, forcing him to turn away his eyes.

When he looked back, he saw concern in Arturo's bleary eyes. The realization that Arturo was his, only his, made him hiss loudly, "She shouldn't have called—"

"Why the fuck not, Sam? She's who I hear from. When I heard from you last?"

"I called you," Sam countered, "just a month ago. I wanted you at the opening of my play."

"Your play," Arturo repeated. "Yeah, man, you did call—a month ago. But other than that? Nada. From you I get visits. Once every ten years or so when some shit in your life starts hitting the fan."

"You know I've been busy—"

"Don't start that, man. "

Sammy saw his brother's face harden, his hands clench into fists. He hadn't wanted it to start like this. This wasn't what he needed. Gently, he asked, "You don't want me here?"

"Esta bien, man. It's your house anyway. I just board here."

"You don't want me here?" Sammy asked again, not so gentle now, and he saw something change in his brother's eyes.

"You could be mi hijo, Sammy. I was already a man when you came. Twenty fuckin' years old, and you the first baby I ever held.

The first." Arturo sat back down on the stoop. "That must do something to you, man. 'Cause, yeah, I want you here. You just shouldn't be here."

"What'd Delilah tell you?"

"Something about some morenita your chorizo has taken to sniffing after."

"Not just my cock."

"What then, man, what could there be you ain't already got with Lilah."

"She's brown, Tootie. Marina. Orizaba. Brown like me."

"Nobody calls me Tootie anymore, Sam. I'm an old man. Art'll do fine." He pushed himself up from the porch as if he couldn't stay still. "Seems to me, though, the world, at least from this front porch, has always been full of morenitas con mamarias that point to heaven—for a few years, anyway, before they fall. How come you missed them then?"

"Delilah got in the way." And she had. She had. Against all of his intentions. He'd been into his first year at Cerritos College when the University of Seven Seas had come calling. He'd applied on a lark his senior year in high school. They'd given him some chickenshit scholarship, but that would have left a thousand dollars. He'd said no. They'd come back with an offer to pick up the whole tab; he was going to say no again, but Arturo had beaten him into changing his mind and told Trujillo, so Sammy had gone—with one twelve-dollar Robert Hall sports coat with polka-dotted lining that had lasted until Barcelona when in a downpour it had shrunk up his arms to the elbows and bled cheap blue dye over his one white shirt. He'd been in one of the washrooms on board the ship trying to save the shirt when Delilah had walked in and shown him how to do it; she'd saved more than the shirt, she saved the trip, a disaster up to then, for he had been the boy with a full scholarship from Carmelas, a brown speck in a sea of monied whiteness who had had no idea how he was going to endure the months that would take him around the world. Delilah, sleek, tall, golden, from Burlingame with money to burn, had chosen him in a washroom and stolen his heart, his soul—against all his true intentions. "She got in the way," he said again.

"She ain't in the way now?" Arturo asked and moved past him up the steps. "Now you got Alma and Lilly standing on each side of her. Seems like you got more in your way, man, than ever before." He went into the house.

Sammy put his hands in his pockets and turned back to Claresa, his narrow street that seemed now so wide and empty. He then lifted his eyes to heaven, the moon and the stars as faint and far away as the street. "Used to be a million stars."

Arturo stepped back out onto the porch. "It's your eyes, man. You gotta be at least forty-five. Eyes go at forty-five—pinga goes a little later—if I remember right."

Sammy laughed. "Papa must have been almost sixty when I was born."

"Pop was special, 'mano. Don't you never forget that," Arturo said.

Pop. So long dead, he was hard for Sammy to conjure up. Not the details of the man, but the wholeness of the image. The color of cinnamon—that's what Mama always said. Canela. A cinnamon-colored man, a bull like Arturo, but shorter, closer to the earth. He'd said he would have been taller had it not been for the short-handled hoe he'd wielded in fields, bent over so many years that when he'd finally been freed from the earth by the job at the Norwalk Dairy building mountains of manure, his body had refused to unfold itself.

"We ain't—either of us—in that old man's league," Arturo reminded solemnly.

And Sam, who said nothing, still knew it to be true. The man had a dignity so strong, so deep, that nothing touched it. Not labor in a field, or labor hip high in shit, not heartbreak at the string of Mama's babies, all born dead save for Arturo at the beginning of their marriage, until Sammy, a blessing, his pop had never tired of telling him, at its end. Dignity, as rich and dark as his eyes, his hair, which had withstood time, Arturo's shame, and the cancer that had robbed him of work, forced his wife into the fields, and taken him before his last, Sammy, was even twelve. Un hombre, a man powerful enough to name himself.

Sammy turned and saw Arturo on the porch, an open coffee can beside him. He was busy rolling a cigarette. When Sammy got closer, he saw it wasn't tobacco.

"It's good shit," Arturo said in response to Sam's look. "Vato got it for me said it was Colombian gold. Fuck it. It gets me there." He lit the joint and sucked on it.

"Same old shit," Sammy said.

Arturo hesitated and then sucked on the joint again. When he exhaled loudly, he said, "How many of us ever change? It's so fuckin' much easier when we just accept it—live with it, man."

"You've changed," Sammy insisted.

"Yeah," Arturo said, laughing. "I cut lawns—other people's lawns. Every fuckin' day of my life—except Sunday, won't get near someone's lawn on Sunday. Pop would be proud. I'm regular. It's all he ever said he wanted. Me to be a regular guy. So, now, at sixty—"

"Sixty-eight," Sammy corrected.

"Sixty-eight," Arturo conceded, holding out the joint, "shit's supposed to hurt only short-term memory, ain't it?" He laughed. "Take a hit, man. It won't kill you." Sammy took the proffered joint and brought it to his lips. Sam passed the joint back. Arturo sucked on it. "I got lawns tomorrow. Can't afford a hangover. It kills the hangover, I swear to God, Sam." He exhaled, saying, "So, tell me about this brown piece—"

"She's a professor where I am—and believe me, she's nobody's piece."

"Delilah says it's been goin' on some time."

Sam nodded. "A year or so."

"So, what're you doin' here?"

"I think this is part of it, Art. I've been needing to come home. I think that's what this thing with Marina's been all about. Getting home."

"Back to brown."

Sam saw the smirk on his brother's face. "I'm serious."

"I ain't?"

"Eschucha me, hermano."

"I'm trying to hear you, Sam."

"I got off somewhere—wrong road—"

"I know about caminos que corren nowhere," Art said and held out his scarred arms, the joint, half gone, trailing smoke from between fat fingers.

"Then understand me. Not all roads to hell are paved with needles, Tootie. Some . . . are paved with blessings."

"Who'd a thought?" Art said, leaning back on the steps, sucking smoke from heavenly shit.

"I was blessed."

"Claro que sí, vato."

"From Carmelas I got to Stanford."

"El solo chico from Carmelas who ever did—but not," Arturo reminded him, "before you went round the world, vato—thanks to us."

Around the world.

When he'd sailed away, his mama had been dead four years. Tía Carmen had been keeping house, seeing Sammy through high school with barely enough money to keep them in beans. Arturo came home that summer before Sammy's leaving, finally released from prison—not even having been allowed home for Mama's funeral. He should have been a stranger, but to Sammy he'd never been really gone. A giant, Art, his giant, his hermano, and, though Art had seemed withdrawn from everyone—pacing through Carmelas that summer like a lion still in a cage—he'd embraced Sammy, pulled him closer than Sammy could have dreamed.

"They say you're smart, carnal," Arturo had said to him one night, the two of them alone on the porch. "What's this smart vato going to do?"

Sammy shrugged. "Cerritos College, I guess. If I can squeeze it in. I got to work."

"You gotta go to school, hombre, that's all you got to do."

So he'd enrolled at Cerritos, Arturo almost turning his VW Bug over to him—Arturo walking to work over at the dairy. When he'd gotten the scholarship letter the second time from the University of the Seven Seas offering a free ride, Arturo had found it—Sammy surprised he hadn't seen the joke in it. "Pinche ship goes around the world," he'd told his brother.

"So?" Art asked.

"So what?" Sammy asked back.

"So go, man."

Sammy had laughed. "I got no money."

"You got a full fuckin' scholarship—"

"I'd need some change in my pockets," he'd said. "And tía. Who'd take care of tía?"

"I'm home now," Art said. "You take care of you—school. All Pop wanted—un hijo with the brains to use 'em."

"Who do you think we are, Tootie," Sammy had asked. "Around the world. I've hardly been out of Carmelas."

"Who do *you* think we are, Sam? That's the question."

Sammy had let it drop, but Arturo changed his mind—the vato had fists like hams, but even more than those fists, Art had thrown him to Trujillo, Sammy's old teacher, and once Trujillo got in the act, everyone in Carmelas knew about Sammy's scholarship. Trujillo wouldn't let it die and pretty soon he had everyone pitching in. Before Sam knew what was going on, Trujillo had collected six hundred dollars.

"It's yours," Mr. Trujillo said, passing the brown bag up to Sam on his porch, Arturo and tía behind. "Six hundred dollars of Carmelas money. Study hard and send us postcards. The only way most us will ever see the world." The neighbors filling the yard behind Trujillo applauded. Sammy had taken the bag, heavy, change rattling, and he'd gone. Around the world. Into Delilah's arms, who refused ever again to let him go, pulling him up to Stanford, from which—until now—he'd never been able to break free.

"Around the world," Sam said aloud to Arturo, feeling older than the years gone by since then could account for, "and farther, Art, so goddamned much farther." Sam extended his hand toward his brother, wanting a hit from Art's number. Art passed the joint, a roach now, and Sammy pulled it to his lips, sucking in the taste, the feel of fire. "When I got back from going around the fuckin' world, I was alone. Pop long dead, Mama, too. Who was here? Just old tía, who could hardly take care of herself. And you—who promised me you'd be here, holding things together—were in prison again. Not for a few years this time. Forever, man, 'cause you killed somebody. You talk about me fuckin' up my life. You're the master fuckup of all time. I got nobody in the world to come home to and you—you get drunk—"

"Not drunk, man," Arturo said, real low, his eyes far off as if he were watching it unfold again. "Stoned on my ass—higher than this kite has ever flown, man—"

"And you off some man—"

"Some brown man, 'mano, as brown as me—"

"And I'm here in Carmelas, with crazy old tía—so what do I do when Delilah chases me down and digs in here with me and tía . . . and tía loves her. What do I do when the offer comes from Stanford? I go—Delilah in tow—I go. And there I was in Stanford—gavachos everywhere."

"Pobrecito," Arturo said loudly. He pushed himself up. "Your ass is in Stanford. You know where my ass was, Sammy?"

Sammy stepped back away from his brother. "I tell you, Art, not a brown face—anywhere up there, 'til '67. But by then, I've got Delilah—she's got me . . . so tight there was no letting go."

"Think about what I was holdin', vato mio."

"I *tried* to get away. Before Delilah got me to marry her, I'd come back here summers to stay with tía. My hands weren't so smooth then. I worked in manure up to my waist like Pop—you—had over at the dairy. I went out with brown girls in Carmelas—trying to cut loose from Delilah—but, Art, we had nothing to talk about."

"But you got out of the manure, come September. My shit went on forever." Arturo sat back down and scooped grass from the open can, rolling first one, then two fat numbers. He put both in his mouth, lit them, sucked greedily and then passed one to Sam, who took it. "Didn't somebody do that to Bette Davis, man, in some movie a hundred years ago?" he said and laughed.

"It wasn't Colombian," Sammy said and took a long pull on the number. "It was different with Delilah—she talked to me. She read books. She knew about art, Tootie. She could take me to a museum and show me things I'd never known were there. She opened doors—and never, Art, never looked down her nose."

"She loves you, man. Delilah loves you."

"Even on a ship full of gringos—she chose me," Sam said.

"I remember," Art said, "the first time you brought her to see me. I was locked up in Lompoc, wasn't I? All I could see at first was that long, hippie yellow hair. But then, she started talkin', man, and you won't believe who she reminded me of."

"Who?"

Arturo shook his head. "Sounds crazy, man, but it's true. Never told anyone until tía. 'Cause she tol' *me*, man. Tía Carmen says to me during a visit—I think Socorro drove her up to Lompoc to see me—she says to me, 'Tootie, that Delilah me acuerda de your mamá'—that's what tía said, and I swear to God, Sammy, that first time in Lompoc, after I could get beyond the fuckin' hair, she reminded *me* of Mama, and she has ever since."

Sammy went to the steps and sat next to his brother. "Mama?" He shook his head in disbelief and took another hit of Art's Colombian.

"So what's this chica Delilah told me about got beside brown chichis?"

At the mention of Marina's breasts, Sammy felt his penis move and thicken in his pants. He closed his eyes. He saw Marina as he'd last seen her, naked on the white sheets in her flat; he was standing in her bedroom doorway on his way out. He'd dallied too long with Marina and now he was already late, for it had been a Thursday and Delilah always cooked on Thursdays and he was always there—on time—honoring this commitment that Delilah seemed to put more store in as other commitments frayed. Marina that day had not lifted the sheet to cover herself, and her openness stopped him in his tracks. Brown flesh from sole to hips to tiny breasts capped in tight copper nipples to neck, an expanse of open brownness he'd never known so nakedly before. She'd laughed from the bed, watching him watching her.

"With me all afternoon," she'd said, "God forbid you should be late for dinner."

All his hurry seemed as silly, as pointless, as the importance he had attached to Thursday dinner. So, he'd gone back to the bed, taking off his clothes again as he moved—knowing all the while that he was turning a corner, deserting Delilah as never before. He'd been naked when he'd reached Marina; she'd lifted her arms. "Make this home," she'd said, running her hands palm down over her body. "Una consumación morena."

Even though Sammy's memory was of Marina's flesh, he said, "It's not her body, man. She talks to me—"

"You said Delilah talks to you."

"Marina," Sam argued, "speaks my tongue."

"Delilah speaks Spanish. She learned it for you."

"It's not the same. Marina's is real."

"As real as yours, 'mano?"

"Como?"

"If you hadn't studied it in school, would your Marina have understood our Carmelas calo?"

"Hablo español, naturalmente, tu tambien. Hablamos español."

"Claro," Arturo said slowly, "pero, mi hermano, have I been dreamin', or hasn't most of our conversation—two-thirds of what we've said tonight—been inglés, vato?"

"So what?"

"You think it's just in the words we use, man?" Art asked.

"I want a brown woman at my side," Sam said flat out, the truth he'd never been able to tell Delilah.

"So no one will doubt your brownness at your book signings, 'mano? Delilah told me you are one vato in demand these days. She said you're getting awards up the nalgas at fancy dinners with Mexicans in tuxedos. Says she doesn't get invited to many of them anymore. You take your doña Marina?"

"Ay que," Sam said turning away, "how could *you* understand?"

In a flash, Arturo was off the steps. He grabbed Sammy's shirt and spun him around, his hands finding Sammy's collar and pulling him so close their lips were almost touching. "Maybe I learned more than you, 'mano. I was forced out into the world long before you, and though I've been pretty much staying put for the last ten years, the twenty, twenty-five, man, before that, I been away. And I learned, you crazy son of a bitch, what you ain't ever learned. It goes with you, man. It's behind the words whatever fuckin' language you use. So you leave your fuckin' gringa wife—you goin' to divorce your little girls, too? What's your Marina bitch have to say about their color, Sammy? They brown enough for her?" He threw Sammy away from him as if he were a piece of trash. Sammy went sprawling through the dust, the earth harder than a floor, hurting.

Arturo strode across and reached down and pulled him up again. "You come back to Carmelas after ten years and you think it's what you left?" Then he threw Sam across the open yard again. Spinning, Arturo pointed to the house. "You know what happened to Mama's Virgin?" he asked, pointing to the alcove Arturo had made for her when he'd stuccoed the house. "Some vatos stole it. I leave my door open, 'cause everyone in the barrio knows I ain't got nothin' to steal except for my lawn mowers locked up in the back yarda. I stuck that stone cupid there just to fill the space and he's perfect. Look at him, Sammy, he's pissin' on the world. You've come home to Carmelas? Well, vato, it's gone. The streets, the names, they're the fuckin' same, but the rest is gone. You're too late. Mine's the only fuckin' house without bars on every window, goddamned pathetic poor people who got nothing to steal and have to hide that behind bars. You think 'cause you remember this place the way it was in summer in those stories and plays you write . . . the way it was when you were a kid . . . the streets full of kids, front yards spillin' people—you think that's enough to make it a place you can come back to when you're scared—that you can pull out of time—whole? Well, look around, you dumb shit. The streets are fuckin' empty. Where are all those people you remember? Gone, vato, gone like Pop, Mama, tía—gone. Trujillo gone to an avocado farm Cruz set up near San Diego and dying in Cruz's fuckin' arms, a man who handled avocados, never the books Trujillo dreamed one of his sons would hold but was son enough to hold *him* as he died. Señora Rosaura? That old Guggisberg bitch—she's dead, too, and you know who turned into her—that granddaughter, the chola with the hair four feet high and the fine, firm nalgas. She still lives in the old lady's house, gone to fat and saddled with Armando and six kids, but except for her, Sam—they're all gone."

"No," Sam said softly.

"*Yes*! The Gils? How long you think those dudes held on to the old man's Horticulture Heaven after he died? La Luna, the old bruja, dried up and blew away. Mark and Contemplación were out of here faster than a vato could say ese. Even Mark's mama, La Lola, who starred in movies, even she—who swore she'd never leave—is gone living somewhere in Riverside with Zapi and Nora. Even the vatos who took no shit from nobody—te acuerdas a Grito Collado? He was taken out in a drive-by—fucker was ridin' pinche bikes with his kids—*by his own primo*—an accident that cabrón Jerry Mendibles on Claresa swore when the police carted him away after finding the gun under his mattress. It'd been dark and Grito, dark as he was, man, was hard to see, but his boys saw it all and their mama Ninfa got them out of here as fast as she could." He paused and then said, "If it's Carmelas you're looking for—I'm it, Sammy. Me! A place full of strangers—and where are they?

"I'll tell you where, Sam—locked up inside on a fuckin' steamin' August night 'cause some vato loco may just go by an' shoot 'em like they did Grito if they dare sit out on the porch like us. So, welcome home, hermano mio." He turned and started toward the house, saying, "Bring that brown woman down for a visit. Maybe I could even get this prick up high enough for both of us to fuck her and give her a real taste of what Carmelas was."

Sammy grabbed Arturo around the ankles and pulled him backward down the steps, tumbling him into the earth like a sack of beans. He climbed over Arturo and straddled his chest, his fist raised high.

Arturo smiled up at him and said, "Bien, bien, hermano. This is what our mama taught us."

Sammy's fists unfurled and he brought them to his eyes. He began to cry.

"La Llorona," Arturo said softly. "Used to be the only way to make you cry. Threaten you with La Llorona."

Sam nodded, wiping his eyes. "Malinche," he whispered.

Arturo reached up and touched Sam's face, his thick hard fingers gentle. "Mama would pull out that old clay pot—remember? Whenever you were bad. She'd done it to me, too. She'd threaten to pull the cork and let her out, releasing La Llorona to chase us through the night."

"Malinche," Sammy said again, remembering the brown woman out of Mexico that time had turned into a monster for walking with the conquerors and used ever after to frighten brown children into obedience. He shuddered, for though now he knew the truth of what Malinche was—had been—she remained in his heart a monster who, if freed, would scream in the night chasing after brown children to betray and devour. "I can see Mama," Sam said, "holding high that Mexican pot, telling me that if she pulled that cork and let her out into the world, she'd catch me, swallow me whole."

"But Mama never pulled the cork, Sammy."

"She never had to," Sammy said. "The threat was enough to keep me in line."

"Me, too," Art said, "for a while." He pushed Sammy off and stood. Sammy rolled onto his back on the hardpacked earth. "I found that old Mexican pot—a year ago," Art said.

Sammy sat up in the dirt. "What'd you do with it—Mama's Malinche pot?"

Arturo stared out at the empty street. "Nothing—forget it—just the dope talking." But Sammy saw in the set of his brother's massive shoulders something—embarrassment? He was holding something back. He got up on his knees. "Art, tell me—the pot, Mama's Mexican pot—"

Arturo turned. "Gone. I . . . I—"

"What?" Sammy demanded, his body taut, leaning toward Arturo.

"I pulled the fuckin' cork."

Sammy laughed, hearing the nervousness at the edges, naked in the night. "Yeah?" Sammy asked.

Art stepped near, a smile tearing his face. "Crumbled, cork crumbled in mi mano—dust." He squatted in front of Sam. His hand reached out and closed on the back of Sammy's neck, gripping it.

"And?" Sammy asked, pulling back from his brother, who gripped his neck harder. "I suppose Malinche climbed from the bottle?" He heard the disdainful tone slap at his brother.

"She did, Samuelito, 'mano mio, whose blood is the same as mine, whose skin is just as brown, she did—"

"You must've been drunk."

Arturo nodded. "Always, hombre—I ain't got a house full of women to lose myself in—no brown pussy waitin' across town to slip into anymore when I'm lost or scared. Maybe drunk I can see clearer than my brother who teaches gringos and doubts our mama's words." He shrugged, pulling Sammy's head closer. "All I know, after the cork went to dust in my fingers, Malinche climbed from out the bottle, rising before me like a genie—tall, long-limbed, beautiful, and brown. She held up her arms and released a cry—"

"La Llorona," Sammy said, calling her by another name, never hers really, but given her by others.

"Not a scream, Sammy, a cry that made me only want to soothe—*her*—so full of pain that—hearing *her* pain—I lost all thought of running." He pulled Sammy close until their foreheads were almost touching. "You know what La Llorona did to me?" Art's eyes were damp, glistening. "She took me in her arms—"

Sammy, unable to bear the closeness of his brother's eyes, forced his head back, saying, "What were you smoking that night, Tootie?" He felt Art's fingers loosen at his neck, release him, this brother who had lied to Papa and Mama all their days, but never to Sammy. "Tell me, big brother, what did she do?"

Arturo took forever before saying, "She embraced me, Sam, all I've ever been, and claimed me."

"Malinche," Sammy said, standing, wanting distance.

Arturo nodded. "The whore of Mexico." He looked up from where he squatted. "She told me that," he said, his eyes boring into Sammy's own. "Then, she walked away," Art said, rising, "right up Claresa into the dark, but not before turning and reminding me she was the mother, too."

"Then, what are we?" Sam asked.

"Malinche's children—no more than that," Arturo said, "wherever, Sam, life may take us—sons of a whore who walked the only road before her."

Inside the house, the phone started ringing, sounding tinny, lonely in the night, becoming, as Sammy listened, a wail calling his name. It rang and rang and he suddenly wanted what Art had said he'd gotten from Malinche the night he'd set her free, a pair of arms to hold him, loving him for all he was, accepting him despite all he'd never be.

But isn't that just what he'd always had with his Delilah? In his mind's eye, he saw Malinche's arms bleed pale and become Delilah's. On each side of the reaching arms, he saw a child, his own girls—Alma and Lilly—each with eyes as black as night—searching only for him. Like Malinche, he saw before him only one road to walk.

Cast of Characters

Chapter 1 Taking Root 1900

—Arnulfo Carmelas, 45 years old, founder of Carmelas, married to Gloria Peralta

—Mario Galvan, 18 years old, marries Chona Contreras

—Paco Valdez, married to Lornita Contreras (Chona's sister)

—Rogelio Sanchez, married to Judith Rodriguez, father of Claresa

—Gilberto Ramirez, married to Maria Ixta

—Diego Reyes, married to Rosaura Flores

—Indio Romero, married to Inez Valparaiso, father of Socorro

—Mr. Hinton, father of Andy

Chapter 2 La Luna 1910

—La Luna, curandera of Carmelas

—Claresa Sanchez, daughter of Rogelio and Judith

Chapter 3 A Tu Servicio 1929

—Benito Juarez de los Rios y Valles, 19 years old, nephew of Arnulfo Carmelas

—Josefa Carmelas Pena, 25 years old, daughter of Arnulfo, marries Jose Pena

—Lola Escalante, 13 years old, daughter of Pepe and Lucia

Chapter 4 Whatever Lola Wants 1934

—Lola Escalante, 18 years old
—Sandy Hinton, 18 years old, daughter of Andy
—Mark, a young Hollywood gofer

Chapter 5 Mi Casa 1947

—Rosa Galvan, marries Rudy Galvan
—Rudy Galvan, son of Mario and Chona
—Chata Escalante Lucero, daughter of Pepe
—Aurora Lucero, daughter of Chata and Henry

Chapter 6 El Bobo Bruto 1951

—Ozzie Gallo, 17 years old, son of Arcadio and Maria Lourdes Gallo
—Gilbert Ramirez, son of Chacho and Serafina
—Arcadio Gallo, 46 years old, marries Maria Lourdes Valdez
—Maria Lourdes Gallo, 40 years old, daughter of Paco Valdez
—Bobby Valdez, 30 years old, son of Paco
—Norma Cienfuegos, 18 years old, granddaughter of Pepe Escalante, daughter of Delia
—Henry Lucero, marries Chata Escalante Lucero

Chapter 7 Contemplacion 1953

—Contemplación Guerra, 18 years old, daughter of Flavio and Margarita Guerra
—Mark de los Rios y Valles, 19 years old, son of Lola Escalante
—Maria Felicia Fuentes, 16 years old, daughter of Mexican gypsy Fabiano Fuentes

Chapter 8 The Whole Enchilada 1958

—Nora Pena de los Rios y Valles, daughter of Josefa and Jose Pena, marries Zapata de los Rios y Valles
—Zapata de los Rios y Valles, son of Benito Juarez de los Rios y Valles, and La Lola

Chapter 9 La Region de las Ilusiones 1960

—Rafael Trujillo, teacher at Ramona, father to Rafa and Cruz, married to Martha
—Les Hutchins, 22 years old, teacher at Ramona
—Mr. Harden, 50 years old, principal of Ramona

Chapter 10 Penneys From Heaven 1961

—Bobby Valdez, son of Paco
—Nadia Valdez, an orphan, marries Bobby Valdez
—Rosie Perez, daughter of Fabiano Fuentes
—Senora de Valle, 89 years old

Chapter 11 Stakes 1962

—Sammy Archuleta, 15 years old

Chapter 12 El Grito de Socorro

—Socorro Romero Collado, daughter of Indio Romero and Inez, marries Cesar Collado
—Cesar Collado, oldest of the Collado boys
—Serafina Ramirez, daughter of Paco Valdez
—Chacho Ramirez, marries Serafina
—Aurora Galvan, daughter of Chata and Henry Lucero
—Father Gomez, priest at St. John in Norwalk

Chapter 13 Desertions 1965

—Dickie Collado, nephew of Cesar and Socorro
—Ramona Pena Collado, marries Dickie

Chapter 14 Price Tags 1966

—Sammy Archuleta, 17 years old
—Remedios Camisa, 18 years old, son of Guillermo and Ruth Camisa
—Arturo Archuleta, brother of Sammy

Chapter 15 Taking Court 1970

—Mickey Escalante, cousin of Lola and Chata
—Blanca Escalante, 19 years old, daughter of Mickey
—Andy Van Der Dander, 19 years old, son of Sandy Hinton and Lucien Van Der Dander
—Indio Escalante, son of Mickey
—Chocolate Escalante, son of Mickey
—Chato, best friend of Mickey

Chapter 16 Las Adelitas 1973

—Adelita Rincon, daughter of Pancho and Armida
—Angel de los Rios y Valles, son of Nora and Zapata de los Rios y Valles

Chapter 17 La Vida Lucky 1976

—Grito Collado, son of Jorge Collado and Plata Fuentes
—Ninfa Galvan Collado, marries Grito, daughter of Aurora and John Galvan

Chapter 18 Days of the Dead 1989

—Mercedes Xiomara Carranza, 85 years old, widow of Victor Carranza
—Felicitación, daughter of Mercedes
—Piedad and Elizabeth, daughters of Mercedes
—Daniel Carranza, son of Mercedes, marries Susana Collado (daughter of Dickie and Ramona), father of Jerry

Chapter 19 Malinche's Children 1994

—Sammy Archuleta, marries Delilah Grayson
—Arturo Archuleta, 68 years old, brother of Sammy

Acknowledgments

A book is like a child—conceived in private, but raised, ideally, in community. I am under no illusion that this book would ever have gotten beyond my own hands had it not been for Susan Vreeland, my dear friend, inspiration, and mentor. When I faltered, she picked up my chronicle, loving it almost as much as I do, and placed it in the hands of her agent (now also mine), the extraordinary Barbara Braun, who joined in the transformation of my work. Let no one tell me about the old days when agents found a writer and schooled him, for Barbara Braun did just that with me before placing this book with the University Press of Mississippi. Fiction editor Moira Crone, who found it in a mountain of manuscripts, perceived in it all the beauty I intended, and helped me see through her objective eyes ways to make it truly shine.

Deep appreciation goes to my Long Beach read-and-critique group: Keith Blanchard, Kate Collins, Kendal Evans, Grant Farley, Sheila Finch, Rose Hamilton-Gottlieb, Harry Lowther, and Susan Vreeland, who saw my creation through all its permutations, caring for me and the book enough to insist that I honor its promise.

Thanks also to the Asilomar Writer's Consortium and its founder, the writer and teacher Jerry Hannah, who took a storyteller and helped him become a writer, getting assistance from the capable brother/sister writers who gather at the edge of the Pacific twice a year in a nurturing community and whose only aim is to assist each other in making their visions live upon a page.

A final word of thanks to El Camino College in Torrance, California, for providing me a working life that permitted me to pursue my passions, and to all my students who convince me daily that the road to liberation and empowerment begins with discovering a voice to tell our tales.